THE MERMAN'S CHILDREN

The bell was lowered beneath the waves. The priest said his foul rite. And the dome of Liri, which had stood since the Great Ice melted, fell to the ocean floor in a thousand shards.

Of the halflings left homeless, Tauno was almost grown; Eyjan was full in the first flush of womanhood; Kennin was strong and bright-eyed, a wild boy. Only Yria, the babe, was too frail to roam the seas.

She would have to be left, clothed in tears, on the shore for Man to find. Thus the journey of the merman's children began in loss and sadness . . .

POUL ANDERSON

POUL ANDERSON

THE MERMAN'S CHILDREN

BERKLEY BOOKS, NEW YORK

MERMAN'S CHILDREN

A Berkley Book / published by arrangement with
the author

PRINTING HISTORY
Berkley-Putnam edition / September 1979
Berkley edition / October 1980

ISBN: 0-425-04643-5

A BERKLEY BOOK ® TM 757,375

PRINTED IN UNITED STATES OF AMERICA

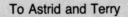
To Astrid and Terry

Author's Note

ONLY Scotland and Russia have from the Middle Ages as rich a heritage of folk ballads as Denmark. Elsewhere, most has perished. It's a pity that so few people outside that country read Danish. No doubt you admire as much as I do "The Battle of Otterbourne"; but the same steel is in "Marsk Stig." For lusty humor we have both "Get Up and Bar the Door" and "Lave and Jon"; for cruelty and bleakness, both "The Twa Corbies" and "Valdemar and Tove"; for death and judgment, both "A Lyke Wake Dirge" and "The Death of Queen Dagmar"; for love that reaches beyond them, both "Clerk Saunders" and "Aage and Else" (with the latter also holding the motif of "The Unquiet Grave"); for a terrifying glimpse of the supernatural, both "Tam Lin" and "Germand Gladensvend"; for one more gentle, both "Thomas the Rhymer" and "The Mermaid's Prophecy." These matchings omit a number which are just as fine.

That is especially true of those dealing with the Otherworld, the halfworld, Faerie, whatever you want to call it. There the Danes have many splendid old verse tales. A jewel among them is *"Agnete og Havmanden"* ("Agnete and the Merman"; the given name is a version of "Agnes").

It happens to be of late date; in his classic essay on these collections, Axel Olrik calls it post-medieval. He adds that it is not of native origin either, but has a German source which in turn draws on Slavic legend. The Northern singer moved the setting of the story to England. Otherwise, though, his (or her) work was no mere derivative, but a creation new and uniquely Danish. In

the nineteenth century it inspired Matthew Arnold to write that
beautiful poem "The Forsaken Merman."

In view of all this, I feel no guilt at having taken a few liberties
of my own. The home of Agnete and her lover has been moved
back to Denmark, where it belongs, and their time, somewhat
arbitrarily, to several hundred years ago. Contradicting the ballad,
I have her bear him daughters as well as sons; after all, that seems
more likely than seven boys in a row. As for the plausibility of
the entire narrative: by definition, fantasies make certain assump-
tions which we take to be factually untrue. The background here
is Catholic, but the religion does not conform to the theology of
St. Thomas Aquinas. Rather, it is the naive, half-pagan mythology
of peasants and seafarers in the early fourteenth century—when
Denmark was enjoying a brief respite in a long period of foreign
and civil wars.

I have tried to be accurate about humans and their societies.
Two persons, Bishop Johan Kvag and Ban Pavle Subitj, are his-
torical.

Those who have visited Yugoslavia will recall that the Dalmatian area is nearly treeless. However, its woodlands were famous in medieval times, even as the cedars of Lebanon had been
in Solomon's.

Climate everywhere was colder than it is today and getting
steadily worse, to culminate in the "little ice age" that prevailed
from about 1430 to 1850.

In describing the locations and fate of the Norse settlements
on Greenland, I have in large part followed Farley Mowat's book
Westviking. His reconstruction is controversial but, to my mind,
makes a good deal of sense. While people of the Dorset culture
appear to have reached Greenland at an early date, they were
replaced—or displaced—by the Eskimos, and there seems to be
no doubt that the latter arrived well after the Norse, who found
no inhabitants (unless possibly a few Irish) when they themselves
first came to the southern end of that country. For the initial scene
in Book Four, Chapter I, I am especially indebted to Peter
Freuchen's account of similar occurrence in his *Arctic Adventure*.

I know of no direct evidence for the class of ships called hulks
or for ratlines bent to shrouds and crow's nests aloft before the
end of the fourteenth century. Yet mariners have always been very
conservative, not without reason. It strikes me as likely that such

innovations would have been in use here and there, by owners of pioneering temperament, some generations before they became so widespread that artists depicted them. Likewise for other items such as spectacles.

For help with certain technical questions and for good advice I am grateful to Karen Anderson, Mildred Downey Broxon, Dorothy Heydt, and Jerry Pournelle. They are not responsible for whatever errors and infelicities remain.

The rest of this note deals with spellings and pronunciations. That is, inevitably, lumpy stuff; you may or may not wish to study it.

Those Danish names which are important in the story go approximately as follows:

Agnete, ow-*nih*-teh; Asmild, *ass*-meel; Dagmar, *dow*-mar; Ingeborg, *ing*-eh-bor; Knud, cnooth, *oo* as in *food*, *th* as in *this*; Kvag, kva, *a* as in *hand*; Margrete, mar-*greh*-teh; Ranild, *ran*-eel; Roskilde, *ross*-keel-eh; Viborg, *vee*-bor.

In general: The combination *aa* may be rendered, inaccurately but recognizably, as *aw*. The combination of *a* and *e* would be written as one character in Danish but for convenience it is two separate letters in this book; the pronunciation resembles *eh*. Terminal *e* is not silent but is sounded, as you will have noted in some of the names above. *J* is like the English consonant *y*, as in *yet*. *Y* itself is equivalent to the German *ü* or roughly, English *ee*.

I have modified some other spellings for your convenience and the printer's: notably the patronymic suffix, meaning "son of," which is here given in its modern form -*sen*.

Even more have I transliterated Croatian in order to eliminate diacritical marks, though this means that numerous spellings are well off target. For present purposes, they follow English rules, with these exceptions: *a* as in *father*; *i* as in *machine*; *o* like *au* in *caught*; *zh* like *z* in *azure*; and both *j* and terminal *e* are employed as they are in Danish, i.e. like our *y* and *eh* respectively.

Hence the surname "Subitj"—which is written differently in its own language—is spoken as "Soo-bit'y," with *t'y* as in "no*t yet*." Readers may find it easier just to say "Soo-bich."

We have no equivalent of the syllabic *r*, e.g., in "Hrvatska," but if you wish you can render it -*ur*.

Names of halfworld creatures and their homes, being imaginary, may of course be sounded in any way the reader chooses. I myself naturally think of them as if they had been transcribed by a Scandinavian.

—POUL ANDERSON

THE MERMAN'S CHILDREN

Prologue

THE coast of Dalmatia rises steeply. A bare league inland, Shibenik town stands high on a hill above the river Krka and sees mountain peaks in the east. Here the water forms a broad basin, which narrows as it moves on to the sea. Upstream, however, it tumbles in ringing cascades out of the lake which it and others have made.

In the days when the Angevin Charles Robert became boy-king of Croats and Magyars, the land along those falls was mostly wildwood. Likewise it was around much of the lake, save where the Krka empties into this. There folk had long since cleared it and laid it under the plow. A little farther up the river, about where the Chikola flows into it, Skradin village clustered by the stronghold of its lord, the zhupan.

Nevertheless, even within castle walls, the wilderness came a-haunting. Not only might one hear wolves howl by night and jackals bark by day, or have one's fields raided by deer and wild boar, or glimpse the horned mightiness of elk and aurochs. Uncanny beings dwelt yonder—Leshy among the trees, a vodianoi in the deeps—and lately, it was whispered, a vilja.

Ivan Subitj, zhupan, paid scant heed to such talk among his serfs. He was a stark man, though just, near kin to the great Ban Pavle and thus aware of a larger world than theirs. Moreover, he had spent years outside, many of them in the wars that hardened and scarred him.

Nor did his eldest son Mihajlo fear woodland bogies. Indeed, this youth had well-nigh forgotten whatever legends he heard early in life: for he had been educated at the abbey in Shibenik, had traveled to the bustling ports of Zadar and Split and once across the narrow sea to Italy. For his part, he wanted wealth and fame, escape from the changelessness wherein he had passed his childhood. To that end, with Ivan's help, he attached himself to the retinue of Pavle Subitj the kingmaker.

Just the same, he remained fond of his home country and often visited Skradin. There they knew him as a merry soul, kindhearted if occasionally thoughtless, who brought with him color, song, and vivid stories from beyond their horizon.

On a certain morn in a new summer, Mihajlo left the castle to go hunting. Half a dozen fellows accompanied him. Three were guards and body servants who had come along from Shibenik. Peace prevailed for the moment, both with the Venetians and among the powerful clans; and Ivan Subitj had beheaded the last bandit in these parts several years ago. Still, few men ventured far alone, and no women. The rest of those with Mihajlo as he rode forth were his younger brother Luka and two free peasants who would be guides and do the rough work. A pack of hounds trotted behind.

The party made a brave sight. Mihajlo was clad in the latest Western fashion, green doublet and hose, saffron shirt, silk-lined cape, Cordovan half-boots and gauntlets, flat velvet cap on long brown curls, face clean-shaven. A hanger slapped at his waist whenever his horse grew frolicsome. He sat the beast as if they were one. His own attendants were hardly less gaudy; their spear-heads flashed aloft. Luka was in much the same knee-length coat, over tunic and cross-gaitered breeches, as the peasants; his garb was simply of better stuff, with finer embroidery along sleeves and hem, his brimless conical hat trimmed with sable while theirs had rabbit fur. He and they alike bore short, recurved bows, as well as knives of a size to cope with bear.

Hoofs racketed in the street, thudded on paths beyond. Unlike Frankish lords, those who were Croatian generally respected their underlings; had Mihajlo ridden across the tender green of crop-lands, he would have answered to his father. Passing a meadow, he did frighten a few calves with a joyful blast on his horn, but rail fences kept them from bolting.

Presently he was in the woods, on a game trail. This was mingled oak and beech forest, soaring boles, over-arching boughs, murmurous leaves, shadowy vaults and reaches where sunlight struck through in flecks and speckles, the hue of gold. Birdsong sounded remote and hushed against the quiet that brooded here. The air was warm, yet carried an edge, and full of odors that had naught to do with house or byre.

The hounds caught a scent. Their clamor awoke.

In the next hours the men took a stag, a wolf, a brace of badger; a wild sow eluded them, but they remained well content. Reaching the lake, they startled a flock of swans, let fly their arrows, brought down three. They thought they might return home.

That happened which God allowed.

Another stag trod onto the shore, a hundred yards from them. Late afternoon sunbeams washed aureate and blue-shadowed across him, for he was white, well-nigh the stature of an elk. Already his growing antlers made a tree athwart heaven.

"By every saint!" shouted Mihajlo, and soared to his feet. A pair of shafts missed the deer, which waited until the men were in the saddle again. Thereafter he fled them. Yet he did not seek thick brush where horses could not follow. He stayed on the trails, ever glimmering in dimness. Vainly, the chase hallooed after. Back and forth he led his pursuers, up and down, round and about, while time waned. The mounts were blown, the dogs gasping, when at last he came back to the lake.

Timber gloomed above its gleam. The sun had sunk and left only a smear of sulfur on western blue. Eastward was purple, swiftly darkening; a star trembled forth. Mist lay in streamers. Bats flitted on high. It was turning cold. Silence filled everything that was.

Like a patch of fog, the crowned animal shivered and was gone.

Mihajlo choked on an oath. Luka crossed himself over and over, as did the servants. Both peasants sprang from their stirrups, down onto their knees, whipped off their hats, and prayed aloud.

"We have been lured," mumbled Sisko, the senior of them. "By who and for what?"

"Let us begone, in God's name," begged his friend Drazha.

"No, hold." Mihajlo rallied his courage. "Our steeds must rest. We could kill them if we push right on. You know that."

"Would you, you spend the night here?" stammered Luka.

"An hour or two, till the moon rises and we can find our way," Mihajlo said.

An attendant of his stared across the quicksilver above the depths, at a ragged murk of foliage beyond, and protested, "Sir, this is no place for Christians. Old heathen things are abroad. That was no buck we hunted, it was the very wind, and now it has vanished to wherever the wind goes. Why?"

"What, and you a city man?" Mihajlo gibed. "Our senses failed us, that's all. Not surprising, weary as we are." He peered through the dusk at their faces. "There is no place on earth which is not for Christians, if they have faith," he said. "Come, let us call on our saints. How then can devils harm us?"

Weakly heartened, they dismounted if they had not already done so, prayed together, unsaddled their beasts, began to rub these down with the cloths. More stars appeared in deepening twilight.

Mihajlo's laughter rattled through the stillness. "Do you see? We had no need of fear."

"No, never," sang a girl's voice. "Is it really you, my dearest?"

He turned and beheld her. Though he and his companions had become blurs among shadows, she stood forth almost clearly, where she came out of the reeds onto land. Her nakedness and the unbound hair were that pale, her eyes that huge and bright. She neared him, arms held wide.

"Jesus and Mary, save us," moaned Drazha at his back. "It is the vilja."

"Mihajlo," she cried low, "Mihajlo, forgive me, I am trying to remember, I truly am."

Somehow he stood his ground, there on the wet lakeside in the gloaming. "Who are you?" he uttered through the earthquake in his breast. "What do you want of me?"

"The vilja," Sisko quavered. "Demon, ghost. Pray it away, men, before it draws us down to its watery hell."

Mihajlo traced the Cross, stiffened his knees, confronted the being and commanded, "In the name of the Father, and of the Son, and of the Holy Spirit——"

Before he could say, "——begone!" she was so close to him that he could make out the sweetly carven features. "Mihajlo," she was pleading, "is that you? I'm sorry if I hurt you, Mihajlo——"

"*Nada!*" he screamed.

She stopped. "Was I Nada?" she asked him, with puzzlement upon her brow. After a while: "Yes, I think I was. And surely you were Mihajlo. . . ." She smiled. "Why, yes, you are. I brought you here to me, didn't I, Mihajlo, darling?"

He shrieked, whirled, and ran. His men fled likewise, every which way into the dark. That made the horses stampede.

When the noise had died, Nada the vilja stood alone. More stars had awakened. The last sunset glow was gone, but the west was yet pale. These different lights sheened off the lake, which cast them onto her until she was a slender curve and ripple of white, a glistening of tears. "Mihajlo," she said. "Please."

Then she forgot, laughed, and flitted into the forest.

——The hunters won home separately but safe. What Sisko and Drazha had to tell made people warier than ever of the wildwood. Mihajlo related no more than he must. Others soon marked that he was no longer the glad youth he had been. Much time did he spend with the chaplain at the castle, and later with his confessor in Shibenik. Next year he entered a monastery. His father the zhupan was less than happy about that.

Book One

KRAKEN

I

THE bishop of Viborg got Magnus Gregersen for his new arch-deacon. This man was more learned than most, having studied in Paris, and he was upright and pious; but folk called him too strict, and said they liked no better to see him coming, with his long lean frame and his long sour face, than they liked to see any other black crow in their fields. The bishop felt one like that was needed, for laxity had set in during the years of strife that harried Denmark after King Valdemar the Victorious died.

Riding along the eastern Jutish coast as episcopal provost, Magnus came to Als, not the island but a hamlet of the same name. It was poor and lonely, deep woods behind it and Kongerslev Marsh to the north. Only two roads served it, one on the strand and one twisting southwesterly toward Hadsund. Each September and October its fishermen would join the hundreds that made catches in the Sound during the great herring run; otherwise their kind saw little of the outside world. They dragged their nets through the water and farmed their thin-soiled acres until time and toil broke them and they laid their bones to rest behind the small wooden church. Many old ways were still followed in steads like this. Magnus thought such doings pagan and bewailed to himself that there was no ready way to stop them.

Thus a baffled zeal grew double strong in him when he heard certain rumors about Als. None there would own to knowledge of what might have been happening since that day fourteen years ago when Agnete came back out of the sea. Magnus got the priest alone and sternly demanded the truth. Father Knud was a gentle man, born in one of those tiny houses, who had long turned a blind eye on what he thought were minor sins that gave his flock some cheer in their bleak lives. But he was aged now, and feeble, and Magnus soon wrung from him the full tale.

The provost returned to Viborg with a holy flame in his gaze.

9

He went to the bishop and said: "My lord, in making my rounds through your diocese I found woefully many signs of the Devil's work. But I had not looked to come upon himself—no, say rather a whole nest of his foulest, most dangerous fiends. Yet this I did in the strand-hamlet Als."

"What mean you?" asked the bishop sharply; for he also dreaded a return of the old witchy gods.

"I mean that offshore is a town of merfolk!"

The bishop eased. "How interesting," he said. "I knew not that any were left in Danish waters. They are not devils, my good Magnus. They lack souls, yes, like other beasts. But they do not imperil salvation as might the dwellers in an elfhill. Indeed, they seldom have aught to do with the tribe of Adam."

"These are otherwise, my lord," answered the archdeacon. "Listen to what I have learned. Two and twenty years ago lived near Als a maiden hight Agnete Einarsdatter. Her father was a yeoman, well-to-do by his neighbors' reckoning, and she was very fair, so she ought to have made a good marriage. But one eventide when she walked alone on the beach, a merman came forth and wooed her. He lured her away with him, and she passed eight years in sin and godlessness beneath the sea.

"At last she happened to bring her newest babe up onto a skerry that it might drink sunlight. This was in earshot of the church bells, and while she sat rocking the cradle, they began to chime. Homesickness, if not repentance, awoke in her. She went to the merman and begged leave to go hear again the word of God. He gave unwilling consent and took her ashore. Beforehand he made her vow not to do three things—let down her long hair, as if she were unwedded; seek out her mother in the family pew; and bow down when the priest named the All Highest. But each of these she did: the first for pride, the second for love, the third for awe. Then divine grace drew the scales from her eyes and she stayed on land.

"Afterward the merman came in search of her. It was another holy day and he found her at Mass. When he walked into the church, the pictures and images turned their faces to the wall. None of the congregation dared lift hand against him, he was so huge and strong. He pleaded with her to return, and well might he have prevailed as aforetime. For this is not a hideous race with fish tails, my lord. Save that they have broad, webbed feet and big, slanting eyes, and the men among them are beardless, and some have green or blue hair—on the whole, they look like beautiful humans. His own locks were golden as hers. And he did not threaten, he spoke in tones of love and sorrow.

"Yet God strengthened Agnete. She refused him and he went back beneath the waters.

"Her father had the prudence, and the dowry, to get her wed inland. They say she was never cheerful, and before long she died."

"If it was a Christian death," the bishop said, "I cannot see that lasting harm was done."

"But the merfolk are still there, my lord!" cried the provost. "Fishermen see them often, romping and laughing in the waves. Does that not make a poor toiler, who dwells in a wretched hut with an ugly wife, ill content, yes, even questioning of God's justice? And when will another merman seduce another maiden, this time forever? That is the more likely now when those children of Agnete and her lover are grown. They come ashore almost as a habit, they have struck up friendships with some of the boys and young men—more than friendship, I heard tell, for the female among them.

"My lord, this is Satan's work! If we let souls be lost that were in our charge, how shall we answer on the Last Day?"

The bishop frowned and rubbed his chin. "You have right. What shall we do, though? If the Alsmen already do what is forbidden, a further ban will hardly check them; I know those stiff-necked fisherfolk. And if we send to the King for knights and troopers, how shall they go beneath the sea?"

Magnus raised a finger. It blazed from him: "My lord, I have studied matters of this kind and know the cure. Those merfolk may not be demons, but the soulless must ever flee when God's word is properly laid on them. Have I your leave to conduct an exorcism?"

"You do," said the bishop shakenly, "and with it my blessing."

So it came about that Magnus returned to Als. More men-at-arms than usual clattered behind him, lest the villagers make trouble. These watched, some eager for any newness, some surly, a few weeping, as the archdeacon had himself rowed out to a spot above the underwater town. And there, with bell, book, and candle, he solemnly cursed the sea people and bade them in God's name forever be gone.

II

TAUNO, oldest child of fair Agnete and the Liri king, had counted his twenty-first winter. There was great merrymaking in his honor, feast, song, dances that wove their flitting patterns north, east, west, south, up, down, and around, between the shells and mirrors and golden plates which flung back the seafire lighting the royal hall; there were gifts, cunningly wrought, not alone of gold and amber and narwhal ivory, but also of pearl and lacy rosy coral, brought from afar by travelers throughout the centuries; there were contests in swimming, wrestling, harpooning, music, and rune-craft; there was lovemaking in dim rooms which had no roof because none was needed, and in the rippling gardens of red, green, purple, and brown weed where jellyfish drifted like white and blue blossoms and true fish darted like meteors.

Afterward Tauno went on a long hunt. Though the merfolk lived off the waters, he fared this time in sport, mostly to visit anew the grandeur of the Norway fjords. With him came the girls Rinna and Raxi, for his pleasure and their own. They had a joyful trip, which meant much to Tauno; he was often a sober one among his lighthearted kindred, and sometimes fell into dark broodings.

They were homebound, Liri was in sight, when the wrath struck them.

"Yonder it is!" Rinna called eagerly. She darted ahead. The green tresses streamed down her slim white back. Raxi stayed near Tauno. She swam laughing around and around him; as she passed below, she would stroke fingers over his face or loins. He grabbed for her with the same playfulness, but always she was out of reach. "Niaah!" she taunted while blowing him bubbly kisses. He grinned and swam steadily on. Having inherited their mother's shape of foot, the halfling children were less swift and deft in the water than their father's race. Nevertheless, a landman would have gasped at their movement. And they got about more readily on

shore than their cousins; and they had been born able to live
undersea, without need for the spells that had kept their mother
from death by drowning, salt, or chill; and the cool-fleshed merfolk liked to embrace their warmer bodies.

Above Tauno sun smote waves, making a roof of bright ripples
that traced its pattern across the white sand beneath him. Around,
the water reached in hues of emerald and amethyst until distance
brought dusk. He felt it slide by, answering the play of his muscles
with caresses like a lover's. Kelp streamed upward from barnacled
rocks, golden-brown, swaying to every current. A crab clanked
over the seabed; a tunny glided farther off, blue and white and
splendid. The water was never the same: here cold, there mild,
here roiled, there calm, and a thousand different tastes and odors
beyond the tang men smell on a strand; and it was full of sounds
for those who could hear, cluckings, chucklings, croakings, chit-
terings, splashings, the hush-hush-hush where it lapped against
land; and beneath each swirl and gurgle Tauno felt the huge slow
striding of the tides.

Now Liri rose clear in his sight: houses that were hardly more
than arbors of seaplants or frames of ivory and whale ribs, delicate
and fantastically scrimshawed in this world of low weight, wide-
spaced among gardens of weed and anemone; in the middle, the
hall of his father the king, big, ancient, stone and coral in subtle
hues, bedight with carven figures of fish and those beasts and
fowl which belong to the sea. The posts of the main door were
in the shapes of Lord Aegir and Lady Ran, the lintel was an
albatross with wings spread for soaring. Above the walls lifted
a dome of crystal, vented to the surface, which the king had built
for Agnete, so that when she wished she might be dry, breathe
air, sit by a fire among roses and what else his love could fetch
her from the land.

The merfolk flitted about—gardeners, craftsmen, a hunter
training a brace of young seals, an oyster gatherer buying a trident
at a booth, a boy leading a girl by the hand toward some softly
lighted cavern. Bronze bells, taken long ago from a wrecked ship,
were being chimed; they pealed more clearly through water than
ever through the air.

"Harroo!" Tauno shouted. He plunged forward in a burst of
speed. Rinna and Raxi fell in alongside him. The three broke into
the "Song of Returnings" he had made for them:

Here may I hail you, my homeland, my heartstrand.
Well for the wanderer's weal is the way's end.
Call up the clamor on conchs and on kettles!
Stories I'll strew from the silver-paved swanroad.
Gold the dawn glittered and glad wheeled the gulls
    when——

Suddenly his companions screamed. They clapped hands to ears, their eyes were shut, they milled about blindly and wildly kicking till the water seethed.

Tauno watched the same craziness take all of Liri. "What is this?" he cried in horror. "What's wrong?"

Rinna wailed her anguish. She could not see nor hear him. He caught her. She fought to break loose. His strength gripped her from behind with legs and one hand. His other hand closed on the silken tresses to hold tight her jerking head. He laid mouth to an ear and stammered, "Rinna, Rinna, it's me, Tauno. I'm your friend. I want to help you."

"Then let me go!" Her shriek was ragged with pain and fright. "The ringing fills the sea, it shakes me like a shark, my bones are coming apart—the light, the cruel blaze, blinding, burning, burning—the words—Let me go or I die!"

Tauno did, altogether bewildered. Rising several yards, he made out the shivering shadow of a fisher boat, and heard a bell . . . was a fire aboard too, and was a voice chanting in some tongue he knew not? No more than that. . . .

The houses of Liri rocked as in a quake. The crystal dome on the hall shattered and rained down in bright shards. The stones trembled and began to slide from each other. That crumbling, of what had stood here since the Great Ice melted, sent its shuddering through Tauno's flesh.

Dimly he saw his father come forth, astride the orca which had its airspace in the hall and which no one else dared mount. Otherwise the king had naught but a trident; and he was clad in naught but his own majesty. Yet somehow his call was heard: "To me, my people, to me! Quickly, before we die! Seek not to save any treasure beyond your children—and weapons—come, come, come if you would live!"

Tauno shook Rinna and Raxi back to a measure of sense, and led them to join the throng. His father, riding about rallying the terrified merfolk, had time to say to him grimly: "You, half mortal, feel it no more than does this steed of mine. But to us, these waters are now banned. For us, the light will blaze and the bell will toll and the words will curse until the Weird of the World. We must flee while we still have strength, to seek a home far and away."

"Where are my siblings?" Tauno asked.

"They were on an outing," said the king. The tone that had trumpeted went flat and dead. "We cannot wait for them."

"*I* can."

The king gripped his son by both shoulders. "That heartens me. Yria and, aye, young Kennin need more than Eyjan to ward them. I know not where we are going. Maybe you can find us later—maybe——" He shook his sun-bright mane. His visage drew into a mask of torture. "Away!" he screamed.

Stunned, beaten, naked, most of them unarmed and without tools, the merfolk followed their lord. Tauno hung, fists clenched on harpoon, until they were out of sight. The last stones of the royal hall toppled, and Liri was a ruin.

III

In the eight years that she dwelt beneath the waters, fair Agnete bore seven children. This was less than a seawife would have done, and maybe the unspoken scorn of those females helped drive her back to land, even as the bells of the little church and the sight of little thatch-roofed timber houses had drawn her.

For though the merfolk, like others of Faerie, knew no aging (as if He Whose name they did not speak thus repaid them for lack of immortal souls), their way of life had its harsh side. Shark, orca, sperm whale, ray, sea serpent, a dozen kinds of killer fish hunted them; the creatures that they in turn hunted were often dangerous; tricks of wind and wave could be deadly; poison fangs and spines, cold, sickness, hunger carried many off. This was most true of their young; they must reckon with losing all but a few. The king had been lucky with those he got with his human mate. Behind his home were only three graves whereon the sea anemones had never been let die.

The four children who remained met in the wreckage of Liri. Round about were the heaped chaos of the hall, the farther-off bits and pieces of lesser homes, gardens already withering, fishflocks already scattered, broken scrimshaw, crabs and lobsters swarming through foodstocks like ravens over a corpse on shore. The meeting spot was where the main door had been. The albatross lay wingless; kindly Lord Aegir had fallen on his face; Lady Ran who takes men in her nets stood above, grinning. The water was chill and waves raised by a storm overhead could be heard mourning for Liri.

The merman's children were unclad, as was usual undersea save at festival times. However, they had gotten knives, harpoons, tridents, and axes of stone and bone, to ward off those menaces which circled closer and closer beyond the rim of their sight. None of them looked wholly like merfolk. But the elder three shared the high cheekbones, slanted eyes, and male beardlessness of their father; and while they had learned the Danish tongue and some of the Danish ways, now it was as merfolk that they talked.

Eldest among them, Tauno took the word. "We must decide where to go. Hard it was to keep death at bay when everyone stayed here. We cannot do it long alone."

He was likewise the biggest, tall, wide in the shoulders, mightily muscled from a lifetime's swimming. His hair, caught by a beaded headband, fell to his collarbones, yellow with the least tinge of green; his eyes were amber, set well apart from the blunt nose, above the heavy mouth and jaw; because he had spent much time on the surface or ashore, his skin was brown.

"Why, shall we not follow our father and tribe?" asked Eyjan.

She had nineteen winters. She too was tall, for a woman, and strong with a strength that lay hidden beneath the full curves of breasts, hips, thighs, until she hugged a lover tight or drove a lance into a wallowing walrus. Hers was the whitest skin, for her hair was bronzy red, floating shoulder-length past a challenging gray gaze and cleanly molded face.

"We know not where they have gone," Tauno reminded her. "It will have to be far, since these were the last good hunting grounds left to our kind around Denmark. And while such merfolk as dwell in the Baltic or along the Norway coast may help them on their way, there's no room for as many more as Liri's people are. The seas are very wide to search, my sister."

"Oh, surely we can ask," Kennin said impatiently. "They'll leave traces. The dolphins are bound to know which way they headed." A sparkle jumped in his eyes, making them more than ever summer-blue. "Haa, what a chance to gad about!"

He was of sixteen winters, had yet to fare far, and knew only youth's eagerness to be off beyond the horizon. He had not gotten his full growth and would never be tall or broad. On the other hand, he was well-nigh as agile a swimmer as a full-blooded merman. His hair was greenish brown, his countenance round and freckled, his body painted in the loudest-colored patterns the dwellers had known. The rest bore no ornament; Tauno was in too stark a mood, Eyjan had always scoffed at the trouble it cost, and Yria was shy.

The last one whispered: "How can you joke when . . . when . . . everything is gone?"

Her siblings moved closer in around her. To them she was still the babe, left in her crib by a mother whom she was coming more and more to look like. She was small, thin, her breasts just budding; her hair was golden, her eyes huge in the tip-tilted, lip-parted face. She had stayed away from revelries as much as a king's daughter might, had never gone off alone with a boy, had spent hours a day learning the womanly arts at which Eyjan jeered—more hours in the dome that had been Agnete's, fondling the treasures that had been Agnete's. Often she lay on the waves, staring at the greenhills and the houses ashore, listening to the chimes which called Christian folk to prayer. Of late she had been going there with one or another of her kin when these would allow, flitting along a twilit strand or behind a wind-gnarled tree or down into the ling like a timid shadow.

Eyjan gave her a quick, rough embrace. "You got too great a share of our mortal side," declared the older sister.

Tauno scowled. "And that is a terrible truth," said he. "Yria is not strong. She cannot swim fast, or far without rest and food. What if we're set on by beasts? What if winter catches us away from the warm shallows, or what if the Liri outcasts move to the Arctic? I do not see how we can take her on any journey."

"Can't we leave her with some foster?" asked Kennin.

Yria shrank into Eyjan's arms. "Oh, no, no," she begged. They could scarcely hear her.

Kennin reddened at his own foolishness. Tauno and Eyjan looked at each other across the hunched back of their little sister. Few were the merfolk who would take in a weakling, when the strong had trouble enough fending for themselves. Now and again one might; but he would do so out of desire. They had no true hope of finding a sea-man who would want this child as their father had wanted a certain grown maiden; nor would that be any kindness to the child.

Tauno must gather his will to speak it aloud: "I think, before we leave, we'd best take Yria to our mother's people.

IV

THE old priest Knud was wakened by a knocking. He climbed from his shut-bed and fumbled a robe on in the dark, for the banked hearthfire gave no real glow; and he felt his way to the door. His bones ached, his teeth clapped with chill. He wondered who might be near death. He had outlived every playmate. . . . "I come, in Jesu name, I come."

A full moon had lately risen. It threw a quicksilver bridge on the Kattegat and made glint the dew on cottage roofs; but the two crossed streets of Als lay thick with shadow, and the land beyond had become a stalking ground for wolves and trolls. Strangely quiet were the dogs, as if they feared to bark; the whole night was cracklingly still; no, a sound somewhere, hollow, a hoof? The Hell Horse grazing among the graves?

Four stood in a cloud of their own breath, unseasonably cold as this night was. Father Knud gasped and signed himself. He had never seen merfolk, besides the one who had come into his church—unless a glimpse in childhood had been more than a marvelous dream. What else could these be, though? He had heard enough accounts from those of his parishioners who met them now and again. The features of the man and woman were cast in that alien mold, the boy's less clearly so, the girl-child's hardly at all. But water dripped and shimmered from her too; she too wore a fishskin tunic and clutched a bone-headed spear.

"You, you, you were to have . . . been gone," the priest said, hearing his voice thin in the frosty quiet.

"We are Agnete's children," said the tall man. He spoke Danish with a lilting accent that was indeed, Knud thought wildly, outlandish. "Because of her heritage, the spell did not touch us."

"No spell—a holy exorcism—" Knud called on God in his mind and squared his narrow shoulders. "I pray you, be not wroth with my villagers. The thing was none of their doing or wish."

"I know. We have asked . . . a friend . . . about what happened. Soon we shall go away. First we would give Yria into your care."

The priest was somewhat eased by this, and likewise by seeing that his visitors' bare feet were of human shape. He bade the four come in. They did, wrinkling their noses at the grime and smells in the single room which the parish house boasted. He stoked the fire, kindled a rushlight, set forth bread, salt, and beer, and, since the newcomers filled the bench, sat down on a stool to talk with them.

Long was that talk. It ended well after he had promised to do his best for the girl. Her three siblings would linger a while to make sure; he must let her go to the strand every dusk and meet them. Father Knud pleaded with them to stay ashore too, but this they would not. They kissed their sister and took their leave. She wept, noiselessly but hopelessly, until she fell asleep. The priest tucked her in and got what rest he could on the bench.

Next day, and more and more in the days of waxing summer which followed, Yria was in better spirits. At last she was quite cheerful. Agnete's kin held aloof, afraid to admit she carried their blood, but Father Knud dealt with her as kindly as his meager means allowed. It helped that the other halflings brought gifts of food fresh-caught from the sea at their regular meetings: which quickly became brief ones. To her, the land was as new and wonderful as she was to the youngsters of the hamlet. Erelong she was daily the middle of a rollicking swarm. As for work, she knew nothing about human tasks but was willing to learn. Kirsten Pedersdatter tried her on the loom and said she could become uncommonly skillful.

Meanwhile the priest had sent a youth to Viborg, asking what should be done about the girl. Could a halfling be christened? He prayed this be so, for otherwise he knew not what would become of the poor darling. The messenger was gone for a pair of weeks; they must be ransacking their books at the bishopric. Finally he returned, on horse this time, accompanied by guards, a clerical amanuensis, and the provost.

Knud had been giving Christian instruction to Yria, who listened wide-eyed and mostly silent. Now Archdeacon Magnus saw her in the parish house. "Do you truly believe in one God," he barked, "the Father, the Son Who is Our Lord and Saviour Jesus Christ, and the Holy Ghost which proceeds from them?"

She quailed before his sternness. "I do," she whispered. "I do not understand it very well, but I do believe, good sir."

After further questioning, Magnus told Knud privately: "There can be no harm in baptizing her. She is not an unreasoning brute, albeit badly in need of more careful teaching before she can be confirmed. If she be devils' bait, the holy water should drive her hence; if she be merely soulless, God will hit upon some way to let us know."

The christening was set for Sunday after Mass. The archdeacon gave Yria a white robe to wear and chose a saint's name for her, Margrete. She grew less afraid of him and agreed to spend the Saturday night in prayer. Friday after sunset, full of eagerness, she wanted her siblings to come to the service—surely the priests would allow it, hoping to win them too—and she cried when they refused.

And so, on a morning of wind, scudding white clouds, dancing glittery waves, before the Alsfolk in the wooden church, beneath the ship model hung in the nave and Christ hung above the altar, she knelt, and Father Knud led her and the godparents through the rites, and signed her and said with joy, "I baptize you in the name of the Father, and of the Son, and of the Holy Ghost. Amen."

She shrieked. Her slight form crumpled. A hissing of breath, some screams and hoarse calls, sounded from the pews. The priest stooped, forgetting his stiffness in his haste, and gathered her to him. "Yria!" he cried. "What's wrong?"

She looked about her, panting and with the eyes of one stunned. "I . . . am . . . Margrete," she said. "Who are you?" Provost Magnus loomed over them. "Who are you?"

Knud cast his tear-streaming gaze up toward the archdeacon. "Is it that, that, that she is in truth soulless?"

Magnus pointed to the altar. "Margrete," he said, with such iron in his tone that the whole rough congregation fell silent, "look yonder. Who is that?"

Her glance followed the knobbly finger. She raised herself to her knees and drew the Cross. "That is Our Lord and Saviour Jesus Christ," she said almost steadily.

Magnus lifted his arms. He likewise wept, but for glory. "Lo, a miracle!" he shouted. "I thank You, Almighty God, that You have let me, most miserable of sinners, witness this token of Your overflowing grace." He swung on the folk. "Kneel! Praise Him! Praise Him!"

Later, alone with Knud, he explained more calmly: "The bishop and I thought something like this might happen. Your message did relate that the sacred pictures had not turned from her. Moreover, in the archives we found a few legends from the days of those apostles to the Danes, Ansgar and Poppo—apocryphal, yet now seen to have embodied some truth. Thus I can interpret what we have seen.

"Like their Faerie parents, halflings have indeed no souls, though doubtless their bodies also are ageless. Yet God is willing to receive even these, aye, even full-fledged beings of that kind. Upon Margrete's baptism, He gave her a soul as He gives a soul to a quickening babe. She has become entirely human, mortal in the flesh, immortal in the spirit. We must see well to it that she loses not her salvation."

"Why can she not remember?" Knud asked.

"She has been reborn. She keeps the Danish language, with what other terrestrial skills she has; but everything that is in any way linked to her former life has been cleansed from her. That must be Heaven's mercy, lest Satan use homesickness to lure the ewe lamb from the fold."

The old man seemed more troubled than pleased. "Her sister and brothers will take this ill."

"I know about them," said Magnus. "Have the girl meet them on the strand in front of those seven trees which grow low and close together. Their branches will screen my men, who will have crossbows cocked——"

"No! Never! I will not have it!" Knud gulped, knowing how scant an authority was his. At length he persuaded Magnus not to ambush the halflings. They were leaving soon. And what might the effect be on Margrete's new soul, that almost the first thing she would remember was a deed of blood?"

Therefore the priests told the men-at-arms to shoot only if ordered. All waited behind the trees, in a cold, blowing dusk. Margrete's white robe fluttered dimly before them where she stood, puzzled but obedient, hands folded over a rosary.

A sound broke through the soughing of leaves and the clashing of whitecaps. Forth from the water waded the tall man, the tall woman, and the boy. It could just be seen that they were unclad. "Lewdness," Magnus hissed angrily.

The man said something in an unknown tongue.

"Who are you?" Margrete replied in Danish. She shrank from them. "I can't understand you. What do you want?"

"Yria——" The woman held out her wet arms. "Yria." Her own Danish was agonized. "What have they done to you?"

"I am Margrete," the girl said. "They told me...I must be brave.... Who are you? What are you?"

The boy snarled and sprang toward her. She raised the crucifix. "In Jesu name, begone!" she yelled, aghast. He did not obey, though he stopped when his brother caught him. The tall man made a strangled noise.

Margrete whirled and fled over the dunes toward the hamlet. Her siblings stood a while, talking in tones of bafflement and dismay, before they returned to their sea.

V

THE island men call Laesö lies four leagues east of northern Jut-land. Sand and ling, windswept from Skagerrak and Kattegat both, it holds few dwellers. Yet the small churches upon it forever banned merfolk from what was once their greatest gathering place—for then it was Hlesey, Hler's Island, with Hler a name of Aegir. Early on, therefore, Christian priests exiled thence, with bell, book, and candle, all beings of heathendom.

But just below it, like a whale calf nigh to its mother, is the islet Hornfiskrön: hardly more than a reef, half a league or so from end to end, though bearing a thin growth of heather. Nobody ever lived there or thought to ban unholiness. Enough of the sea god's older power lingered that merfolk could approach from the south and go ashore.

Thither Vanimen, their king, had brought the Liri tribe, on a day when rain was blowing in from the west. It had taken them longer than a healthy adult would have needed, for many small ones were among them. Besides, that large a band could not well live off the waters as it fared, and hunger soon weakened everyone.

Wading to land, they felt the wind run bleak across their bodies, and the first stinging drops. It hooted, skirled, piped, while steely waves with flying manes chopped and growled beneath. Sand hissed white. Westward loomed a darkness where lightning scrib-bled runes; the eastern sky was hidden by a low wrack.

Vanimen climbed onto the highest dune close by—the grittiness hurt his footwebs—and waited for his followers to settle down. A goodly sight he gave them, standing trident in hand for a sign of majesty. He was bigger than most, sculptured with muscle below the snow-fair skin; the scars thereon reminded of how many centuries he had endured, how many frightful battles he had won. Golden hair hung wet past his shoulders, around a face much like that of his son Tauno, save that his eyes were sea-green. Calm rested there, strength, wisdom.

That was a mask he put on. Without hope, they were foredoomed. Shattered by what had happened, they looked out of their wretchedness to him alone.

Alone forsooth, he thought. The longer he lived, the lonelier he grew. Few merfolk reached his age; none else had done so in Liri; something took them, oftener soon than late, unless they had rare skill and luck. No friends of his boyhood remained, and his first sweetheart had been a dream these hundreds of years. For a short while he had dared believe that with Agnete he had found what mortals called happiness. Well had he known it could only last a blink of time, until her flesh withered and she went wherever humans did. He had imagined her children might keep a measure of joy for him. (Oh, bitterest of everything, maybe, was that he could no more tend the graves of the three who died.) Tauno, who carried his father's bardic gift on to something higher; Eyjan's healthy beauty; Kennin's promise; Yria's trustfulness, her likeness in looks to her mother—but the bearers were gone, left behind, and could they ever search the great seas enough to rejoin him?

He must not be weak, Vanimen remembered. As if with a bodily heave, he put grief aside and regarded his people.

They numbered about sevenscore, he saw. Belike it was the first time anyone had cared to count them, and even today, he the sole one who thought to do so. His long life, the ever-growing weight of experience and of reflection thereupon, had taken away the easygoing nature common to his race, given him a mind that could brood like a human's.

More than half the gathering were children. (At that, several had died on the flight hither.) They clustered about their mothers— a babe at a breast, a toddler whom she tried to shield from the weather, a bairn whose limbs were lengthening but who still clung to a lock of her hair while staring out of wide eyes at a world gone harsh and strange. . . . Grown males and unencumbered females stood apart from this huddle. Fatherhood among the merfolk was nearly always a matter of guesswork, and never of import. Offspring were raised loosely by their mothers, whatever lovers these chanced to have at the moment, female friends and *their* lovers, ultimately by the tribe.

Save for Agnete's, of course. . . . How she had striven to build into them a sense of what she held to be right and decent. After she departed, Vanimen had given them what he could of their earthside heritage; after all, he had seen something of that over the centuries. Now he wondered if he had done them any service.

Well, but those haggard faces were turned his way. He must offer them more than the empty wail of the wind.

He filled his lungs till his voice could boom forth: "People of Liri that was, here we must decide our course. Wallowing blindly about, we will die. Yet every shore we ken that might nourish us is either forbidden to beings of Faerie—most of them are—or hold as many of our kind as can live there. Where then shall we seek?"

A quite young male called, with a lilt of eagerness: "Do we need a coast? I've kept myself for weeks in the open ocean."

Vanimen shook his head. "You could not for years, Haiko. Where would you go for rest or refuge? Where would you raise a home, or find the very stuff you need for its making? The deeps we may enter for a short while, but we cannot stay in them; they are too cold, black, and barren; the ooze covers all that we dig from skerries and eyots and shoals. Without an abiding place, presently without tools or weapons, you would be no more than a beast, less fitted for life than the shark or orca which would hunt you down. And before you perished, the children would, the hope of our blood. No, we are like our cousins the seals, we need earth and air as much as we need water."

Fire, he thought, was kept for men.

Well, he had heard of the dwarfs, but the thought of living underground was shuddersome.

A lean female with blue tresses took the word: "Are you sure we can find no place nearby? I've cruised the Gulf of Finland. At the far end of it are rich fishing grounds which none of our sort inhabit."

"Did you ever ask why, Meiiva?" Vanimen replied.

Surprised, she said, "I meant to, but always forgot."

"The careless way of Faerie," he sighed. "*I* found out. It nearly cost me my life, and nightmares rode me for years afterward."

Their looks at him sharpened. That was at least better than the dullness of despair. "The mortals there are Rus," he told them, "a different folk from Danes, Norse, Swedes, Finns, Letts, Lapps, any in these parts. The halfworld beings that share their land with them are ... different also: some friendly, but some weird and some altogether terrible. A vodianoi we might cope with, but a rousalka——" Memory bit him, colder than wind and thickening rain. "Each river seems to have a rousalka. She wears the form of a maiden, and is said to have been one until she drowned; but she lures men into the depths and takes them captive for frightful tortures. I too was lured, on a moonlit night in the tidewater, and what happened, what I saw—well, I escaped. But we cannot live along shores thus haunted."

Silence fell, under the lash of the downpour. Color was gone, vision found naught save grays and darknesses. Lightning flared close; thunder went rolling down unseen heaven.

Finally an elder male—born when Harald Bluetooth reigned in Denmark—spoke: "I've given thought to this as we traveled. If we cannot enter as a group where our kind dwell, can we not by ones and twos, into the various domains? They could take us in piecemeal, I believe. They might even be glad of the newness we'd bring."

"For some, that may be the answer," Vanimen said unwillingly; he had awaited the idea. "Not for most of us, though. Remember how few nests of merfolk are left; we were the last on a Danish strand. I do not think they could, between them, add our whole number without suffering for it. Surely they would be loth to have our little ones, who must be fed for years before they can help bring in food."

He straightened, to stand as tall as might be in the storm. "Also," he called to them, "we *are* the Liri dwellers. We have our shared blood, ways, memories, all that makes us ourselves. Would you part from your friends and lovers, would you forget old songs and never quite learn any new, would you let Liri of your forebears—your forebears since the Great Ice withdrew—die as if it had never been?

"Shall we not aid each other? Shall we let it become true what the Christians say, that Faerie folk cannot love?"

They gaped at him through the rain. Several babies cried. At length Meiiva responded: "I know you, Vanimen. You have a plan. Let us judge it."

A plan——He lacked power to decree. Liri had chosen him king after the last leader's bones were found on a reef, a harpoon head between the ribs. He presided over infrequent folkmoots. He judged disputes, though naught save a wish to keep the general esteem could enforce his decisions upon the losers. He dealt on behalf of his people with communities elsewhere; this was seldom necessary. He led those rare undertakings that required their united effort. He was master of their festivals.

His highest duties lay outside of tradition. He was supposed to be the vessel of wisdom, a counselor to the young and the troubled, a preserver and teacher of lore. Keeper of talismans, knower of spells, he guarded the welfare of Liri against monsters, evil magic, and the human world. He interceded with the Powers . . . aye, he had guested Ran herself. . . .

His rewards were to dwell in a hall, rather than the simple home of an ordinary merman; to have his needs provided for when he did not choose to do his own hunting; to have splendid things brought him as gifts (though he in his turn was expected to be hospitable and openhanded); to be highly respected by a tribe not otherwise prone to reverence.

The rewards were gone, save perhaps the last, and it a heavy part of the duty which remained.

He said: "This is not the whole universe. In my youth I wandered widely, as a few of our breed have done sometimes. Westward I came as far as Greenland, where I heard from both merfolk and men of countries beyond. No living member of either race had ever visited there, but the knowledge was certain; dolphins confirmed it for me. Many of you will remember my bespeaking this now and then. Those appear to be wonderful shoals and shores, that Christendom hardly is aware of and has no dominion in. If we went thither, we would have them to ourselves—vastness, life, and beauty to grow into, free and at peace."

Astonishment replied in a babble. Haiko was the first to exclaim above it: "You've just avowed we can't stay in midocean. Can we—our young, indeed, and most of us who are grown—can we outlive that long a swim? There's the reason why nobody like us dwells yonder!"

"True, true." The king lifted his trident. A hush fell. "But hear me," he said. "I too have been thinking. We could make the passage with scant losses or none, were islands along the way for rest, refuge, and refurbishing. Not so? Well, what of a floating island that came with us? Such is called a ship.

"Men owe us for the harm they have done us, who never

harmed them. I say: let us seize a ship of theirs and steer for the western lands—the new world!"

By eventide, the storm had gone away. Likewise had the storm among the people; after hours of dispute, they were agreed. For the main part they sought sleep against the morrow, curled up behind dunes, though a number went out after game to keep alive on.

Vanimen paced with Meiiva, around and around the islet. They were close to each other, often lovers before and after Agnete. Less flighty, more feeling than most, she could frequently cheer him.

Eastward the sky was a violet-blue chalice for the earliest stars. Westward it fountained in red, purple, and hot gold. The waters moved luminous and lulling. The air was quiet and faintly softer than hitherto; it smelled of kelp and distances. A person could set aside hunger, weariness, woe, to enjoy an hour's hope.

"Do you honestly feel this can be done?" Meiiva asked.

"Yes," the king declared. "I've told you how I've been on the prowl about that harbor, again and again, the latest time not long ago. We may have to lurk, watching for our chance. However, at this season I expect that will be no great while; the town does much trade. Nobody will dare pursue us at night, and by dawn we should be well away, unfindable."

"Do you know how to handle a ship?" she pounced. "That's something which didn't get talked about today."

"Well, only a little, from what I've seen for myself or garnered from men—I have had friends among them once in a while, you recall," Vanimen said. "But we can learn. There should be no big danger in it if we keep plenty of sea room. Nor should there be any haste." His tone quickened. "For we *will* have our island. Able to rest on it by turns, we'll need far less food; thus we can sustain ourselves by hunting. And, of course, we needn't fret about fresh water as humans must. And we can find our way more readily than they can. The simple surety that we have a land to steer for, and not an edge where the seas roar down to the nether gulf—that alone should make the difference which saves us."

He gazed from sand and scrub, to the glimmer of sunset upon the western horizon. "I know not whether to pity or envy the children of Adam," he murmured. "I know not at all."

Meiiva took his hand. "You're strangely drawn to them," she said.

He nodded. "Aye, more and more as the years flow onward. I do not speak of it, for who would understand? Yet I feel . . . I know not . . . more is in Creation than this glittering, tricksy Faerie of ours. No matter that humans have immortal souls. We've always reckoned that too low a price for being landbound. But I have wondered"—his free hand clenched, his visage worked—"what do they have in this life, here and now, amidst every misery, what do they glimpse, that we are forever blind to?"

Stavanger, in the south of Norway, dreamed beneath a waning moon. That light made a broken bridge across the fjord, where holms rose darkling, silvered the thatch and shingle of roofs, softened the stone of the cathedral and came alive in its windows, turned the streets below the house galleries into even deeper guts of blackness. It touched the figureheads and masts of vessels at the wharf. . . .

Candle-glow through thin-scraped horn shone on the aftercastle of a particular ship. She was from the Hansa city of Danzig: one-masted like a cog but longer, beamier, of the new sort that were known as hulks. Day would have shown her clinker-built hull bright red, with white and yellow trim.

Moon-ripples trailed the stealthily swimming mermen. They felt no chill, no fear; they were after quarry.

Vanimen led them to his goal. The freeboard was more than he could overleap, but he had earlier gone ashore and stolen what he would need. A flung hook caught the rail amidships. From it dangled a Jacob's ladder up which he climbed.

Quiet though he sought to be, his noise reached the watchman. (The crew were visiting the inns and stews.) That fellow came down from the poop bearing his lanthorn and pike. Dull gleams went off the steel, and off the gray streaks in his beard; he was no young man, but portly and slow. "Who goes?" he challenged in German; and as he saw what confronted him, a howl of terror: "Ach, Jesus, help me! Help, help——"

He could not be let rouse the harbor. Vanimen unslung the trident from his shoulders and gave it him in the belly, a full thrust that shocked back through the merman's own muscles while it skewered the liver. Blood spurted forth. The guard fell to the deck. He writhed about. "Johanna, Peter, Maria, Friedrich," he gasped—the names of wife and children? His look swirled to Vanimen. He half raised a hand. "God curse you for this," came from him. "St. Michael, my namesake, warrior angel, avenge——"

Vanimen put a tine through an eye, straight into the brain, and the watchman grew still. Mermen were swarming up the ladder. They paid scant heed; none but their king knew German. He stood for a moment, heartsick at what he had done, before he pitched the corpse out and took command of the ship.

That was no easy task, when his followers were quite ignorant of her use. Surely their awkwardness and gropings about reached ears on land. They were ready to fight if they must. But no more humans appeared. It was unwise for a common person to seek after a racket heard in the night, and whatever burgher guard was in Stavanger doubtless decided that nothing untoward was likely going on—a brawl, maybe, or a drunken revel.

The mooring lines were slipped. The sail, unfurled, caught the land breeze for which Vanimen had waited until this late hour. There was ample light for Faerie vision to steer by. The hulk stole down the bay. As she passed an island, the mermaids and children started coming aboard.

By dawn she had left Norway well behind her.

VI

INGEBORG Hjalmarsdatter was an Alswoman of about thirty winters. She had been orphaned early and married off to the first younger son who would have her. When she proved barren and he went down with the boat whereon he worked, leaving her nothing, no other man made an offer. The parish cared for its paupers by binding them over for a year at a time to whoever would take them. Such householders knew well how to squeeze out their money's worth in toil, without spending unduly on food or clothes for their charges. Ingeborg, instead, got Red Jens to give her passage on his craft to the herring run. She plied what trade she could among the booths on shore, and came back with some shillings. Thereafter she made the trip yearly. Otherwise she stayed home, save when she walked the woodland road to Hadsund for market days.

Father Knud implored her to mend her life. "Can you find me better work than this?" she laughed. He must needs ban her from Communion, if not the Mass; and she seldom went to the latter, since women hissed her in the street and might throw a fishhead or a bone at her. The men, easier-going on the whole, did agree she could not be allowed to dwell among them, if only because of their goodwives' tongues.

She had a cabin built, a shack on the strand several furlongs north of Als. Most of the unwed young men came to her, and the crews of vessels that stopped in, and the rare chapman, and husbands after dark. Had they no coppers, she would take pay in kind, wherefore she got the name Cod-Ingeborg. Between whiles she was alone, and often strolled far along the shore or into the woods. She had no fear of rovers—they would not likely kill her, and what else mattered?—and little of trolls.

On a winter evening some five years past, when Tauno was

just beginning to explore the land, he knocked on her door. After she let him in, he explained who he was. He had been watching from afar, seen men slink in and swagger out; he was trying to learn the ways of his lost mother's folk; would she tell him what this was about? He ended with spending the night. Since, he had many times done so. She was different from the mermaids, warmer somehow in heart as well as flesh; her trade meant naught to him, whose undersea fellows knew no more of marriage than of any other sacrament; he could learn much from her, and tell her much, murmured lip to lip as they lay beneath the coverlet; he liked her for her kindliness and toughness and wry mirth.

For her part, she would take no pay from him, and few gifts. "I do not think ill of most men," she said. "Some, yes, like that cruel old miser Kristoffer into whose hands I would have fallen had I not chosen this way. My skin crawls when he comes smirking." She spat on the clay floor, then sighed. "He has the coin, though. . . . No, mainly they are not bad, those rough-bearded men; and sometimes a lad gives me joy." She rumpled his hair. "You give me more, without fail, Tauno. Can you not see, that's why it would be wrong for you to hire me?"

"No, I cannot," he answered in honesty. "I have things you say men reckon precious, amber, pearls, pieces of gold. If they will help you, why should you not have them?"

"Well," she said, "among other reasons, word would come to the lords around Hadsund, that Cod-Ingeborg was peddling such wares. They'd want to know how I got them. I do not wish my last man to wear a hood." She kissed him. "Oh, let us say what's better, that your tales of your undersea wonderland give me more than any hand-graspable wealth may buy."

She dropped a number of hints that she longed to be taken away as was fair Agnete. He was deaf to them, and she gave up. Why should he want a barren burden?

When Provost Magnus exorcised the merfolk, Ingeborg would see no person for a week. Her eyes were red for a long time afterward.

Finally Tauno sought her again. He came from the water, naked save for the headband that caught his locks and the sharp flint dagger belted at his hip. In his right hand he carried a barbed spear. It was a cold, misty twilight, fog asmoke until the lap-lapping wavelets were blurred and the stars withheld. There was a scent of kelp, fish, and from inland of damp earth. The sand gritted beneath his feet, the dune grass scratched his ankles.

A pair of fisher youths were nearing the hut, with a flaming link to show the way. Tauno saw farther in the dark than they could. Under the wadmal sameness of cowl, smock, and hose, he knew who they were. He trod into their path. "No," he said. "Not this night."

"Why . . . why, Tauno," said one with a foolish grin. "You'd not bar your chums from their bit of fun, would you, or her from this fine big flounder? We won't be long, if you're so eager."

"Go home. Stay there."

"Tauno, you know me, we've talked, played ball, you've come aboard when I was out by myself in the jollyboat, I'm Stig——"

"Must I kill you?" asked Tauno without raising his voice.

They looked at him by the guttering link-flare, towering over them, hugely thewed, armed, hair wet as a strand-washer's and faintly green under its fairness, the mer-face and the yellow eyes chill as northlights. They turned and walked hastily back. Through the fog drifted Stig's shout: "They were right about you, you're soulless, you damned *thing*——"

Tauno smote the door of the shack. It was a sagging box of logs weathered gray, peat-roofed, windowless, though a glow straggled outward and air inward where the chinking moss had shriveled. Ingeborg opened for him and closed behind them both. Besides a blubber lamp, she had a low fire going. Monstrous shadows crawled on the double-width sleeping dais, the stool and table, the few cooking and sewing tools, clothes chest, sausage and stockfish hung from the rafters, and those poles across the rafters which skewered rounds of hardtack. On a night like this, smoke hardly rose from hearthstone to roofhole.

Tauno's lungs always burned for a minute after he had come ashore and emptied them in that single heave which merfolk used. The air was so thin, so dry (and he felt half deafened among its muffled noises, though to be sure he saw better). The reek here was worse. He must cough ere he could speak.

Ingeborg held him, wordlessly. She was short and buxom, snub-nosed, freckled, with a big gentle mouth. Her hair and eyes were dark brown, her voice high but sweet. There have been princesses less well-favored than Cod-Ingeborg. He did not like the smell of old sweat in her gown, any more than he liked any of the stenches of humankind; but underneath it he caught a sunny odor of woman.

"I hoped . . ." she breathed at last, "I hoped. . . ."

He shoved her arms away, stood back, glared, and hefted the spear. "Where is my sister?" he snapped.

"Oh. She is—is well, Tauno. None will harm her. None would dare." Ingeborg tried to draw him from the door. "Come, my unhappy dear, sit, have a stoup, be at ease with me."

"First they reaved from her everything that was her life——"

Tauno must stop anew to cough. Ingeborg took the word. "It had to be," she said. "Christian folk could not let her dwell unchristened among them. You can't blame them, not even the priests. A higher might than theirs has been in this." She shrugged, with her oft-seen one-sided grin. "For the price of her past, and of growing old, ugly, dead in less than a hundred years, she gains eternity in Paradise. You may live a long while, but when you die you'll be done, a blown-out candle flame. Myself, I'll live beyond my body, most likely in Hell. Which of us three is the luckiest?"

Still grim but somewhat calmed, Tauno leaned his weapon and sat down on the dais. The straw ticking rustled beneath him. The peat fire sputtered with small blue and yellow dancers; its smoke would have been pleasant if less thick. Shadows crouched in corners and under the roof, and leaped about, misshapen, on the log walls. The cold and dankness did not trouble him, unclad though he was. Ingeborg shivered where she stood.

He peered at her through the murk. "I know that much," he said. "There's a young fellow in the hamlet that they hope to make a priest of. So he could tell my sister Eyjan about it when she found him alone." His chuckle rattled. "She says he's not bad to lie with, save that the open air gives him sneezing fits." Harshly again: "Well, if that's the way the world swims, naught can we do but give room. However . . . yestre'en Kennin and I went in search of Yria, to make sure she wasn't being mistreated. Ugh, the mud and filth in those wallows you call streets! Up and down we went, to every house, yes, to church and graveyard. We had not spied her from afar, do you see, not for days. And we'd have known were she inside anything, be it cabin or coffin. She may be mortal now, our little Yria, but her body is still half her father's, and that last night on the strand it had not lost its smell like daylit waves." Fist thudded on knee. "Kennin and Eyjan raged, would have stormed shore and asked at harpoon point. I told them we'd only risk death, and how can the dead help Yria? Yet it was hard to wait till sunset, when I knew you'd be here, Ingeborg."

She sat down against him, an arm around his waist, a hand on his thigh, cheek on shoulder. "I know," she said most softly.

He remained unbending. "Well? What's happened, then?"

"Why, the provost took her off with him to Viborg town——Wait! No harm is meant. How could they dare harm a chalice of Heavenly grace?" Ingeborg said that matter-of-factly, and afterward she fleered. "You've come to the right place, Tauno. The provost had a scribe with him, and that one was here and I asked him about any plans for keeping our miracle fed. They're not unkindly in Als, I told him, but neither are they rich. She has no more yarns to spin from undersea for their pleasure. Who wants a girl that must be taught afresh like a babe? Who wants a foster-daughter to find a dowry for? Oh, she could get something—pauper's work, marriage to a deckhand, or that which I chose—but was this right for a miracle? The cleric said no, nor was it intended. They would bring her back with them and put her in Asmild Cloister near Viborg."

"What's that?" Tauno inquired.

Ingeborg did her best to explain. In the end she could say: "They'll house Margrete and teach her. When she's of the right age, she'll take her vows. Then she'll live there in purity, no doubt widely reverenced, till she dies, no doubt in an odor of sanctity. Or do you believe that the corpse of a saint does not stink as yours and mine will?"

Aghast, Tauno exclaimed, "But this is frightful!"

"Oh? Many would count it glorious good fortune."

His eyes stabbed at hers. "Would you?"

"Well . . . no."

"Locked among walls for all her days; shorn, heavily clad, ill-fed, droning through her nose at God while letting wither what God put between her legs; never to know love, children about her, the growth of home and kin, or even wanderings under apple trees in blossom time——"

"Tauno, it is the way to eternal bliss."

"Hm. Rather would I have my bliss now, and then the dark. You too—in your heart—not so?—whether or not you've said you

mean to repent on your deathbed. Your Christian Heaven seems
to me a shabby place to spend forever."

"Margrete may think otherwise."

"Mar—aah. Yria." He brooded a while, chin on fist, lips taut,
breathing noisily in the smoke. "Well," he said, "if that is what
she truly wants, so be it. Yet how can we know? How can *she*
know? Will they let her imagine anything is real and right beyond
their gloomy cloi—cloister? I would not see my little sister
cheated, Ingeborg."

"You sent her ashore because you would not see her eaten by
eels. Now what choice is there?"

"None?"

The despair of him who had always been strong was like a
knife to her. "My dear, my dear." She held him close. But instead
of tears, the old fisher hardheadedness rose in her.

"One thing among men opens every road save to Heaven," she
said, "and that it does not necessarily bar. Money."

A word in the mer-tongue burst from him. "Go on!" he said
in Danish, and clutched her arm with bruising fingers.

"To put it simplest: gold," Ingeborg told him, not trying to
break free. "Or whatever can be exchanged for gold, though the
metal itself is best. See you, if she had a fortune, she could live
where she wished—given enough, at the King's court, or in some
foreign land richer than Denmark. She'd command servants, men-
at-arms, warehouses, broad acres. She could take her pick among
suitors. Then, if she chose to leave this and return to the nuns,
that would be a free choice."

"My folk had gold! We can dig it out of the ruins!"

"How much?"

There was more talk. The sea people had never thought to
weigh up what was only a metal to them, too soft for most uses
however handsome and unrusting it might be.

At the end, Ingeborg shook her head. "Too scant, I fear," she
sighed. "In the ordinary course of things, plenty. This is different.
Here Asmild Cloister and Viborg Cathedral have a living miracle.
She'll draw pilgrims from everywhere. The Church is her guardian
in law, and won't let her go to a lay family for your few cups and
plates."

"What's needed, then?"

"A whopping sum. Thousands of marks. See you, some must

be bribed. Others, who can't be bought, must be won over by grand gifts to the Church. And then enough must be left for Margrete to be wealthy.... Thousands of marks."

"What weight?" Tauno fairly yelled, with a merman's curse.

"I—I—how shall I, fisherman's orphan and widow, who never held one mark at a time in this fist, how shall I guess?... A boatful? Yes, I think a boatload would do."

"A boatload!" Tauno sagged back. "And we have not even a boat."

Ingeborg smiled sadly and ran fingers along his arm. "No man wins every game," she murmured. "You've done what you could. Let your sister spend threescore years in denying her flesh, and afterward forever in unfolding her soul. She may remember us, when you are dust and I am burning."

Tauno shook his head. His eyelids squinched together. "No...she bears the same blood as I...it's not a restful blood...she's shy and gentle, but she was born to the freedom of the world's wide seas...if holiness curdles in her, during a lifetime among whisker-chinned crones, what of her chances at Heaven?"

"I know not, I know not."

"An unforced choice, at least. To buy it, a boatload of gold. A couple of wretched tons, to buy Yria's welfare."

"Tons! Why—I hadn't thought—less than that, surely. A few hundred pounds ought to be ample." Eagerness touched Ingeborg. "Do you suppose you could find that much?"

"Hm...wait. Wait. Let me hark back——" Tauno sat bolt upright. "Yes!" he shouted. "I do know!"

"Where? How?"

With the mercury quickness of Faerie, he became a planner. "Long ago was a city of men on an island in midocean," he said, not loud but shiveringly, while he stared into the shadows. "Great it was, and gorged with riches. Its god was a kraken. They cast down weighted offerings to him—treasure, that he cared not about, but with it kine, horses, condemned evildoers; and these the kraken could eat. He need not snatch aught else than a whale now and then—or a ship, to devour its crew, and over the centuries he and his priests had learned the signals which told him that such-and-such vessels were unwanted at Averorn.... So the kraken grew sluggish, and appeared not for generations of men; nor was there any need, since outsiders dared no longer attack.

"In time the islanders themselves came to doubt he was more than a fable. Meanwhile a new folk had arisen on the mainland. Their traders came, bearing not goods alone, but gods who didn't want costly sacrifices. The people of Averorn flocked to these new gods. The temple of the kraken stood empty, its fires burned out, its priests died and were not replaced. Finally the king of the city ordered an end to the rites that kept him fed.

"After one year, dreadful in his hunger, the kraken rose from the sea bottom; and he sank the harbored ships, and his arms reached inland to knock down toers and pluck forth prey. Belike he also had power over quake and volcano—for the island was whelmed, it foundered and is forgotten by all humankind."

"Why, that is wonderful!" Ingeborg clapped her hands, not thinking at once of the small children who had gone down with the city. "Oh, I'm so glad!"

"It's not that wonderful," Tauno said. "The merfolk remember Averorn because the kraken lairs there yet. They give it a wide berth."

"I—I see. You must, though, bear some hope if you——"

"Yes. Worth trying. Look you, woman: Men cannot go undersea. Merfolk have no ships, nor metal weapons that don't soon corrode away. Never have the races worked together. If they did—maybe——"

Ingeborg was a long time quiet before she said, almost not to be heard, "And maybe you'd be slain."

"Yes, yes. What is that? Everybody's born fey. My people stand close—they must—and a single life is of no high account among us. How could I range off to the ends of the world, knowing I had not done what I might for my little sister Yria who looks like my mother?" Tauno gnawed his lip. "But the ship, how to get the ship and crew?"

They talked back and forth, she trying to steer him from his course, he growing more set in it. At last she gave in. "I may be able to show you what you want," she said.

"What? How?"

"You understand the fishing craft of Als are too cockleshell for what you have in mind. Nor could you hire a ship from a

respectable owner, you being soulless and your venture being
mad. However, there is a cog, not large but still a cog, that works
out of Hadsund, the town some miles hence at the end of Mariager
Fjord. I go to Hadsund on market days, and thus have come to
know her men. She's a cargo tramp, has fared as widely north as
Finland, east as Wendland, west as Iceland. In such outlying parts,
the crew have not been above a bit of piracy when it looked safe.
They're a gang of ruffians, and their skipper, the owner, is the
worst. He came of a good family near Herning, but his father
chose the wrong side in the strife between kings' sons, and thus
Herr Ranild Grib has nothing left to him besides this ship. And
he swears bitterly at the Hansa, whose fleets are pushing him out
of what business he could formerly get.

"It may be he's desperate enough to league with you."

Tauno considered. "Maybe," he said. "Um-m-m . . . we merfolk are not wont to betray and kill our own kind, as men with
souls are. I can fight; I would not fear to meet anyone with any
weapon or none; still, where it comes to haggling and to being
wary of a shipmate, that might be hard for us three siblings."

"I know," Ingeborg said. "Best I go along, to dicker and keep
an eye open on your behalf."

He started. "Would you indeed?" After a moment: "You shall
have a full share in the booty, dear friend. You too shall be free."

"If we live; otherwise, what matter? But Tauno, Tauno, think
not I offer this out of lust for wealth——"

"I must speak with Eyjan and Kennin, of course—we must
plan—we must talk further with you—nonetheless——"

"Indeed, Tauno, indeed, indeed. Tomorrow, forever, you shall
have what you will from me. Tonight, though, I ask one thing,
that you stop this fretting, cast off that veil which covers your
eyes, and let us be only Tauno and Ingeborg. See, I've drawn off
my gown for you."

VII

WHEN the black cog *Herning* stood out of Mariager Fjord, she caught a wind that filled her sail and sent her northward at a good clip. On deck, Tauno, Eyjan, and Kennin shed the human clothes—foul, enclosing rags!—that had disguised them during their days of chaffer with Ranild Espensen Grib. A lickerish shout lifted from six of the eight men, at sight of Eyjan white in the sunlight, clad only in dagger belt and tossing bronze mane. They were a shaggy, flea-bitten lot, those men, scarred from fights, their leather jackets, wadmal shirts and breeks ripe with old grease stains.

The seventh was a lad of eighteen winters, Niels Jonsen. He had come to Hadsund a couple of years before, seeking deckhand work to help care for widowed mother and younger siblings on a tiny tenant farm. Not long ago, the ship whereon he served had been wrecked—by God's mercy without loss of life—and he could get no other new berth than this. He was a good-looking boy, slender, flaxen-haired, blue-eyed, with straightforwardly shaped fresh features. Now he blinked away tears. "How beautiful she is," he whispered.

The eighth was the captain. He scowled and came down off the poopdeck that sheltered the man at the tiller. (There was also a deck over the bows, through which the forepost jutted. Below and between these reached the main deck, with mast, two hatches, tackle, cooking-hearth, and what cargo was carried topside. Among this last were a red granite boulder, three feet through and about a ton in weight; and a dozen extra anchors; and much cable.)

Ranild went to the halflings, where they and Ingeborg stood on the port side watching Jutland's long hills slide by. It was a clear day; the sun cast dazzling glitter across gray-green-blue whitecaps. Wind skirled, rigging thrummed, timbers creaked as

41

the cog's cutwater surged with a bone in its teeth. Overhead, gulls
mewed and made a snowstorm of wings. A smell of salt and tar
blew around.

"You!" Ranild barked. "Make yourselves decent!"

Kennin gave him a look of dislike. Those had been hard hours
of bargaining, in a back room of an evil inn; and merfolk were
not used to a tongue like Ranild's, rougher than a lynx's. "Who
are you to speak of decency?" Kennin snapped.

"Ease off," Tauno muttered. He regarded the skipper with no
more love but somewhat more coolness. Not tall, Ranild was thick
of chest and arm. Black hair, never washed and scanty on top,
framed a coarse broken-nosed pale-eyed countenance; snag teeth
showed through a beard that spilled halfway down the tub belly.
He was dressed like his crew, save that he bore a short sword as
well as a knife and floppy boots rather than shoes or bare feet.

"What's the matter?" Tauno asked. "You, Ranild, may like
to wear clothes till they rot off you. Why should we?"

"*Herr* Ranild, merman!" The shipmaster clapped hand on hilt.
"My folk were Junkers when yours dwelt among the flatfish—I'm
noble yet, the Fiend thunder me! It's my vessel, I laid out the
costs of this faring, you'll by God's bones do what I tell you or
swing from the yardarm!"

Eyjan's dagger whipped out, to gleam near his gullet. "Unless
we hang you by those louse-nest whiskers," she said.

The sailors reached for knives and belaying pins. Ingeborg
pushed between Eyjan and Ranild. "What are we doing?" she
cried. "At each other's throats already? You'll not get the gold
without the merfolk, Herr Ranild, nor they get it without your
help. Hold back, in Jesu name!"

They withdrew a little on either side, still glowering. Ingeborg
went on quietly: "I think I know what's wrong. Herr Ranild, these
children of the clean sea have been rubbed raw by days in a town
where hogs root in the streets, by nights in a room full of stink
and bedbugs. Nevertheless, you, Tauno, Eyjan, Kennin, should've
listened to a rede well meant if not so well spoken."

"What is that?" Tauno asked.

Ingeborg flushed; her eyes dropped and her fingers wrestled.
She said quieter yet: "Remember the agreement. Herr Ranild
wanted you, Eyjan, to go below for him and his men. You would
not. I said I . . . would do that, and thus we came to terms. Now

you are very fair, Eyjan, fairer than any mortal girl can be. It's not right for you to flaunt your loveliness before those who may only stare. Our voyage is into deadly danger. We can't afford strife."

The halfling bit her lip. "I had not thought of that," she admitted. Flaring: "But rather than wear those barn-rug rags when we've no need of disguise, I'll kill the crew and we four will man this ship ourselves."

Ranild opened his mouth. Tauno forestalled him: "That's empty talk, sister mine. See here, we can stand the horrible things till we pass Als. There we'll dive down to where Liri was, fetch garments fit to use—and cleanse the filth of these off us on the way."

Thus peace was made. Men kept leering at Eyjan, for the rainbow-hued tunic of three-ply fishskin that she donned after going underwater showed cleft of breasts and hardly reached past her hips. But they had Ingeborg to take below.

The human clothes had been from that woman, who walked alone through rover-haunted woods to Hadsund, got Ranild interested, and met the siblings on the shore of Mariager Fjord to guide them to him. Once the bargain was handselled, he had to persuade his men to go along. Gaunt, surly, ash-pale Oluv Ovesen, the second in command, had not hesitated; greed ruled his life. Torben and Lave said they had faced edged steel erenow and looked at the end to face nooses; therefore, why not a kraken? Palle, Tyge, and Sivard had let themselves be talked over. But the last deckhand quit, which was why young Niels Jonsen was taken on.

No one asked Ranild what had become of his former crewman. Secrecy was important, lest priest forbid or noble thrust into the undertaking. Aslak was simply never seen again.

That first day *Herning* passed the broad beaches and thunderous surf of the Skaw, and from the Skagerrak entered the North Sea. She must round Scotland, then work southwest to a locality well beyond Ireland. In spite of being a good sailer, she would need Godsend winds to make it in less than two weeks—which in truth was how long the time became.

Since she was traveling in ballast, there was ample room below decks, and that was where the men slept. The halflings disdained such a gloomy, dirty, rat-scuttering, roach-crawling cave, and took their rest above. They used no bags or blankets, only straw ticks. Often they would spring overboard, frolic about the ship, maybe vanish beneath the waves for an hour or two.

Ingeborg told Tauno once that she would have liked to stay topside with them; however, Ranild had ordered her to spend the nights in the hold, ready for whoever might want her. Tauno shook his head. "Humans are a nasty lot," he remarked.

"Your small sister has become human," she answered. "And have you forgotten your mother, Father Knud, your friends in Als?"

"N-n-no. Nor you, Ingeborg. After we're back home—but of course I'll be leaving Denmark."

"Yes." She glanced away. "We have another good fellow aboard. The boy Niels."

He was the sole crewman who did not use her, and yet who was always cheerful and polite toward her. (Tauno and Kennin likewise stayed clear of that pallet in the hold; those who now shared her were not honest yeomen and fishers, and for themselves they had billows to tumble in, seal and dolphin to play with, flowing green depths to enter.) Mostly Niels followed Eyjan about with his eyes and, shyly when off watch, himself.

The rest of the crew had no more to do with the halflings than they must. They took the fresh fish brought aboard, but would not speak with the bringers while it was eaten. To Ingeborg they grumbled words like, "Damned heathen...uppity...talking beasts...worse than Jews...we'd be forgiven many sins if we cut their throats, wouldn't we?...well, before I put my knife in that bare-legged wench, I've something else...." Ranild kept his own counsel. He too stayed aloof from the three after his few tries at friendliness were rebuffed. Tauno had sought to respond; but the skipper's talk bored when it did not disgust him, and he had never learned to dissemble.

He did like Niels. They seldom had converse, though, for Tauno was close-mouthed save when chanting a poem. Moreover, in age Niels was nearer to Kennin, and those two found a deal of memories and jokes to swap. Among other jobs, hours a day were spent in weaving the extra cable into a great net. Niels and Kennin would sit together at this work, paying no heed to the sullen men around, and laugh and chatter:

"——I swear that was one time an oyster showed surprise!"

"Hm, I mind me of years back when I was a sprat. We kept a few cows, and I was leading one of 'em to a kinsman's bull. By the road was a gristmill with a waterwheel, and from afar I saw it begin work. A cow has dimmer eyes than a human; this lovesick creature knew only that something big stood in the offing and bellowed. Away she went, me galloping after and yelling till the halter was yanked from my hand. But I soon caught her, oh yes. When she found it was no bull, she stopped, she looked like a blown-up bladder that's been blade-pricked; she merely stood till I took the halter, and afterward she shambled along meek as if she'd been poleaxed."

"Ho, ho, let me tell you about when we boys dressed a walrus in my father's robe of state——"

Eyjan would frequently join in the merriment. She did not follow ladylike ways, even in the slight degree that most mermaids did. She haggled her red locks off at the shoulders, wore no ring or necklace or golden gown save at festivals, would rather hunt or challenge the surf around a skerry than sit tame at home. On the whole, she scorned landfolk (in spite of which, she had prowled the woods with cries of delight for blossoms, birdsong, deer, squirrel, autumn's fiery leaves and the snow and icicles that glittered after). But of some she was fond, Niels among them. Also, she did not lie with her brothers—a Christian law which Agnete had gotten well into her older children ere leaving them—and the mermen were gone to an unknown place and the lads of Als were far behind.

Herning plowed through day and night, squall and breeze, until she raised what Tauno and Ranild agreed were the southern Orkney Islands. That was toward evening: mild weather, fair wind, clear summer night and a full moon due. They saw no reason not to push on through the narrows after sunset, the more so when the brothers offered to swim ahead as waterline lookouts. Eyjan wanted to do the same, but Tauno said one must stay back against possible disaster like a sudden onslaught of sharks; and when they drew lots, hers was the short straw. She cursed for minutes without repeating herself before she calmed down.

Thus it happened that she stood alone on the main deck, near the forecastle. Another lookout was perched aloft, screened from her by the bellying sail, and a helmsman was under the poop, hidden in its shadow. The rest, who had learned to trust the halflings in watery matters, snored below.

Save for Niels, who came back and found Eyjan there. The moonlight sparkled on her tunic, sheened on her face and breast and limbs, lost itself in her hair. It washed the deck clean, it built a shivering road from the horizon to the laciness of foam on small waves. They slapped very gently on the hull, those waves, and Niels, who was barefoot, could feel it, because the ship was heeled just enough that he became aware of standing. The sail, dull brown with leather crisscrossing by day, loomed overhead like a snow-peak. The rigging creaked, the wind lulled, the sea murmured. It was almost warm. Far, far above, in a dreamy half-darkness, glinted stars.

"Good evening," he said awkwardly.

She smiled at the tall, frightened boy. "Welcome," she said.

"Have you . . . may I . . . may I join you?"

"I wish you would." Eyjan pointed to where the luminance picked out a couple of widely spaced roilings on the port and starboard quarters. "I long to be with them. Take my mind off it, Niels."

"You—you—you do love your sea, no?"

"What better thing to love? Tauno made a poem once—I cannot put it well into Danish—let me try: *Above, she dances, clad in sun, in moon, in rain, in wind, strewing gulls and spindrift kisses. Below, she is green and gold, calm, all-caressing, she whose children are reckoned by shoals and herds and pods and flocks beyond knowing, giver and shelterer of the world. But farthest down she keeps what she will not ever let the light see, mystery and terror, the womb wherein she bears herself. Maiden, Mother, and Mistress of Mysteries, enfold at the end my weary bones!* . . . No." Eyjan shook her head. "That is not right. Maybe if you thought of your earth, the great wheel of its year, and that . . . Mary? . . . who wears a cloak colored like the sky, maybe then you could—I know not what I am trying to say."

"I can't believe you're soulless!" Niels cried softly.

Eyjan shrugged. Her mood had shifted. "They tell me our kind was friendly with the old gods, and with older gods before them. Yet never have we made offering or worship. I've tried and failed to understand such things. Does a god need flesh or gold? Does it matter to him how you live? Does it swerve him if you grovel and whimper? Does he care whether you care about him?

"I can't bear to think you'll someday be nothing. I beg you, get christened."

"Ho! Likelier would you come undersea. Not that I could bring you myself. My father knows the magic for that; we three don't." She laid a hand over his, where he gripped the rail till his fingers hurt. "Yet I would fain take you, Niels," she said low. "Only for a while, only to share what I love with you."

"You are too . . . too kind." He started to go. She drew him back.

"Come," she smiled. "Under the foredeck are darkness and my bed."

"What?" He could not at once comprehend. "But you— but——"

Her chuckle cuddled him. "Fear not. We sea-wives do know the spell that keeps us from conceiving unless we wish it."

"But—only for sport—with *you*——"

"For sharing of more than pleasure, Niels." However gentle, the pull of her hand on his arm became overwhelming.

Tauno and Kennin did not swim watch for naught. They called up warning of a rock, and alter of a drifting boat, perhaps broken loose from a ship that was towing it. These were trafficked waters this time of year. Ranild felt cordial toward the brothers when they came aboard at dawn.

"God's stones!" he bawled, laying hand on Kennin's shoulder. "Your breed could turn a pretty penny in royal fleet or merchant marine."

The boy slipped free. "I fear the penny must be prettier than any they own," he laughed, "to make me stand in an outhouse breath like yours."

Ranild cuffed after him. Tauno stepped between. "No more," the oldest halfling rapped. "We know what work is to be done and how the gains are to be shared. Best not overtread—from either side."

Ranild stamped from them with a spit and an oath. His men growled.

Soon afterward Niels found himself circled by four off watch, up on the poop. They cackled and nudged him, and when he would not answer them they drew knives and spoke of cutting him till he did. Later they were to say it was not really meant. But

that was then. At the time, Niels broke through, tumbled down
the ladder, and ran forward.

The merman's children lay asleep beneath the forecastle. It
was a blue day of blithe winds; a couple of sails were on the
horizon, and gull wings betokened the nearness of land.

The slumberers woke with animal quickness. "What's wrong
now?" asked Eyjan, placing herself beside the human youth. She
drew the steel dagger that, like her brothers, she had gotten Ingeborg to buy for her with a bit of Liri gold. Tauno and Kennin
flanked them, harpoons in hand.

"They—oh—they——" Red and white flew over Niels'
cheeks. The tongue locked in his mouth.

Oluv Ovesen shambled ahead of Torben, Palle, and Tyge.
(Ranild and Ingeborg slept below; Lave was at the helm, Sivard
on lookout in the crow's nest; these last watched with drool and
catcalls.) The mate kept blinking his white lashes and peeling lips
back from his yellow teeth. "Well, well," he hailed, "who's next,
good slut?"

Eyjan's eyes were flint gray, storm gray. "What mean you,"
she answered, "if ever a yapping cur means anything?"

Oluv stopped two ells short of those threatening spears. Angrily, he said: "Tyge was at the tiller last night and Torben at the
masthead. They saw you go beneath the foredeck with this milksop
boy. They heard you two whispering, thrashing, thumping, and
moaning."

"And what has my sister to do with you?" Kennin bristled.

Oluv wagged a finger. "This," he said: "that we went along
as honest men with leaving her alone; but if she spreads her legs
for one, she does for all."

"Why?"

"*Why?* Because we're all in this together, you. And anyway,
what right has a sea cow to give herself airs and pick and choose?"
Oluv sniggered. "Me first, Eyjan. You'll have more fun with a
real man, I promise you."

"Go away," said the girl, shaking with fury.

"There's three of them," Oluv told his crewfolk. "I don't count
little Niels. Lave, lash the tiller. Hallohoi, Sivard, come on down!"

"What do you intend?" Tauno asked in a level voice.

Oluv picked his teeth with a fingernail. "Oh, nothing much,
fish-man, if you and your brother are sensible. We'll hogtie you
for a while, no more. Else——Easy with that lance. We've pikes

and crossbows we can fetch, remember, and we're six against you." He laughed. "Six! Your sister'll soon be thanking us."

Eyjan yelled like a cat. Kennin snarled, "I'll see you in the Black Ooze first!" Niels groaned, tears breaking loose; one hand drew his knife, the other reached for Eyjan. Tauno waved them back. His mer-face was quite still within the wind-blown locks.

"Is this your unbreakable will?" he asked tonelessly.

"It is," Oluv replied.

"I see."

"You, she . . . soulless . . . two-legged beasts. Beasts have no rights."

"Oh, but they do. However, turds do not. Enjoy yourself, Oluv." And Tauno launched his harpoon.

The mate screamed when those barbs entered his guts. He fell and lay flopping on the deck, spouting blood, yammering and yammering. Tauno leaped to snatch the now loosened shaft. Wielding it like a quarterstaff, he waded into the crewmen. His siblings and Niels came behind. "Don't kill them!" Tauno roared. "We need their hands!"

Niels got no chance to fight. His comrades were too swift. Kennin drove stiffened fingers into Torben's midriff and, wheeling, kneed Palle in the groin. Tauno's shaft laid Tyge flat. Eyjan bounded to meet Lave, who was running at her from aft; she stopped when they had almost met, caught his body on her hip, and sent him flying to crack his pate against the foredeck ladder. Sivard scrambled back aloft. And that was that.

Ranild came howling from the hold. Confronted by three half-lings and a strong lad, he must needs agree, no matter how sulkily, that Oluv Ovesen had fallen on his own deeds. Ingeborg helped by reminding everyone that this meant fewer to share the booty. A kind of truce was patched together, and Oluv's corpse sent overside with a rock from the ballast lashed to his ankles so he would not bring bad luck by rising to look at his shipmates.

Thereafter Ranild and his men spoke no unnecessary word to the merman's children—or to Niels, who slept with the latter lest he get a knife in the kidneys. Given such close quarters, the boy could do nothing to Eyjan save adore her. She would smile and pat his cheek, but absently; her mind was elsewhere, and often her body.

Ingeborg sought out Tauno in the bows and warned him that

the crew did not mean for those they hated to live many days past the time the gold was aboard. She got them to talk by herself pretending loathing for the Liri folk, claiming to have befriended these in the same spirit as one might lure an ermine into a trap for its pelt.

"Your word is no surprise," Tauno said. "We'll stand watch and watch, the whole way home." He considered her. "How haggard you've grown."

"Easier was it among the fishermen," she sighed.

He took her chin in his palm. "When we get back, if we do," he said, "you'll have the freedom of the world. If we don't, you'll have peace."

"Or Hell," she said tiredly. "I did not come along either for freedom or for peace. Now best we stay apart, Tauno, so they won't think we're of the same heart."

What kept Eyjan busy, and her brothers, was the search for lost Averorn. Merfolk always knew where they were; but the halflings did not know where their goal was, within two or three hundred sea-miles. They swam out to ask of passing dolphins—not in just that way, for those beings did not use language of the same kind; yet merfolk had means for getting help from creatures they believed to be their cousins.

And directions were indeed gotten, more and more exact as the ship drew nearer. Yes, a bad place, said Fishgrabber, a kraken lair, ah, steer clear . . . it is true that krakens, like other cold-blooded things, can lie long unfed; however, this one must be ravenous after centuries with naught but stray whales . . . he stays there, said Sheerfin, because he still thinks it is his Averorn, he broods on its drowned treasures and towers and the bones that once worshipped him . . . he has grown, I hear tell, until his arms reach from end to end of the ruined main square . . . well, for old times' sake we'll guide you thither, said Spraybow, seeing as how the moon wanes toward the half, which is when he goes to sleep, though he is readily aroused . . . but no, give you more than guidance, no, we have too many darlings to think about. . . .

In this wise did *Herning* at last reach that spot in the ocean beneath which lay sunken Averorn.

VIII

THE dolphins took hasty leave. Their finned gray backs were rainbowed by the morning sun, in mist off the froth cast up by their flukes. Tauno felt sure they would go no farther than to the nearest edge of safety; that was an unslakably curious and gossipy breed.

He had laid a course to bring the cog here at this time, giving a full day's light for work. Now she lay hove to and the broad-beamed hull hardly rocked at rest. For it was a calm day, with the least of breezes in an almost cloudless heaven. Waves went small and chuckling, scant foam aswirl on their tops. Looking overside, Tauno marveled, as he had done throughout his life, at how intricately and beautifully wrinkled each wave was, no two alike, no one ever the same as its past self. And how warmly the sunbeams washed over his skin, how coolly the salt air blessed him! He had not broken his fast, that being unwise before diving to the uttermost deeps, and was thus aware of his belly, and this too was good, like every awareness.

"Well," he said, "soonest begun, soonest done."

The sailors goggled at him. They had brought out pikes, which they clutched as if trying to keep afloat on them. Behind suntan, dirt, and hair, five of those faces were terrified; Adam's apples bobbed in gullets. Ranild stood stoutly, a crossbow cocked on his left arm. And while Niels was pale, he burned and trembled with the eagerness of a lad too young to really know that young lads can also die.

"Get busy, you lubbers," jerred Kennin. "We're doing the work that counts. Can't you turn a windlass?"

"I give the orders, boy," said Ranild with unwonted calm. "Still, he's right. Hop to it."

Sivard wet his lips. "Skipper," he said hoarsely, "I . . . I think best we put about."

"After coming this far?" Ranild grinned. "Had I known you're a woman, I could have gotten some use out of you."

"What's gold to an eaten man? Shipmates, think. The kraken can haul us undersea the way we haul up a hooked flounder. We——"

Sivard spoke no more. Ranild decked him with a blow that brought nosebleed. "Man the tackle, you whoresons," the captain rasped, "or Satan fart me out if I don't send you to the kraken myself!"

They scurried to obey. "He does not lack courage," Eyjan said in the mer-tongue.

"Nor does he lack treachery," Tauno warned. "Turn never your back on any of that scurvy lot."

"Save Niels and Ingeborg," she said.

"Oh, you'd not want to turn your *back* on him, nor I mine on her," Kennin laughed. He likewise felt no fear, he was wild to be off.

Using a crane they had fitted together and braced against the mast, the sailors raised that which had been readied while under way. A large piece of iron had been hammered into the boulder till it stood fast; thereafter the outthrusting half was ground and whetted to a barbed spearhead. Elsewhere in the rock were rings, and the huge net was secured to these at its middle. Along the outer edges of the net were bent the twelve ship-anchors. All this made a sort of bundle lashed below a raft whose right size had been learned by trial and error. The crane arm dangled it over the starboard bulwark, tilting the cog.

"Let's go," said Tauno. He himself was unafraid, though at the back of his head he did think on the fact that this world—that entered him and that he entered through senses triply heightened by danger—might soon crack to an end, not only in its present and future but in its very past.

The siblings took off their clothes, save for the headbands and dagger belts. Each slung a pair of harpoons across the shoulders. They stood for a moment at the rail, their sea ablaze behind them, tall Tauno, lithe Kennin, Eyjan of the white skin and the comely breasts.

To them came Niels. He wrung their hands, he kissed the girl, he wept because he could not go with them. Meanwhile Ingeborg held hands and eyes with Tauno. She had braided her hair, but

a stray brown lock fluttered across her brow. Upon her snub-
nosed, full-mouthed, freckled face had come a grave loneliness
he had never known before, not ever among the merfolk.

"It may be I will not see you again, Tauno," she said, too low
for others to listen, "and sure it is that I cannot and must not speak
what is in my heart. Yet I'll pray for this, that if you go to your
death, on your errand for a sister's sake, God give you in your
last moment the pure soul you have earned."

"Oh . . . you are kind, but—well, I fully mean to come back."

"I drew a bucket of sea water ere dawn," she whispered, "and
washed myself clean. Will you kiss me farewell?"

He did. Her pretense of dislike was no longer needful, he
supposed; his alliance could guard her, as well as each other, on
the homeward voyage. "Overboard!" he shouted, and plunged.

Six feet beneath, the sea took him with a joyful splash. It
sheathed him in aliveness. He savored the taste and coolness for
a whole minute before he called, "Lower away."

The sailors cranked down the laden raft. It floated awash,
weight exactly upheld. Tauno cast it loose. The humans crowded
to the rail. The halflings waved—not to them but to wind and
sun—and went under.

The first breath of sea was always easier than the first of air.
One simply blew out, then stretched wide the lips and chest. Water
came in, tingling through mouth, nostrils, throat, lungs, stomach,
guts, blood, to the last nail and hair. That dear shock threw the
body over to merfolk way; subtle humors decomposed the fluid
element itself to get the stuff which sustains fish, fowl, flesh, and
fire alike; salt was sieved from the tissues; interior furnaces stoked
themselves high against the lamprey chill.

That was a reason why merfolk were scarce. They required
more food afloat than men do ashore. A bad catch or a murrain
among the shellfish might make an entire tribe starve to death.
The sea gives; the sea takes.

Vanimen's children placed themselves to manhandle their
clumsy load and swam downward.

As first the light was like new leaves and old amber. Soon it
grew murky, soon afterward blackness ate the last of it. No matter
their state, the siblings felt cold. Silence hemmed them in. They
were bound for depths below any in Kattegat or Baltic; this was
the Ocean.

"Hold," Tauno said, in the dialect of the mer-tongue that was used underwater, a language of many hums, clicks, and smacks. "Is she riding steady? Can you keep her here?"

"Aye," answered Eyjan and Kennin.

"Good. Let this be where you wait."

They made no bold protests. They had worked out their plan and now abode by it, as those must who dare the great deep. Tauno, strongest and most skilled, was to scout ahead.

Strapped on the left forearm, each of them carried a lanthorn from Liri. This was a hollowed crystal globe, plated with varnished silver on one half and shaped into a lens on the other half, filled with that living seafire which lit the homes of the merfolk. A hole, covered with mesh too fine for those animalcules to escape, let them be fed and let water go in and out. The ball rested in a box of carven bone, shuttered in front. None of the lanthorns had been opened.

"Fare you lucky," said Eyjan. The three embraced in the dark. Tauno departed.

Down he swam and down. He had not thought his world could grow blacker, bleaker, stiller, but it did. Again and yet again he worked muscles in chest and belly to help inside pressure become the same as outside. Nevertheless it was as if the weight of every foot he sank were loaded on him.

At last he felt—as a man at night may feel a wall in front of him—that he neared bottom. And he caught an odor...a taste ...a sense...of rank flesh; and through the water pulsed the slow in-and-out of the kraken's gills.

He uncovered the lanthorn. Its beam was pale and did not straggle far; but it served his Faerie eyes. Awe crawled along his backbone.

Below him reached acres of ruin. Averorn had been large, and built throughout of stone. Most had toppled to formless masses in the silt. But here stood a tower, like a last snag tooth in a dead man's jaw; there a temple only partly fallen, gracious colonnades around a god who sat behind his altar and stared blind into eternity; yonder the mighty wreck of a castle, its battlements patrolled by spookily glowing fish; that way the harbor, marked off by mounds that were buried piers and city walls, still crowded with galleons; this way a house, roof gone to show the skeleton of a man forever trying to shield the skeletons of a woman and child; and everywhere, everywhere burst-open vaults and warehouses, the upward twinkle of gold and gems on the seabed!

And sprawled at the middle was the kraken. Eight of his darkly gleaming arms reached into the corners of the eight-sided plaza that bore his mosaic image. His remaining two arms, the longest, twice the length of *Herning*, were curled around a pillar at the north side which bore on top the triskelid disc of that god he had conquered. His terrible finned head sagged loosely over them; Tauno could just glimpse the hook beak and a swart lidless eye.

The halfling snapped back the shutter and started to rise in lightlessness. A throbbing went through the ocean, into his bones. It was as if the world shook. He cast a beam downward. The kraken was stirring. He had awakened him.

Tauno clenched his teeth. Wildly he dug hands and feet into that frigid thick water; he ignored the pain of pressure too hastily lifted; yet icily with merfolk senses he noted which way he moved. It rumbled below him. The kraken had stretched and gaped, a portico had been knocked to pieces.

At the verge of daylight, Tauno halted. He hung afloat and blinked with his lanthorn. A vast shadowiness swelled beneath.

Now, till Kennin and Eyjan got here, he must stay alive—yes, hold the monster in play so it would not go elsewhere.

In the middle of that rising stormcloud body, he saw a baleful sheen of eyes. The beak clapped. An arm coiled out at him. Upon it were suckers that could strip the ribs of a whale. Barely did he swerve aside from its snatching. It came back, loop after loop of it. He drove his knife in to the hilt. The blood which smoked forth when he withdrew the blade tasted like strong vinegar. The arm struck him and he rolled off end over end, in pain and his head awhirl.

Another arm and another closed in. He wondered dazedly who he was to fight a god. Somehow he unslung a harpoon. Before the crushing grip had him, he swam downward with all his speed. Maybe he could get a stab into that mouth.

A shattering scream blasted him from his wits.

He came to a minute later. His brow ached, his ears tolled. Around him the water had gone wild. Eyjan and Kennin were at his sides, upholding him. He glanced blurrily bottomward and saw a shrinking inkiness. The kraken hooted and threshed as it sank.

"Look, oh, look!" Kennin jubilated. He pointed with his own lanthorn. Through blood, sepia, and seething, the wan ray picked out the kraken in his torment.

Brother and sister had towed their weapon above him. They had cut it free of its raft. The spear, with a ton of rock behind it, had pierced the body of the kraken.

"Are you hurt?" Eyjan asked Tauno. Her voice wavered through the uproar. "My dear, my dear, can you get about?"

"I'd better be able to," he mumbled. Shaking his head seemed to clear away some of the fog.

The kraken sank back into the city he had murdered. The spear wound, while grievous, had not ended his cold life, nor was the weight of the boulder more than he could lift. However, around him was the outsize net.

And now the merman's children came to grab the anchors on the rim of that net and make them fast in the ruins of Averorn.

Desperate was their work, with the giant shape threshing, the giant arms flailing and clutching. Cast-up ooze and vomited ink blinded eyes, choked lungs, in stinking clouds; cables whipped, tangled, and snapped; walls broke under blows that sent Doomsday thunders through the water; the hootings beat on skulls and clawed at eardrums; the attackers were hit, cast bruisingly aside, scraped by barnacled skin until their own blood added iron taste to the acid of the kraken's; they were a battered three who finally pegged him down.

But bind him they did. And they swam to where his huge head throbbed and jerked, his beak snapped at the imprisoning strands, his arms squirmed like a snakepit under the mesh. Through the murk-mists they looked into those wide, conscious eyes. The kraken stopped his clamor. They heard only a rush of current, in and out of his gills. He glared unflinchingly at them.

"Brave have you been," said Tauno, "a fellow dweller in the sea. Therefore know that you are not being killed for gain."

He took the right eye, Kennin the left. They thrust their harpoons in to the shaft ends. When that did not halt the strugglings which followed, they used their second pair, and both of Eyjan's. Kraken blood and kraken anguish drove them off.

After a while it was over. Some of their weapons must have worked into the brain and slashed it.

The siblings fled from Averorn to the sunlight. They sprang into air and saw the cog wallowing in billows that the fight in the deeps had raised. Tauno and Eyjan did not bother to unload their lungs, though air-breathing they would be lighter than the water. They kept afloat with gentle paddling, let the ocean soothe and croon to their aching bodies, and drank draught upon draught of being alive. It was young Kennin who shouted to those clustered white-faced at the bulwarks: "We did it! We slew the kraken! The treasure is ours!"

At that, Niels ran up the ratlines, crowing like a cock, and Ingeborg burst into tears. The other sailors gave a cheer that was oddly short; thereafter they kept attention mainly on Ranild.

Through the waves leaped the dolphins, twoscore of them, to hear the tale.

Work remained. When the swimmers signed that they had rested enough, Ranild cast them a long weighted line with a sack and a hook at the end. They took it back under.

Already the ghost-fish he had been too slow to catch were nibbling on the kraken. "Let's do our task and be away from here as fast as we can," said Tauno. His companions agreed. They liked not poking around a tomb.

Yet for Margrete who had been Yria they did. Over and over they filled the bag with coin, plate, rings, crowns, ingots; over and over they hung on the hook a golden chest or horn or candelabrum or god. A signal would not travel well along this length of rope; the crew simply hauled it in about every half hour. Tauno discovered he had better attach his lanthorn, for, although the sea above had quieted, *Herning* did drift around and the line never descended to the same place. Between times the merman's children searched for new objects, or took a little ease, or fed themselves off the cheese and stockfish Ingeborg had laid in the sack.

Until Tauno said wearily: "We were told several hundred pounds would be ample, and I swear we've lifted a ton. A greedy man is an unlucky man. Shall we begone?"

"Oh, yes, oh, yes." Eyjan peered into the glooms that bulked around their sphere of weak light. She shivered and huddled close to her elder brother. Rarely before had he seen her daunted.

Kennin was not. "I begin to know why the landfolk are so fond of looting," he said with a grin. "There's fun in an endlessness of baubles as in an endlessness of ale or women."

"Not truly endless," Tauno answered in his sober fashion.

"Why, is it not endlessness if you have more of something than you can finish off in your lifetime, gold to spend, ale to drink, women——?" Kennin laughed.

"Bear with him," Eyjan said into Tauno's ear. "He's a boy. All Creation is opening for him."

"I'm no oldster myself," Tauno replied, "though the trolls know I feel like a mortal one."

They rid themselves of the remaining lanthorns, putting these in the last bagful. It would rise faster than was wise for them. Tauno gestured salute to unseen Averorn. "Sleep well," he murmured; "may your rest be unbroken till the Weird of the World."

From cold, dark, and death, they passed into light and thence into air. The sun cast nearly level beams out of the west, whose sky was greenish; eastward, amidst royal blue, stood forth a white planet. Waves ran purple and black, filigreed with foam, though the breeze had stopped. Their rush and squelp were the lone sounds in that coolness, save for what was made by the lolloping dolphins.

These wanted at once to know everything, but the siblings were too tired. They promised full news tomorrow, coughed the water from their lungs, and made for the cog. None waited at the rail save Herr Ranild. A rope ladder dangled down amidships.

Tauno came first aboard. He stood dripping, shuddering a bit from exhaustion, and looked around. Ranild bore crossbow in crook of arm; his men gripped their pikes near the mast—— The kraken was dead. Why this tautness among them? Where were Ingeborg and Niels?

"Um-m-m . . . you're satisfied?" Ranild rumbled in his whiskers.

"We have plenty for our sister, and to make the lot of you rich," Tauno said. His flesh dragged at him, chilled, bruised, worn out. The same ache and dullness were in his head. He felt he ought to be chanting his victory; no, that could wait, let him only rest now, only sleep.

Eyjan climbed over the side. "Niels?" she called.

A glance across the six who stood there sent the knife hissing from her scabbard. "Treachery—this soon?"

"Kill them!" Ranild shouted.

Kennin had just come off the ladder. He was still poised on the rail. As the sailors and their pikes surged forward, he yelled and pounced to the deck. None among those clumsy shafts had swiftness to halt him. Straight at Ranild's throat he flew, blade burning in the sunset glow.

Ranild lifted the crossbow and shot. Kennin crashed at his feet. The quarrel had gone through breastbone, heart, and back. Blood poured across the planks.

It stabbed in Tauno: Ingeborg had warned of betrayal, but Ranild was too shrewd for her. He must have plotted with man after single man, in secret corners of the hold. The moment the swimmers went after their booty, he gave the word to seize her and Niels. And slay them? No, that might leave traces; bind them, gag them, lay them below decks, until the trusting halflings had returned.

Eyjan's quick understanding, Kennin's ready action had upset the plan. The onrush of sailors was shaken and slowed. There was time for Eyjan and Tauno to dive overboard.

A couple of pikes arced harmlessly after them. Ranild loomed at the rail, black across the evening. His guffaw boomed forth: "Maybe this'll buy your passage home from the sharks!" And down to them he cast the body of Kennin.

IX

THE dolphins gathered.

With them, after the manner of merfolk, Tauno and Eyjan left
their brother. They had closed the eyes, folded the hands, and
taken the knife—steel beginning to rust—that it might go on in
use as something that had known him. Now it was right that he
should make the last gift which was his to give, not to the conger
eels but to those who had been his friends.

The halflings withdrew a ways while the long blue-gray shapes
surrounded Kennin—very quietly, very gently—and they sang
across the sunset ocean that farewell which ends:

> Wide shall you wander, at one with the world,
> Ever the all of you eagerly errant:
> Spirit in sunlight and spindrift and sea-surge,
> Flesh in the fleetness of fish and of fowl,
> Back to the Bearer your bone and your blood-salt.
> Beloved:
> The sky take you.
> The sea take you.
> And we will remember you in the wind.

"But oh, Tauno, Tauno!" Eyjan wept. "He was so young!"

He held her close. The low waves rocked them. "Stark are the
Norns," Tauno said. "He made a good departure."

A dolphin came to them and asked in dolphin wise what more
help they wished. It would not be hard to keep the ship hereabouts,
as by smashing the rudder. Presently thirst would wreak justice.

Tauno glanced at the cog, becalmed on the horizon, sail furled.
"No," he said, "they hold hostages. Nevertheless, something must
be done."

"I'll cut open Herr Ranild's belly," Eyjan said, "And tie the end of his gut to the mast, and chase him around the mast till he's lashed to it."

"I hardly think him worth that much trouble," Tauno replied. "Dangerous is he, though. To attack the ship herself, with the dolphins or by swimming beneath and prying strake from strake, is no trick. To seize her, on the other hand, may be impossible. Yet must we try, for Yria, Ingeborg, and Niels. Come, we'd better take food—our cousins will catch us some—and rest. Our strength has been spent."

——A while after midnight he awoke refreshed. Grief had not drained from him; however, the keenness for rescue and revenge filled most of his being.

Eyjan slept on, awash in a cloud of her hair. Strange how innocent, almost childlike her face had become, lips half parted and long lashes down over cheekbones. Around her were the guardian dolphins. Tauno kissed her in the hollow where throat met breast, and swam softly away.

It was a light night of Northern summer. Overhead, heaven stood aglow, a twilight wherein the stars looked small and tender. The waters glimmered, barely moving, a lap-lap-lap of wavelets above the deeper half-heard march of the tide. The air was hushed, cool, and damp.

Tauno came to *Herning*. He circled her with the stealthiness of a shark. Nobody seemed to be at the helm, but a man stood at either side of the main deck, pike agleam, and a third was in the crow's nest. Lanthorns were left dark so as not to dazzle their eyes. That meant three below. They were standing watch and watch. Ranild was taking no chances with his foes.

Or was he? The rail amidships lay scarcely more than a fathom above the water. One might find means to climb—

And maybe kill a man or two before the racket fetched everybody else. Useless, that. Vanimen's children had beaten the whole crew erenow; but that had been when no sailor carried more than a knife, and none really looked for a battle, and anyhow—once Oluv was out of the way—it had been no death-fight.

Also, Kennin was gone.

With naught save his upper countenance raised forth, Tauno waited for whatever might happen.

At length he heard a footfall, and the man who blotted the

starboard sky called, "Well, well, do you pant for us already?"

"You're on watch, remember," came Ingeborg's voice—how dragging, how utterly empty! "I could grit my teeth and seduce you if I thought the skipper would flog you for leaving your post; but so such luck. No, I left that sty in the hold for a breath of air, forgetting that here also are horrible swine."

"Have a care, harlot. You know we can't risk you alive for a witness, but there are ways and ways to die."

"And if you get too saucy, we may not keep you till the last night out," said the man on the larboard side. "That gold'll buy me more whores than I can handle, so why bother with Cod-Ingeborg?"

"Aye, piss on her," said the man aloft, and tried to. She fled weeping under the poop. Laughter bayed at her heels.

Tauno stiffened for a moment. Then, ducking silently below, he swam to the rudder.

Its barnacles were rough and its weeds were slimy in his grasp. He lifted himself with more slowness and care than he had used in scouting the kraken's den. Because of sheer the tiller was about eight feet overhead, in that cavern made by the upper deck. Tauno caught the post with both hands, curved his chine, and got toes in between post and hull, resting on a bracket. In a smooth motion, not stopping to wince as the bronze dug into his flesh, he rose to where he could crook fingers on the after rail; and thus he chinned himself up.

"What was that?" cried a sailor on the twilit main deck.

Tauno waited. The water dripped off him no louder than wavelets patted the hull. It felt cold.

"Ah, a damned dolphin or something," said another man. "Beard of Christ, I'll be glad to leave this creepy spot!"

"What's the second thing you'll do ashore?" A coarse three-way gabbing began. Tauno reached Ingeborg. She had drawn one breath when she saw him athwart silvery-dark heaven. Afterward she stood most quiet, save for the wild flutterings of her heart.

He caught her to him in the lightlessness under the poop. Even then he marked the rounded firmness of her, the warm fragrance, the hair that tickled his lips laid close to her ear. But he whispered merely: "How goes it on board? Is Niels alive?"

"Until tomorrow." She could not respond with quite the steadiness that Eyjan would have shown; but she did well. "They tied and gagged us both, you know. Me they'll keep a while—did you hear? They're not so vile that Niels has any use for them. He lies bound yet, of course. They talked about what to do with him while he listened. Finally they decided the best sport would be to watch him sprattle from the yardarm tomorrow morning." Her nails dug into his arm. "Were I not a Christian woman, how good to spring overboard into your sea!"

He missed her meaning. "Don't. I couldn't help you; if naught else, you'd die of chill. . . . Let me think, let me think. . . . Ah."

"What?" He could sense how she warned herself not to hope.

"Can you pass a word to Niels?"

"Maybe when he's haled forth. They'll surely make me come along."

"Well . . . if you can without being overheard, tell him to lift his heart and be ready to fight." Tauno pondered a minute. "We need to pull eyes away from the water. When they're about to put the rope around Niels' neck, let him struggle as much as he's able. And you too: rush in, scratch, bite, kick, scream."

"Do you think—do you believe—really——Anything, I'll do anything. God is merciful, that He . . . He lets me die in battle at your side, Tauno."

"Not that! Don't risk yourself. If a knife is drawn at you, yield, beg to be spared. And take shelter from the fighting. I don't need your corpse, Ingeborg. I need you."

"Tauno, Tauno." Her mouth sought his.

"I must go," he breathed in her ear. "Until tomorrow."

He went back to the sea as cautiously as he had left it. Because his embrace had wet her ragged gown, Ingeborg thought best to stay where she was while it dried. She wouldn't be getting to sleep anyway. She fell on her knees. "Glory to God in the highest," she stammered. "Hail, Mary, full of grace—oh, you're a woman, you'll understand—the Lord is with you——"

"Hey, in there!" a sailor shouted. "Stow that jabber! Think you're a nun?"

"How'd you like me for a divine bridegroom?" called the masthead lookout.

Ingeborg's voice fell silent; her soul did not. And erelong the watchers' heed went elsewhere. Dolphins came to the ship, a couple of dozen, and circled and circled. In the pale night their wake boiled after them, eerily quiet; their backfins stood forth like sharp weapons; the beaks grinned, the little eyes rolled with a wicked mirth.

The men called Ranild from his bunk. He scowled and tugged his beard. "I like this not," he mumbled. "Cock of Peter, how I wish we'd skewered those last two fishfolk! They plot evil, be sure of that. . . . Well, I doubt they'll try sinking the cog, for how then shall they carry the gold? Not to speak of their friend the bitch."

"Should we maybe keep Niels too?" Sivard wondered.

"Um-m-m . . . no. Show the bastards we're in earnest. Cry over the waters that Cod-Ingeborg can look for worse than hanging if they plague us further." Ranild licked and lifted a finger. "I feel a breath of wind," he said. "We can belike start off about dawn, when Niels is finished with the yardarm." He drew his shortsword and shook it at the moving ring of dolphins. "Do you hear? Skulk back into your sea-caves, soulless things! A Christian man is bound for home!"

——The night wore on. The dolphins did nothing more than patrol around the ship. At last Ranild decided they could do no more, that his foes had sent them in the hollow hope they might learn something, or in hollower spite.

The breeze freshened. Waves grew choppy and smote louder against the hull, which rocked. Across the wan stars, inexplicable, passed a flight of wild swans.

Those stars faded out at the early summer daybreak. Eastward the sky turned white; westward it remained silver-blue, bearing a ghostly moon. The crests of waves ran molten with light; their troughs were purple and black; the sea overall shimmered and sparkled in a green like the green of certain alchemical flames. It whooshed and cast spray. Wind whittered through the shrouds.

Up the forward ladder from the hold, men prodded Niels at pike point. His hands were tied behind him, which made the climbing hard. Twice he fell, to their blustery glee. His garments were foul and bloodstained, but his blowing hair and downy beard caught the shiningness of the still unseen sun. He braced legs wide against the role of the ship and drank deep of the wet wild air.

Torben and Palle kept watch at the bulwarks, Sivard aloft. Lave and Tyge guarded the prisoner. Ingeborg stood aside, her face blank, her eyes smoldering. Niels looked squarely at Ranild, who bore the noose of a rope passed over the yardarm. "Since we

have no priest," the boy asked, "will you let me say one more
Our Father?"

"Why?" the skipper drawled.

Ingeborg trod near. "Maybe I can shrive you," she said.

"Hey?" Ranild was startled. After a moment, he and his men
snickered. "Why, indeed, indeed."

He waved Lave and Tyge back, and himself withdrew toward
the bows. Niels stood hurt and astounded. "Go on," Ranild called
through the wind and wave-rush. "Let's see a good show. You'll
live as long as you can play-act it, Niels."

"No!" the captive shouted. "Ingeborg, how could you?"

She caught him by the forelock, drew his countenance down
to hers in spite of his withstanding, and whispered. They saw him
grow taut, they saw how he kindled. "What'd you say?" Ranild
demanded.

"Keep *me* alive and I might tell you," Ingeborg answered
merrily. She and Niels mocked the last rites as best they were
able, while the sailors yelped laughter.

"*Pax vobiscum*," she said finally, who had known clerics.
"*Dominus vobiscum*." She signed the kneeling youth. It gave her
a chance to murmur to him: "God forgive us this, and forgive me
that He is not the lord on whom I called. Niels, if we ever see
each other beyond today, fare you well."

"And you, Ingeborg." He rose to his feet. "I am ready," he
said.

Ranild, puzzled, more than a bit uneasy, came toward him
carrying the noose.

And suddenly Ingeborg shrieked. "*Ya-a-a-a-ah!*" Her nails
raked at Lave's eyes. He lurched. "What the Devil?" he choked.
Ingeborg clung to him, clawing, biting, yelling. Tyge dashed to
help. Niels lowered his head, charged, and butted Ranild in the
stomach. The captain went down on his arse. Niels kicked him
in the ribs. Torben and Palle sprang from the bulwarks to grab
the boy. Sivard gaped from above.

The dolphins had been swimming in their ring for so many
hours in order that the crew might come to think no trouble was
to be expected from the water and stop watching for it. Too late,
the man in the crow's nest cried warning.

Out from under the poopdeck burst Eyjan. Her knife flared in
her grasp.

Up from the sea came Tauno. He had emptied his lungs while he clung to the barnacled hull, hidden by the forecastle bulge. Now a dolphin rose beneath him. With fingers and toes, Tauno gripped the backfin, and the leap carried him halfway from water to gunwale. He caught the rail and vaulted inboard.

Palle started to turn around. The merman's son snatched the pikeshaft lefthanded; his right hand slid dagger into Palle, who fell on the deck screaming and pumping blood like any slaughtered hog. Tauno rammed the butt of the pike into Torben's midriff. The sailor staggered back.

Tauno slashed the rope on Niels' wrists. He drew the second of the knives he carried. "Here," he said. "This was Kennin's." Niels uttered a single yell of thanks to the Lord God of Hosts, and bounded after Torben.

Lave was having trouble yet with Ingeborg. Eyjan came from behind and drove her own blade in at the base of the skull. Before she could free the steel, Tyge jabbed his pike at her. With scornful ease, she ducked the thrust, got in beneath his guard and to him. What happened next does not bear telling. The merfolk did not make war, but they knew how to take an enemy apart.

At the masthead Sivard befouled himself and wailed for mercy.

Stunned though Torben was, Niels failed to dispatch him at once, making several passes before he could sink knife in gut; and then Torben did not die, he threshed bleeding and howling until Eyjan got around to cutting his throat; and Niels was sick. Meanwhile Ranild had regained his feet. His sword flew free; the cold light ran along it. He and Tauno moved about, searching for an opening.

"Whatever you do," Tauno said to him, "you are a dead man."

"If I die in the flesh," Ranild gibed, "I will live without end while you're naught but dung."

Tauno stopped and raked fingers through his hair. "I don't understand why that should be so," he said. "Maybe your kind has more need of eternity."

Ranild thought he saw a chance. He rushed in. Thus he took Tauno's lure. He stabbed. The halfling was not there, had simply swayed aside from the point. Tauno chopped down on Ranild's wrist with the edge of his left hand. The sword clattered loose. Tauno's right hand struck home the knife. Ranild fell to the deck. The sun rose and all blood shone an impossibly bright red.

Ranild's wound was not mortal. He stared at Tauno above him and gasped, "Let me . . . confess to God . . . let me escape Hell."

"Why should I?" Tauno said. "I have no soul." He lifted the feebly struggling body and threw it overboard for the dogfish. Eyjan swarmed up the ratlines to make an end of Sivard's noise.

Book Two

SELKIE

I

VANIMEN, who had been the Liri king and was now the captain of a nameless ship—since he had thought *Pretiosissimus Sanguis* boded ill—bound for an unknown shore, stood in her bows and peered. Folk aboard saw how his great form was stiff and his face grim.

Aft of him the sail rattled, spilling wind. The hull creaked aloud, yawed in the waves that already had it rolling and pitching, took a sheet of spray across the main deck. The passengers who crowded there, mostly females and young, jostled together. Angry cries rose from among them.

Vanimen ignored that. His gaze swept around the waters. Those ran gray as iron, white as sleet, in ever higher crests, beneath tattered, murky clouds. The wind hooted, shrilled in rigging, strained, smote, struck icicle fangs into flesh. Rain-squalls walked the horizon. Ahead, a cavern of purple-black had swallowed the afternoon sun. Gaping wider by the minute, it flared with lightnings, whose thunders toned across leagues.

Sensing trouble on its way, the travelers who were in the sea made haste to return. The ship could not hold them all, but their help might be needed. Vanimen saw them glimpsewise, fair forms among billows that fought them. Nearby lifted the backfin of his orca, loyal beast.

Meiiva climbed the ladder to join him. Braided, her blue mane did not fly wildly as did his golden, and she had wrapped a cloak from a clothes chest around her slenderness. She must bring her lips against his ear to say: "The helmsman asked me to tell you he fears he can't keep her head to the waves as you ordered, once the real blow sets in. The tiller is like an eel in his hands. Could we do something to the sail?"

"Reef it," Vanimen decided. "Run before the storm."

"But that's from . . . northwest. . . . Haven't we had woe aplenty
with foul winds, calms, and contrary currents since we left the
Shetlands behind us, not to lose the distance we've made?"

"Better that than lose the ship. Oh, a human skipper might
well broach a wiser scheme. We, though, we've gained a little
seamanship in these over-many days, but indeed it is little. I can
only guess at what might work to save us."

He laid palm above brow to squint into the blast. "This I need
not guess at," he added. "I've known too many weathers through
the centuries. That is no gale which will exhaust itself overnight.
No, it's a monster out of Greenland and the boreal ice beyond.
We'll be in its jaws for longer than I want to think of."

"This is not the season for such . . . is it?"

"No, not commonly, though I've watched a gathering cold
breed ever more bergs and floes and storms during the past few
hundred years. Call this a freak, and us unlucky."

Within himself, Vanimen wondered. The watchman he slew
to gain his vessel, a man who deserved no such fate, had cursed
him first . . . and called on the Most High and his own saint. . . . The
king had never told anyone. He did not believe he ever would.

If they sank—— His glance went to the main deck and lingered.
Most of them would die, the lovely mermaids who gave and took
so much joy, the children who had yet to learn what joy truly was.
He himself might win to some alien shore, but what use in that?

Enough. Let him do whatever was in his might. No matter
how long a life you might win for yourself, who in the end escaped
the nets of Ran?

Vanimen sent a boy to summon the strongest males up the
Jacob's ladder. Meanwhile he rehearsed in his mind what commands to give. At least his tribe had learned quick obedience to
their captain, a thing altogether new in the history of the race.
But they had not learned many mariner skills. His own were
scarcely superior.

The call for help was none too soon. Shortening sail proved
a wild battle in the swiftly rising wind. Cloth and lines flayed
blood out of crew while the hulk staggered prey to surge after
surge. No few passengers were washed overside. One babe perished, skull smashed against a bollard. While death was familiar
to the merfolk, Vanimen would not soon forget that sight, or the

mother's face as she gathered the ruin in her arms and plunged into a sea that might be kindlier.

That was a dangerous thing to suppose, Vanimen knew. The water embraced a person, gave shelter from sun and weather, brought forth nourishment; but it sucked warmth from the body that only huge eating could replace, and in its reaches laired killers untold. He caused lines to be trailed from the deck, to which swimmers might cling for a time of rest if they could not come aboard. This might also help prevent them getting lost from the ship.

By then, the full storm was almost upon her. Vanimen sought the aftercastle. In the stern below the poop, two mermen stood at the helm. That watch was less arduous now that they were simply letting the wind take them whither it listed. He gave them advice, promised relief in due course, and turned away. Built into either side were a pair of tiny cabins, starboard for the captain, larboard for his officers. On this voyage they were seldom used, for merfolk found them confining. He wanted a while away from the elements. He opened the door of the master's.

A lamp swung from a chain, guttered, cast dull light and troll-shaped shadows and rank smoke. Who had kindled it——? A moan brought his glance to the bunk. The girl Raxi and the youth Haiko were making love.

To interrupt would be bad manners. Vanimen waited, braced against the crazy lurching and swaying around him, frostily amused at what agility their act required of them here. Above the head of the bunk was a crucifix; above the foot, where a man could regard it as he lay, was a painting of the Virgin, crude, dimly seen, yet somehow infinitely tender. The images had not turned their backs—this was not the church he had dared enter, seeking for Agnete—but he felt anew his strangeness to everything they were. He felt his aloneness.

The rutting couple finished, with a shared cry. Presently they noticed Vanimen. Haiko grew abashed; Raxi grinned, waved, and eased out from beneath her partner.

"Why are you in my berth?" Vanimen demanded through wind-howl, thunder-crash, wave-roar, timber-groan.

"The others are full," Raxi answered. "We knew not you'd come, nor thought you'd mind."

Did Haiko flush? "It . . . it would be unwise to . . . do this in the water," he mumbled. "We might lose sight of the hull. But we may soon be dead."

Raxi sat up and reached out her arms. In the narrow space, she touched Vanimen. "Will you be next?" she invited. "I'd like that."

"No!" he heard himself snap. "Get out! Both of you!"

They did, with hurt looks. The door closed behind them, leaving him altogether solitary. Through foul gloom he stared into the eyes of the Holy Mother and wondered why he had been angered. What had those two done that was wrong . . . in her very sight? They were soulless; they could not sin, any more than an animal could. Nor could he.

"Is that not true?" he asked aloud. There was no answer.

Day and night, day and night, day and night, until counting drowned in weariness, the storm drove the ship before it.

Afterward hardly any of that span abode in memory. It was nothing but chaos, struggle, half-perceived pain, and loss. Sharpest in Vanimen's heart was that his orca disappeared. Maybe it got stunned into bewilderment and drifted elsewhere, as several merfolk did. He saw it no more.

Somehow he and his people kept their vessel afloat, though in the end she was leaking so badly that the pumps could never stop. Somehow they outlived the tempest. In all else it had its will of them——

——until it was finished.

The hulk lay outside the Gates of Hercules. Vanimen recognized those dim blue masses on the world-rim, Spain and Africa, from a time past when he had adventured south. The seas still ran heavy, but azure and green beneath a sky washed utterly pure; glitter danced along every movement. Warmth spilled from the sun, calling forth odors of tar to mingle with salt and flavor the breeze. A throb and a murmur went through planks, ears, bones: a song of peace.

No craft had thus far ventured out of port. Insatiably curious, dolphins flocked about this one. Vanimen left on deck a crowd as gaunt and shaky as himself. He dived, struck, went below, rose anew to continue breathing air. His flesh felt each ripple through the cleanliness that upbore him. He addressed the dolphins.

What could they tell him of the Midworld Sea? On his earlier faring he had not swum much beyond a great lionlike rock in the straits. Christendom had prevailed hereabouts for long and long; little or naught of Faerie seemed to remain. Today was different for him. His ship would never cross the ocean. He would be lucky if she made another thousand leagues before foundering, and that would have to be through waters more mild than stretched westward. Did any refuge exist to which she might bring the Liri folk?

The dolphins chattered among themselves. They sent messengers off, a-leap in prismatic spray, to seek additional counsel. It took time. Meanwhile the people rested, hunted, regained strength. By fortune, a dead calm fell and lasted a considerable period; hence no humans sailed near to inquire who this might be.

An answer of sorts emerged. Most lands inside the Gates doubtless would be inhospitable. Fishermen were too plentiful and, the Church aside, would not welcome fish hunters. The African coast might be better, save that mankind there was of a faith which kindled still more zeal against Faerie than Christendom generally did.

But . . . a certain shore on the eastern marge of a narrow sea was otherwise. The dolphins had trouble explaining. They knew merely that nothing like merfolk dwelt yonder, yet Faerie was not wiped out as it had been in, say, Spain. No, to judge from glimpses and encounters the dolphins had had, that country teemed with nonhuman beings. Were the mortals more tolerant than elsewhere? Who knew?

Much shipping went back and forth in those parts, as well as trawling. Nevertheless, food ought to be ample for a few score settlers. The coast was rugged, too, often heavily wooded, rich in islands; surely someplace was a site for New Liri.

Vanimen's pulse thudded. He made himself be patient, asking and asking. The dolphins could describe more or less what the men looked like that they had observed, how they dressed, what kind of sacred or magical objects they carried. (Many had come to grief at sea; the dolphins occasionally helped swimmers reach land, and always studied the drowned with interest.) It was hard to understand the accounts. These creatures did not think or even see quite like him. Slowly, he puzzled out a portion. More helpful was their relation of what mortals *said*. They had a range and keenness of hearing, an exact memory for what they heard, such as were given to no life elsewhere.

Vanimen joined what he got from them to what he had garnered on his travels or from men he had known. A few of the latter—decades or centuries down in dust—were educated, eager both to learn and to teach, willing to take him for what he was if word about it did not get around . . . King Svein Estridsen, Bishop Absalon. . . .

That seaboard, on the far side of Italy, was called Dalmatia. Nowadays it was part of a realm called Hrvatska, or Croatia in the Latin tongue. The folk were akin to the Rus, but of Catholic belief. Nor did the dolphins know of anything among them like the northern rousalkai. That was as much as Vanimen could piece together.

Perhaps what waited yonder was the final working out of a curse. But perhaps not. And had the merfolk much to choose from?

II

THE storm overtook the cog *Herning* on her journey back to Denmark. That had already been a hard passage through hostile winds. She could tack, awkwardly and never pointing close, but this was a matter of straining at sheets and braces to reset, while tightly keeping the helm lest she lose steerage way or go worse out of control. In these airs, it must be done again and again, day or night, with scant warning or none.

Ingeborg could just cook and keep house, work amply rough. Eyjan had the strength to stand watches and help at lines and tiller; she brought fresh fish aboard, aided by several dolphins whose curiosity kept them nearby; she navigated in mermaid wise. Mainly the undermanned craft depended on Tauno's muscles. Yet he—regretting now that none of the original crew had been spared, dangerous though that would have been afloat and at home—could not have been the sole deckhand. He needed the lesser might of Niels, as well as the boy's redes.

It was not that Niels was experienced, even as much as a fisher lad his age. He had only been on a few short trips before this one. But he was quick to learn, eager to ask; he dreamed of a berth on a better vessel and maybe, maybe, in a far tomorrow, if God willed, a captaincy of his own. What shipmates could or would not explain, he got from other men when in port, his friendly manner making them glad to oblige him. In this present peril, he observed more keenly than ever, and from this he also learned, fast.

Thus, too busy to notice it, he found himself skipper. If he had any thoughts to spare before tumbling into what little sleep offered itself, they were of Eyjan. She readily smiled at him. A few times she gave him a quick hug or kiss, when something had gone well, and his spirit soared on gull wings to the sun. But there

had been no further lovemaking—scant moments for it, and belike
the merman's children with no heart for it, so soon after their
brother's death.

Early on, Niels decided to work north. In the neighborhood
of Iceland they should get a favoring current, and improve the
chance of a wind fair for their goal. Indeed, erelong they were
making good speed. Cheer lightened weariness.

Then the tempest smote.

Darkness raved. Ingeborg knew day must be aloft—in Heaven,
if no place else, where the Lord sat in judgment on sinners—for
she was not altogether blind. Nonetheless, vision barely reached
the length of the hull.

She had no duties left on deck; any fire in the clay hearth upon
it was doused at once and food became a swallow of salt flesh,
dry cheese, stockfish, sodden flatbread, wormy biscuit. At last,
however, the gloom and stench of the hold grew unendurable, and
she groped her way topside. Wind and hail harried her into what
shelter was beneath the poop. There she waited alone, since the
helm was lashed and Niels slumbered exhausted below.

When the weather first turned menacing, he had had a sea
anchor built and cast out and the sail struck. To run before the
blast could all too well mean piling into a reef or island of the
many that ring northern Scotland ... unless a following billow
came over the stern and broke the vessel asunder. His device
would keep her bow on, for the least possible damage, and he
could ray for an end to the blow before she drifted to her doom.
Meanwhile, he and his crew would not be idle. They must man
the pumps for hours each day as seams opened, they must hasten
to make repairs or make things fast afresh when the waters hammered and hauled, they must maintain what lookout they were
able against the dread sight of breakers.

Time had gone on, measureless as a nightmare.

Ingeborg took hold of the tiller to steady herself against wild
leaps and plunges. The gale struck inward, plastered the drenched
garments to her skin, dragged at her like a river in spate. She was
drowned in its clamor, in the earthquake rumble of waves and
their roars when they burst, in cold that bit through her very
numbness.

Straining ahead, she saw the mast reel across murk, amidst

hail and scud. Its top whipped. Though the yard was down, secured on deck, how long could wood and rope take that strain? Combers boomed ahead, onrushing mountains, black and iron-gray under the jaggedness of their crests. Spray sheeted when they passed the bow; the hull shuddered. Brawling onward, they loomed above the rails. Often and often *Herning* did not respond soon enough to her tether, and fury cataracted across her main deck. Hatch coamings sprung, the hold had become swamp-wet.

Through driving spindrift and ice, Ingeborg made out Tauno and Eyjan, shadowy at the forecastle. They seemed to be in converse. (How?) Abruptly Ingeborg choked on a scream. Tauno had vaulted overboard.

But he is the son of a merman! she swore to herself. He can live in that. Yes, he's spoken of a nether, eternal peace. . . . Mary, ward him. . . .

Eyjan came aft, which brought her into clearer view. Nude save for headband and knife belt, she seemed free of chill. Rather, her red locks, heavy with water, made the single touch of warmth inside a hidden horizon. The pitching of the craft did not trouble her panther gait.

She entered the aftercastle. "Ah, Ingeborg," she greeted, now sufficiently close to be heard. "I spied you clambering out—for a breath of air, however bitter, no?" She reached the woman and stopped. Through hands cupped between mouth and ear, her tones were more distinct. "Let me keep you company. It's my watch, but I can as well sense danger from here—maybe better, without that cursed hail stinging me."

Ingeborg lifted a palm from the tiller to screen her own voice: "Tauno, where has he gone?"

The cleanly molded visage starkened. "To ask the dolphins if they can find help for us."

Ingeborg gasped. "God have mercy! Do we need it that much?"

Eyjan nodded. "We're nigh to land. He and I have felt how the sea is shoaling when we've ventured into it. Its pulse—aye, we've caught the first echoes of surf. And the weather shows no sign of letting up."

Ingeborg stared into the gray eyes. "At least, if we're wrecked, he can live——" She realized she had whispered.

Perhaps Eyjan guessed. "Oh, poor dear!" she cried. "Can I give you comfort?"

Her tall form stepped between the woman and the wind. She held out her arms. Ingeborg released the helm and stumbled into that embrace. It upbore her against lunge and roll, heat flowed from softness of breasts and live play of muscles, she could cling as if to the mother she half remembered.

Talk went easier, too. "Fear not, beloved friend," Eyjan murmured. "If we see shipwreck before us, Tauno and I will take you and Niels on our backs, well clear of breakers. We'll bring you ashore at a safe place, and afterward fetch aid from your own kind."

"But the gold will be lost." Ingeborg felt the grasp around her tighten. "He couldn't likely get another ship, could he? Everything he fared after and staked his life for; everything it means to him— and he could still die. Could he not? Eyjan, I beg you, don't . . . you two . . . risk yourselves for us——"

Agnete's daughter held her close and crooned to her while she wept.

Tauno came back with word that the dolphins were in search. They knew of a creature that might be able to help, could they find him. Little more had they said, because they themselves understood little. They were unsure whether the being would understand them in his turn or be willing.

That was all Tauno related, for he had barely returned when the forestay parted. The end of it, lashing back, passed an inch from Eyjan's neck. Appalled, he chased after it, caught and fought it as if it were a bad beast, got it hitched to the mast: where he saw that that was beginning to crack. Eyjan resisted when he would bend on a new stay. He could fall down onto the deck, to death or the slower death of crippling. Let him pump instead, if he could not take a moment's ease.

Night fell, the short light night of Northern summer gone tomb-black and age-long.

Morning brought dusk again. Spindrift hazed the world; a wrack flew low overhead. The seas were massive as before, but choppier, foam-white, turbulence waxing in them as they neared the shallows and the rocks beyond. Anchor or no, the cog reeled like a man who has taken a sledgehammer in his temple.

Tauno and Eyjan had spent the darkest hours topside and were still on watch, a-strain after signs of ground. The gale had drained strength from them at last; they huddled in each other's arms against its cold and violence. Once he wondered aloud if power remained for him to keep a mortal's face above water.

"Maybe we cannot," Eyjan replied through shrieks and rumbles. "If things come to swimming, do you take Ingeborg and I Niels."

"Why?" Tauno asked, dully surprised. "He weighs more than she does."

"That makes small difference afloat, you know," she told him, "and if they must die, they would liefest it were thus."

He did not pursue the question; and presently they both forgot it.

A shape had appeared alongside. Glimpsed among waves, whenever the cog dipped her larboard rail, it was that of a large gray seal. They had wondered why such an animal would accompany them. Afterward they believed that already they had snuffed an odor of strangeness, though the storm confused every sense too much for them to mark this at the time.

Suddenly *Herning* stood well-nigh on her beam ends. A wave climbed aboard. Upon it, amidst it, rode the seal. The ship rolled back and forth toward a more even keel. Water torrented through her scuppers. The seal stayed behind. He raised himself on front flippers . . . change boiled through his flesh . . . a man crouched there.

He rose to confront the stupefied siblings. They saw he was huge, a head above Tauno, so broad and thick that he seemed squat. Hair and beard grew sleek over his head, gray in color, as was the woolliness which everywhere covered his otherwise naked form. The skin beneath was pale. He reeked of fish. His face was hideous, save for the eyes—low and cragged of brow, flat of nose, gape-mouthed, the heavy jaw chinless. Those eyes, though, shone between lashes a queen might envy: big, softly golden brown, without whites: unhuman.

Tauno had clapped hand to knife. Stiffly, he let go the hilt and raised his arm. "Welcome, if you come in friendship," he said in the Liri tongue.

The stranger answered with a deep, barking tone but with mortal words. "Dolphins tauld that wha' drew me. Could be a woman here, to reck by their chatter. You're no true woman or man, from your smell, nor true merfolk, from your looks. Wha', then, and who?"

The speech he used was intelligible, akin to Danish. Norse settlers had come to the islands off Scotland in Viking times; most of those places remained under the Norse crown; the tongue of the ancestors lived on in a western version, side by side with Gaelic.

"We're in sharp need," Eyjan said. "Can you help us?"

The reply cut straight through every storm-noise: "Maybe, if I will. Small mercy ha' I known for mysel'. Ha' ye more aboard?"

"Yes." Tauno lifted the nearest hatch and shouted a summons to Niels and Ingeborg, who slept.

They scrambled up within heartbeats, alarm stretching their countenances. When they saw the newcomer, they halted, drew breath, unthinkingly linked hands.

The were-seal's glance fell on Ingeborg and stayed. Step by step, he crossed the deck toward her. She and Niels stood fast, apart from their struggle not to fall. She paled and the youth stiffened as his hairy fingers, with nails like claws, reached forth to stroke her cheek. The mark of desire rose before them.

And yet he was gentle, merely touched her, joined gazes only while his lips trembled upward in shyness. Thereupon he turned back to the siblings and said, "Aye, I'll help, for her sake. Thank this lady, the three o' ye. Hoo could I let her droon?"

Hauau, he named himself, and told that he dwelt on Sule Skerry. Few of his kind were left; maybe he was the last. (That was believable, since no one in Liri had ever heard of them.) From earliest days, men had hated the selkie race and hunted it down. Hauau thought that might be because its members raided the nets of fishers, like their kin the true seals but with human skill and cunning. He was not sure, for he had been alone since he was a pup, with just a dim recollection of his mother and what she sang to him. He had escaped after men arrived in a boat, cornered her, and cut her apart. It seemed to him he had heard them calling on Odin; be that as it may, the thing happened long ago.

This came out in scattered words, as did the story of the travelers. Foremost was the toil of surviving. *Herning* could no more be let drift; lee shores were too close. Besides a stay snapped, with need for replacement, the mast was now badly cracked and must be reinforced. A pair of extra spars fetched from below, lashed tight, should serve. . . .

Hauau's strength was enormous. He held Tauno and Niels on his shoulders while they worked on the pole. Without him, worn as they were, belike they could never have raised the yard and its sodden sail, nor hauled hard enough on the sheets to keep mastery. Forsooth, were he not there to do a triple share of pumping, the hull would have filled.

Still more astonishing was his seamanship. Having explained to his companions what each order he gave would mean, and drilled them in this, he took the helm when they saw surf rage upon clustered rocks. Battered, leaky, sluggish, the cog nonetheless came alive in his hands. It was very near, but they did claw off that trap, and the next and the next. They stayed afloat, they even won back sea room.

As if realizing it could not have them, the storm departed.

III

"AYE, well can I see ye hame," Hauau growled. "But first we maun caulk, sprung as this old tub is, or she'll nae last half the coorse."

Bast for that purpose was stowed aboard. Ordinarily the ship would have been careened, but Tauno's crew lacked the needful manpower, besides not daring to lie ashore. Worse than the alienness of Faerie folk, the gold would rouse murder against them. Siblings and selkie could work beneath the waterline, hammering fiber into manifold leaks. Best would have been to tar it on the outside. Since this was impossible, Ingeborg started fire anew on the cooking hearth and kept hot a kettleful of pitch for Niels, who applied it inboard. After a pair of hard days, the task was done. *Herning* still required occasional pumping, her entire hull remained badly weakened, but Hauau deemed her close enough to seaworthy.

When his fellows had enjoyed a long sleep and broken their fast, he gathered them on deck. It was a quiet morning above mirror-bright water. Gulls cruised air which was blue, with a few clouds as white as their wings, and growing warm. On the horizon off the starboard bow lay a streak of solidity, Ireland.

Tauno and Eyjan sprawled their big fair bodies naked on the planks. Ingeborg was likewise unclad, her filthy raiment soaking overside at the end of a line. So was Niels', but he kept a cloak tightly around himself, and would not sit. Whenever his glance touched the female forms, flame and snow chased each other through the down on his cheeks.

Hauau hulked in front of them, his hugeness grotesque athwart the day. The hoarse tones coughed from him: "I think we'd be rash tae try beating back aroon' Scotland and across the North Sea. The vessel wants nursing every fathom o' the way. Best we pass doon through the Irish Sea, aroon' through the English Chan-

nel, and thence past Friesland tae Denmark. 'Tis nae doot a length-
ier passage, but belike milder. Too, coasting, should worst come
tae worst, we'll know we can get the humans tae shore alive."

"Can you pilot?" Tauno asked. "We're none of us familiar
with these parts."

"Aye, that I can, and warn ye as well wha' kinds o' ship tae
steer clear o' when we spy their topmasts. The King o' England
has captains wha' be harder tae deal wi' than pirates."

Eyjan stirred. Her gaze upon the selkie grew intent. "You've
saved us from wreck, you'll bring us to haven," she said low.
"What reward shall be yours?"

Hauau's chest swelled, he struggled to speak, it broke forth
in a bellow: "Ingeborg!"

"What?" the woman cried. She raised knees in front of breasts,
clutched them with her left arm, traced the Cross with a right hand
that shook.

The were-seal half reached toward her. He also shivered.
"Whilst we, we sail," he stammered. "Only whilst we sail. I'll
be gentle, I promise. Och, 'tis been lang alane——"

She looked from him, to Tauno. The halfling's face drew into
bleak lines. "You've done too much for us that we should force
you," he said.

Silence grew while she stared at him.

Hauau stirred at last. His shoulders slumped. "Aye, grumly
am I," he mumbled. "I'd stay on anyhoo, but I couldna stand tae
see—Farewell. I think ye can mak' hame wi'oot me. Fare ever
well." He moved toward the rail.

Ingeborg sprang up. "No, wait," she called, and ran to him.
He stopped, agape. She took the great clawed hand in hers. "I'm
sorry," she said; her voice wavered and tears stood in her eyes.
"I was just startled, do you understand? Of course I——"

He barked wild laughter and caught her in a bear hug. She
wailed for pain. He let go. "Forgi' me," he begged. "I forgot. I'll
be gentle, I will."

Niels stepped forward, bleached about the nostrils. "No, Ingeborg, don't," he said. "We've sin aplenty on our souls—and
you——"

Her own laughter clattered. "Why, you know what I am," she
retorted. "Here is naught really new . . . is there?"

Eyjan rose, took Niels by the shoulder, whispered into the
tangled blond locks that hid his ears. He gasped.

Tauno found his feet. He and Hauau locked eyes. "You *will* treat her kindly," he said, fingers on the haft of his knife.

Nights were lengthening and darkening as summer wore on, but this one was clear, countlessly starry, ample light for Faerie vision. *Herning* sailed before a breeze that made the channel blink with wavelets. It rustled and gurgled along the bows; now and then an edge of sail flapped, a block rattled, a timber creaked— small sounds, lost in the hush—until Hauau roared in the forepeak.

Later he came forth beside Ingeborg, to stand looking outward. Tauno had the helm, Eyjan was in the crow's nest, but neither paid them any open heed. "I thank ye, lass," the selkie said humbly.

"You did that already," the woman replied, with a nod at the darkness under the foredeck.

"I canna do it again?"

"No need. A bargain is a bargain."

He continued to gaze across the water. His grip closed hard on the rail. "Ye dinna like me at all?"

"I meant not that," she protested. Inch by inch, she moved a hand until it lay across his. "You're our rescuer and, yes, you are better to me than many I remember. But we are of, well, sundered kin, mortal and, and other. What closeness can ever be between us?"

"I've watched your een upon Tauno."

In haste, Ingeborg asked, "Why didn't you try Eyjan? She's beautiful where I'm plain, she's of your halfworld, and I think she might enjoy—not that I regret, Hauau, sweet."

"Ye'll grow used tae the smell," he promised bitterly.

"But why will you have *me?*"

He stood long mute. Finally he turned to her, fists clenched, and said: "Because ye be in truth a woman and nae fay."

She raised her glance toward his. The stiffness began to leave her body. "My folk slew yours," she said as if in confessional.

"That was hundreds o' years agone. We're well-nigh forgotten on land, and the auld grudge wi' us. I dwell in peace, afar on Sule Skerry—wind, waves, gulls the ainly speakers, limpets and barnacles the ainly neighbors—at peace, save for storm and shark, whilst winter follows winter—but sometimes it grows dreegh, d'ye ken?"

"Bare rock, bare sea, sky without Heaven.... Oh, Hauau!" Ingeborg laid her cheek on his breast. He stroked her with clumsy care.

"But why have you not sought elsewhere?" she wondered after his heart had tolled threescore slow beats.

"I did when younger, wide aboot, and many's the kittle thing I did see. But by and large, wha' Faerie people I met wad ha' small part o' me. They saw me as ugly and looked na deeper, for tae them, naught lies below the skin."

Ingeborg lifted her head. "That's not true. Not of every half-worlder, at least. Tauno—Tauno and Eyjan——"

"Aye, so it do seem. 'Tis good o' them tae provide for their sister. Natheless... in humans like you is more. I canna name it. A warmth, a, a way o' loving... is it that ye know ye maun dee and therefore cleave tegither the wee span ye hae, or is it a spark o' eternity... a soul? I dinna ken. I know nobbut that in some men, and in more women, I hae felt it, like a fire on a cauld night.... Ye hae it, Ingeborg, bright and strong as e'er I cheered mysel' by. Reckon yoursel' lucky in your sorrows, for that ye can love as much as ye do."

"I?" she asked, astounded. "A whore? No, you're wrong. What can you tell about mankind?"

"More than ye might think," he said gravely. "Frae time tae time I hae entered your world, and not always been cast right oot; for though I be bad tae see and smell, I'm a strong, steady worker. Hoo else might I hae learned the tongue or the sailor's craft? I've had feres amang men, and certain women hae made me welcome in their hames, and a few—can ye believe?—a very few hae gi'en me love."

"I see why they would," she breathed.

Pain twisted his visage. "Na wedded love. Hoo could a monster like me hae a kirkly wedding? 'Tis been but for short whiles. Langer amang men, aye; we'd make voyage after voyage. In the end I maun leave them too, o' coorse, syne they were growing old and I na. Tens o' years wad pass on my skerry ere I had courage tae seek out mortals again. 'Twas langer yet if there had been a woman's kiss."

"Must I too hurt you, then?" Ingeborg stood on tiptoe and drew his neck downward. Mouth met mouth.

"'Twill be worth it, dear," he said. "Wha' dreams I'll weave

in the clouds, wha' songs the wind will sing o' ye! And every
calm, starlit night will bring back this, till the day o' my weird."

"But you will be so alone."

He tried to ease her: "'Tis as well. When my death comes,
'twill be because o' a woman."

She stood back. "What?"

"Och, naught." He pointed aft. "See hoo shining wheels the
Wain o' Carl."

"No, Hauau," she urged, and shivered beneath the cloak she
had cast over her before leaving the forepeak. "Say forth, I beg
you." She paused; he gnawed his lip. "We'll be . . . mates . . . for
this journey. I've seen more witchiness of late than I dare dwell
upon. Another mystery, that may touch me——"

He sighed, shook his head, and answered, "Nay, na ye, Ingeborg, fear na that. I . . . by mysel' the most o' my life, brooding
over the deeps . . . hae gained a measure o' the second sight. I
foreknow summat o' my fate."

"And?"

"The hour will come when a mortal woman bears me a son;
and later I will tak' him awa' wi' me, lest they burn him for a
demon's get; and she'll wed a man wha' shall slay us both."

"No, no, no."

He folded his arms. "I'm na afeared. Sad for the bairn, aye.
Yet in those days Faerie will be a last thin glimmer ere it fades
oot fore'er. Thus I can believe 'tis a mercy for him; and mysel',
I'll be at one wi' the waters."

Ingeborg wept, quite quietly, under the stars. He did not venture to touch her.

"I am barren," she gulped.

He nodded. "I know full well ye're nae my doom. Your ain
fate——" His teeth snapped air. After a moment: "Ye're weary
frae all ye hae suffered. Come, let me tak' ye below tae sleep."

It was still dark when the hourglass called time for a change
of watch, though dawn was not far off. The crew had agreed that
two Faerie folk should always be on duty at night, and laid out
a scheme of shifts. On this occasion Hauau took over steering and
Tauno went aloft.

Eyjan, freed, swung lithely down a hatch to the quarters rigged
in the hold. Enough light for her came from the constellations

framed in that opening; had the hatch been on, she could have found her way by touch, odor, a mermaid's sense of direction and place. Niels and Ingeborg slumbered on pallets side by side, he stretched out, she curled like an infant, an arm across her eyes. Eyjan squatted beside the youth, stroked his hair, said low into his ear: "Come, sluggard. It's our time now."

"Oh . . . oh." He jerked to wakefulness. Before he could speak aloud, she stopped his lips with hers.

"Softly," she cautioned. "Disturb not that poor woman. Here, I'll guide you." She took his hand. Rapturous, he followed her to ladder and deck.

Westward the stars glittered, but eastward a horned moon had risen and the sky beneath was turning argent. The sea shimmered ever more bright; Eyjan stood forth against shadow as if a lamp glowed cool from within her. Wind had freshened, it strummed on the rigging and bellied out the sail, *Herning* heeled over a bit, aquiver. Waves whooshed.

Niels halted. "Eyjan," he cried, "you're too fair, your beauty burns me."

"Soft, soft," she said, with a hasty glance up the mast. "This way, to the forepeak." She danced ahead, he bumbled after.

Blackness no longer dwelt under the bow deck: instead, a twilight wherein he could see her clearly, till she cast her body against his and he was caught in the whirlwind of her kiss. Trumpets, drums, and exploding flames burst loose in him. "Get those stupid clothes off," she soon commanded, and plucked at them herself.

——They lay resting for the next passage. "I love you," he said into the fragrance of her hair. "With my very soul, I love you."

"Hush," she warned. "You're a man—yes, a man, however young—and christened."

"I care not!"

"You will. You must." Eyjan leaned on an elbow to look down at his countenance. Most gently, her free hand descended on his breast. "You have an immortal spirit to ward. Need has made us shipmates, but I'd not be the means of your ruin, darling friend."

Blinded by sudden anguish, he groped at her bosom and gasped, "I can't leave you. Never can I. And you—you'd not leave me, would you? Say you won't!"

She calmed him with kisses and embraces till he could listen
to her: "We'll not fret about the morrow, Niels. What can that do
save spoil the today that is ours? No more talk of love." She
chuckled. "Rather, good, honest lust. You're a most rousing fellow, did you know?"

"I, I *care* for you——"

"And I for you. We'll share in many ways, at work, at talk,
at song, at gaze over sea and sky...close comrades...." Again
she laughed, deep in her throat. "At this hour, though, we've else
to do, and I feel that you—how marvelous."

——In the crow's nest, Tauno heard the noises they made. His
mouth grew tight; he beat fist into palm, over and over.

Easy weather prevailed, and *Herning* limped south faster than
might have been awaited. When she passed near craft plying between England and the Pale, Hauau, clad like a man, shouted in
the English language that she was whatever he and Niels deemed
would be plausible at a given encounter. Since they were clearly
on no mission of war or robbery, that sufficed. Once they did
heave to and wait for night in order to steal past a royal ship which
Hauau took a near look at in his seal form. She could have stopped
them on suspicion of spying or smuggling.

On a cloudy eventide Tauno came back with a fine big salmon
in his grip. He swung himself up the rope ladder that trailed from
the waist and cast the fish onto the planks. "Ho, ho!" boomed the
selkie from the dark in the aftercastle where he steered. "Will ye
cut me a chunk o' that the noo?"

Tauno nodded and brought it to him. In the dull light of a
lanthorn which illuminated the floating compass needle, Hauau
bulked less human-looking than by day. He snatched the raw meat
and tore at it greedily. The siblings did not care for cooked fish
either, and Ingeborg prepared it only for Niels and herself. Yet
a touch of disgust passed across Tauno's face before he could
check it.

Hauau noticed. "Wha' ails ye?" he asked.

Tauno shrugged. "Naught."

"Nay, summat, and tae do wi' me, I'm thinking. Spit it oot.
We canna afford tae let angers rankle."

"Why, I've no plaint against you." Tauno's voice remained
sullen. "If you must know my fancy, I'll say that we were more
mannerly about our eating in Liri."

Hauau studied him a moment before he said in chosen words: "Ye'd na let that itch, save tae tak' your mind off a pain. Wha's the matter, lad?"

"Naught, I told you!" Tauno snapped, and turned to go.

"Hold," the selkie called out. Tauno did.

"Is it that there's nae wench for ye, when Niels and I hae 'em?" Hauau probed. "I believe Ingeborg wad mak' ye welcome, and sure I'd na begrudge ye the pleasure."

"Do you imagine *she*——" Tauno broke off. This time he did leave.

Dusk was thickening outside. A dim shape slid down a shroud and reached deck with a thump. Tauno trod close. Niels must strain to see, but the halfling easily recognized confusion upon the other.

"What were you doing there?" he demanded.

"Why, why, Eyjan has the crow's nest, you know," Niels replied in a voice that trembled the least bit. "We were talking till she warned I'd better leave while I can make out what's around me."

Tauno nodded. "Yes, you'd miss no chance of her company, would you?"

He stared onward. Niels caught him by the wrist. "Tauno . . . sir . . . I pray you, hear me," the youth pleaded.

The Liri prince halted. "Well?" he said after a partial minute.

Niels swallowed. "You've grown aloof. Cold to me—to everybody, it seems, but most to me. Why? Have I wronged you in any way? I'd not do that for the world, Tauno."

"What makes you suppose you could do me harm, landling?"

"Well, your sister—your sister and I——"

"Huh! She's a free being. I'm not such a fool as to judge her."

Niels reached out in the gloaming that separated him from Tauno. "I love her," he said.

"How can you? We're soulless, she and I, remember?"

"You can't be! She . . . she's so wonderful, so wonderful. I want to marry her . . . if not in sight of man, then sight of God . . . abide with her, cherish her, till death comes for me. Tauno, I'd be a good husband. I'd provide well for her, and the children. My share of the gold, I know how to make that fruitful——Will you speak to her, Tauno? She'll not let me talk of it, but will you, for my sake—and hers? Why, she could be saved, even——"

The babble strangled as the halfling took Niels by the arms and shook him, back and forth till teeth rattled. "Hold your mouth," Tauno snarled. "Not another word, or I'll smite you flat. Enjoy your little romp while it lasts. That's what it is to her, you understand, a romp, the latest of dozens. Naught else. Be glad for what she has a whim to lend you, and pester us not with your whining. Do you hear me?"

"Yes, forgive me, I'm sorry," sobbed Niels. When Tauno let go, he sank to the deck.

The merman's son loomed above him for a span, though it was aloft that his glance sought. Nothing stirred yonder save a wind-tossed lock of hair. He opened his lips to form speech in the Liri tongue, but closed them.

Slow resolve came over him. "Stay topside, Niels, till I say you may come below," he ordered.

Swiftly, then, he sought a hatch. He did not trouble to put cover on coaming, which would have muffled sounds. Straight to Ingeborg's pallet he went and roused her.

Rain blew soft from Ireland and blurred the world into dove color. It whispered louder than the breeze as it struck the waves and dimpled them. Through coolness and damp, each breath one drew carried a ghost of green fields.

A masthead lookout being useless, Tauno and Eyjan swam ahead, scouts. The cog was dim in their sight; they were together by themselves for the first time in a long stretch. At the pace of sailing today, they moved easily, well able to converse.

"You were cruel to Niels," she said.

He chopped a splash out of the water. "You heard us?"

"Of course."

"What have you told him?"

"That you were in a bad mood and he must not take it to heart. He was grieving. Speak kindly to him, Tauno. He worships you."

"And adores you. Young dolt!"

"Well, I am his first, his very first, did you know?" Eyjan smiled. "He learns quickly and well. Let him gladden many more in his life after we've parted."

Tauno scowled. "I hope he'll not brood over you till he mislays what wits were ever his. He and Ingeborg—who else have we to deal for us on Yria's behalf? You and I could scarcely pass ourselves off as earthfolk, let alone Danish subjects."

"Yes, we've spoken about that, he and I." Eyjan was likewise worried. "At least he knows he must be careful, him a mere sailor finding his way through laws that are meant to bind him fast in his lot." Earnestly: "I've hopes, though, for he is clever, and with depth in him for growth." Her tone sank. "On that account, maybe he'll not ease me out of his breast as he should——" Briskly: "Well, besides, he'll have Ingeborg's counsel, and she's seen every kind of man, I suppose."

"She's a strong creature," Tauno agreed without eagerness.

Eyjan swirled herself to a sideways position, that she might regard him. "I thought you were fonder of her than that."

Tauno jerked a nod. "I like her, aye."

"And her, about you—— There in the crow's nest, I could hear from down in the hold the joy wherewith she awakened to you. She was never loud, but I still heard." Eyjan winced and paused before she went on: "Next day we talked, she and I. Woman talk. She wondered, against all reason, if we might settle near her—the gold would buy a shoreside place—and not fare off afar in quest of our people. When I told her this was impossible, she looked away from me. Afterward she looked back and chattered on, very lightly. But I had been watching her shoulders and hands." Eyjan sighed. "Indeed it is not well for mortals to have doings with Faerie."

"Nor for us," Tauno rasped.

"True. Poor Ingeborg. And yet how could we abide as the last two merfolk in Denmark? Can we not find our father, we must seek to join a different tribe. Hard enough will it be for us to search across the world."

"Yes . . . hard," Tauno said. They stared at each other. He went pale, she flushed. Abruptly he dived, and did not broach for an hour.

Herning rounded Wales, passed by the white cliffs of England, followed the Lowlands on toward home.

IV

THE ship of the Liri people had come better than halfway up the Dalmatian coast when the slavers espied her.

At first none of them, not even Vanimen, feared evil. On their passage from the Gates of Hercules they had spoken many vessels; these were busy waters. Since he took care to keep well away from land, nobody challenged them. Likewise he ordered that everyone on deck wear clothes by day, taken out of sailors' chests, and that swimmers be submerged until after dark. The Northern craft, plainly storm-battered, drew curiosity and sometimes—he thought—offers of help. He would gesture off those who steered nigh and shout in what Latin he had that nothing was needed, he was bound for a nearby port. It served, though he wasn't sure whether that was because his language was near enough to the vernaculars or because skippers grew leery of as ragged and odd-looking a gang as they saw. Notwithstanding, the presence of females and young, whom he purposely had in view, said they were not pirates; hence no warcraft lay alongside.

Had that happened, they would have abandoned ship. He was reluctant to do so otherwise. Despite her poor condition, slowness, clumsiness, incessant labor at the pumps, she remained their shelter—and a disguise, in a narrow sea divided between Christian and Mussulman with naught of Faerie surviving. Therefore he drove her onward, day and night, day and night. When wind failed, and the sun was down or humans absent, he had his folk tow. Thus she made better speed than any mortal crew could have gotten out of her. Still, the weeks grew weary before she entered the Adriatic mouth. Without the waves to seek for hunt, frolic, renewal, the wanderers might well have perished of despair.

Now travel became even more creeping and cautious, because they must hug the eastern shores in order that parties be readily

able to search these out. Such a route much raised the likelihood
of being investigated by a naval patrol of whoever ruled on land.
Just the same, hearts lightened, song broke forth, for here was
lovely country, steep, full of woods, rich in fish. Vanimen would
keep sailing while he was able, unless he found the perfect place
first, but having to flee the hulk should not be catastrophic.

So he thought.

Indeed the halfworld lived yet along this littoral, and surely
too in the mountains which reared behind it. Swimming thither,
emerging on a strand, he sensed magic as a thrill in his blood,
after the barrenness through which he had lately fared; he glimpsed
creatures shy or sinister which were not of ordinary flesh. Strange
they were to him, and when they did not flit off as though in
dread, they threatened and he withdrew. But they were his kin in
a way that Agnete had finally known she could never be.

Some spots had been interdicted by exorcism. He cast what
questioning spells lay in his power and learned that for the most
part this had happened in recent years. A new faith seemed to
have appeared among men, or rather a new sect—since he observed naught but the Cross anywhere—which disdained the easygoing ways of earlier Christians. Oftener he simply observed too
much cultivation, or a thriving town, which by its mere presence
would ban a colony. Well, the dolphins had told him he must seek
further north.

As he did, he began to come on the multitudinous islands they
had bespoken, and no eternal curses laid by priests. The creed that
actively hated everything smacking of joy in life—for after all,
Vanimen reflected, that was what the Faërie races who would fain
be friends to men brought them, no doubt at peril to their souls
but nevertheless joy—the new creed must not have penetrated this
far. Somewhere here, he dared to hope, lay the goal of his dreams.

Wryness added: It had better. The hull was coming apart beneath him. No longer could pumps hold the water at bay. Daily
deeper sunken, crankier, less movable by any wind, his ship would
soon be altogether useless. True, then his band could search onward by themselves. . . .

Thus matters stood when the slavers found her.

It was a day to keep fishers at home and merchants at wharfs.
Ever strengthening, squalls blew from the west, whistle, white-

caps, rain-spatters out of flying gray overhead. Vanimen tried to work clear of the lee shore, but recognized anon that there was no way. Forward of him, across a pair of riotous miles, he descried a substantial island, close in against the mainland. He gauged he could make the channel between, which would give shelter. Roofs warned of human habitation, but that couldn't be helped and they were not many.

He placed himself on the poop deck, where he could stand lookout and shout commands to a crew that had gained a little skill. Naked for action, they scampered about or poised taut for the next duty. Much larger was the tale of females and young whom he sent below to avoid their becoming a hindrance. Those could have joined the swimmers, as a few like them had done; but most mothers feared what riptides and undertows might do to snatch their infants from them, among the rocks of these unknown shoals.

Another craft came over the vague horizon while the merfolk were making their preparations. She was a galley, lean, red-and-black painted, her sail furled and she spider-walking on oars. The figurehead glimmered gilt through spume, a winged lion. From this and her course, Vanimen guessed, out of his scanty information, that she was Venetian, homeward bound. Puzzlement creased his brow; she was no cargo carrier—and would have been in convoy were that the case—but seemed too capacious for a man-of-war.

He cut off his wondering and gave himself to the rescue of his own vessel. It took experience and wit, as well as an inborn feeling for the elements, to guess what orders he should give helmsman and deckhands. Therefore, in the following hour, he paid the stranger small heed . . . until Meiiva, who had been on watch in the bows, breasted the wind and joined him.

She tugged his elbow, pointed, and said above shrillness: "Look, will you? They're veering to meet us."

He saw she spoke truth. "When we've naught for hiding our nature!" he exlaimed. After a moment wherein he stood braced against more than rolling and pitching, he decided: "If we scurried to don clothes, it might well seem odder than if we stay as we are. Let's trust they'll suppose we've simply chosen to be unencumbered; we've seen sailors naked ourselves, you recall, since we passed the straits out of the ocean. Likeliest the master only wants to ask who we are. He'll hardly draw so close that he can tell we're not his kind—too dangerous in this weather—and wet hair won't unmistakably proclaim that it's blue or green— Pass word among the deckhands to have a care how they act."

When Meiiva returned to him, the galley was straight upwind and Vanimen wrinkling his nose. "Phew!" he said. "Can you smell? She reeks of dirt, sweat, aye, of misery. What devilment does she bear?"

She squinted. "I see a number who wear metal, and I see weapons," she replied. "But who are those in rags, huddled amidships?"

That became clear when the distance between had shortened. Men, women, children, dark-skinned, heavy-featured, were chained at wrists and ankles. They stood, sat, slumped, shuddered with cold, sought what tiny comfort was in each other's nearness, beneath the pikes of lighter-complexioned guards. Unease gripped Vanimen. "I think I know," he told Meiiva. "Slaves."

"What?" She had never met the human word.

"Slaves. People taken captive, sold and bought and forced to toil, like the beasts you've watched drawing plow and cart. I've heard of the practice from men I've talked with. No doubt yonder vessel is returning from a raid on southerly foreigners." Vanimen spat to leeward, wishing he could do it oppositely.

Meiiva winced. "Is that true?"

"Aye."

"And yet the Maker of Stars favors their breed above all else in this world?"

"I cannot understand, either. . . . Hoy, they're hailing us."

No real speech could cross the barriers of wind and language. A lean man, smooth-shaven, in corselet and wildly plumed helmet, peered until Vanimen's skin crawled. At last, however, the galley fell off and the Liri king gusted a breath of relief.

By now the island loomed dead ahead, with nasty surges at its foot. His whole attention was required to maneuver the hulk into the safety of the channel. Right rudder! Heave the yard about! Pole out the starboard clew! Feel violence go through timbers— did the keel grate on something?—suddenly she finds calm, but that means loss of steerage way——

Incredibly, the ship came to rest.

Vanimen stared back and forth. They were in a strip of water which merely chopped. Shores rose on either hand like walls. The storm hooted, but save for sparse, vicious raindrops was blocked off; air felt less raw here than outside. The mainland was wooded behind a strip of beach. Trees and ruggedness half hid a cluster of buildings on the island. No people or dogs were in sight. Nor was other bottom, whose presence he had awaited and planned against.

He turned his mer-senses upon the water itself, and found its saltiness was thinned. A bit further north, a river must flow from the continent into the sea. No doubt the estuary contained a harbor, which he guessed was fair-sized; pieces of trash and globs of tar bobbed in his view. That would be where humans docked. The conformation of land hid it from him, and him from it.

He felt certain the blow would end before nightfall. Then the quest could continue. Meanwhile— He sagged back against the taffrail. Meanwhile, here was peace. Let there be sleep. The need for it took him like a billow.

Meiiva screamed.

Vanimen slammed awake. Around a cliff came the galley. Her oars churned a storm of their own. She was upon the hulk ere the menfolk below were out of the hatches. Their king had an instant to remember that he captained a ship whereon a man he murdered had cursed him.

Grapnels bit fast. A boarding bridge thunked down. Over it, armed and armored, boiled the Venetians. They had sent their merchandise to the hold and were after more.

When they suddenly noticed the strangeness of these victims, web feet, hues of hair, eldritch features, several of them recoiled. They cried out, crossed themselves, made as if to stampede back. Tougher ones bellowed, swung swords on high, urged the attack onward. Their chief whipped a crucifix from about his neck and raised it next to his own blade. That gave courage. The prey were naked, nearly all unarmed, mostly female or small.

Under bawled commands, the raiders deployed, formed a line, advanced to box Vanimen's followers in the stern. Weapons, helms, mail—no mere strength could stand before that. Nor did merfolk know aught of war. Those on deck retreated in horror; those who had not emerged ducked back down into the hold.

Swimmers came to the surface and raged around. "Don't!" the

king shouted as they sought to climb the rope ladder. "It's death or worse!"

Easy would be to join them and escape. He saw the first passengers jump from deck. But, leaped through him, but what of those who were trapped below? Already the enemy surrounded the hatches.

He himself would embrace oncoming spearheads before he went into fetters, a market, the dust and dung, whippings and longings that would be his existence as a slave. Or he might be made a show... once when ashore he had seen a bear, weeping pus around the ring in its nose, dancing without hope at the end of a chain while onlookers laughed.... Did those who trusted him not have a right to the selfsame choice?

And they bore too much of Liri; the sea-wives loose in the water were too few to keep the tribe alive.

He was their king.

"Forward!" he roared. Planks thundered beneath his charge.

His trident lay in a cabin, but he had his thews. A pike thrust at him. He caught the shaft, wrenched it free, whirled the butt around, dashed a brain from the skull. Clubbing, stabbing, kicking, trampling, bellowing, he waded in among the foe. A man got behind him and lifted an ax to cleave his spine. Meiiva arrived, knife in her grasp, hauled back the fellow's chin and laid his throat open. Mermen who had been deckhands rallied, joined those twain, cast their might and deep-seated vitality against whetted steel. They cleared a space around one of the hatches. Vanimen called to the mermaids. They and their children poured forth, to the rails and overboard. For them, his little band stood off the humans.

On the castle of the galley, crossbowmen took aim.

The merfolk might well have won that battle—had war been in their tradition. They had no training, though, no skill at the slaughter of people they had never met before. Vanimen should not have bidden the swimmers stay. He realized that after the iron closed back in on him, and cried out for their help; but they heard him not through the din, and merely moved about, bewildered. Some took crossbow quarrels in their bodies, as the shooters noticed them.

Two or three on board died likewise. The Venetians there recovered formation, counterattacked, made a melee that smeared the deck with blood. Most of those they slew were females and young on the way out, but they got every merman on the hulk save for Vanimen.

Dimly, he felt himself pierced and slashed. Somehow—Meiiva beside him, striking out like an angry cat—he forced a path. Together they reached the side and sprang.

Salt water took him as once his mother had. He sank into cool green depths, his friends swarmed close, none but their dead were left behind, he had saved them from slavery, his task was done and now he could rest. . . .

No. The blood streamed out of him, dark to see, bitter to taste. Those were great wounds; he must go ashore where they could be properly stanched, or else join the slain. Likewise others, he saw through tides of murk. Female after female, child after child, had suffered hurt.

"Come," he did or did not tell them.

They reached the mainland, coughed their lungs clear, and crept from their sea.

No doubt the Venetians too were shaken by the encounter. They kept to galley and hulk for an hour or more. Meanwhile, in their sight, the fugitives cared as best might be for the injured, with moss, cobwebs, woven grass that bound a gash tight.

Once more their lack of soldierliness betrayed that folk. They should have swum off as soon as treatment was done, despite certain loss of the most badly lacerated. Vanimen would have made them do so. But he lay half in a swoon and there was no proper second in command. The rest crouched where they were, frightened, desultorily talking, never agreeing to a single action.

The slavers observed and plucked up resolution. Weird though yonder beings were, they could be overcome, to sell for a much higher price than any Saracens or Circassians would fetch. The master of the galley was a bold man. He reached his decision and issued his orders.

Carefully but swiftly, he rowed toward land. Alarmed, a number of Liri people ran right and left, where they might re-enter the channel. Crossbow volleys sent them scuttling back, save for a couple who were killed. With determined leadership, the whole group could have won past. However, Vanimen was barely returning to wakefulness. It was patent that he could not swim any distance. Meiiva laid his arm across her shoulders, upheld his weight, and took him lurching inland, where forest offered concealment. For lack of any better example, the tribe milled after them. It was exactly what the Venetian had hoped for. If they scattered into the brush, many would elude him, but he would take many others. Ducats danced before his eyes.

The ground sloped sharply. Guided by his leadsman, he cast anchor just within the galley's draught and dropped the boarding bridge to a point higher up. Men who ran down it found themselves in water only to their stomachs, and hurried ashore. The prizes were vanishing under trees, among brakes and soughing shade. The hunters followed.

They might well have seized some of their quarry, to sell into mills or circuses or peculiar brothels or, maybe, fisher servitude like a falcon's in air. The rest would have escaped them and gone on to the fate that awaited. However, bad luck struck down on misjudgment—unless everything was the will of Heaven—and thwarted them.

Dwellers on the island had been watching. What those saw from afar was enough to alarm; they remembered piracy and war too well, too well. Word had flown on nimble feet and a hard-driven rowboat, to the Ban's harbor outpost and thence, on horseback, to his garrison in Shibenik. A warcraft glided forth; a troop quickstepped along shore.

When he saw that metal gleam into view, the slaver captain knew he had overreached himself. He had had no business in territorial waters of the Croatian kingdom. Since it was presently at peace with the Republic, he would never have gone against one of its ships. A clearly foreign vessel, clearly in distress, had been too big a temptation. Now he had better make off, and trust the Signory's embassy to deny that any Venetian could by any stretch of the imagination have transgressed in such wise.

A trumpet brought his men back. The Croatians for their part made no haste, after it grew evident that the stranger did not want a fight. They let him go. Their officers were curious as to what had attracted him in the first place. They set squads to beating the bush.

All this Vanimen learned much later, mostly from Father Tom-

islav, who in his turn deduced a good deal of it on the basis of
what he heard. At the time Vanimen knew simply pain, faintness,
and an uproar which sent his band groping ever further inland.

Water was their first need, more terrible for each hour that
passed. Yet they dared not return at once to the sea, when armed
humans ramped along its edge and blundered in their wake.
Through leafy distances they smelled a river, but also a town upon
it. That they must give a wide berth.

Unsuccessful and unprepared for a real effort, the pursuers
soon gave up. It was but a tiny consolation to the merfolk. Led
by Meiiva, since the king could do no more than stumble along
if he had someone to lean on, they battled the woods, the always
rising hills, their own thirst, hunger, exhaustion, dread, the burden
of the wounded among them, the sobbing of their children. Stones,
twigs, thorns cut tender webs; branches clutched; crows gibed.
As wind died out, warmth and quiet lifted from the earth—heat
and deafness, to these beings out of another world. Here were no
tides or currents, waves or fresh breezes, food to catch or deeps
to shelter in; here was just a directionless maze, the same and the
same and the same. Barely could they pick a way onward.

Infinite though it seemed, the forest was a patch, whose verge
the wanderers reached about nightfall. That was a fortunate time,
letting them strike across farmland to find the stream. Vanimen
mumbled that they should stay on paths, which hurt feet that were
already bleeding but would not leave a trail like grainfields. Otherwise, the trek went easier than heretofore, in cool air under
kindly stars. No buildings were near. The terrain climbed and
climbed.

By midnight they sensed that more than a river lay ahead; there
was a lake. Withered gullets contracted when trees appeared like
black battlements over a ridge they mounted. Wildwood barred
off the water. Strengthless as they now were, few of them could
face another struggle through thickets: certainly not at night, when
beings that wished them no good were likely a-prowl. Unnutar,
whose nose was the keenest in the tribe, said that he snuffed a
wrongness in the lake itself; something huge lurked there.

"We must soon drink, or we die," Rinna whimpered.

"Be still," snarled a mother whose babe lay fainted in her arms.

"Food also," Meiiva said. Though her race needed much less

nourishment on land than at home, none were used to going this many hours hungry. Scores of the group were reeling in weakness; children had drained away their tears pleading for any mouthful.

Vanimen strove to clear his mind. "Farmstead," he croaked. "A well. Larder, granary, cows, pigs. We . . . outnumber the owners . . . scare them off . . . help ourselves, and quickly double back to the coast——"

"Aye!" rang Meiiva's voice. "Think, all of you. If we've seen no homes, then these acres belong to a large household, rich, well-fed; it can't be much farther off." She took them on around the forest border.

After a couple of hours, they did smell water closer by, plus man and cattle. They had rounded the lake and reached the upper river that emptied into it. Indeed, two streams were flowing together, with settlement near that point. The merfolk broke into a shambling run. Eastward, false dawn tinged the sky.

Again ignorance ruined their cause. They knew so little of humankind, and that only in a corner of the North. They took it for given that cultivation would center on a single estate or, at most, a hamlet—not a sizeable village of serfs guarded by a castleful of men-at-arms. Some among them noticed, but had no chance to warn before madness laid hold of the rest. Like lemmings, the Liri people sought to the water and cast themselves in.

Dogs did not clamor, but showed instant fear. Soldiers yawning away the tail end of a night watch, came alert and shouted for comrades who were beginning to grumble out of the blankets. Even this early, it was possible to see what a wild gang were at the ford—but unclad and mostly unarmed. Ivan Subitj, zhupan at Skradin, kept his forces always on the ready. In minutes they were out of the gates. Pulsebeats later, horsemen had crossed a bridge, surrounded the strangers, urged back at lance point those who attempted flight. The riders were not many, but foot were on the way too.

Vanimen raised both hands. "Do likewise," he told his folk, with the last remnants of intelligence that he could summon. "Yield. We are taken."

V

Not far north of Als, forest gave way to marsh. This ran for two or three leagues behind a road that was a mere track along the strand and little used, as much from fear of halfworld creatures as because habitation was sparse between here and the Skaw. Archdeacon Magnus had not been afraid to ride past with his entourage, but he was a crusader whom God made invincible against demons. Common folk had no such comfort.

There *Herning* dropped anchor, one chilly eventide. Eastward the Kattegat glimmered away till it lost itself in dusk. Westward the shore lay darkling. A last smear of sunset cast red across the water, broken by reeds, hummocks, gnarly willows. The land breeze smelled of mire and damp. A bittern boomed, a lapwing shrieked, an owl hooted, lonesome noises.

"Strange to end our quest here," Ingeborg murmured.

"No, we do not," Eyjan said. "Here we begin."

Niels blessed himself, for the place was eerie in truth, and like every dweller thereabouts he had heard stories . . . nicors, elves? . . . did he truly see a will-o'-the-wisp dance blue yonder, for luring men to doom? He wondered if the holy sign would avail him, after all his heathen doings. His hand groped for Eyjan's, but she had moved aside, starting work.

First she, Tauno, and Hauau aided their shipmates to land. Then for hours they went back and forth, fetching the gold of Averorn from the deck where they had lately restowed it. Niels and Ingeborg kept watch, to warn of unlikely human arrivals—though an outlaw or two might perhaps lair nearby—or visitants less welcome. Naught happened. They shared a cloak and soon a standing embrace against the cold; they shivered together through the night.

Dawn saw the unloading finished, but no sun. Thick mists had arisen, the world was a dripping dankness, drenched with silence.

Tauno and Eyjan, who knew the marsh well, had foreseen that; they had indeed held the cog out a whole day after making landfall, till they could count on this veil. Hauau felt as easy in fog as they did. Guided by these companions, youth and woman splashed wearily, wretchedly, to help in the next part of the task.

The gold must be hidden. Tauno remembered a lightning-blasted tree that was readily findable from the road. A measured number of paces due west of it was a pool, shallow, scummy, as if created to keep secrets. A platted mat of withes, which would last for years underwater, kept mud at the bottom from swallowing what the wanderers laid down. Transport went faster than before, with the added hands; besides, a person could carry more afoot than swimming, and whatever the stuff weighed, it filled a rather small space altogether.

Still, haste was necessary. Often this caused a bearer to crumple soft metal into a less awkward shape. Seeing Tauno thus wreck the spiderweb fragility of a tiara, Ingeborg mused sadly, "What lover once gave that to his lady, what craftsman wrought it with love of his own? There went the last glimpse of their lives."

"We've lives to live *now*," he snapped. "You'll have to melt most of this down anyhow, or cut it in small pieces, won't you? Besides, their souls endure, and doubtless remember."

"In some gray place outside of time," Eyjan said. "They were not Christian."

"Yes, I suppose we're luckier," Tauno answered. He went on picking things up. Even close by, he seemed unreal in the fog. Ingeborg winced, began to draw the Cross, stopped her finger and likewise returned to work.

Toward noon, slowly freshening airs tattered the vapors and drove them seaward. Light reached earth in spearcasts, which more and more often left rents to show the blue beyond. It grew warmer. Waves clucked on the beach.

Their labor completed, the party ate cold rations and drank sour wine brought from the ship—hardly a farewell banquet, there beside the road, but the best they had. Afterward Tauno drew Niels out of earshot.

They stood for a mute moment, nude halfling towering above slim, ill-clad human, Tauno stern, Niels tired and timid. Finally the Liri prince found words: "If I have used you ill, I beg your pardon. You deserved better of me. I tried, in the later part of our voyage,

but—well, I'd overmuch on my mind, and could forget what I owed
you."

Niels raised his eyes from the ground and said in a kind of desper-
ation, "That's nothing, Tauno. It's my debt to you that is immeasur-
able."

A grim smile: "For what, my friend? That you faced hardship and
peril of life again and again in a cause that was not yours? That you
have worse before you?"

"How? Wealth; everything it means, an end to want and toil and
groveling for my kinfolk—Margrete, Yria, of course, but will I not
be amply rewarded as well?"

"Hm. I'm not learned in earthling ways, but I can guess what odds
are against you; and if you fail, men will give you an ending far more
terrible than any the ocean or its monsters could. Have you thought
about this, Niels?" Tauno demanded. "Truly thought about it? I ask
on Yria's account, lest she be dragged down too; but also on yours."

Steadiness came over the young man. "Yes, I have," he said.
"You know whom it is that in my heart I serve. Well, I would not serve
her badly, so I've spent every free hour making plans. Ingeborg will
be my first counselor, she's more worldly-wise, but she'll not be the
only one. What happens lies with God, yet I am hopeful." He drew
breath. "You know, don't you, that rashness would destroy us? We
must make sure of every step ere we take it."

"Aye. When might you be done? In a year?"

Niels frowned and plucked at his wispy beard. "I would guess
longer. Surely for me to establish myself—but that's not what you
want to hear about, is it? Yria . . . if all goes well . . . we *might*
have her ransomed in a year. It depends on what allies we can
find, you see. . . . Oh, say that a twelvemonth hence we'll know
better how things are going."

Tauno nodded. "As you like, Eyjan and I will return then for
news."

Niels' mouth fell open. "You'll be gone that long?"

"Why should we linger, when we'd fain be searching for our
people?"

Niels gulped hard. His hands wrestled. In a while he could
ask: "Where will you seek?"

"West," said Tauno, more softly than heretofore. "Toward
Greenland. Hauau and I spoke of this, one moonlit night in the
sea. He has foreknowledge. About me it was hazy; but he did say

there was a whisper in his skull, that somewhere thither, a part of my fate lies waiting."

Sunlight blinked upon him, to turn his head amber. As if that recalled him to the everyday, he shrugged and finished, "It's a reasonable direction. We may learn something helpful along the way, as at Iceland."

"You'll not lead Eyjan into danger, will you?" Niels implored.

Tauno rapped forth a laugh. "She's hard to keep out of it." After regarding the countenance before him, he added, "Let's not borrow trouble. Enough comes as a free gift. Let's plan how we may meet again."

Niels threw himself into that matter as if escaping. Talk went back and forth. The siblings must needs inform him when they arrived, and thereafter wait for him to come. This was a bad spot for them to do so. It had little cover ashore; if Alsmen in fishing boats glimpsed them, that would awaken dangerous gossip. For his part, Niels would be taking ample risks whenever he came back to raise more gold. Best that otherwise he do nothing overly remarkable in neighborhoods where he was known—and he was bound to become noticed throughout the kingdom.

They decided on the island of Bornholm, away off in the Baltic Sea. Tauno knew and liked the place, which had but few clusters of settlement. Niels had been to that fief of the Lund archbishopric too, on an earlier trip, and there met an old salt, crusty and trusty, who owned a boat in Sandvig. Let the merman's children seek him out, passing themselves off as human foreigners, and give him a carefully worded message. For payment—they had both donned golden arm coils, off which bits could be sliced—he should be willing to go to Denmark, track Niels down, and deliver the report.

"Next year, if we are alive—aye!" said Tauno. He and his comrade handselled it.

Ingeborg and Hauau stood among wet swirls that an unseen sun turned silvery. The Kattegat leaped at their feet.

"I maun be awa' the noo, ere the weather breaks and reveals us," he told her. The scheme was for him to steer *Herning* well out, then turn the cog loose, to smash beyond recognition on a Norse or Swedish coast where nobody knew her anyway. Meanwhile a gray seal would be swimming toward Sule Skerry.

She embraced him, forgetful of the fishy stench that rubbed off on her gown. "Will I ever see you again?" she asked through tears.

Surprise made fluid the heavy features, the blocky, shaggy frame. "Och, lass, why'd ye wish that?"

"Because you, you are good," she stammered. "Kind, caring——How many care, in this world...or beyond?"

"Wha' gowk yon halfling be," Hauau sighed. "But nay, Ingeborg, seas will sunder us."

"You could come back sometime. If everything goes well—I'll have me an island or a strip of beach to dwell on——"

He clasped her by the waist and looked long into her eyes. "Are ye that lanely?"

"You are."

"And ye think we might tegither——" He shook his head. "Nay, my jo. Ye hae your ain doom, I hae mine."

"B-before those claim us——"

"Nay, I said." He fell quiet. Mist blew by, waters murmured.

At last, slowly, as if each word were a burden: "Wha' I hae found dear in ye is your mortal womanness. But my second sight— och, I dinna ken, for 'tis all blurred, yet—o' a sudden I grow frightened o' ye. Such strangeness blaws doon the wind, oot o' your tomorrow."

He let her go and trod backward. "Forgi' me," he mumbled, his palms raised as though in defense. "I shouldna hae spoken. Farewell, Ingeborg." He turned and walked from her.

"Whilst I beget my son," he called through a drifting curtain of mist, "I will be thinking o' ye."

She heard him wade outward. She heard him swim. When the fog had lifted, the ship was on the horizon.

There could be no real leavetaking. Persons had done what they were able, two by two, before the anchor sank. Niels and Ingeborg gazed north until the last sight of their lovers was lost among waves. Heaven stood open; rays from the west made waters blaze; distant and black winged a flight of cormorants.

He shook himself. "Well," he said, "if we want to reach Als before dark, best we start off."

They meant to sleep that night in her hut. If it had been torn down during her absence, maybe Father Knud would share his roof. In the morning they must confront the terrestrial world, but at least that could begin among folk who knew them.

Ingeborg fell into step. Sand scrunched underfoot. "Remember," she said, "at first, let me carry most of the speech. You're not used to lies."

He grimaced. "Especially lies to those who trust me."

"Whereas a whore is faithless."

So harsh was her tone that he broke stride and swung his head—stiffly, in his weariness—around for a glance at her. She stared straight down their path. "I meant no harm," he blurted.

"I know," she said as if by rote. "However, do curb your tongue until you're out of this dream you're awash in, and have your judgment back."

He flushed. "Yes, I miss Eyjan, that's a loss which flenses, but—oh——"

She relented, reached up to stroke his hair as they walked, said mildly, "Later you, the man of us, will take the lead. It's only that I know men in Hadsund who I think will aid us for a pinch of gold, without asking many questions . . . and tell us somewhat about men of power whom we'll approach afterward. We've talked of this erenow."

"Indeed."

"Nevertheless, best we keep sure that we're in full understanding, you and I." Her laughter was brittle. "Has Faerie ever held anything more outlandish than our intent?"

They trudged on south.

Book Three

TUPILAK

I

A FEW leagues inland from the Adriatic coast, hills began swelling into mountains. That rise, the edge of the Svilaja Planina, was also the border of the district, reaching further on into the true highlands, for whose peace the zhupan Ivan Subitj was responsible. Yet his castle did not stand near the middle of it, but at Skradin, not far at all from Shibenik. Partly this was because the village was the largest community in the zhupe, partly so that if need be he could summon quick help from the town. Besides, little warding was generally required; much of the country was wilderness, and the dwellers peaceable. Indeed, this was a wholly different world from the littoral, its ships and cities and outlook to the West. Here ancient ways endured, and ancient things.

Father Tomislav seemed to embody them as he passed through Skradin. He stumped along faster than would have been awaited in a man so burly. His oaken staff would be a fearsome weapon were he ever attacked. The cassock he had tucked up above dusty old boots was of the coarsest linsey-woolsey, faded and darned. The rosary that swung at his side, making the crucifix bounce, was of wooden beads carved by a peasant. His face was likewise of the peasantry, broad, round-nosed, weather-beaten, small russet eyes a-twinkle over the high cheekbones, scant gray hair but a grizzled bush of beard spilling over the chest almost to the paunch. His hands were big and calloused.

As he passed down the street, he received many hails from people. He replied boomingly, save when a child would skip near enough for him to rumple its locks. A few persons called—had he learned something about the aliens, were they dangerous, what did they portend? "You'll hear in time, in God's good time," he told them, without pause in his stride. "Meanwhile, have no fear. We've sturdy saints looking after us."

113

At the castle, a sentry notified him, "The zhupan said he will meet you in the Falcon Chamber." Tomislav nodded and bustled on across the cobbles of the courtyard, into the keep. This was a minor fortress built of tawny limestone quarried nearby more than a hundred years ago; it lacked glass, proper chimneys, any modern comfort. At the north end it sported a watchtower, below whose roof was a room whence men could look widely over the landscape and sometimes loose their hawks. There, too, they could talk in private.

Having climbed, Tomislav leaned out for the view while he puffed. Below him was the daily tumult, servants, artisans, dogs, poultry, sound of voices and footfalls and clattering metal, whiffs of smoke and dung and bread in the oven. Beyond were grainfields mellowing toward harvest, a-ripple under a breeze that sent a few clouds white across blue overhead. Birds filled the sky, doves, crows, thrushes, rooks, larks. On the southern horizon, wildwood made a green wall to cut off all but a glimpse of the lake.

His gaze sought back along the Krka that, passing by Skradin, emptied into yonder water. A mile outside the village, some apple trees grew by the stream, fenced off lest pigs take fallen fruit or boys take unfallen. Tomislav saw the helm and lancehead of a horseman flash beside the rails. More guards surrounded the entire orchard. Under its leaves, the strangers sat captive.

Steps on the staircase caused the priest to turn around. The zhupan entered—a tall man, craggy-featured, the scar of a sword-slash twisting his mouth and seaming his cheek on the left. He wore his white-shot black hair at shoulder length but trimmed his beard close. His garb was as usual, an embroidered blouse, breeks tucked into half-boots, a dagger at his belt, no jewelry.

"God give you a good day," Tomislav greeted with a sign of blessing. He would have said the same to the humblest old granny.

"That may depend on you as well," Ivan Subitj replied wryly.

Tomislav could not quite halt a scowl when the castle chaplain, Father Petar, came in behind. This was a gaunt fellow who seldom smiled. The priests exchanged stiff nods.

"Well, have you a useful word for us?" Ivan demanded.

Tomislav grew more hesitant than was his wont. "I may or I may not. My wits don't reach to understanding this thing at once."

"Scarcely a surprise," Petar snapped. "My son, I warned you

it was a waste of time sending for...for one whose pastorate huddles afar in the woods. No offense, Tomislav. I hope you will agree this is a matter for learned doctors to study, for the Ban or perhaps the King's own regents to decide about."

"We'd not hear from them soon," Ivan said. "Meanwhile, we've more than a hundred eldritch incomers to guard and feed. It strains us, keeping them, not to speak of the unease their presence wakens in the commoners."

"What have you learned from Shibenik?" Tomislav inquired.

Ivan shrugged. "What I told you, however briefly, when you arrived yesterday. A foundering wreck of a foreign ship; dead bodies of this race, and of what appear to be Italians—likeliest Venetians—that must have fought them; that's what the satnik's men collected. Wisely, he's taken steps to keep news from spreading. The corpses were buried in secret, the soldiers got strict orders to say nothing to anybody. Rumors are bound to spread regardless, but we can hope they'll stay mere rumors and die out after a while."

"Save here," Petar muttered, and ran fingers through his blond beard. His other hand sent clicks along his rosary.

"Yes. Well, not much traffic goes in or out of Skradin," Ivan said. "I've sent a request for help—food and reinforcements—but had no answer yet. Doubtless the satnik has a letter on its way to Ban Pavle, asking for instructions, and is wary of acting till he hears. This leaves me holding the entire burden, wherefore I seek what counsel I can get."

"From anybody whatsoever?" Petar scoffed.

Tomislav bristled, gripped hard his staff, and growled back, "What would *your* advice be?"

"Safest to slay them" Petar said. "They may or may not be human, but Christian they surely are not—not Catholics of the Western rite, mauger that one of them knows Latin, nor of ours; not Orthodox schismatics, not even of the abominable Bogomil heresy, not even Jews or paynim." His voice grew high; between the chill stone walls, he sweated. "Naked, shameless, seen freely copulating...why, the very heathen have some decency, some kind of marriage....And nothing like a prayer, a sacrifice, any act of worship, nothing like that has been observed among them in their plight."

"If this be true," Tomislav said, turning mild, "why, the worst of sins would be to slaughter them, when we might instead lead them to God."

"We cannot," Petar insisted. "They are beasts, they have no souls, or they are something worse, something out of Hell itself."

"That remains to be seen," Ivan interrupted.

Petar clutched at the zhupan's wrist. "Lord—my son—my son, dare we risk damnation such as they could bring? The Holy Glagolitic Church is beleaguered already—by the Pope, who should be our loving father, by the Orthodox of Serbia and the Empire, by the Satan-inspired Bogomils——"

"Enough!" Ivan freed himself. "I bade Father Tomislav come here and meet those beings for sound reasons. Must I repeat them to you? I know him of old as a man wise in his fashion; he's no ignoramus either, he studied in Zadar and later served its bishop; as for devilment or witchcraft, he lives where folk know more about that than we do. He himself has been touched——"

There appeared that on Tomislav's face which caused the warrior to break off his speech and finish lamely; "Have you, then, discovered aught?"

The rustic priest stood a moment, fighting down his feelings, before he replied. Then it was with a trudging calmness. "I may have. Petar addressed their leader wrongly when he showed he commands a bit of Latin. That person is proud, he's suffering from his wounds, he's sick with fear on his people's behalf. Shout at him like at a slave, rail at him about their ways, which have harmed no one unless maybe themselves . . . how do you expect he'll behave? Naturally he turned his back. You did better for us, Zhupan, when you sent in your military chirurgeon to treat their hurts."

"Well, then, you spoke softly to the chief," Ivan said. "What has he told you?"

"Little as yet. However, I feel sure that's not out of unwillingness. His Latin is scant and bears a grievous accent." Tomislav chuckled. "I confess my own has gathered rust, which didn't help matters. Moreover, we're entirely foreign to each other. How much can we explain in a few hours?

"He did convey to me that they came hither not as enemies but only in search of a home—beneath the sea." That occasioned less surprise than it might have, for the looks of the merfolk had immediately raised speculation. "They were driven out of their country in the far North; I've not learned how or why. He admits they're not Christian, though what they are is still a mystery to me. He promised that if we let them go, they'll seek the water and never return."

"Lies are cheap," said Petar.

"Do you think he was truthful?" Ivan queried.

Tomislav nodded. "I do. Of course, I can't take my oath on it."

"Have you any notion about their nature?"

Tomislav frowned out at the sky. "Um-m-m . . . a guess or two, maybe. Just guesswork, founded on certain things they know or believe in my flock, on what I've read or heard elsewhere, and on my own . . . my own experience. Most likely I'm wrong."

"Are they of the mortal world?"

"They can be slain, the same as us."

"That is not what I asked, Tomislav."

The priest sighed. "My guess is that they are not of Adam's blood." In haste: "That doesn't mean they're evil. Think of Leshy, domovoi, poleviki, such-like harmless sprites—well, sometimes a touch mischievous, but sometimes good friends to poor humans——"

"On the other hand," Petar said, "think of viljai."

"Be still!" Ivan shouted in a flash of wrath. "No more croaking out of you, hear me? I may well ask the bishop to send me a different confessor."

He turned back to Tomislav. "I'm sorry, old fellow," he said.

"I . . . am not . . . that tender-skinned," the priest of the zadruga answered with difficulty. "It seems to be true, in the past few years a vilja has been flitting about my neighborhood. God forgive the malicious gossipers."

He squared his shoulders. "My guess is that we'd do best, both for ourselves and in the sight of God, to let those people go," he said. "Take them back to the sea, under spears if you like, but take them back and bid them farewell."

"I dare not do that, save at the behest of an overlord," Ivan replied. "Nor would I if I could, before we are quite certain that no harm can come of it."

"I know," Tomislav said. "Well, then, here's my advice. Keep them prisoners, but treat them kindly. And let their headman go home with me, that we may get acquainted."

"What?" shrilled Petar. "Are you mad?"

Ivan himself was startled. "You're reckless, at least," he said. "That wight is huge. When he has recovered, he could rip you asunder."

"I hardly think he'll try," Tomislav answered low. "At worst, what can he slay but my flesh, whereafter my parishioners will cut him down? I've long since lost any fear of departing this life."

The zadruga was a hamlet of less than a hundred souls, whose families were close kin. It lay a full day's travel from Skradin, on a path that wound northerly, then westerly, through the woods around the lake, though never in sight of yon water. Here men had once cleared land along a brook and settled down to live by farming, with timber cutting, charcoal burning, hunting, and trapping on the side. They worked the soil in common, as they would have done were they free peasants. Most of them were actually serfs, but it made small difference, for the nobles of Hrvatska were seldom oppressive or extortionate, and nobody wanted to leave.

The thorp formed a double row amidst croplands, shaded by trees left standing. Of wood, one- or two-roomed, thatch-roofed, houses stood off the ground, with stalls beneath for livestock and gangplanks to the living quarters. The lane between them was muddy when it was not dusty, and thick with dung. Smells were not offensive, though; sweet green distances swallowed them up. Nor did dwellers pay much heed to the flies of summer. Behind each home was a kitchen garden.

Granaries stood about, small, slat-sided, elevated on skinny boles whose roots made birdlike feet, as on Baba Yaga's famous abode. A couple of sheds held tools and related necessities. Two-wheeled carts were parked beside when not in use; these were gaily painted. At one end of the lane was a little workshop, at the opposite end the chapel, hardly larger, also colored in fanciful designs, the shakes of its roof bulging to form an onion dome that upheld the Cross. There was no mill, but foundations and the crumbled remnants of an earthen dam showed there formerly had been.

Nowhere did fields and meadows reach beyond sight. The forest encompassed them. Some places it was at a distance, other places it crowded close, but everywhere it brooded, crowns in sunlight but full of shadows beneath. Most of the trees were oak or beech, with a mingling of different kinds. Brush grew dense between.

In many ways the settlement reminded Vanimen of Als. As time passed, he came to understand how shallow the likeness was.

The journey here, on a borrowed ass, had been agony. Once in Tomislav's house, with a bed to rest in and plenty of hearty food, the merman healed faster than a human would have done. A second Faerie gift was the speed wherewith he mastered the Hrvatskan language. Erelong he and the priest began to hold real discourse, which day by day grew less halting. After people lost fear of him, he came to know them also, and somewhat about their lives.

He sat with Tomislav, sharing a bench, on the gangway landing below the long-raftered roof. It was Sunday, when men rested after their worship. The priest had been laboring at harvest as hard as anyone; Vanimen, now hale, had lent strength which was great if unskilled.

Summer was yielding to autumn. Leaves seemed paler green than erstwhile, a few already brown, red, gold; the sky too had gone wan, pierced by geese whose cries awoke wordless longings; when the sun went under the treetops, a breeze that had been cool became chill. Most persons idled at home. Those who passed by simply hailed Tomislav and his guest. That sight had grown familiar. Clad like the rest, aside from bare feet, Vanimen could almost have passed for a human of mighty stature.

The two were drinking beer out of wooden bowls and had grown a trifle tipsy. "You're a good sort," the merman remarked. "Would that I might help you live better."

"That's the kind of wish that makes me think you can indeed receive God's grace if only you'll choose," Tomislav said eagerly.

As his own distrust faded, Vanimen had gotten frank. The priest had softened the story when he wrote it in the reports he dispatched, by a boy, to Ivan. "I'll not lie to him, but I'll not needlessly worsen hostility against you," he had explained.

For his part, Tomislav had tried to make clear what sort of

land this was. Hrvatska shared monarchy with Hungary. Richly endowed by nature, with numerous seaports for trading abroad, it was an important realm in its own right. It would have been more so, save that the great clans were generally at odds, sometimes at outright war. Alas, then foreigners, notably the damnable Venetians, took advantage of chaos and occupied what was not theirs. At the moment, peace prevailed. An alliance of the Subitj and Frankapan septs gave strong government. Most powerful was the Count of Bribir, Pavle Subitj, who had won to the position of Ban—provincial ruler, save that *his* province today was the whole country. Ivan was kin to him.

This eventide Vanimen evaded talk of the Faith by saying; "Toil and poverty may purify the soul, but they're hard on body and mind. Why, you've not even a proper housekeeper." Women came in by turns to work, but none had much time or strength to spare. Often the priest must do his own cooking—which went rather well, for he enjoyed food—and cleaning; always did his own gardening and brewing.

"I need none, really. My wants are simple. I get my share of jollity. You'll see when we hold harvest festival." Tomislav paused. "Indeed, my earthly lot became easier in several ways when my poor wife passed away. She was long helplessly ill, needing my care." He crossed himself. "God called her to come and be healed. I'm sure she's in Heaven."

Astonished, Vanimen said, "Were you wedded? I know clergymen formerly were, at least in the North, but I hadn't heard of it for generations."

"Aye, we're Catholic, yet of the Glagolitic rite, which is not Rome's. Though the Popes have ever misliked that, they've not outright forbidden our usages."

Vanimen shook his head. "I'll never grasp why you humans wrangle about such snailshell matters—how you can do it, when you might be savoring this world." He saw his host would fain avoid dispute, and went on, "But tell me, if you will, of your past. I've heard mere shards thus far."

"There's naught to tell," answered Tomislav. "A most ordinary, stumbling mortal life. It can't interest you, who for centuries have known marvels beyond my imagining."

"Oh, it would," Vanimen murmured. "You are as strange to me as I to you. If you would let me glimpse your inwardness, I might see—well, not only how the tribe of Adam inhabits earth, but why. . . ."

"You might see what God means!" Tomislav exclaimed. "Ha, that chance is worth baring my breast to you.

"Not that I've much to reveal. Ask what questions you will as I go along." Talking, the man let his voice drop. His gaze went outward, over the roof opposite, to trees and sky—to lost years, Vanimen supposed. Now and then he took a swallow of beer, but not with his customary gusto; it was a thing his body did to keep his throat moist.

"I was born a serf, though not here: in Skradin, 'in the shadow of the castle,' as the saying goes. My father was a groom there. The chaplain of that time thought me worth teaching to read and write. When I reached the proper age, fourteen, he recommended me to the bishop. Thus I went to Zadar to study for holy orders—hard work in truth, for both flesh and spirit. Nonetheless, there was a city full of liveliness, men from beyond every horizon, worldly goods, worldly pleasures. I confess, for a while I fell into sin. Afterward I repented, and dare believe I've been forgiven, and may have gained a little insight into my fellow creatures.

"Repentance made me long back, however, long for my birth-land, simple ways, my own kind of people. No pastorate here-abouts fell open for several years. During them, I was amanuensis to the bishop.

"Meanwhile I'd turn lust into lawful conjugality by arranging to marry a woman from these parts. In fact, because of my wish still more than canonical requirement, that was before I entered orders. Ah, lovely in her youth was my Sena!

"But early on, sadness came over her. At first it may have been due to her new environs. Crowds, noise, chaffering, intrigue, restlessness, ever-changefulness, those things frightened her and weighed on her soul. Besides, we lost two children to sickness. She found less comfort in the three that lived than I did, or than I hoped she would.

"Finally I got this church. The bishop grumbled at letting me go, but relented when I made clear what it should mean to Sena.

"Well, it was of no avail. More babies of hers died or were stillborn. Worse, our three growing children found this life as bad as she'd found the city. They missed the outside world; they chafed, waxed rebellious. My ordination had freed my whole family from serfdom. Thus no law bound them in place. One by one, when they grew old enough, they defied us and broke away.

"First Franjo went to sea. After a few voyages, his ship was never heard of again. It may have been wrecked, it may have fallen to pirates or slavers. Could be, this moment, my son is a eunuch in some Turk's harem. *Kyrie eleison.*

"It was less bad for Zinka. She wed a merchant she met once when we were in Shibenik—wed him without our leave, almost the day afterward. We could do naught, for the priest was a countryman of his and he took her home with him to Austria. Never a word has come since. I pray she is happy. *Christe eleison.*

"Later our younger son, Juraj, ran off. He's in Split, working for a Venetian factor—Venice, the ancient enemy. I hear about him from time to time, through the kindness of a tradesman I know; but I never hear from him. *Kyrie eleison.*

"Maybe you can guess how this clawed Sena's heart, which she could never harden. A few years after she bore her last child, she withdrew into silence, and scarcely moved . . . only lay there in bed, empty-eyed. Though I wept when she died, ten years ago, I knew it was God's mercy. And our little daughter was still alive then, still alive for her."

Tomislav shook himself. He uttered a laugh. "You must think me sodden with self-pity," he said as he came back to awareness of the evening. "Not at all, not at all. God gives me many consolations: Himself, the greenwood, music, merrymaking, fellowship, the trust of my flock, and, yes, the love of their small children——"

He stared into his bowl. "This is empty," he announced. "Yours too. Let me go tap the keg. We've time before vespers."

When he returned, Vanimen said with care: "I also have lost children." He did not add that he had lost them forever. "Tell me, you bespoke a girl who came late. Did she likewise die?"

"Yes," Tomislav told him, plumping back onto the bench. "She was a lovely maiden."

"What happened?"

"No man knows. She drowned in the lake, where she had wandered. Maybe she stumbled, hit her head on a root. For once, it can't have been the vodianoi's doing, because after many days of search we did find her body afloat——"

——bloated and stinking, Vanimen knew.

"I, I did not have her buried with her mother and the rest," Tomislav said. "I carted the casket to Shibenik."

"Why?"

"Oh, my thought was—oh, maybe she'd lie easier—I was dazed, you understand. The zhupan helped me get permission."

As if springing to an attack, Tomislav leaned close and went on: "I warned you, mine would not be a very stirring tale. Besides, you've yet to outlive your own woes."

While Vanimen had more steadiness of mind than most merfolk, he could shift a topic or a mood as swiftly as seemed desirable. "Aye, for my whole tribe," he said. "I meant to raise this matter with you."

"You've done that"—Tomislav attempted a smile—"in words which got pungent."

"Merely to complain that they're still kept penned; and with females and young apart from males, I hear."

"Well, their conduct *was* unseemly. Talk about it became a threat to public morals, Petar claimed."

"How long must this go on?" Vanimen smote his thigh. "I see before me—how sharply I see, feel, hear, smell, taste—their misery in unfreedom."

"I've told you," Tomislav said. "The Ban's decision is that they be held, properly cared for, till he's gotten full information about them. I think that time draws nigh. You and I between us, we've learned much. Now that you've got the Hrvatskan tongue, you can speak with him yourself. He desires that."

The Liri king shook his head. "When? I gather he's busy, fares up and down the realm, may be gone for weeks at a stretch. Meanwhile, I say, my people are in quiet torment. Your baron may think he feeds them well, but my own belly tells me there's too much grain and milk, not enough fish. They'll sicken—from lack of water, too. Doubtless they get ample to drink, but when were they last swimming, when were they last down below, as nature meant for them? You let me refresh myself in the brook here, but even so, I sense how my flesh is slowly parching."

Tomislav nodded. "I know, Vanimen, friend. Or what I don't know, I can guess. Yet what may be done?"

"I've thought on that," the merman said with rising spirit. "A short ways hence is a lake. Set us free there. A part of us on any given day, no doubt; the rest will be hostages, abiding their turns.

It won't be as good as the sea, but it will sustain us, it will bring us back from what's half death.

"Besides, I gather that nobody fishes the lake. *We* could and would. It must be aswarm. We'd fetch back plenty to share with you humans. It'll more than pay the cost of keeping us. Would that appeal to your baron?"

Tomislav frowned. "It might, were the lake not accursed."

"How?"

"A vodianoi lairs there, a water monster. It plundered nets that fishermen cast forth. When they sent boats with armed men after it, their weapons would not wound. The boats got sunken, and brave lads who could not swim were drowned. Once folk wanted a mill here, that grain need not go clear to Skradin for grinding. When they'd well-nigh finished, the vodianoi came upstream and wallowed in the millpond. Such was the terror that men destroyed what they'd made, so that it'd go back to the lake."

Vanimen forced himself to ask: "Why has a priest like you not banned it?"

"The folk would not have that. Church and nobility think it best to heed their wish. An exorcism would drive off all beings of the halfworld from these parts, and some are believed to bring good luck. Better be denied use of the lake, and in the wildwood sometimes be tricked by Leshy—better that than have no polevik to keep blight from the crops, no domovoi to embody a household and its well-being, no Kikimora that may get the whim to aid a wife overwhelmed by work...." Tomislav sighed. "Pagan, yes, but a harmless paganism. It touches not the true faith of the people, and it helps them endure lives that are often charged with sorrow. The Bogomils have expelled every such olden survival, wherever their sect prevails; but the Bogomils are joyless, they hate this world that God made beautiful for us."

After a breath of two, Tomislav added in a near whisper, "Yes, that which haunts the waters and the wildwood can also be beautiful...."

Vanimen scarcely heard. His words blazed forth, as he sprang to his feet and lifted a fist against the evening star:

"Why, this is just where we can help you, we merfolk! A chance to prove our goodwill! I myself will lead the troop that drives the monster away!"

II

THERE was a man in Hadsund called Aksel Hedebo, a well-to-do dealer in the horses that were a Danish export. Ingeborg had often been with him. However, it was a surprise when she appeared at his establishment, accompanied by a straightforward-looking young fellow, and requested a confidential meeting. "We have a favor to ask," she said, "and would make you a small gift to win your kindness."

The finger ring she revealed, cupped in her palm to be hidden from his apprentices, was no trinket. He guessed its worth at five silver marks. "Follow me, then," he replied, mask-faced, and led the visitors from the working part of the house to the residential, and through a door which he closed.

The room beyond was darkly wainscotted, massively furnished, with excellent glass in the windows. Aksel curtained these, which brought a dusk suitable for secrets. Taking the ring, he seated himself at a table and regarded the curious figures in the gold. "Sit down, you two," he ordered rather than invited.

They sank to the edges of chairs. Their gaze sought him, anxious. He was fat, blue-jowled, heavy-mouthed, clad in rich garb which gave off a stronger than common smell of stale sweat. After a while he looked up. "Who are you?" he addressed Niels.

The latter stated his name, birthplace, and seafaring trade. The merchant's eyes probed and probed. They saw him, like the woman, clean, well-groomed, attired in new clothes. But the marks of sun, wind, hardship were as yet little softened upon either of them.

"What will you of me?" Aksel queried.

Ingeborg spoke: "It's a long tale. As a trader yourself, you'll understand if we hold much of it back. The short of the business is that we've come into some fortune and need help placing it.

Niels, here, thinks we might best buy our way into shipping. You deal with captains, you have outland connections—surely with the . . . the Hanseatic League, is that right, Niels? If you can send us to a suitable man, with your own persuasion that he hearken"— she flashed the smile she had used in the marketplace—"you'll not find us niggards."

Aksel tugged at a lock of black hair. "A queer offer, from such as you," he said presently. "I must know more. How big is this fortune, and how did you win it?"

His glance went to the purse which hung plump at Niels' belt. Within that leather were coins of the realm, which should excite no remark. Ingeborg had gotten them from a goldsmith in town whom she likewise knew, a man ready to run his risk of the law finding him out when she would sell him a lump of precious metal at well below its true value. She and her companion bore far more wealth on them in the form of pieces sewn into their garments, but this was against unforseen need in the near future.

Her tone remained cool: "What the sum truly comes to, that'll depend on what we can do with it—wherefore we seek your counsel. It's treasure trove, you see."

Aksel stiffened. "Then it's the Crown's! Do you want to be hanged?"

"No, no, naught like that. Let me tell. You must remember Herr Ranild and his cog, how he left earlier in the year on a voyage that he was close-mouthed about, and has not been heard of since. Niels was a crewman, and Ranild brought me along."

"Hoy?" The dealer recovered from his surprise. "Hm, well, folk hereabouts did wonder what had become of Cod-Ingeborg. But a woman at sea, she's bad luck."

"No," Niels denied in quick anger.

Ingeborg gestured him to keep still and went on: "He was shorthanded and in haste. I could be useful."

"Yes," Aksel snickered. Niels glared at him.

Ingeborg kept her head aloft. "Besides," she said, "word had come to me, as word of this or that often does. Put together with what Ranild heard in different wise, it pointed at a treasure to be gotten, out of a heathen burial in a midocean place. Thus, no robbery, no sacrilege, no withholding of anybody's due.

"Gold awakened greed, though, and led to killing. You recall what ruffians those were, save for Niels. Afterward a terrible

storm smote. The upshot was that only we two are left alive of
the souls who fared forth upon *Herning*, and the ship is lost. But
we brought certain metal ashore, and now we mean to have the
good of it."

Silence fell, until Aksel snapped. "Is this true?"

"I'll swear to you by every saint, or whatever oath you wish,
that each last word is true," Ingeborg said. "So will Niels."

The youth nodded violently.

"Hm, hm." Again Aksel tugged his greasy hair. "You've spun
me half a thread of your yarn."

"I told you we would. The reasons why need not trouble you."
Ingeborg grinned. "What did you ever tell your wife about me?"

She grew earnest again, tautened still more, and urged, "You
stand to gain much for slight effort and no hazard. We seek not
to overstep the law. Rather, we want guidance to keep us within
it. At the same time, it'd be foolish to blab, when a mighty man
can always find some pretext to strip us bare."

"Ye-e-es," Aksel agreed. "you're clever to see from the outset
that you need a patron, who'll shield you and get you into a trade
where you can prosper quietly." He frowned at the ring, which
he turned over and over on the table before him.

"The Hansa," Niels blurted. "Their ships carry most cargoes
throughout the North, don't they? I hear how the cities of the
League grow ever greater—kings fear them——Could I become
a shipowner of theirs——"

Aksel shook his head. "Scant hope there, lad. I know them
well. They're grasping devils, jealous of what they have, un-
friendly to outsiders, chary of aught that might upset by the least
bit the power of a magnate or a guild. For instance, Visby on the
island of Gotland, Visby grants broad freedoms to merchants, but
only if they're Gotlander born. I think if you went to one of those
uncrowned princes, he'd just lead you on till he saw how to get
you wrung dry, and belike me into the bargain."

Niels flinched. Ingeborg laid a hand over his. "There must be
somewhere to go!" he protested.

"Maybe, maybe," Aksel said. "You've caught me off guard.
Let me think——" He set the ring twirling on the table. Its whirr
seemed unnaturally loud. "Um-m-m . . . Copenhagen . . . big
seaport, enfeoffed to the bishop of Roskilde, who lets no guilds
take root there . . . aye, each burgher pursues his trade under license

of his own from the city authorities. . . . Maybe. I know hardly anything more, for little of my stock goes that way."

"You see," Ingeborg said, "if you allow yourself to, you can help us. Take time to think onward. First, if I know you, you'll dicker about your price."

Aksel lifted his face. They saw it harden. "Why are you sure I will?" he demanded.

"What mean you?" Ingeborg replied. Niels stared in dismay.

"You've told me well-nigh naught, and what you did tell is doubtless lies."

"Remember, we'll both swear before God to the truth of it."

"Perjury would be petty among your sins, Cod-Ingeborg." Aksel thrust forward his jaw. "Your story strains belief. Far likelier is that you twain unearthed a hoard in Denmark—unless you committed murder on the high seas; and the gallows punishes that too. Would you drag me down with you? Wariness beseems me."

The woman considered him. "You act the coward, then."

"I'm a law-abiding man who has a household to support."

"Shit! I said you *act* the coward, like a strolling player. I know you, I know your kind," Ingeborg avowed in huge scorn. "You've decided, all at once, you'll rob us yourself. Well, you can't do it. Dismiss us to try elsewhere, or bargain like a decent scoundrel."

Niels shifted about and laid hand to the sailor's knife he wore.

Aksel made a smile. "Ah, now, my dear. It's only that I've no wish either to flirt with the hangman. I need assurance—to start with, a look at that hoard."

Ingeborg rose. "Come, Niels. Here is nothing for us."

"Wait." Aksel's tone stayed calm. "Sit down. Let's talk further."

Ingeborg shook her head. "The years have given me a nose for treachery. Come, Niels."

The youth found his feet. Aksel raised an arm. "I bade you wait," he said. "Or must I call my apprentices to seize you?"

"Never will they!" Niels yelled.

Ingeborg hushed him. "What have you in mind?" she asked quite coolly.

"Why, this," Aksel answered with his ongoing smile. "I suspect you're guilty either of piracy or of stealing royal property. Certain it is that you've not so much as wondered what tax may be due on your gains. Now, you are paupers and without families of your own, but God has called me to a higher station in life; I've more, far more to lose. Why should I risk ruin . . . for anything less than the entire hoard?"

When they stood moveless, he added, "I'd give you something, of course."

They stayed mute. He scowled. "Very well," he said, and slapped the table. "Be clear in your minds that I did *not* offer to become your accomplice. I just put a question to see how you'd behave. My duty is to report this matter—no, not to the sheriff; direct to the baron. Meanwhile, I can't let you escape, can I?

"Think well, you twain. I've heard that Junkèr Falkvor's executioner is more skillful than most. He'll get your whole tale out of what is left of you, for his lord."

"And you'll have a nice reward, no doubt," the woman fleered.

"That is the cautious course for me," Aksel pursued. "I'd be sorry to follow it, for I've happy memories of you, Ingeborg, and your comrade has a whole life before him. Therefore sit down, and let me try bringing you to reason."

"Niels," Ingeborg said.

Her friend understood. His knife came forth, of terrifying size in that dim room.

"We are going," he said. "You'll take us out. If we have any trouble, you'll die first. Up!"

Abruptly blanched, Aksel rose. This was no longer a boy who confronted him. Niels sheathed the blade but kept him close by. Ingeborg dropped the ring down her bosom.

They left the house as three. In an alley some distance off, Niels released Aksel. After the trader had stumbled into the street, Ingeborg's bitterness broke loose: "I thought he was the least bad of the lot. Where in Christendom is mercy?"

"Best we move on ere he raises hue and cry," Niels warned.

They made a devious way to the waterfront on Mariager Fjord. A small ship lay awaiting the tide, to depart for ports along the Sound. They had already engaged passage on her deck and brought aboard what would be needful for them. It had seemed a wise precaution. Since they had additionally paid the captain for a night's worth of drinking their health, he let them rest in his compartment until he sailed.

III

A FULL moon stood aloft in a frosty ring. Few stars shone through its brightness, that turned hoar the treetops around the lake and tinged each wavelet with silver. A breeze bore autumn's chill and rattled leaves which were dying.

The vodianoi rose from the bottom and swam toward shore. He grew old when the moon waned, young when it waxed; this night he was in the flush of power and hunger. The bulk of three war horses, his body, on which grew moss and trailing weeds, was like a man's save for thick tail, long-toed feet, webbed and taloned forepaws. The face was flattened, with bristles around its cavern of a mouth. Eyes glowed red as coals.

When belly touched ground, he stopped. Through the murk below the trees there reached him a sound of brush being parted and footfalls drawing near. Whatever humans wanted here after dark, maybe one of them would be careless enough to wade out. The vodianoi moved no more than a rock. The argent ripples he had raised faded away.

A shape flitted out of shadow, to poise on the grass at the water's edge: upright, slim, white as the moon. Laughter trilled. "Oh, you silly! Let me show how to lurk." Wind-swift, it swarmed into an oak nearby. "Let me feed you." Acorns flew, to bounce off the monster's hide.

He grunted thunder-deep wrath. These past three years the vilja had teased him. He had even wallowed onto land a few painful yards, seeking to catch her, gaining naught but her mirth. Soon she must leave the wood, to spend winter beneath lake and stream, but that availed not the vodianoi. Though cold made her dreamy, she never grew too unaware or too slow for him. Besides, when she was not actually rousing him to fury, he knew in his dim-witted fashion that it was unlikely he could harm such a wraith.

The only good thing was that in that season she merely greeted him, like a sleepwalker, when they met.

"I know," she called. "You hope you'll grab you a fine, juicy man. Well, you shan't." With a gesture, she raised a whirly little wind around him. "They're mine, those travelers." Her mood swung about. The wind died away. "But why do they fare at night?" she asked herself in a tone of bewilderment. "And they bring no fire to see by. Men would bring fire—would they not? I can't remember. . . ."

She hugged her knees where she sat on high, rocked back and forth, let her hair blow cloudy-pale on a breeze that hardly stirred the locks of those who approached. All at once she cried, "They are *not* men—most of them—not really," and climbed higher to be hidden.

The vodianoi hissed after her, hunched back down, and waited.

The mermen came out of the forest. They numbered a score, led by Vanimen, naked save for knife belts but carrying fish spears and hooped nets. Ivan Subitj was among the half-dozen humans who were along to observe. Guided through gloom by companions with Faerie sight, they had made stumbling progress, and blinked as if dazed when suddenly moonlight spilled across them.

"Yonder he is!" Vanimen called. "Already we've found him. I thought an absence of flame would aid us in that."

Ivan peered. "A boulder?" he asked.

"No, look close, espy those ember eyes." Vanimen raised steel and shouted in his own tongue.

The mermen splashed out. Bellowing in glee, fangs agleam, the vodianoi threshed after the nearest. The fleet creature eluded him. He chased another, and failed.

Now he and they were swimming. The mermen closed in, jeered, pricked with their forks. The vodianoi dived. They followed.

For a minute, water roiled and spouted.

Silence fell, the lake rocked back toward calm, heaven again dreamed its icy dreams. A soldier's voice was lost in that immensity: "The fight's gone too deep for us to see."

"If it is a fight," a companion said. "That thing's immortal till Judgment. Iron won't bite on it. What hope have those hunters of yours, lord, witchy though they be?"

"Their headman has told me of several things he can try," Ivan answered. He was not one to confide in underlings. "Which is best, he must find out."

"Unless it slays his band," a third man said. "What then?"

"Then we must abide here till dawn, when we can find our way home," the zhupan stated. "The beast can't catch us ashore."

"There's other things as might." The second trooper stared around him. Moonbeams glimmered in his eyeballs, making them blank.

Ivan raised a cross he wore around his neck. A crystal covered a hollow theren. "This carries a fingerbone of St. Martin," he said. "Pray like true Christians, and no power of darkness can harm us."

"Your son Mihajlo thought different," a soldier dared mutter.

The zhupan heard, and struck him on the cheek. The slap woke an echo. "Hold your tongue, you oaf!" Men signed themselves, thinking dissension boded ill.

Slow hours passed. Frost deepened. Those who waited shivered, stamped feet, tucked hands in armpits. Breath smoked from them. Something white stirred restlessly at the top of a great oak, but nobody cared to peer closely after it.

The moon was sinking when a cry tore out of their throats. A blackness had broken the glade. A hideous shape moved toward them. It halted some distance off, near enough that they could see the mermen tread water to ring the vodianoi in.

Vanimen entered the shallows, stood up, walked to the humans. Wetness dripped from him like mercury. Pride blazed forth like the sun that was coming. "Victory is ours," he proclaimed.

"God be praised!" Ivan jubilated. After a moment, warrior hardheadedness returned. "Are you sure? What did you do? What's to happen next?"

Vanimen folded arms across his mighty chest and laughed. "We could kill him, aye. But on this very night of his greatest strength, we could outswim him. Our weapons gave pain. None of us did he seize, the while we tormented him till it grew beyond bearing. Also, we showed him how we take fish. In that, he cannot match us either. We can snatch them before he does, scare them off, leave him famished.

"At least we made him know, with the help of a spell for understanding, that we would do this as long as needful. Best he spare his own anguish and depart forthwith. We'll escort him up the river, past your town, and let him go on thence, into unpeopled highlands. He'll grieve you no more."

Ivan embraced him. Men cheered. Mermen responded lustily from the water. The vodianoi brooded.

"Follow along the edge," Vanimen advised. "We'll keep in sight of you." He turned to rejoin his folk.

The white shape flitted down through withering leaves. Many came along when it sprang from a lower branch to earth. "Ah, no," it sang, "would you drive the poor old ugly hence? This is his home. The lake will be lonely without him, a wonder will be gone, and who shall I play with?"

Vanimen saw the form dance over glittery grass, the form of a naked maiden, lovely to behold but colorless, seeming almost transparent. No mist of breath left nostrils or lips. *"Rousalka!"* he bawled, and fled into the lake.

The being stopped. "Who are you?" she asked the zhupan in her thin, sweet voice. "Should I remember you?"

Sweat studded Ivan's skin, he shuddered, yet it was with hatred and rage rather than fear that he advanced. "Demon, ghost, foul thief of souls!" he shrilled. "Begone! Back to your grave, back to your hell!"

He slashed with his sword. Somehow it did not strike. The vilja lifted her hands. "Why are you angry? Be not angry," she begged. "Stay. You are so warm, I am so alone."

Ivan dropped his blade and raised his cross. "In the name of the Holy Trinity, and St. Martin whose banner St. Stefan bore into battle, go."

The vilja whirled about and ran into the wood. She left less mark by far in the hoarfrost than a woman would have done. They heard her sobbing, then that turned into laughter, then there was no more trace of her.

Bells pealed rejoicing till all Skradin rang. No person worked, save to prepare a festival that began in the afternoon and continued past sunset.

The sight had been awesome for those who were awake before dawn, when the vodianoi passed by under guard of the mermen. It was as if, for a moment, the world—castle, church, town, houses, fields, ordered hours and the cycle that went measured from Easter to Easter—had parted like a veil, men glimpsed what it had hidden from them, and that was no snug Heaven but ancient, unending wildness.

By early daylight, when Vanimen's hunters returned with the zhupan and his band, fright was forgotten. Talk aroused of starting fishery. True, the deep forest was still a chancy place to enter, and would not be cleared away for generations. Yet logging proceeded, year by year; plowland stretched outward, homes multiplied; cultivation had tamed a sizeable arc of the lakeside. The monster gone, it should be safe to launch boats from that part, if one did not row too near the wooded marge.

The zhupan confirmed the good news. He had seen the vodianoi leave his conquerors and make a slow way on upstream, panting, sometimes able to swim, sometimes groping over rocks that bruised, till lost from sight. The creature moved brokenly. Belike doom would overtake him long before Judgment; hopelessness might well make him lay down his bones to rest.

Father Petar conducted a Mass of thanksgiving, with a somewhat sour face. Thereafter, merriment began. Presently the nearest meadow surged with folk in their holiday garb, embroidered vests, flowing blouses, wide-sweeping skirts for the revealing of an ankle in the dance. An ox roasted over a bonfire, kettles steamed forth savory smells above lesser flames, barrels gurgled out beer, mead, wine. Bagpipes, flutes, horns, drums, single-stringed fiddles resounded through the babble.

Freely among the peasants moved the Liri folk. Ivan Subitj had taken it on himself to release them. He had no fret about their breaking parole and fleeing. Friendship laved them today and their morrow looked full of hope. For decency's sake he had arranged that they be clad, though this must for the most part be in borrowed clothes that were old and fitted poorly. That meant little to them, especially in their happiness at being back together. Anyhow, garments were readily shed when male and female had left the village and found a bush or a tree-screened riverbank.

The noisiest, cheeriest celebrant was Father Tomislav. He had come hither with Vanimen after Ivan approved the merman's idea, and only with difficulty had he been restrained from joining the expedition. Now, when men linked hands around a cauldron to dance the kolo, his vigor sent whipcracks through their circle. "Hai, hop! Swing a leg! Leap like David before the Lord! Ah, there, my dears,"—to pretty girls as he whirled by them—"just you wait till we and you make a line!"

Vanimen and Meiiva had repaid long separation. They entered the meadow when the kolo was ending. Luka, son of Ivan, pushed through the crowd to greet them. He was a slender lad, whose bright outfit was in scant accord with his thoughtful mien. From the beginning he had been greatly taken by the merfolk, eager to learn about them, ever arguing for their better treatment. After Vanimen's exploit, he approached them with adoration.

"Hail," he said through the racket around. "You look somber. You should be joyous. Can I help you in any way?"

"Thank you, but I think not," The Liri king replied.

"What's wrong?"

"I'll speak of it later with your father. Let me not shadow your pleasure."

"No, I pray you, tell me. Maybe I can do something."

"Well——" Vanimen decided. Meiiva, who spoke no Hrvatskan as yet, slipped quietly into the background. "Well, since you'll have it so, Luka. Have you heard that we met a rousalka by the lake?"

The stripling blinked. "What said you?"

"Rousalka. The revenant of a maiden that haunts the water where she drowned."

"Oh." Luka's eyes widened; he caught his breath. "The vilja. You saw her?" He paused. "No, I've not heard. It's a thing that men would avoid talk of."

"Is 'vilja' your word?" Vanimen spoke stiffly. "I had to do with one of the kind once, afar in the North. Thus I recognized this for what it was. Terror overwhelmed me and I fled. The shame of that is a gnawing in my breast. Your father drove it off, but when afterward I sought to explain why courage had left me, he said he'd liefer not hear."

Luka nodded. "Yes, he has his reasons. However, I think he'll yield if you press him. The matter's no secret—woeful, but not disgraceful."

"Such a . . . vilja . . . mocks our triumph," Vanimen said. "I hear men bleat about fishing, my tribe for helpers. Are they witless? The vodianoi could merely devour them. How can they fail to dread what the vilja will do?"

"Why, what might that be?" Luka asked in surprise. "Minor mischief, as the Leshy inflict—a wind to blow somebody's washing off the grass, a nursling taken from its mother when she isn't looking, but always soon given back—and a sprig of wormwood will keep her at a distance. No doubt a man who let her beguile him would be in mortal sin. But surely none will, nor does it seem she's even tried. After all, a ghost is terrifying in itself. I know that, sir, I know it better than I wish I did."

The merman gave the lad a close look. "How?"

Luka shivered in the sunlight, the noise and music and smoke. "I was with my brother on that hunt where she found him, two years agone. I too saw her face, the face of Nada who drowned herself the year before——"

A hand grabbed him by the neck, flung him to the ground. "You lie!" Father Tomislav screamed. He had wandered up, unnoticed, and overheard. "Like the rest of them, you lie!"

Standing over the sprawled boy, amidst a stillness that spread outward, amidst eyes that stared inward, the priest mastered his fit. "No, you don't, I'll believe you don't," he said thickly. "A chance likeness or a sleight of Satan deceived you. I'm sorry, Luka. Forgive my foul temper." He looked from person to person. The tears broke out of him. "My daughter was not a suicide," he croaked. "She is not a condemned shade. She rests in Shibenik, in holy earth. Her, her soul...in...Paradise——" He stumbled off. The gathering parted to let him go.

Rain dashed against castle walls, in a night that howled. Cold crept out of the stone, past the tapestries, and darkness laid siege to lamps. Ivan Subitj sat across a board from Vanimen of Liri. He had dismissed his servants, keeping his wife awake. She sat in a corner, warming herself as best she could at a brazier, till he signaled for more wine.

"Yes," he said, "I'd better give you the whole tale. Else you might shun the lake; and I do have hopes of your settling down amongst us, enriching us by your fisher skills. Besides, there's no shame for my family in what happened—not really. Grief——" He gusted a sigh. "No, disappointment; and I'm well aware I do wrong to feel thus."

He stroked the scar that puckered his countenance. "No shame to you either, Vanimen, that you recoiled from her: not if such

beings are as fearsome in the North as you've related. I could tell
you of horrors I'll bear inside me to the grave, and I reckon myself
a brave man. But—I know not why; maybe we're different from
the Rus in some way that endures after death itself—whatever the
cause, a vilja is not the grisly sort of thing that you say a rousalka
is. Oh, a man would be unwise to follow her...but he'd have
a soul to lose. You——" Ivan chopped his words off short.

Vanimen flashed a hard smile.

Ivan drank. Thereafter he said hastily: "My grudge against
Nada is just that she caused my older son to forsake the world.
Well, I think she did. I could be wrong. Who knows the well-
springs of the heart, save God? But Mihajlo was such a lively
youth; in him, I saw myself reborn. And now he's in a monastery.
I should not regret that, should I? It makes his salvation likelier.
Luka seems more cut out for a monk than ever Mihajlo was; and
it's become Luka who inherits—— No, he won't, for a zhupan
is elected by the peers of his clan, or appointed out of it by the
Crown, and they'll see he's not a fighter."

Goblets went to mouths for a time in which the storm alone
had voice. Finally Vanimen asked low, "Was the vilja indeed once
the daughter of Tomislav?"

"He cannot endure that thought," Ivan replied, "and those who
care for him do not bespeak it in his hearing. I forgive what he
did to my son this day. No real harm, and Luka should have been
more alert.

"Nevertheless—well, let me share with you what everybody
hereabouts knows. Maybe you, who are of Faerie, can judge better
than we've done, we humans.

"You must understand that Sena, Tomislav's wife, was a
woman born to sorrow. Her father was a bastard of the zhupan
before me, by a serf girl, whom they say was of rare beauty. He
manumitted his son, who became a guslar—a wandering musician,
a ne'er-do-well—and at last shocked people by bringing home a
bride from the Tzigani, those landless pagans who've lately been
drifting in. She herself was Christian, of course, though it's unsure
how deep the conversion went.

"Both died young, of sickness. Their daughter Sena was raised
by kinfolk who—I must say—blamed every childish wrong she
did on her heritage. I've often wondered if it was pity as much
as her loveliness that made Tomislav seek her hand.

"You've heard of their afflictions. A while after Nada was born, Sena sank into dumb, helpless mourning, and lay thus until she died. What memories of her mother did the girl afterward carry around? In haphazard fashion, Nada learned from neighbor women what she was supposed to know, more or less. Her father spent his whole love upon her, who was all he had left, but what good can a man do? He may have confided in her more than he should—a priest does carry the woes of many others—he may have made her see too early that this world is full of weeping. I know not. I'm only a soldier, Vanimen."

Ivan drank, summoned fresh wine, sat again mute before he went on:

"I remember Nada well, myself. As zhupan, I travel much about in the hinterland, to keep abreast of what the knezi—judges over villages—and pastors and such are doing. Besides, Tomislav brought his family here whenever he could, as on market days. We've no proper marketplace here, but folk do meet to trade back and forth. I suppose in part he hoped to ease the restlessness of his older children.

"Oh, Nada became fair! I heard, too, that she was quick-witted, and kinder-hearted, even toward animals, than is best for a peasant. Certainly I saw her laughterful and frolicsome. Yet already then, and seldom though we did meet, I would also see her withdrawn, silent, sad, for no clear cause.

"I suppose that's a reason she had no suitors, however gladly the young men would dance and jest with her when she was in the mood. Besides, her dowry would be very small. And she was overly slender; how well could she bear babe after babe, to keep a household alive? Fathers must have weighed these things on behalf of their sons."

Ivan swallowed, put his goblet down, stared at a shuttered window as if to look beyond and lose himself in the rain. "Well," he said, "here comes the part that's hard for me to tell. Let me go fast.

"She had broken into bloom when Mihajlo, my older son, came visiting and saw her here in Skradin. At once he began paying her court. He'd ride through the woods to her zadruga, and how could Tomislav refuse hospitality? He'd arrange that she come to Skradin for this or that celebration—oh, everything quite proper, but he wanted her and meant to have her.

"Mihajlo was...is...a charming fellow. Nada's two brothers and her sister had flown the nest, and doubtless she'd heard somewhat herself of a wider realm outside, a realm where maybe her choices were not merely to become a drudge or a nun...I know not. I know only that her father, Tomislav, sought me and asked if Mihajlo intended marriage.

"What could I say? I knew my boy. When he wedded, it would be for gain; meanwhile he'd have his sport, also afterward. Tomislav thanked me for my frankness, and said those two must stop seeing each other. Because I think well of him, I agreed. Mihajlo wrangled with me, but in the end gave his promise. She was not that much to him."

"But he to her——" the merman said, half under his breath. "And her father—she must have loved him too. The melancholy caught her when she was torn asunder——"

"She was found floating in the lake," Ivan interrupted roughly. "Since then, it seems, she haunts it. You've naught to fear from her, though, you merfolk. Need we carry this sad little story onward?" He lifted his vessel. "Come, let's get drunk together."

Tomislav went home in the morning. First he met with Vanimen to bid farewell.

That was in a dawn which the rain had washed pure. The two of them stood at the edge of woods. Above, the sky was white in the east, blue overhead, violet enough in the west to hold a planet which trailed the sunken moon. Trees had come all bronze and brass and blood, while fallen leaves crunched underfoot. Stubblefields lay misty. Cocks crowed afar, the single sound in the chill.

Tomislav leaned his staff against a bole and clasped Vanimen's right hand in both of his. "We'll meet again, often," he vowed.

"I would like that," the merman answered. "Be sure, at least, I will not leave these parts without calling on you."

The man raised brows. "Why should you ever go? Here you are loved, you and your whole tribe."

"As a dog is loved. We were free in Liri. Should we become tame animals, no matter how kindly our owners?"

"Oh, you'd never be serfs, if that's what troubles you. Your skills are too valuable." Tomislav paused. "True, you'd better become Christians." It kindled in him; suddenly his face was not homely. "Vanimen, take baptism! Then God will give you a soul that outlives the stars, in the glory of His presence."

The merman shook his head. "No, good friend. Over the centuries, I've witnessed, thrice, the fate of those folk of mine who did that."

"And——?" the priest asked after a silence.

"I daresay they gained what they yearned for, immortality in Heaven. But here on earth, they forgot the lives they had had. Everything they were went a-glimmering, as if it had never been— dreams, joys, farings, everything that was them. There remained meek lowlings whose feet were deformed." The sea king sighed. "Tomislav, I do not hate oblivion that much. My kindred feel likewise."

The man stood undaunted; his beard bristled gray at the earliest whisper of a breeze. "Vanimen," he urged, "I've thought about such things, thought hard"—for an instant, his mouth twisted— "and it seems to me that God makes nothing in vain. Nothing that is from Him shall perish for aye. Yes, this may be heresy of mine. Nonetheless, I can hope that on the Last Day, whatever you forsake will be restored to you."

"You may or may not be right," Vanimen said. "If you are, I still disdain it, I who've hunted narwhals under the boreal ice and had lemans that were like northlights"—his voice sank—"I who lived with Agnete—— He took his hand free. "No, I'll not trade that for your thin eternity."

"But you don't understand," Father Tomislav responded. "Oh, I've read legends; I know what commonly happens when Faerie folk are received into Christendom. But this needen't always be. It's simply for their own protection, I believe. Chronicles tell of a few halfworld beings that got baptism and kept full memory." He cast his arms around the merman. "I'll pray for a sign that you will be given this grace."

IV

JOHAN KVAG, bishop of Roskilde, often had business in Copenhagen, for he was its liege. In a private room of the house he kept
there, he sat long silent while he considered, from his seat whereon
were carved the Apostles, the young man in a plain chair before
him. Ordinary clothes and Jutish brogue hardly accorded with the
gold, given to Mother Church, that had persuaded his major-domo
to arrange this audience.

"You have told me less than you could, my son," he finally
said.

Niels Jonsen nodded. His self-possession, at his age and station
in life, was remarkable too. "Aye, my lord," he admitted. "Some
might suffer, did the whole tale come out. But I swear before God
that I've spoken no lie to you, and won the treasure in no wrongful
way."

"And now you would share it with my see. If your reckoning
of its worth is correct, that would be a donation an emperor could
scarcely match."

"I'll leave the dividing to you, and trust in your fairness."

"You've small choice," the bishop said dryly. "You'll not stay
alive, let alone grow wealthy, without protection."

"I know it well, reverend excellency."

Johan cupped his chin. "And still you bargain," he murmured.
"You forget the danger to your spirit that lies in worldly riches."

"My priest can steer me clear of that, I hope," said Niels.

"You are a cocky one, aren't you?"

"No disrespect, sir. But if naught else, I've people I'd like to
help, beginning with my mother and her brood. Besides, the way
the Hansa's pushing in, meseems the kindgom should be glad of
a big shipowner who's Danish."

The bishop's gravity broke in a laugh. "Well spoken!"

Niels' countenance lightened. "Then you'll take me on?"

"Not that fast, my son, not that fast. There are certain conditions to meet. First, though you keep a secret or two from me, you must tell all to a priest, that he may shrive you." The sunburnt face drew downward. Johan smiled and added: "I'll send you to Father Ebbe of St. Nicholas'. That's your patron, and Ebbe is of seafaring stock himself, lenient about things that others might find overly peculiar."

"A thousand thanks, my lord."

"Next you must lead trusty men to the hoard, unbeknownst, for them to examine it." The bishop bridged his fingers. "We must be careful. If it's as great as you claim, we cannot bring it forth overnight. Wars would ensue for its possession, on whatever pretext. Few years ago, this city was under Norwegian attack; and when I think of the German dukes—— Yes, I suspect our wisest plan in the end will be to leave the major part buried."

"But you can do so much good with it," Niels protested.

"Gold cannot buy more in aid of the poor than the land can produce. Nor are clergy immune to temptations, of which the worst may be those of power."

Johan raised a reassuring palm. "Certainly we'll have use for considerable amounts," he went on. "They can be introduced in discreet fashion. Likewise for your career, my son. Not only dare you not burst flamelike into opulence; you've much to learn ere you can successfully lead a company.

"We'll explain that you've come into an inheritance, and that I have found you worthy of my favor. This should raise few questions. Folk will suppose you're the bastard of a well-off man, perhaps kin of mine, who's died." At Niels' scowl: "Nay, no reflection on your mother's honor. It's merely what they'll take for granted, a common kind of event which occasions short-lived gossip, if any.

"In due course, I'll have you made a burgher, and you can get your licenses for trade.... Look less impatient, lad," the bishop chuckled. "I've no intolerable length of time in mind."

"You're generous, your reverence." Niels clenched fist on knee. "But some matters can't wait very long."

Johan nodded. "True. You bespoke your family. And doubtless you anticipate pleasures. No vast harm in that, if amidst them you still remember God. And maybe you've a venture or two you'd like to begin on at once, that's within your present abilities? Well, none of these things is impossible, for you will admittedly have money. Your need is just to hold covered how large the sum is." Joy blazed at him. "Go with my blessing. We'll talk further tomorrow."

The moats, walls, watchtowers that guarded Copenhagen were stately. Within them, however, most of the city was houses wooden and thatch-roofed, jammed together along narrow, crooked, mucky streets. The folk who crowded it were mainly laborers, their drabness relieved here and there by the flamboyant rags of a juggler or fiddler; traffic was mainly afoot, save for wagons forcing through with a bow wave of curses. Beggars and foreign seamen gave strangeness but hardly more color. A mounted knight, a rich merchant, a famous courtesan in her litter, would stand out as much by rarity as by finery. Swine, poultry, dogs, children wandered about. Noise went like surf, voices, feet, wheels, hammers. Raw beneath a low gray sky, the air reeked of smoke, dung, offal, graveyards.

And yet, Niels thought, the saying was true: this was indeed free air. It bathed him with hope, made him drunk on dreams. Here was the womb of the future. He could almost set aside the longing for Eyjan that ever querned within him—almost—in this place so utterly sundered from everything of hers.

He reached the inn where he was staying, hurried through the taproom with a bare wave to the landlord and the drinkers, thudded upstairs and along a hallway. The Blue Lion was for those who could afford the best that became a commoner: clean, safe, with a pair of bedroom for hire in addition to the general one. He knocked on a door of the former.

Ingeborg let him in. She had bought an image of the Virgin and stood it on a shelf. He saw from wrinkles in her gown that she had been praying. Her gaze sought his, she trembled and parted her lips but could not speak.

He closed the door. "Ingeborg," he said, "we've won."

"O-o-oh. . . ." A hand went to her mouth.

"The bishop agrees. He's a fine fellow. Well, he does want to move slowly, but that's all right, that's wise. Our luck has turned." Niels whooped. He danced where he stood, for the bed left scant floor space. "Our luck, Ingeborg! No more poverty, no more toil, no more whoredom—the world is ours!"

She crossed herself. "Mary, I thank you," she whispered.

"Aye, me too, we'll light many candles, but first let's rejoice," Niels babbled. "We'll feast this eventide, I'll have the kitchen get whatever you like and cook it for you, we'll have wine and tapers and music——Oh, Ingeborg, be glad. You deserve gladness."

He clasped her waist. She regarded him through tears. "Teach me how to be happy," she asked.

He fell moveless, staring down at her. It came suddenly to him that she was fair to see, full figure, gentle features, luster of brown eyes and billowing hair. They had kissed before, but quickly, in simple friendliness. Now the whiplash need was off him—off them both. He'd wondered in fleeting moments how that would feel, being free to remember Eyjan all the time. Now he knew; but here was Ingeborg.

"You're beautiful," he said, amazed.

"Niels, no," She tried to draw back. He pulled her against him. Her mingled scents of woman were dizzying. The kiss went on and on.

"Niels," she breathed shakily into his bosom, "do you understand what you seek?"

"Yes, Ingeborg, darling." He lowered her to the bed.

——Afterward, as they lay resting in embrace, she said, "I beg one thing of you, Niels."

"It's yours." He stroked the softness of her back.

"Never call me 'love,' or 'dearest,' or any such word, as you were doing."

He lifted his head off the bolster, astonished. "What? Why not?"

"We have only each other. Gold or no, it'll be long before we've friends we can trust. Believe you me. Then let there be no lies between us."

"I care for you!"

"And I for you. Very, very much." Her lips brushed his cheek. "But you are too young for me, too good——"

"No."

"And it's Eyjan you yearn for."

He had no answer to that.

She sighed. "It's Tauno for me, of course," she owned. "I fear we've neither of us any chance. Well, maybe I can guide your heart toward a mortal maiden."

"What of you?" he asked through her tresses.

He felt her shrug. "I'm tough. Besides, whatever happens, while we stay honest, we have each other."

V

A MARBLE fireplace made warm a chamber which maroon hangings and Persian rug softened. While window glass gave a view—hardly distorted at all—of an inner court where blooming had long since ended, roses from a solarium planter filled a crystal vase on an inlaid table. Books numbered a score, both Greek and Latin. Pavle Subitj, Ban of Hrvatska, was in his heart more a man of the West than of the East.

Tall in a silken robe, white hair and beard neatly trimmed, he seemed no less than the Liri king, though Vanimen, likewise attired in what was his gift, did loom above him. Both had grown too intense in their discourse to remain seated.

"Yes, I hope your tribe will stay in this realm," he was saying. "Perhaps I've not made sufficiently clear how much I want it. Your unique abilities—as fishermen, sailors, pilots you'll be valuable. But a new war is brewing with Venice. In that, you could be priceless." He studied the other. "Of course, I'd reward such service as best as I was able."

Vanimen scowled. "Why should we enter a quarrel that's none of ours?" he retorted.

"It will be yours, for you will be our countrymen."

"Indeed? That was not what we came in search of."

"I know. You wanted to rebuild a Faerie life, which impinged little on mortal mankind. Well, you've found what is better. Highest is salvation, immortal souls and the fatherhood of God. However, scoff not at material gains, which themselves comfort the spirit. For instance, you've related, in these past days of your visit, how hard and perilous it actually was undersea, how often you knew bereavement. Would you deny your people—your children—liberation from the shark?"

The merman began pacing, back and forth, hands gripped together behind him. "We'd readily be your friends," he said.

"Grant us an islet where we can remain ourselves, and you'll find us stout partners in work, trade, seafaring . . . yes, even in war, if that is inescapable. But you demand more. You'd make us into something altogether alien. Why do you require we be christened?"

"Because I must," Pavle told him. "It would ruin me, before Church and throne and populace alike, if I let a colony of halfworld creatures take root; and who then would be your protector? As it is, I've worked harder than you imagine, to contain the news of you. Outside the Skradin vicinage, there go naught but rumors. In that wise I gained peace for everyone to become acquainted. It cannot last.

"Even when you join us, I'll strive that that happen quietly. No public tidings, no dispatches to King or Pope. Most of you will stay where you now are, or move to the coast nearby if you prefer nautical trades. Those who travel farther, with naval commanders or merchant adventurers, they'll go one or a few at a time—remarkable, yes, but in human company of limited size.

"That's for your good as well as mine, Vanimen. Did your story spread wide, excitement might easily take a dangerous turn. Fear of the unknown could link you in ignorant minds with the Devil. It could end with your being hunted down, the fortunate among you butchered, the unfortunate burnt at the stake."

"Aye," the merman growled, "you're right . . . and nonetheless you'd have us become like your kind?"

He halted, straightened to his full height, and said, "No. We'll return to the waters and our quest. You'll be rid of us."

"Suppose I forbid your departure," the Ban said quietly.

"We'll elude your troops, or break through them, or die in our freedom." Vanimen's tone was as soft.

Pavle smiled sadly. "Peace. I won't. If indeed you would go, you have my leave. Yet where will you seek, and how? You must needs be barred from this kingdom, and likeliest no Mediterranean coast will have you. If you win back to the ocean, well, you can swim south along Africa, though the toll as you fare will be dreadful. But can you endure the tropics, you breed of the North?"

Vanimen stood mute.

After a minute, Pavle went on: "Let's imagine you do in some way find a home. What will you have gained? At best, a few centuries. Then Faerie must depart existence, and you with it."

"Think you so?" Vanimen asked. "Why?"

Pavle clapped his shoulder and said, most gently, "I wish I did not. Too much beauty and wonder will perish with the halfworld, and I've a feeling that whatever replaces them will have less in common with humanity than it did."

Faint through walls came the sound of cathedral bells. "Hark," Pavle said. "The time of yon ringing was ordered not by sun, moon, or stars. A clock has taken that part, a hard, artificial thing, devoid of mystery.

"In my own lifespan I have seen wax the power of bombard, rocket, sapper. In them is the doom of knighthood, which—Arthur, Orlando, Ogier, Huon—ever linked warriors to the Otherworld.

"Wilderness melts away before ax and plow. Meanwhile everything that matters is forgathering in the cities, where all is manmade and the smallest hob-sprite can find no home.

"Yearly farther, in yearly greater numbers, ships ply the seas, guided by compass and astrolabe rather than birdflight, landmarks, a mariner's sense of oneness with the billows. They will round the earth someday, and Christian steeples rise above the last places where Faerie had refuge.

"For the earth is a globe, you may know, of measurable size. The very tracks of the stars are being measured, closer than the ancients could, and learned men are calculating the architecture of the universe. Their schemes have no room for awe or magic.

"Look here." Pavle sought the table and picked up two lenses in a wire frame. "This is something I heard was newly invented in Italy, and sent for. As I've aged, my eyesight has been failing me at short range, till I could scarcely read or write. Today I slip this thing over the bridge of my nose, and it's almost like being young again." He handed them to Vanimen. "A beginning," he foretold. "The progenitor of instruments which make vision keener than an eagle's, closer than a mole's. My descendants will turn them outward on the heavens, inward on themselves. Perhaps God will then terminate the world, lest men question His ways too closely. Or perhaps not. But sure I am that they will have questioned Faerie out of it."

The merman stared at the spectacles. He held them in his palm as if they were freezing cold.

"Therefore," Pavle finished, "are you not well advised to accept your fate, gratefully, and seek your home in Paradise?

"I won't press you, save that I must have your decision within a few more months. Think. Go back to Skradin and tell your folk. Speak, too, with that priest in the zadruga whom Ivan esteems. Ask him to pray for you."

Alone, Father Tomislav knelt. Winter night engulfed him, still and bitter, making the clay floor gnaw at his knees. He could barely glimpse Christ on the Cross, above the altar, by the light of a candle he had lit to the saint whose name his church bore, and whose effigy he beseeched.

"Holy Andrei," he said, his voice as lost as the flame, "you were a fisherman when Our Lord called you to come follow Him. Did you ever afterward long back to the sea . . . just the least bit, maybe? Waves alive around you, a salt wind, a gull gliding—oh, you know what I mean. You didn't regret your ministry. Nothing like that. But you remembered, sometimes—didn't you? I myself miss the water shiny at the foot of Zadar, and going out in a boat—what a romp, what bigness and freshness!—and me a land-lubber born.

"You should understand how the merfolk feel. It isn't their fault they have no souls, and so can't properly crave salvation. The paynim among humans don't crave it either, do they? God made the merfolk for His seas. If they forget the nature He gave them, well, I suppose they could still breathe down below, that kind of thing, but what use would it be? Like a man forgetting how to walk. They'd never learn again aright, I think.

"Mostly, though, the sea's been their life, their love. Yes, love. Even a dog can love, and the merfolk have minds as good as any man's. Would I choose to forget my Sena? No. The memories hurt, but I cherish them. You know that, as many Masses as I've offered for her soul's repose.

"Holy Andrei, seafarer, speak to God on behalf of the poor merfolk. Explain how they'll accept baptism if it doesn't cost them their memories. They aren't being defiant of Him or anything. It's simply their way. When they have souls, they'll be different. But why take away from them what they were before? Instead, leave them able to tell men of the wonders He's created in the deeps, that we may worship Him the more. Isn't that reasonable?

"Holy Andrei, grant me a sign."

The crude wooden image stirred. Lips curved in a smile, hand reached out in the gesture of benediction.

For a moment Tomislav gaped. Then he fell prostrate, weeping. "Glory be to God, glory be to God!"

When at last he got back on his knees, all was as erstwhile. The candle guttered low, the cold ascended, stars above the roof marched on toward midnight.

"Thank you, Andrei," Tomislav said humbly. "You're a true friend."

After a minute, in sudden shock: "*I've* been vouchsafed a miracle! Me!" He folded his hands. "Lord, I am not worthy."

He would keep vigil till dawn. "Our Father, Who art in Heaven, hallowed be Thy name———"

Near morning, when weariness had dazed him, he lifted a timid gaze to the saint's face. "Andrei," he mumbled, "they say such terrible things about my little daughter. Could you maybe give me another sign? I know the stories aren't true. Nada's where you are. Could be she's right there at your side looking down on her old dad. If only people would see that. Can't you show them?"

The carving never stirred. Tomislav lowered his head. Blood trickled into his beard. When daylight glimmered, he rose, bowed before the altar, and departed.

Vanimen and Meiiva walked down the wagon track that went through the forest. Snow had fallen of late, an inch or two that soon melted off bare dirt but abided in purity under the trees. Boughs and twigs reached austere across blueness. The air was quiet and nearly warm.

"His honesty is above challenge," the merman said. "However, half asleep, he may well have imagined that that happened which he desired so much to happen."

Meiiva shivered, not from cold. "Or else the dead man he invoked was playing a trick," she said.

"No, I don't ween the Most High would allow that. He is just."

She gave him a startled glance. "Never erenow have you spoken thus."

"We've none of us been wont to talk, or think, about such matters. They were beyond us, as the fashioning and use of a knife are beyond a dolphin. We knew only blind luck, which might be good or might be bad, save that in the end, soon or late, it was always fatal. God did not care about us . . . we supposed . . . and we had naught to do with Him.

"Today I wonder," Vanimen said when they had laid several more yards behind them. He grinned as he used to when confronting a threat. "I'd better, hadn't I?"

"Do you really hold that we should forsake Faerie?" Meiiva plucked at the gown, dun and itchy, which closed her off from a living world. "We had the freedom of the swan's road."

"I fear Pavle Subitj is right," Vanimen answered heavily. "For the children if not ourselves, we should yield."

"Will their lives be worth the cost? Man's lot is seldom happy."

"Our people can do well enough. Their swimming skills are in demand; they are liked; already, you must have noticed, mermen and maidens, mermaids and youths, begin to sigh for each other, and heads of households ponder the advantages of marriage alliances with persons of such excellent prospects."

Meiiva nodded. "Indeed. The offspring of those unions will be more terrestrial than our kind. The next generation after them will be entirely human—drownable. We've witnessed this down the centuries, have we not? In one or two hundred years, the blood of Liri will be mingled unto evanishment, the memory of Liri be a myth that no sensible man believes."

"Save in Heaven," he reminded her.

A raven croaked.

"I wish——" he started to say, and stopped.

"What, dear?" Her fingers caressed his arm.

"I wish I were doing this because I truly want to be with God," he got out. "I ought not come to Him as a pauper."

"*You*, Vanimen?" she whispered.

"Aye," he said. They halted. She saw him square his shoulders inside the peasant's coat. "Let me go first, so the rest of you may see what happens and thereafter choose for yourselves.

"I am your king."

Father Petar was grossly offended that the ceremony would take place off in the woods, with Father Tomislav officiating. The zhupan must point out that this was at the Ban's express command, because having many observers who often went to Shibenik or farther would be impolitic.

Having received religious instruction, Vanimen excused himself and went alone down to the coast. He spent the day and night of the equinox at sea. What he did or thought then was something whereof he later kept silence.

His return was on the eve of St. Gabriel. Next morning, after Mass had been sung, he entered the church. The inhabitants of the zadruga stayed there as onlookers. No image denied him. Outside, his people waited under budding leaves, in a hard rain.

He came forth with arms widespread and cried in their own tongue: "Oh, hasten, hasten, beloved! Christ bids you welcome to blessedness!"

VI

TAUNO and Eyjan reached Greenland months after leaving Denmark. First they had searched the nearer waters, albeit with scant expectation. Their tribe could only be living in those parts in dispersal, and that might well itself prove impossible. Everywhere from North Cape and the Gulf of Bothnia to the Galway coast and Faeroes, what few hunting grounds remained—not yet overrun by humans or barred by curse of a Christian priest—had long been held by others, who numbered about as many as could support themselves.

Though friendly enough to the siblings, these dwellers had no knowledge whatsoever of where the exiles might have gone. That was strange, as widely as news traveled with merfolk roving singly or in small bands, and with the dolphins. A few persons had heard of a migration up the Kattegat and across the Skagerrak, but there the trail ended.

Hence the siblings went on to Iceland, arriving about midwinter. They got no help from the three surviving settlements along yonder shores either, save hospitality during a season more stern than Tauno and Eyjan had known in their young lives. Elders who had seen several hundred years go by told them that through the past eight or nine decades cold had been deepening. Pack ice groaned in every fjord which once had been clear, and bergs laired in sea lanes which Eric the Red had freely sailed three centuries ago.

But this was of no large moment to merfolk, who, indeed, found more life in chill than in warm waters. The king of Liri might well have led his community to unclaimed banks off Greenland. In spring, Tauno and Eyjan sought thither.

On the way, they encountered some dolphins who confirmed what they had suspected. Vanimen and his following had taken a ship westward from Norway. Alas, a mighty storm arose and blew the vessel farther off course than any of those animals—whose territories are large but nevertheless territories—chose to go.

"If she foundered," Tauno reasoned, "the sailors would be swimmers again. Where they made for would depend on where they were, but they'd strive toward the goal they had if it seemed at all reachable. If she did not go under, then they'd beat back toward that same goal. As close as we ourselves are to Greenland, our chances are best if we continue." Eyjan agreed.

They spent that summer on the eastern side, fruitlessly for their search. What gatherings of their father's sort that they met were uncouth barbarians who had never heard the name of Liri—for merfolk had less occasion to make this crossing than the sons of Adam had had. When they came upon a group of Inuit, the half-lings joined those in hope of some tidings.

At home they had barely gotten rumors of a new human breed moving southward through the great glacier-crowned island. Tauno and Eyjan found them to be hardy, skilled, helpful, open-handed, merrier companions and lustier lovers than most shore-dwellers of Europe, heathens who felt no guilt at welcoming Faerie kind into their midst. But after a few months, their way of life took on a sameness which chafed. Having learned somewhat of the language, and the fact that nobody had the longed-for information, brother and sister bade farewell and returned to the sea.

Southbound among early ice floes, they soon left behind them all trace of Inuit, who had not yet gotten that far down from the north. Rounding the cape at the bottom of the island, the pair met dolphins who did bear a word to stir hearts—word of magic a-prowl farther up the west coast. The dolphins could scarcely say more; yonder wasn't their range, and what they got was mere gossip such as they loved to pass onward. Nor did they care to go look; the whisper went that this was a very dangerous sorcery.

It might simply appear to be so, Tauno and Eyjan decided. For instance, the founding of a New Liri could well frighten creatures who had never seen or dreamed of an underwater town. And, whatever was going on, they had a need to know about it more nearly.

From humans back home to whom they had been close, they were aware of how matters stood ashore in Greenland. The Norse had three settlements on this side, where climate was less harsh than elsewhere. Oldest, biggest, and southernmost was the Eastern, the Ostri Bygd. Not far from it lay the Mid Bygd. A goodly way north, despite its name, was a later Western settlement, the Vestri Bygd. The tales of menace came out of that last.

Tauno and Eyjan swam toward it. The season was now well along into fall.

VII

An umiak was traveling with land to starboard, at the center of a school of kayaks. The merman's children broached half a mile off, cleared their lungs, and poised where they were that they might take stock in safety. Shark, orca, storm, reef, riptide had winnowed faintheartedness out of their bloodline, but had also taught caution.

"Deeming by what the dolphins said, the . . . thing . . . hereabouts is a foe to white men," Tauno reminded. "Thus, if the matter isn't just that our kith have had to defend themselves against attack, it must be Inuit work. I'd as soon not get a harpoon in me because I'm taken for a white man."

"Oh, nonsense!" Eyjan answered. "I'd never known folk can be as gentle as those who guested us."

"A different set from these, sister mine. And I heard stories about murders done once in a while."

"If naught else, they'll see we can't be of common earth. What we must avoid is not assault, but frightening them off. Let's go ahead slowly, wearing our cheeriest faces."

"And ready to plunge. Aye, then."

Air-breathing, they slanted to intercept the convoy. They felt the frigidity of the water, but not in the torn and gnawed way that a mortal would; to them, it slid caressingly past every muscle, stoking warmth up within them, tasting not alone of salt but of countless subtler things, life and deeps and distances. Choppy, it rocked them as they went—whitecaps a thousand shades of blue black overlaid by a shimmer of green. It whooshed and gurgled; afar on the coast it roared. A west wind blew sharp-edged under a silver-gray sky where wrack flew like smoke. Gulls filled heaven with wings and cries. To right the land rose steeply, darkling cliffs, glimpses of autumn-yellowed meadows tucked in sheltered nooks, peaks where snow lay hoar, and beyond these a bleak brightness that told of inland ice.

Their attention was mainly on the boats. Those within must have gone on some such errand as fowling, and be homebound; no Inuit dwelt quite as far south as the Norse. The umiak was a big canoe, leather across a framework of whalebone and driftwood, paddled by a score of women. As many kayaks accompanied it, each bearing its man. All the gang were merry; their shouts and laughter blew among the gulls' mewings, the waves' squelpings. Tauno and Eyjan saw one young fellow lay alongside the skin boat and speak to a woman who had to be his mother, nursing her newest babe: for she dropped her paddle, hoisted her jacket, and gave him a quick drink at her breast.

Another spied the swimmers. A yell awoke. Sword-blade-thin, the kayaks darted toward them.

"Keep behind me, Eyjan," Tauno said. "Hold your spear under the surface ready to use." He himself trod water, repeatedly lifting his hands to show they were empty. His thews thrummed.

The first kayak foamed to a stop before him. He inside could well-nigh have been a merman too, or rather a sea-centaur, so much did he and his craft belong together. The hide that covered it was laced around his sealskin-clad waist; he could capsize, right himself, and get never a drop on his boots. A double-ended paddle sent him over the waves like a skimming cormorant. A harpoon lay lightly secured before him; the inflated bladder bobbed around.

For several heartbeats, he and the halflings regarded each other. Tauno tried to peer past his astonishment and guage him as a man. He was youthful, even more powerfully built than most of his stocky brethren, handsome in a broad-featured, small-eyed, coarsely black-maned fashion. Beneath grease and soot, his complexion was of an almost ivory hue, and bore the barest trace of whiskers. He recovered fast, and surprised the siblings by asking in accented Norse, "You castaways? Need help?"

"No, I thank you, but we belong here," Tauno replied. The Danish he knew was sufficiently close to the tongue of the colonists—closer, in fact, than to Hauau's dialect—that he expected no trouble in understanding. He smiled, and rolled around to let the Inuk see him better.

In looks he might well have been a Norseman, long and thick-muscled, save for beardlessness, amber eyes, and the tinge of green in his shoulder-length hair. But no earth-born man could have rested at ease, naked off Greenland in fall. A headband, a belt to hold a pair of obsidian knives, and a narrow roll of oiled leather strapped to his shoulders beneath a spear whose head was of bone were his whole clothing.

Eyjan was likewise outfitted. She also smiled, and dazzled the Inuk.

"You . . . are——" A protracted native word followed. It seemed to mean "creatures of magic."

"We are your friends," Tauno said in that language; it was his turn to speak haltingly. He gave the names of his sister and himself.

"This person is called Minik," the young man responded. He was emboldened, more than his companions, who hovered nervously farther off. "Will you not come aboard the umiak and rest?"

"No——" protested somebody else.

"They are not of the Neighbors," Minik said.

Reluctant, the rest yielded. Such inhospitality was unheard of among their race. It could not be due to fear of wizardry. They did live in a world of spirits which must forever be appeased, but here were simply two manlike beings who made no threat and could surely relate wonders. Something terrible must have happened between them and the Vestri Bygd. And yet——

Eyjan noticed first. "Tauno!" she exclaimed. "They've a white woman among them!"

He had been too alert to the harpoons to pay much heed to the boat he was approaching. Now he saw that about at its middle, staring dumfounded as the rest, knelt one who overtopped them; and above a thrown-back parka hood, her braids shone gold.

The merman's children climbed over the side, careful not to upset the craft, more careful to squat in the bows prepared for a leap. The hull was ladend and bloody with a catch of auks. Tauno and Eyjan aimed their awareness at the single man there, a passenger in the stern, grizzled, wrinkled, and snag-toothed. He made signs at them, gasped, yelped, then grew abruptly calm and called out: "These bear no ills for us that I can smell." And to them: "This person is called Panigpak and said by some to be an angakok"—a shaman, sorcerer, familiar of ghosts and demons, healer, foreseer, and, at need, wreaker of harm upon foes. For all his modesty, customary among his people, and for all the shriveling that age had brought upon him, he had an air of wild-animal pride; Tauno thought of wolf and white bear.

The women squealed and chattered; a few cackled half terrified laughter; their eyes darted like black beetles above the high, wide cheekbones. There drifted from them a secnt of fleshly heat and, not unpleasantly, of smoke and oil and the urine wherein they washed their hair. The men crowded their own craft around. They held themselves a bit more reserved—just a bit.

The Norsewoman alone kept still. She wore the same skin coat and trousers and footgear as the rest, she was as greasy as they, but her gaze burned blue. That, her fair and cleanly molded face, her stature and slenderness, roused longings in Tauno which no Inuk woman could altogether quell. He draped a hand between his thighs to hide those thoughts, and took the word:

"Forgive how lamely somebody talks. We learned among a distant band of the People. With them we hunted, fished, feasted, swapped gifts, and became friends. Here we will not linger. We search for our family, and ask no more from you than whatever knowledge you may have of it."

Wind blew, waves trundled, the boat swayed in shrill cold. But it was as if the blond girl spoke through silence, in her birth-tongue: "Who are you? What are you? Not true merfolk . . . I think. Your feet are not webbed."

"Then you know of our kind?" Eyjan cried gladly.

"Through tales I heard at the fireside, most from the old country. Naught else."

Eyjan sighed. "Well, you are right about our nature. But see how you bewilder us, even as we bewilder you."

The woman hugged to her an infant that, like most of her fellow paddlers, she had along. Hers was towheaded. "Can we indeed talk freely?" she breathed.

A couple of men objected to this lingo they did not understand. Were things not uncanny enough already? She answered them more handily than the halflings could have done. These swimmers could best use Danish. Was it not wisest to let them, so that they might explain swiftly and rightly? Afterward she would make clear what they had told. She appealed to Minik and Panigipak. The angakok's jet eyes probed at the strangers. After a while he agreed.

Minik was her man, Tauno realized. How had that happened?

"I, I hight Bengta Haakonsdatter," she stammered. A pause,

a clouding over. "I was Bengta Haakonsdatter. I am Atitak. And my daughter"—she held the one-year-old very close—"she was Hallfrid, but we call her Aloqisaq for Minik's grandmother, who died on a floe soon before we came to him."

"Were you stolen away?" Eyjan asked low-voiced.

"No!" Bengta's free hand snatched over the side, caught Minik's shoulder, and clung fast. He flushed, embarrassed at a show the Inuit did not put on; but he let her hand upon him remain. "Tell me of yourselves," she begged.

Eyjan shrugged. "My brother and I are half human," she said, and went on to relate briefly what had happened. She finished in a tone not quite steady: "Have you heard aught of merfolk arriving?"

"No," Bengta mumbled. "Though I may well not have, the way my life has gone of late."

"Speak to your comrades, dear. Tell them merfolk are not their enemies. Rather, sea dwellers and air breathers together could do what neither alone is able to."

The singing language went back and forth. Often Panigpak put a question straight to the halflings, aided at need by the Norse-woman. The facts emerged piecemeal. No, these Inuit knew nothing of any advent. However, they spent most of their time ashore, hunting, and seldom went far out at sea—never as far as the white men, who in days gone by had sailed beyond the horizon to fetch lumber (Bengta spoke of a place she called Markland) and were still wont to take their skiffs on recklessly long journeys in summer. (They huddled at home throughout the winter, which was when the Inuit traveled—by dog-hauled sleds, overland or across the ice along the coasts.) Hence they in the Bygd might have ken of happenings on some island of which poor ignorant people in kayaks could say naught. Were that so, surely Bengta's father would know, he being the mightiest man in the settlement.

Tauno and Eyjan could not miss the horror wherewith the name of Haakon Arnorsson was uttered. His own daughter flinched, and her voice harshened.

Just the same—— "Well, we had better go to see him," Eyjan murmured. "Shall we carry a message from you, Bengta?"

The girl's will broke. Tears burst forth. "Bring him my curse!" she screamed. "Tell him...all of them...leave this land... before the tupilak dooms them...that our angakok put on them ...for *his* misdeeds!"

Minik clutched his harpoon. Panigpak crouched deeper, secretive, into his furs. Women and kayaks edged back from the two in the bows. Infants sensed unease and wailed. "I think we'd best get out of here," Tauno said at the corner of his mouth. Eyjan nodded. In twin arcs, the merman's children dived over the side of the umiak and vanished beneath restless bitter waters.

VIII

THE talk had revealed where Haakon's garth lay on the great bight that sheltered the Vestri Bygd. The short gray day had turned to dusk when the halflings found it. That gloom hid them while they donned the garb rolled into their packs. It would hardly disguise what they were. Instead of cloth, which dampness would soon have rotted, the stuff was three-ply fishskin, rainbow-scaled, from Liri. Though brief, those tunics would not offend Christians as badly as nakedness did. Out of waterproof envelopes they took steel knives; however, they did not lay aside their rustfree weapons of stone and bone, and they bore their spears in their hands.

Thereafter they walked to the steading. Wind whined sharp-toothed; waves ground together the stones of the beach. Faerie sight brought more out of the murk than a human could see; but the view between hunchbacked hills was everywhere desolate. The settlement was not a town, it was homes scattered across many wild miles: for brief bleak summers made this land a niggard. Since grain often failed, grass, as pasture and hay for livestock, was the only crop the dwellers dared count on raising. Stubble, thin beneath their bare feet, told the wayfarers how scant the latest harvest had been. A paddock, fenced by bleached whale ribs, was large, must formerly have kept a fair number of beasts, but now held a few scrawny sheep and a couple of likewise wretched cows. A small inlet ended here, and three boats lay drawn aground. They were six-man skiffs, well-built, well suited to this country of countless winding fjords; but beneath the pungent tar that black-ened them Tauno descried how old their timbers were.

Ahead loomed the buildings, a house, a barn, and two sheds ringing a dirt courtyard. They were of dry-laid rock, moss-chinked, turf-decked, barely fit for the poorest fishermen in Den-mark. Peat-fire smoke drifted out of a roofhole. Gleams trickled through cracks in warped ancient shutters. Four hounds bounded clamorous from the door. They were big animals, wolf blood in them, and their leanness made them appear twice frightful. But when they caught the scent of the halflings, they tucked down their tails and slunk aside.

The door opened. A tall man stood outlined black between the posts, a spear of his own at the ready. Several more gathered at his back. "Who comes?" he called distrustfully.

"Two of us," Tauno answered from the dark. "Fear not if we look eerie. Our will toward you is good."

A gasp arose as he and Eyjan stepped into the fireglow, oaths, maybe a hurried prayer. The tall man crossed himself. "In Jesu name, say what you are," he demanded, shaken but undaunted.

"We are not mortals," Eyjan told him. The admission always scared less when it came from her sweetly curved lips. "Yet we can speak the name of Jesu Kristi as well as you, and mean no harm. We may even help, in return for an easy favor we hope you can grant us."

The man drew a loud breath, sank his weapon, and trod forward. He was as gaunt as his dogs, and had never been stout; but his hands were large and strong. His face was thin too, in cheeks, straight nose, tightly held mouth, plowshare chin; faded blue eyes, framed by gray hair and cropped gray beard. Beneath a long, plain woolen coat with hood thrown back could be seen stockings and sealskin shoon; nothing smelled well. A sword, which he must have belted on when he heard the noise, hung at his waist. To judge from the shape, it had been forged for a viking. Were they truly that backward here, or could they afford nothing new?

"Will you give us your names too, and name your tribe?" he ordered more than asked. Defiantly: "I am Haakon Arnorsson, and this is my steading Ulfsgaard."

"We knew that," Eyjan said, "since we inquired who the chief man is in these parts." In about the same words as she had used to his daughter, she told of the quest up to yesterday—save for merely relating that Liri had become barren, not that the cause of the flight therefrom was an exorcism. Meanwhile the men of the household got courage to shuffle nigh, and the women and children to jam the doorway. Most were younger than Haakon, and stunted by a lifetime of ill feeding; some hobbled on bowed legs or in unmistakable pain from rheumatism and deformed bones. The night made them shiver in their patched garments. A stench welled from the house which the eye-smarting smoke could not altogether blanket, sourness of bathless bodies that must live packed in a narrow space.

"Can you tell us anything?" Eyjan finished. "We will pay . . . not gold off these rings of ours, unless you wish it, but more fish and sea-game than I think you'd catch for yourselves."

Haakon brooded. The wind moaned, the folk whispered and made signs in the air, not all of the Cross. At last he flung his head on high and snapped: "Where did you learn of me? From the Skraelings, no?"

"The what?"

"The Skraelings. Our ugly, stumpy heathen, who've been drifting into Greenland from the west these past hundred years." A snarl: "Drifting in together with frosty summers, smitten fields, God's curse on us—that I think their own warlocks brought down!"

Tauno braced muscles and mind. "Aye," he answered. "We met a party of them, and your daughter Bengta, Haakon. Will you trade your knowledge for news of how she is?"

An outcry lifted. Haakon showed teeth in his beard and sucked air in between them. Then he stamped spearbutt on earth and roared, "Enough! Be still, you whelps!" When he had his silence, he said quietly, "Come within and we'll talk."

Eyjan plucked Tauno's elbow. "Should we?" she questioned in the mer-language. "Outdoors, we can escape from an onset. Between walls, they can trap us."

"A needful risk," her brother decided. To Haakon: "Do you bid us be your guests? Will you hold us peace-holy while we are beneath your roof?"

Haakon traced the Cross. "By God and St. Olaf I swear that, if you plight your own harmlessness."

"On our honor, we do," they said, the nearest thing to an oath that Faerie folk knew. They had found that Christians took it as mockery if soulless beings like them called on the sacred.

Haakon led them over his threshold. Eyjan well-nigh gagged at the full stink, and Tauno wrinkled his nose. The Inuit were not dainty, but the ripeness in their quarters betokened health and abundance. Here——

A miserly peat fire, in a pit on the clay floor, gave the sole light until Haakon commanded that a few soapstone lamps be filled with blubber and kindled. Thereafter his poverty became

clear. The house had but a single room. People had been readying
for sleep; straw pallets were spread on the platform benches which
lined the walls, in a shut-bed that must be the master's, and on
the ground for the lowly. The entire number was about thirty. So
must they lie among each other's snores, after listening to whatever
hasty lovemaking any couple had strength for. An end of the
chamber held a rude kitchen. Smoked meat and stockfish hung
from the rafters, flatbread on poles in between, and were grue-
somely little when the wind was blowing winter in.

And yet their forebears had not been badly off. There was a
high seat for lord and lady, richly carved though the paint was
gone, that had doubtless come from Norway. Above it gleamed
a crucifix of gilt bronze. Well-wrought cedar chests stood about.
However rotted and smoke-stained, tapestries had once been beautiful. Weapons and tools racked between them remained good to
see. It was all more than these few dwellers could use. Tauno
whispered to Eyjan, "I reckon the family and retainers used to live
in a better house, a real hall, but moved out when it got too hard
to keep warm for a handful, and built this hovel."

She nodded. "Aye. They'd not have used the lamps tonight,
had we not come. I think they keep the fat against a famine they
await." She shivered. "Hu, a lightless Greenland winter! Drowned
Averorn was more blithe."

Haakon took the high seat and, with manners elsewhere long
out of date, beckoned his visitors to sit on the bench opposite. He
ordered beer brought. It was weak and sour, but came in silver
goblets. He explained he was a widower. (From her behavior
toward him, they guessed the child was his which bulged the belly
of a young slattern.) Three sons and a daughter were alive—he
believed; the oldest lad had gotten a berth on a ship bound back
to Oslo, and not been heard of for years. The second was married
and on a small farm. The third, Jonas, was still here, a wiry
pointy-nosed youth with lank pale hair who regarded Tauno in fox
wariness and Eyjan in ill-hidden lust. The rest were poor kin and
hirelings, who worked for room and board.

"As for my daughter——"

Bodies stirred and mumbled among thick, moving shadows.
Eyes gleamed white, fear could be smelled and felt in the smoke.
Haakon's voice, which had been firm, barked forth: "What can
you tell of her?"

"What can you tell of merfolk?" Tauno retorted.

The Norseman curbed his wits. "Something . . . maybe."

It gasped and choked through the dimness. "I doubt that," Eyjan breathed in her brother's ear. "I think he lies."

"I fear you're right," he answered as low. "But let's play his game. We've a mystery here."

Aloud: "We found her at sea, not far hence, amidst Inuit—Skraelings, do you call them? She and her baby looked well." They looked better than anybody here, he thought. Belike Haakon had seen to it that she got ample food while growing, because he wanted her to bear him strong grandsons or because he loved her. "I warn you, though, you'll not like what she told us to tell you. Bear in mind, this was none of our doing. We were on hand for a very brief time, and we don't even understand what she meant by her words."

The father's knuckles stood white around his swordhilt. Jonas his son, seated on the bench next to him, likewise grasped dagger.

"Well?" Haakon snapped.

"I am sorry. She cursed you. She said everybody should depart this country, lest you die of a—a tupilak, whatever that is—which a magician of theirs has made to punish a sin of yours."

Jonas sprang to his feet. "Have they taken her soul out of the body they took?" he shrieked through a hubbub.

Did Haakon groan? He gave no other sign of his wound. "Be still!" he required. The uproar waxed. He rose, drew his sword, brandished it and said flatly: "Sit down. Hold your mouths. Whoever does not will soon be one less to feed through the winter."

Quiet fell, save for the wind piping around walls and snuffing at the door. Haakon sheathed blade and lowered his spare frame. "I have an offer for you two," he said, word by word. "A fair trade. You've told us you're half human, but can breathe underwater as well as a real merman, and swim almost as well. By your weapons, I ween you can fight there too."

Tauno nodded.

"And you ought not to fear sorcery, being of the Outworld yourselves," Haakon went on.

Eyjan stiffened. Jonas said in haste, "Oh, he doesn't mean *you* are evil."

"No," Haakon agreed. "In truth, I've a bargain to strike with you." He leaned forward. "See here. There is indeed . . . a flock

of what must be merfolk . . . around an island to the west. I saw
them shortly before, before our woes began. I was out fishing.
Sturli and Mikkel were along," he added to the astounded household, "but you remember that the tupilak got them afterward. We
were . . . alarmed at what we saw, unsure what Christian men
should do, and felt we'd best hold our peace till we could ask a
priest. I mean a wise priest, not Sira Sigurd of this parish, who
can't read a line and who garbles the Mass. I know he does; I've
been to church in the Ostri Bygd and heeded what was done and
sung. And surely he's failed to pray us free of the tupilak. Folk
around here are sliding fast into ignorance, cut off as we mostly
have been——" His features writhed. "Aye, sliding into heathendom."

He needed a minute to regain his calm. "Well," he said. "We
meant to seek counsel from the bishop at Gardar, and meanwhile
keep still about the sight lest we stampede somebody into foolishness or worse. But then the tupilak came, and we—I never had
the chance to go." He caught the eyes of his guests. "Of course,
I can't swear those beings are your kin. But they are latecomers,
so it seems reasonable, no? I doubt you could find the island by
yourselves. The waters are vast between here and Markland. You'd
at least have a long, perilous search, twice perilous because of
the tupilak. I can steer by stars and sunstone and take you straight
there. But . . . none from the Vestri Bygd can put to sea and live,
unless the tupilak be destroyed."

"Tell us," Eyjan urged from the bottom of her throat.

Haakon sat back, tossed off his beer, signaled for more all
around, and spoke rapidly:

"Best I begin at the beginning. The beginning, when men first
found and settled Greenland. They went farther on in those days—
failed to abide in Vinland, good though that was said to be, but
for a long time afterward would voyage to Markland and fetch
timber for this nearly treeless country of ours. And each year ships
came from abroad to barter iron and linen and such-like wares for
our skins, furs, eiderdown, whalebone, walrus ivory, narwhal
tusk——"

Tauno could not entirely quench a grin. He had seen that last
sold in Europe as a unicorn's horn.

Haakon frowned but continued: "We Greenlanders were never
wealthy, but we flourished, our numbers waxed, until the land-

hungry moved north and started this third of our settlements. But then the weather worsened, slowly at first, afterward ever faster—summer's cold and autumn's hail letting us garner scant harvest any more; storms, fogs, and icebergs at sea. Fewer and fewer ships arrived, because of the danger and because of upheavals at home. Now years may well go by between two cargoes from outside. Without that which we must have to live and work, and cannot win from our home-acres, we grow more poor, more backward, less able to cope. And . . . the Skraelings are moving in."

"They're peaceful, are they not?" Eyjan asked softly.

Haakon spat an oath, Jonas onto the floor. "They're troll-sly," the older one growled. "By their witchcraft they can live where Christians cannot; but it brings God's anger down on Greenland."

"How can you speak well of a breed so hideous, a lovely girl like you?" Jonas added. He tried a smile in her direction.

Haakon's palm chopped the air. "As for my house," he said, "the tale is quickly told. For twenty-odd years, a Skraeling pack has camped, hunted, and fished a short ways north of the Bygd. They would come to trade with us, and Norsemen would less often visit them. I thought ill of this, but had no way to forbid it, when they offered what we needed. Yet they were luring our folk into sin—foremost our young men, for their women have no shame, will spread legs for anybody with their husbands' knowledge and consent . . . and some youths also sought to learn Skraeling tricks of the chase, Skraeling arts like making huts of snow and training dogs to pull sleds——"

Pain sawed in his tone: "Four years ago, I married my daughter off to Sven Egilsson. He was a likely lad, and they—abode happily together, I suppose, though his holding was meager, out at the very edge of the Bygd, closer to Skraelings than to any but one or two Christian families. They had two children who lived, a boy and girl, and a carl to help with the work.

"Last summer, want smote us in earnest. Hay harvest failed, we must butcher most of our livestock, and nevertheless would have starved save for what we could draw from the sea. A frightful winter followed. After a blizzard which raged for days—no, for an unguessable part of the nearly sunless night which is winter here—I could not but lead men north to see how Bengta fared. We found Sven, my grandson Dag, and the carl dead, under skimpy cairns, for the earth was frozen too hard to dig a grave in. Bengta and little Hallfrid were gone. The place was bare of fuel. Traces—sled tracks, dog droppings—bespoke a Skraeling who had come and taken them.

"Mad with grief and wrath, I led my men to the stone huts where those creatures den in winter. We found most were away, hunting, gadding about, I know not what. Bengta too. Those who were left said she had come of her free will, bringing her live child—come with a male of theirs, come to his vile couch, though he already had a mate—— We slaughtered them. We spared a single crone to pass word that in spring we'd hunt down the rest like the vermin they are, did they not return our stolen girls."

Shadows closed in as the fire waned. Dank chill gnawed and gnawed. Eyjan asked mutedly, into Haakon's labored breathing:

"Did you never think they might have spoken truth? There were no marks of violence on the bodies, were there? I'd say hunger and cold, when supplies gave out, were the murderers, or else an illness such as your sort brings on itself by living in filth. Then Minik—the Inuk, the man—he went yonder, anxious about her, and she took refuge with him. I daresay they'd long been friends."

"Aye," Haakon confessed. "She was ever much taken by the Skraelings, prattled words of theirs as early as she did Norse, hearkened to their tales when they came here, the dear, trusting lass. . . . Well, he could have brought her to me, couldn't he? I'd have rewarded him. No, he must have borne her off by might. Later—what you heard in the boat is proof—that damned old witch-man cast a spell on her. God have mercy! She's as lost and enwebbed as any traveler lured into an elfhill—lost from her kin, lost from her salvation, she and my granddaughter both—unless we can regain them——"

"What happened next?" Tauno asked in a while.

"They abandoned that ground, of course, and shifted to somewhere else in the wilderness. Early this spring, hunters of ours came on one of theirs and fetched him bound to me. I hung him over a slow fire to make him tell where they were, but he would not. So I let him go free—save for an eye, to prove I meant what I said—and bade him tell them that unless they sent me my daughter and granddaughter, and for my justice the nithings who defiled her, no man in the Bygd will rest until every last troll of them is slain; for all of us have women to ward.

"A few days afterward, the tupilak came."

"And what is that?" Tauno wondered. His spine prickled.

Haakon grimaced. "When she was a child, Bengta passed on to me a story about a tupilak that she had from the Skraelings. I thought it was a mere bogy tale that might give her nightmares. Then *she* consoled *me* and promised not. Oh, she was the most loving daughter a man could have, until——

"Well. A tupilak is a sea monster made by witchcraft. The warlock builds a frame, stretches a walrus hide across, stuffs the whole with hay and sews it up, adds fangs and claws and—and sings over it. Then it moves, seeks the water, preys on his enemies. This tupilak attacks white men. It staves in a skiff, or capsizes it, or crawls over the side. Spears, arrows, axes, nothing avails against a thing that has no blood, that is not really alive. It eats the crew. . . . What few escaped bear witness.

"This whole summer, we've been forbidden the sea. We cannot fish, seal, fowl and gather eggs on the rookery islands; we cannot send word to the Ostri Bygd for help. Men set out overland. We've heard naught. Maybe the Skraelings got them, though like as not, they simply lost their way and starved in that gashed and frozen desert. The southerners are used to not hearing from us for long at a time; in any case, they have troubles of their own; and if they did send a boat or two, the tupilak waylaid those.

"We've barely stocks on hand to last out the winter. But next year we die."

"Or you go away," Tauno said into his anguish. "Now I see what Bengta meant. You must leave, seek new homes to south-ward. I suppose the angakok will call off his beast if you do."

"We'll be go-betweens if you wish," Eyjan offered.

Some of the men cursed, some shouted. Jonas drew his knife. Haakon sat as though carved in flint, and stated: "No. Here are our homes. Our memories, our buried fathers, our freedom They're not much better off in the south than we are here; they can take us in; but only as hirelings, miserably poor. No, I say. We'll harry the Skraelings instead till they are gone."

Once more he leaned forward, left fist clenched on knee, right hand raised crook-fingered like the talons of a Greenland falcon. "Thus we arrive at my bargain," he told the merman's children. "Let us take the boats out tomorrow. The tupilak will know, and come. While we fight it from the hulls, you attack from beneath.

It can be slain—cut to pieces, at least. That story Bengta heard was of how a valiant man got rid of a tupilak. He invented the kayak, you see, to capsize on purpose and get at the thing's underside. Belike that's an old wives' tale in itself. Anyhow, no man of us has skill with those piddleboats. Still, it shows what the Skraelings believe is possible, and they ought to know; right?

"Help free us from our demon, and I'll guide you to your people. Otherwise"—Haakon smiled stiffly— "I'd not be surprised if the creature took you for Norse and slew you. You are half of our breed. Be true to your race, and we will be true to you."

Again was a windy hush. Tauno and Eyjan exchanged a look. "No," said the brother.

"What?" burst from Haakon. He tried to jeer: "Are you afraid? When you'd have allies? Then flee these waters at dawn."

"I think you lie to us," Tauno said. "Not about your bloodiness toward the Inuit, nor about their revenge, no—but about those merfolk. It rings false."

"I watched faces," Eyjan put in. "Your own following doesn't swallow that yarn."

Jonas grabbed at his dagger. "Do you call my father a liar?"

"I call him a desperate man," Tauno said. "However"—he pointed to the crucifix above the high seat— "take that sign of your God between both hands, Haakon Arnorsson. Kiss your God on the lips, and swear by your hope of going to Him after you die, that you have spoken entire truth to us, your guests. Then we will fare beside you."

Haakon sat. He stared.

Eyjan rose. "Best we go, Tauno," she sighed. "Goodfolk, we're sorry. But why should we risk our lives for nothing, in a quarrel not ours and unjust to boot? I rede you to do what Bengta said, and leave this land of ill weird."

Haakon leaped erect. His sword blazed forth. "Seize them!" he shouted.

Tauno'a knife sprang free. The sword whirred down and struck it from his grasp. Women and children screamed. But from fear of what might happen if the halflings escaped, the men boiled against them.

Two clung to either arm of Tauno, two to either leg. He banged them around. A club struck his head. He roared. The club thudded twice, thrice. Agony and shooting stars flashed across his world.

He crumpled. Between raggedy-clad calves he glimpsed Eyjan. She had her back to the wall. Spears hemmed her in, the sword hovered aloft, Jonas laid steel at her throat. Tauno fell into nothingness.

IX

Day broke as a sullen red glimmer through clouds, a steel sheen on the murk and chop of the fjord. Wind blew whetted. Tauno wondered if the wind was always keening around this place. He awoke on the straw where he had been laid out, to see Haakon towering above him as a shadow. "Up!" called the chieftain, and men grumbled about in the house-dark, babies wailed, older children whimpered.

"Are you well?" Eyjan asked from across the room. Like him, she had spent the night on the floor, wrists and ankles bound, neck leashed to a roofpost.

"Stiff," he said. After hours of sleep, his temples no longer throbbed as when first he regained awareness. Blood clotted his hair, though, thirst his mouth. "You, my sister?"

Her chuckle came hoarse. "Well, that Jonas lout crawled by ere dawn to fumble at me, then dared not untie my legs. I could have made do, but it was a sort of fun to pretend I couldn't. Shall I tell the rest?" They were using their father's language.

"Not unless you do want him upon you, and belike more than him. We're soulless—animals—to be used however men see fit—remember?"

Haakon had come near saying as much when he had them secured: "Never would I have laid hand on any human whom I'd declared a guest, not even a Skraeling. But you aren't. Does a man break faith when he butchers a sheep he's kept? My sin would be *not* to force you, for the saving of my people." He added: "Tomorrow you'll help us fight the tupilak, Tauno. Eyjan stays behind, hostage. If you win, you both go free. That oath I will give you upon the Cross."

"Can we nonetheless believe a traitor?" she snarled.

His mouth twisted upward. "What choice have you?"

This morning he had men stand around, clad in shirt and breeks, weapons bared, while he released Tauno. The halfling rose, flexed the cramp out of his limbs, went to Eyjan and kissed her. Jonas shifted from foot to foot. "Well," the youth said around a mouthful of cheese and hardtack, "well, let's away and get the thing done."

Tauno shook his head. "First, food and water for my sister and me. As much as we need, too."

Haakon frowned. "Best to eat lightly, or not at all, before battle."

"Not for beings like us."

A middle-aged, brown-haired man, who hight Steinkil, guffawed. "Right. Haakon, you know how seals gorge."

The leader shrugged. He must struggle to hold back dismay when he saw what pounds of meat his captives put down. At the end, he snapped. "Now will you come?" and stalked for the door.

"A little span yet," Tauno said.

Haakon wheeled about. "Have you forgotten what you are, here?"

Tauno gave him stare for stare. "Have you forgotten what captaincy is ... even here?"

Then the Liri prince knelt by his sister, took her in his arms, and murmured into the fresh fragrances of her hair and flesh, "Eyjan, mine is the better luck. If I die, it will be cleanly. You— they're women, brats, and oldsters who'll guard you. Can't you play on their fears, or trick them somehow, and——?"

"I'll try," she answered. "But oh, Tauno, I'll think of you the whole while! If only we went together this day!"

They looked into each other's eyes as they voiced the "Song of Farewells":

Hard is the heartbeat when loves must take leave,
Dreary the dreeing, sundered in sorrow,
Unless they part lively, unweighted by weeping,
Gallantly going and boldly abiding,
Lightened by laughter, as oftentimes erstwhile.
Help me to hope that I'll see you right soon!
I'll lend you my luck, but back must you bring it——

He kissed her again, and she him. He got up and went outside.

Eleven ablebodied men and lads came along. They could handle two of the three skiffs that Haakon had from of old. Jonas had wanted to send for more from neighboring farms. "If we fail and perish," he said, "this house is stripped of strength."

Haakon denied him: "If we fail, everybody will perish. A fleet of boats could not overcome the tupilak. That was tried, you know. Three got away while it was wrecking the rest. Our main hope this time is our merman, and he's single. Also"—for an instant, glory flickered through his starkness—"I bear the name of king's reeve for this shire, not to risk lives but to ward them. Let us win as we are, and we will live in sagas as long as men live in Greenland."

While the hulls were launched, Tauno stripped and bathed. He would not get weapons until the onslaught came. Most of the crew dreaded him too much, nearly as much as they did the monster. Well had they struck him down and bound him, but he stayed eldritch, and maybe no will less unbendable than Haakon's could have made them venture forth in his company.

Silent, they took their seats. Oars creaked in tholes, splashed in water, which clucked back against planks and made the skiffs pitch. Spindrift spread salt on lips. Meadows of home fell away aft; the fjord broadened, dark and foam-streaked, between sheer cliffs. Against the overcast wheeled a flock of black guillemot. Their cries were lost in the sinister singing of wind. The sun was a dull and heatless wheel, barely above the mountains; it was as if cold radiated from their snows and the glacier beyond.

Each man had an oar, Tauno also. He sat by Haakon in the bows. Before him were Jonas and Steinkil; the remaining pair in this craft were grubby drawfs whose names he did not know or care about. The second boat paced them, several fathoms to starboard. He leaned into his work, glad of the chance to limber and warm up, dismal though the task was. Erelong Haakon said, "Go easier, Tauno. You're outpulling us."

"Strong as a bear, ha?" Steinkil flung over his shoulder. "Well, could be I'd liefer have a bear aboard."

"Tease him not," said Jonas unexpectedly. "Tauno, I . . . I'm sorry. Believe we'll keep troth with you. My father is a man of honor. I try to be."

"As with my sister last night?" gibed the halfling.

Haakon missed a stroke. "What's this?"

Jonas cast Tauno a pleading glance. The latter took swift thought and said, "Oh, anybody could see how he hankered." He felt no real anger at the attempted ravishment. Such matters meant little to him or Eyjan; if she'd had fewer partners than he, it was because she was two years younger; she knew the small spell that kept her from conceiving against her wish. He himself would happily tumble Jonas' sister Bengta, should that unlikely chance come—the more so when he and his own sister had had ever worse trouble holding back from each other on their long journey, for the sake of their mother who had abhorred that.... Besides, they could lose naught by his making the younker look pitifully grateful.

"Mortal sin," Haakon growled. "Put that desire from you, boy. Confess and—ask lax Sira Sigurd to set you a real penance."

"Blame him not," Steinkil urged. "She's the fairest sight I've ever seen, and brazenly clad."

"A vessel of Hell." Haakon's words came ragged. "Beware, beware. We're losing our Faith in our loneliness. I shudder to think where our descendants will end, unless we—— When we've finished with the tupilak—when we have, I say—I will go after my daughter.... What made her do it?" he almost screamed. "Forsake God—her blood, her kind—aye, a house around her, woven clothes on her back, white man's food and drink and tools and ways, everything we've fought through lifetimes to keep— play whore to the wild man who violated her, huddle in a snow hut and devour raw meat—— What power of Satan could make her do it?"

He saw how they stared from the other skiff, clamped his lips, and rowed.

They had been an hour under way, and begun to hear thunder where open sea surfed on headlands, when their enemy found them.

A man in the next boat howled. Tauno saw foam around a huge brown bulk. It struck yonder hull, which boomed and lurched. "Fend it off!" Haakon bellowed. "Use your spears! Pull, you cravens! Get us over there!"

He and Tauno shipped their oars and crouched on their feet. The halfling reached low, took from the bilge a belt bearing three sheath knives which he had asked for, and buckled it on. Not yet did he go overboard. He watched what they neared, his eyesight gone diamond sharp, ears keen to every splash and bang and curse and prayer, nostrils drinking deep of the wind to feed lungs and slugging heart. His will shrank at what he saw, until Eyjan's image made him rally.

The tupilak had hooked a flipper, whereon were a bear's claws, across a rail. Its weight was less than a live animal's, but the boat was still canted so that men must struggle to keep afoot and aboard. Two shafts were stuck in the wrinkled hide—they wagged in horrible foolishness—and the broken halves of two more from earlier combats. No blood ran thence. At the end of a long, whipping neck, the head of a shark gaped and glassily glared. The limb jerked, the boat rocked, a man fell against the jaws, they sheared. Now blood spurted and bowels trailed. The wind blew away the steam off their warmth.

A rower aft in Haakon's boat yammered his terror. Steinkil leaned to cuff him, then doggedly returned to his oar. They closed from behind. Haakon braced his legs wide and hacked with a bill. Tauno knew he sought to tear the walrus skin, let out the stuffing of hay and rotten corpses——

The flukes of a killer whale lashed back, up from roiled water, down on the prow. Wood splintered. Haakon tumbled. Tauno dived.

He needed a split minute to empty his lungs, let in the brine, and change his body over to undersea breathing. The icy green currents around him dimmed and shortened vision—he saw churned chaos above and ahead—battle clamor crashed blow after blow on his eardrums. The currents were tainted by the iron smell and taste of human gore. The dead man sank past, slowly twirling on his way to the eels.

"We'll keep the thing busy as long as we can, while you hit from below," Haakon had said. "That won't be very long."

Ready, Tauno gripped a blade between his teeth and surged forward. Attacking, he lost both fear and self. There was no Tauno, no tupilak, no band of men; there was a fight.

The hulls were shadows, breaking and re-forming, on the splintery bright ceiling of his green world. Clearer was the tupilak, the curve of its paunch . . . he saw how thongs stitched it together, he caught an ooze of mildew and moldered flesh. Claws scythed on the rear flippers. Tauno swooped inward.

The knife was now in his hand. His legs drove him past as he cut. A long gap in the seam followed the blade. He swung beyond reach of a foot that swatted at him.

Arcing back in a stream of bubbles, he saw some bones of sailors drop out. Mindless, the tupilak raged yet against the Norse. He glimpsed how the tail battered, and the noise shook him.

In again—hold underwater breath against graveyard foulness, slice away from the seam, grab that corner, heave the flap of skin wide—a slash caught him along the ribs, he lost his knife, he barely kicked free.

The beast sounded. The shark snout turned about in search. Paddles and tail sent the gross form toward him. He thought fleetingly that had those been Inuit in the boats, they'd have known to sink many harpoons in the body, trailing bladders to hamper it. Well, at best the man-eater was slow and awkward. He could swim rings around it. To get close, however, was . . . something that must be done.

The maw flapped hollow about a skeleton that, yes, seemed to be coming apart here and there. But feet and tail still drove, jaws still clashed. Tauno got onto the back, where nothing could reach him. He clamped thighs tight, though barnacles chewed them. He drew a second blade, and worked.

He could not reach clear around that bulk. But when he let go, the tail threshed feebly, half severed. Dizziness passed in dark rags before his eyes. He must withdraw for a short rest.

Did a dim knowledge stir in the tupilak, or was it driven to fulfill the curse? It lumbered back to the boats.

If it sank those, whether or not it outlasted them, would Eyjan's captors ever let her go? He heard the mass ram on strakes, and rose for a look through air.

The second skiff drifted awash, helpless till the four crewmen left could bail out the hull and retrieve their floating oars. The tupilak struck again and again on Haakon's vessel, whose stem was broken and whose planks were being torn free of the ribs. Neck and head reached in after prey. Where was the sheriff? His son Jonas hewed bravely with an ax—likewise, beside him, Steinkil. As Tauno watched, Steinkil stumbled into the teeth. They shut. Blood geysered. He reeled back, clasping the wrist where his right hand had been.

Haakon stood forth. He must have been knocked out. Crimson smeared his own face and breast, the last bright hue under wolf-gray heaven. Somehow he spied Tauno, yards away. "Do you want help, merman?" he shouted.

From under a thwart, he lifted the boat's anchor, wooden-shanked but with ring, stock, and flukes of iron from former days, made fast by a leather cable to what remained of the stempost. Jonas had drawn back when Steinkil was crippled. The other two cowered behind him. Haakon staggered aft. The jagged mouth yawned ready. He brought the anchor on high, crashed it down. A fluke put out the right eye and caught in the socket.

The jaws had him. Riven, he pulled free. "Men, swim!" he cried. "Tauno, take the beast——" He crumpled.

The halfling had strength back, and arrowed forward. Reckless of claws, he ripped. On the edge of sight, he saw Haakon's crew go into the bay. The tupilak did not give chase. Tauno was harming it too much.

It plunged when he did, seeking to seize him. But a Greenland skiff dragged behind. Hardly more could it move than if the sea had frozen around it.

Tauno's knives bit. Each piece that he cut away returned to the death whence the angakok had raised it.

Finally an empty hide floated and a shark's head sank down into darkness. The waves cleansed themselves. When Tauno, air-breathing, reached the second boat, he felt the wind on his brow like an austere benediction.

Though now made useable again, the craft was not for him to board safely. Nine men were already an overload in a hull so splintered and sprung—nine, for by use of flotsam, both Haakon and Steinkil had been brought across. Tauno hung on the rail. The hale looked dazedly at him, drained of everything save awe. Steinkil's bandaged stump looked as though he would live. Haakon would not. From breastbone to manhood, he was flayed open. His long frame sprawled in blood and entrails between two thwarts.

Yet he clung to wakefulness. His eyes and Tauno's met, dimming blue on hot amber. The Liri prince could just catch a harsh whisper: "Merman, I thank you.... Honor my oath, Jonas. ... Merman, forgive me my lie about your people."

"You had yours to think of," Tauno said gently.

"And my daughter.... She'll speak to you.... I've no right to beg ... but will you find her and——" Haakon strove for breath. "Beseech her—but if she won't, tell her I ... I never disowned my Bengta ... and in Purgatory I'll pray for her——"

"Yes," Tauno said, "Eyjan and I will do that."

Haakon smiled. "Maybe you do have souls, you merfolk."

Soon afterward he died.

X

FAERIE senses found spoor that mortals could never. Tauno and Eyjan cast about for a mere brace of days—though they did travel too through most of the enormous late-autumn nights—before they discovered the Inuit's new camp.

That was in a valley, small and snug above a high-walled bight. From the meadow a trail wound down toward the glimpsed gleam of water. A fresh spring bubbled out of turf gone sere but still soft underfoot. Dwarf birch and willow stood scattered, clinging to a last few yellow leaves. Elsewhere reared mountains, gray-blue where snow did not lie. Through an eastward cleft flashed a mysterious green off the inland ice. A haloed westering sun slanted rays through air brilliant, breathless, and boreal.

Dogs bayed when the two big figures in fishskin tunics strode nigh, then caught the scent and quieted; they did not cringe like white men's hounds. Hunters came out bearing harpoons, knives, or bows; they did not bluster. Women stayed at their tasks, bidding children stay close by; they did not voice fear or hatred.

Everybody seemed to be at home, enjoying the spoils of a chase that had gone well. Over fire, meat of both seal and bear made savory smoke. More was hung on poles for safety; the larger hides were being scraped clean; women had begun chewing on the smaller to supple them. While stone huts were there against winter, as yet families used their conical tents. Passing by one of these, the newcomers saw a half-completed piece of work, a carving in ivory of a musk ox. It was exquisite.

They raised palms and called, "Peace! Remember us from the umiak. We are your friends."

Weapons sank or fell to earth. Bengta's man took the word: "We could not see you well. The sun dazzled us. Somebody is ashamed."

She herself hastened forth to meet the siblings. "You won't betray us to the Norse, will you?" she pleaded in that tongue.

"No," Tauno said. "We do bear a message from them."

"And hard news for you, dear," Eyjan added. She caught both Bengta's hands. "Your father is dead. The tupilak got him as he and Tauno fought it. But he is avenged, the monster is slain, and before he went, he blessed you."

"O-o-oh——" The girl stood moveless for a space. Her breath fogged the crackling cold, till it lost itself in a sky the color of her eyes. Smoke had dulled her hair, which she wore now in a knot, Inuit fashion. But she stood straight and healthy, in furs a queen might covet. "Oh, Father, I never dreamed——" She wept. Eyjan hugged and comforted her.

Minik had followed the talk. Clumsily, he patted her shoulder. "Excuse her," he said in his own speech. "She is . . . not as well versed in right ways . . . as one hopes she will become in due course. Kuyapikasit, my first wife, will make food and roll out bedding for you." He smiled, shy through sorrow on her behalf.

Panigpak the angakok came likewise from the ring of staring folk. Trouble touched his worn features. "Somebody thinks he heard something about a tupilak," he forced out. However Tauno loomed above him, his gaze and his stance were steady.

"You heard aright," the halfling replied. He and Eyjan had worked out beforehand what to say in the Inuit. Thus he told of the battle in swift strokes of speech.

The people buzzed their horror. Panigpak was worst hit. "I am a fool," he groaned. "I brought that danger on you, who never harmed us."

"Who could have foreseen?" Tauno consoled. "And, hark, there is more.

"When we returned, Jonas Haakonsson sent his carls to summon the men of the Vestri Bygd to a Thing, a meeting where decisions are made. My sister—he listened to her, and spoke as she counseled him. The rest listened to me. We frightened them, you understand, although they did suppose we had been sent for their rescue by the Great Nature." That was as close as Inuit could come to "God."

Tauno went on: "We soon saw that little but the masterfulness of Haakon had kept them where they are. They heeded our warning, what wise sea dwellers had told us, that this land will grow less and less fit for them until those who remain must starve.

"They voted to depart for the south. The lot of them. First they need to be sure nothing will set on their boats. That is my sister's errand and mine—to get your promise of safe passage come summer. Thereafter the whole north country is yours."

The people yelled, danced, surged about; yet they seemed more excited than joyful, and joyful more because the feud had ended than because the victory was theirs. "I will, I will!" Panigpak sobbed. "Yes, my sending will go forth as soon as can be, to bargain with Sedna for calm weather and many fish. And my sending will likewise ask if she who rules the deeps knows aught of your folk."

"Then, Bengta," Eyjan said low, "you must decide your own tomorrows, and your child's."

Haakon's daughter drew free. Tears had made runnels through the soot on her face; the skin shone hawthorn blossom fair. But she wept no more, her head was aloft, her Norse rang: "That I did last year, when I chose Minik for us twain."

The visitors gave her an astonished regard. She clenched her fists and met it. Silence dropped over the Inuit.

"Yes," she said. "Did you think he took me away out of lust? Never would he force a woman, or deceive her; he knows not how to. And we were playmates once. He would have brought Hallfrid and me to my father. I begged him otherwise, and in charity he yielded. Charity. He had a good and able wife— who has also made me welcome. Few Inuit want two, when at need they can borrow; I think you of Faerie can see how clean a help that is between friends. I? I knew not an art of the many an Inuk woman must know. I could only swear I would try to learn. Give me time, and I hope to be no longer a burden on him."

"So you love him?" Eyjan murmured.

"Not as I loved Sven," Bengta said. "But for what Minik is, yes, I do."

It was not clear how well her husband had followed her waterfall of words. He did flush and, in an abashed way, looked pleased.

"My hope is in him, and Hallfrid's," she said. "Where else is any? I talked with these folk through my whole life, every hour I could. I too, like you, became aware of the Fimbul Winter on its way; for they told how, year by year, they watched the glaciers grow and the sea lie ever earlier frozen, ever later thawed. When at last I sat in an ill-made house, fireless, among three corpses, my baby weakly mewing in my arms for hunger, I was sure of our doom. We in the Vestri Bygd could hang onto our misery till it strangled us; or we could go down to the Mid and Ostri Bygds— if those hold out—and be paupers. Whereas the Inuit——Look around you. They've done what the Norse will always be too stubborn for, they've learned how to live in this country that, after all, is my home—live well.

"If you were me, Eyjan, would you not have snatched at a chance to join them?"

"Of course," the other girl answered. "But I am not Christian."

"What's the Church to me?" Bengta cried. "The maunderings of an ignorant dodderer. I'll take my hazard of Hell-flames, I who have been through Hell's ice."

Her pride melted. Suddenly she covered her eyes and gasped, "But that I wrought my father's death . . . I will be long in atoning for."

"Why do you say so?" Eyjan asked. "When you ran away, he harried innocent and helpless people. I doubt you ever guessed that stern man bore so wild a love for you. When the deed was done, should not their kith seek revenge, and an end to the threat?"

"The tupilak was mine!" Bengta shrieked. "I thought of it, when they wanted to send me back for the sake of peace. I wore down Panigpak till he made it. Mine!"

She sank to her knees. "I told him and everybody—whatever they did, quarrels and killings must worsen with worsening years—as long as the Norse remained—whereas if we drove them out, though it cost lives of theirs—it would be a mercy to them also—and I believed this. Holy Mary, Mother of God, witness I believed it!"

Eyjan raised her and embraced her again. Tauno said slowly, "I see. You wanted your kin, the darlings of your youth, you wanted them out before too late. But the angakok would have recalled and dismantled his creature next spring, whatever happened, would he not?"

"Y-y-yes," she stammered on Eyjan's breast. "Then it slew my father."

"We told you, he blessed you ere he died," Tauno said. He

ran fingers through his locks. "And yet . . . strange . . . how strange . . . the tupilak sent not in hate but in love."

Presently Atitak, Minik's second wife, was calm enough to help prepare a feast. That night the northlights came forth in such splendor that they covered half of heaven.

XI

SUMMER had passed, fall come back. The Danish ling bloomed purple, rowan flared, aspen trembled in gold. Down from the hunter's moon drifted a lonesome wander-song of geese. In the mornings breath smoked and puddles crunched underfoot.

Sunlight and cloud shadows chased each other across the land, on the wings of a chilly wind. Asmild Cloister took no heed. Foursquare among oaks that soughed with their last leaves, its bricks seeming doubly red against the heath beyond, it looked across a small lake to Viborg—cathedral towers, spire of the Black Friars' church, walls of a guardian castle—as if yonder market town were unreal. That was not true of the sisters themselves, who carried on many charitable works; but here they had their retreat, whose harmony the world could not trouble.

Or so it had seemed.

Three came riding from Viborg, in accordance with earlier messages back and forth. They appeared respectable, in good but sober garb, on horses of the best stock. Dismounting at the nunnery, the slender young man with flaxen hair assisted the pretty though clearly older woman down with due courtesy. His servant, who took charge of the beasts, was a burly fellow; but he must double as a bodyguard, and his own manners were seemly. The first two requested admittance and entered with every deference.

Notwithstanding, the prioress received them bleakly. "I must obey the bishop's command," she said. "Nevertheless, the saints bear witness that this is most irregular. Know I shall be praying that you do not succeed in bereaving us of our fairest jewel."

"That's not our aim, reverend mother," Niels Jonsen avowed in his mildest tone. "You'll recall from the correspondence that we twain are paying a debt of honor."

"Little enough have I been given to read, and that as it were

185

a palimpsest," the prioress snapped. "I am not so innocent that I cannot tell when there has been conniving—bargains struck, pressure brought to bear, temptations dangled—yes, even among lords of the Church."

"Those are grave charges, reverend mother," Ingeborg Hjalmarsdatter warned. Realizing that she had indeed said too much, the prioress paled. Ingeborg smiled. "I understand. The girl has become dear to you, right? Then surely it should please you that now she'll have a choice which was not hers before, and if she chooses to stay here—as well she may—it's because her devotion is freely given."

"You speak of devotion, you? I've had inquiries made. Your presence besmirches this house."

"I've always heard as how anger is amongst the deadly sins," Niels said, his own brow flushed. "Shall we get on with our business, reverend mother?"

Thus the episcopal will was done. Niels and Ingeborg were led to the courtyard. Nobody else remained to listen, though doubtless several peered from windows beyond earshot.

Margrete, whose flesh had been Yria, came out into the cloister arcade and halted. Not yet a novice, she was attired in a gown and wimple that suggested the black Augustinian habit. While she had gained inches and the shapeless raiment could not entirely hide waxing fullness of breasts and hips, it was still as if a child stood there, huge-eyed in the delicate face, lips timidly parted.

Ingeborg advanced to take her hands, "Margrete, dear," she greeted. "You know us not, but you know of us. We're your friends, come to help you."

The girl shrank back. "They told me I must see you," she whispered.

"Ha! What else have they told you about us?" Niels snorted. "You're a prize they'll not gladly yield. The pilgrim trade——"

Ingeborg frowned over her shoulder. "Hush," she said. "This is no time for bickering." To Margrete: "All we wish of you is that you listen to us, and ask whatever questions you like. It's in private because some persons might be harmed, did the tale go abroad. You must swear you'll breathe no word of it yourself, unless you hear something wicked that you'd sin if you kept hidden. You won't, I promise. The tale is of those who cared for your wellbeing enough to stake their lives in the cause—your brothers and sister, Margrete."

"I haven't any," the maiden stammered. "Not any more."

"Would you disown them? Why, you'd be in the sea today, unless you'd died the way an animal dies, save that they brought you ashore. Sit down." Ingeborg urged Margrete to a bench. "Pay heed."

A flaw of wind swooped into the court, raw and boisterous. A cloud passed overhead like a white banner. Crows laughed.

The story of the merman's children was soon told, for Niels and Ingeborg softened it much. Margrete's pallor grew more deep at first, but later blood coursed visibly through her cheeks.

"The upshot is this," Niels finished. "The lords temporal and spiritual who're concerned know only that I'd fain honor a pledge to a comrade, and that my confessor gives me leave. The bishop of Roskilde has supported me stoutly throughout; we've become friends of a sort. Besides, donations in my name, made in . . . hm . . . thankfulness to the saints . . . they bring more of the gold to the Church as a whole, without drawing dangerous remark. Also, he agrees it's right you should have an inheritance from your kin— for of course he's aware by now that they, the halflings, led that faring, though I've held back from letting out more to him.

"Well, a fortune awaits you in Copenhagen. Bishop Johan's found a family—the man's a rich merchant—who'll be glad to adopt you, see to your upbringing, make you a fine marriage. You're welcome to ride thither with us, if you want."

"I've met the family," Ingeborg added. "They're good, kindly, sensible; there's peace in that home."

"Liveliness too," Niels smiled. "You'll enjoy yourself."

"Are they pious?" Margrete asked.

"The bishop picked them, didn't he?"

The girl sat mute for a spell, in the blustery day. "I had some forewarning of this," she said finally, staring at the flagstones. "Mother Ellin was hard set against it——"

"Are you happy here?" Ingeborg inquired.

"What has become of . . . Tauno and Eyjan?"

Margrete did not see the pain that crossed the others. "We know not," said Niels. "Since more than a year."

Ingeborg laid an arm around the girl. "Are you happy here?"

she repeated. "If you truly are, why, stay. You can deed your legacy to the convent, or do whatever else you want with it. We came just to give you your freedom, darling."

Margrete drew a sharp breath. Her fingers clung to her knees. "The sisters . . . are . . . kind. I . . . am learning things——"

Ingeborg nodded. "But you share Tauno's blood."

"I ought to stay. Mother Ellin says I ought!"

"Those who rank her say you needn't," Niels reminded.

"Oh, I *would* like children——" The slight form bent over in weeping.

Ingeborg sought to embrace her. Margrete pulled away, rose, retreated to a pillar and hugged that while the sobs racked her. Man and woman waited.

Presently, still hiccoughing but with calm welling up from within, the maiden turned around to them and said:

"Yes, I must pray for guidance, but I do think I'll go. Best it not be with you, though. Could you get me a different escort for, oh, next week?"

"We can abide that long in Viborg," Niels offered.

Margrete stood stiffly before them and forced the words forth: "No, please not. I should see you two no more than needful, ever. For I am a living sign of God's grace, and you—I've heard about your ways—oh, do mend them, do marry! Shun those halflings, too, for your salvation's sake, unless you can get them to take baptism. But I don't suppose you can, and—yes, they were very good to me, I'll pray for them if the priest says I may—but impurity and soulless things out of heathendom are not for Christian people to consort with, are they?"

Book Four

VILJA

PANIGPAK said it was necessary to wait until snow had fallen and igloos could be built. That time soon came. For three days and the three nights in which they were but a glimmer, the angakok fasted. Thereafter he went alone into the mountains while men made a house of a size that would hold everybody. They lined it with tent hides, but over a ledge opposite the doorway they laid a bearskin.

When folk were gathered there after dark, Panigpak's name was called thrice before he entered. "Why are you here?" he said. "This person cannot help you. I am only an old fool and liar. Well, if you will have it so, I will try to bamboozle you with my silly little tricks."

He went to the ledge and stripped himself naked. The others already were unclad to the waist, or altogether, for the heat in the igloo was stifling. Lamps made sweat sheen, eyes glisten; the sound of breath was like surf. He sat down, and a man called Ulugatok bound his arms and legs with thongs that cut into the flesh. Panigpak gasped for pain but otherwise uttered naught.

The helper laid a drum and a dried sealskin nearby, before he joined the crowdedness on the floor. "Put out the lamps," he said. "Stay where you are, whatever happens. To go to him now is death."

Blackness rolled in, save for one tiny flame which did not make the angakok visible. He began to sing, a high-pitched rhythmic chant, louder and louder. The drum beat, the dry skin rattled, sounds which came from elsewhere in the murk, sometimes here, sometimes there, sometimes overhead, sometimes below ground. Slowly the people started singing with him. It came to possess them, they lost themselves in it, swayed back and forth, writhed across each other, spoke in tongues, howled and screamed.

The madness gripped Tauno and Eyjan as well, until even with Faerie sight they did not know when or how Panigpak departed.

He was gone. The song quavered onward, endless as winter night. The Inuit were beside themselves, out of themselves.

Now, said their belief, the angakok swam downward through the rock to the underworld, and out below the waters. He passed the country of the dead; he passed an abyss where whirled eternally a disc of ice and boiled a cauldron full of seals; he got by a guardian dog, greater than a bear, which bayed and snapped at him; he crossed a bottomless chasm on a bridge that was a knife blade; and thus at last he came before huge, one-eyed, hostile Sedna, whom some call the Mother of the Sea.

It was as if time had gone on to Doomsday Eve when finally Ulugatok called, "Quiet! Quiet! The shadow ripens." He dared not give aught its true name here—a man must be a shadow, his approach must be its ripening—lest the spirits hear and strike. He quenched the single flame, for it would kill Panigpak did anyone see the angakok before he had put his skin back on, that he left behind when he went below.

Utter lightlessness brought a sense of spinning, falling, rushing helpless on a stormwind whose noise echoed off unseen heaven. Then the drum began anew, and the crackling sealskin. Ulugatok droned forth a long magical chant in words that nobody else knew. Perhaps its chief purpose was to bring calm. He did not stop until the only sound was the crying of frightened children.

Panigpak's voice came weary: "Two of us must die this winter. But we will find abundance of meat, the fish will swarm, spring and summer will be mild, the Neighbors will go away. I have also word for our guests, but must speak to them later, alone. It is done."

A man groped through the dark, sought a nearby hut for fire, returned and kindled the lamps. Panigpak sat on the ledge, bound by the thongs. Ulugatok went to release him. He fell back and lay swooned for a while. When he opened his eyes, he saw Tauno and Eyjan among those beside him. He tried feebly to smile. "It was nothing," he muttered. "Just lies and tomfoolery. I am an old swindler, and no wisdom is in me."

The Inuit did not talk about such things once they had happened. It was with diffidence that Panigpak himself sought out the siblings, after he had had rest and nourishment. The three went off to the strand.

That was in weather clear and cold. After a glance at the world, the sun was slipping back down, afar in the south. Its rays made steely and blue the forms of two icebergs which plowed by through gray waters. Sheet ice was forming along the coast, though as yet too thin to venture forth upon. Fulmars went skimming above; their cries came faintly to those who stood on the snow-covered shingle.

"Nothing in the sea is hidden from her beneath it," Panigpak said, more gravely than was his wont. "Well did she know of your people, Tauno and Eyjan. Somebody had to compel her to disgorge a word, as he must compel her—if he can—to release the seals in a season when they are few for our hunting. She is not friendly, Sedna."

Tauno clasped the angakok's shoulder. Silence lengthened.

Eyjan lost patience, tossed her ruddy locks, and demanded, "Well, where are they?"

Wrinkles tightened in Panigpak's face. He stared outward and said low, "It is hard to understand. Something has happened that vexes even her. You must help this lackwit speak, for you will grasp much that he cannot. Thus, while dry land is beyond Sedna's ken, she does have names for many parts along the coasts. She got them from drowned sailors, I think. I remember the sound of them—one does not forget anything out of that place—but they mean nothing to my ignorant self, though doubtless they will to you."

Given what he related, his interrogators could piece together much of the tale. The Liri folk had taken a ship, belike seized by them, from Norway. They were bound for Markland or Vinland— the Norse hereabouts no longer knew just which of the regions west of them lay where—when a tempest smote. That must have been the same whose edge battered *Herning*. The other vessel suffered its full might and duration. She was driven clear back to Europe. From their father's teaching, Tauno and Eyjan were sufficiently well versed in that geography to recognize that he had then steered into the Mediterranean. The spot where he ended his voyage was in no part of their information, but Panigpak did give them names—the island of Zlarin, the mainland of Dalmatia— which they could inquire about later. It seemed the merfolk had there been attacked, and had fled afoot.

What followed was perturbing, baffling. They must be in the same vicinity, those who lived, for they still appeared offshore: one or a few at a time, for short spans. Otherwise Sedna marked them no longer. And something had changed them, they were different from erstwhile, in a way she could not speak of but which filled her, the very Mother of the Sea, with foreboding.

——Tauno scowled. "Ill is this," he said.

"Maybe not," Eyjan replied. "Maybe they've found a charm that lets them enjoy a new home inland."

"We must seek them out and learn. We'll need human help for that."

"Aye. Well, we were going to Denmark anyhow, on Yria's account."

Panigpak studied the twain with eyes that had seen a lifetime's worth of grief. "Perhaps," he said quietly, "someone can give you a little help of another sort."

On a calm night, stars filled the jet bowl above until it was well-nigh hidden, save for the silver band across it. Their light, cast back off snow, let Bengta Haakonsdatter, who was now Atitak, walk easily along a slope above the dale. Breath wafted white as she spoke, though it did not frost the wolfskin fur of her parka hood. Footfalls crunched; else her voice alone broke the silence.

"Must you leave this soon? We would be happy to keep you among us—and not really because of the fish and seal you take in such plenty. Because of yourselves."

Beside her, Tauno sighed: "We've kindred of our own yonder, who may be in sore plight, and whom we miss. In spite of the kayaks promised us—they should indeed let us travel faster than by swimming—the journey will take weeks upon weeks. We must hunt along the way, remember, and sleep, and often buck foul winds. We're well rested, after the tupilak business. Truth to tell, we've lingered more time by far than was needful. Soon the Inuit will be rambling about. If we went along, we could hardly start home before spring."

The woman gazed at his starlit nakedness, took his hand in her glove, and dared ask, "Why have you stayed at all, then? Eyjan is restless, I know. It's been you who counseled waiting."

He stopped; she did; he faced her, reached into the hood to stroke her cheek, and answered, "Because of you, Bengta."

He had been living as part of Minik's household, and Minik was glad to lend her to him. They were only apart when it seemed, mutely, that she should join her husband for a sleep, and Tauno the first wife Kuyapikasit, lest feelings be hurt. (Eyjan bore herself not like a female, but like a hunter who shifted from family to family as the whim took her. She had enjoyed every man in the camp.)

Bengta stood quiescent. He could barely hear her: "Yes, it's been wonderful. If you must go, will you return afterward?"

He shook his head. "I fear not."

Hers drooped. "Your merman heart—" She looked up again. "But what about me has kept you? That I seem more like a woman of your race than any Inuk does? Well, Europe is full of white women."

"Few so fair, Bengta."

"I think I know the reason," she began, "though maybe you don't yourself——" and broke off.

"What?"

She bit her lip. "Nothing. I misspoke me." She started downhill. "Come, let's go back, let's seek the ledge."

The snow cried out under their scarring feet. "What did you mean?" he said roughly.

"Nothing, nothing!"

He took her elbow. Through fur and leather she felt that grip, and winced. "Tell me." She saw his mouth stretched wide, till teeth gleamed under the stars.

"I thought," she blurted, "I thought I'm the nearest thing you have to Eyjan...and it will be a long journey with none save her—— Forgive me, Tauno, beloved. Of course I was wrong."

His countenance grew blank, his tone flat. "Why, there's naught to forgive. What affront in your fancy, to a being that has no soul?"

Abruptly he halted again, drew her around before him smiled, and kissed her with immense tenderness.

——On the furs of their ledge, in the darkness of the hut, she whispered, "Let the seed in my womb be yours. It could be; I've counted. Minik is a dear man and I want his children too, but may his gods give me that much remembrance of my Tauno."

Day had become a fugitive, scarcely into sight before darkness hounded it away. Night was no blindfold to Faerie eyes, but the siblings departed under the sun because then the Inuit could more easily bid them farewell.

The whole band was there, as far out on the ice as appeared safe. Land was white at their backs, save where a cliff or crag upheaved itself. Ahead reached the sea, grizzly, choppy, and noisy. Clouds blew low on a wind that stung.

Panigpak trod forth from the gathering, to where brother and sister waited. In his hand was a bone disc, slightly inward-curving, hung on a loop of sealskin that went through a hole near the edge. It spanned perhaps an inch-and-a-half.

"Vastly have you aided us," he told them. "Tauno destroyed the tupilak that this person's folly brought forth. Thus he won the awe of our enemies, and we have peace. Eyjan,"—he shook his gray head, chuckled, blinked hard—"Eyjan, when I am too old to be of any use, and go forth to sit on the ice alone, your memory is what will warm me."

"Oh, you've returned whatever we did in heaped-up measure," Tauno said, while his sister brushed lips across the angakok's brow. She had told her brother that he was not strong to be with, but he was sweet.

"One does not count between friends," Panigpak reminded. Had he never dealt with the Norse, he would not have know what to say. "Somebody would fain make a parting gift."

He handed over the disc, which Tauno laid in his palm and considered. Graven in the hollow and blackened to stand forth against its yellowish white were signs: a bird with dark head and crooked beak winging before a crescent moon. Eeriness thrilled through him as he felt an enchantment cool inside.

"You will be seeking strange lands," Panigpak said. "Their dwellers may speak tongues unknown to you. Whoever wears this amulet will understand whatever is heard, and can reply in the same tongue."

Eyjan touched fingertips to it. "With such things, care is ever needful," she murmured. "Your spells are not like ours. What should we know about it?"

"It is a deep magic," the angakok told them as softly. "To make it taxed somebody's poor powers to the uttermost. I must begin by opening my father's cairn to take a piece of his skull—oh, he is not angry; he feels dim pleasure among the shades because he could help. . . .

"The amulet links spirit to spirit. Beware of gazing long upon the sigil—yes, best wear it under clothing, or with the blank side outward—for a soul can be drawn in if it feels any wish to leave the world, and that is death." He paused. "Should this happen, the trapped ghost can come out again, into whoever wears the amulet, if that person desires. But who might want to become half a stranger?"

Tauno hastily closed his hand on the thing.

Eyjan's fingers plucked his open. She hung it around her neck in the way Panigpak had advised. "Thank you," she said, a bit unsteadily.

"It is nothing," he answered. "It is only what an old fool can offer."

When a few more words had passed, and the last embraces, the merman's children took up their kayaks and walked outward. The ice broke under them, making a floe from which they lowered the boats. They got in, laced their coats fast, untied the paddles. With a wave and shout, they swung southward. The Inuit and Bengta watched until they were gone out of seeing.

II

ONCE while homebound, Tauno encountered a pod of Greenland whale on their way around the brow of the world, and heard their route song. Few merfolk had ever done that, for the lords of the great waters rarely came nigh land—and who would seek them out, what would he say to them in their majesty?

Tauno was hunting. Eyjan was elsewhere, towing his sealed kayak behind hers. They did this by turns, lest the craft, untended, drift unfindably far off course. When they eased cramped limbs with a frolic in the waves, they took care to stay close by; when they slept afloat, they tethered hulls and themselves together. It was troublesome, and certainly they could have hunted better as a team, but on the whole they were traveling faster and easier than if they had swum.

He had gone under, in hopes of a large fish. Lesser ones were hardly worth the killing to be the fuel bodies needed for warmth and work. Thus sound reached him far more readily than through air, and toned in thews, blood, bone as well as in ears. Through chill, sliding gray-green came a throb. Faint at first, it made him veer in its direction. He continued after he knew what stroked and clove so resistlessly, for the passage would alarm many creatures and he could well seize prey among them. Then the whales began to sing.

Almost helpless, Tauno went on, mile after mile farther than he had intended, until at last he saw them—their backs that rose like skerries, their bellies and enormous, feeding mouths down below, each fin more big than a man, flukes raising swells and currents as they drove, steadily onward, forms which outbulked most ships. The slow thunder of that hundredfold movement rolled as a part of the music, which boomed and trilled, dived and soared,

through ranges no human could have heard. The song took him
from within, made a vessel of him for itself, for its might and
mystery.

He knew little of the language, and Eyjan had the sigil. None
of his father's breed were much wiser, because it was not a speech
remotely akin to any humankind or Faerie. The sounds were not
words but structures or events, each as full of meanings—none
altogether utterable—as a library of books, or as a life looked
back upon when death draws near. Tauno bore in his mind a
double heritage, and he was a poet. Afterward he recreated a
fragment of what he had heard. But he knew, with longing, that
what he then had was the merest shard, chance-splintered off a
whole to whose shape and purpose it gave never a clue.

Lead bull:—All that is life did come out of the tides
That follow the moon, as in hollowness yonder
It circles this world, and the wake of its coursing
Lays hold on the seas, draws them upward in surges
More strong than the sun can arouse from remote
              ness——
The sun and the moon and this globe in a ring-dance
Through measureless deeps and a spindrift of stars.
Old cows: Yes, they circle, they circle,
Like the memory held
Of a calf that has died
When its mother cannot
Bring herself to the weaning
And release it to swim
From her side into strangeness.
Young bulls: Heavy under heaven
Heaves the main in winter;
Warm are yet the wishes
Wakened by that rushing.
Summer also sees us
Seeking for each other.
Lustily may love go.
Laugh in your aliveness!"
Young cows: Be you the quickening light,
Be you the wind and the rain

Begetting billows,
We are the ocean and moon,
We are the tides that for aye
Renew your mother.
Calves: Brightness of salt scud,
Wings overhead, scales beneath,
Milk-white foam—new, new!
Old bulls: The seasons come and the seasons go,
From the depths above to the depths below,
And time will crumble our pride and grief
As the waves wear even the hardest reef.
We cruise where grazing is found far-flung
And the orcas lurk to rip loose a tongue.
Though we are they whom the waters bless,
Our bones will sink into sunlessness.
The race is old, but the world more so,
And a day must come when the whales must go.
The world forever cannot abide,
But a day must come of the final tide.
Old cows: Yet we have lived.
Young bulls: Yet we do live.
Calves: Yet we will live.
Young cows: Yet we make live.
Old bulls: It is enough.
Lead bull: Fare onward.

Through Pentland Firth go monstrous currents, and there are places where violence grows worse; one must pass by the Merry Men of Mey, and between the Swalchie and the Wells of Swona, and around the Bores of Duncansbay. Before daring these, the merman's children found a lee on the Caithness coast, where they could mend their sea-weary kayaks and rest their sea-weary selves.

Cliffs stood ruddy on either side of an inlet which was hardly more than cleft in them. At its end was a strip of sand with a border of turf behind, boggy but soft. Thence a V-shaped slope led upward. A footpath wound through its boulders and sparse worts, but clear was to see that this site got few visitors, surely none in winter.

It was less cold here than might have been looked for, and to

the travelers felt almost balmy after what they had known in the
past weeks. Sunlight did not enter, so that the wavelets lapped
dim silver in shadow; but reflections of it off the strait which
churned beyond gave some warmth to the cliffs, that glowed
downward in turn. Winds were only a whistling past their heights.
Tauno and Eyjan brought the kayaks above high-water mark. Over
the turf they spread skins of seals newly taken. Blubber helped
flint and steel start a fire in twigs gathered above, which kindled
driftwood from below. Besides the flesh, they had an auk to roast
and fish to eat raw.

"Ah," said Tauno. "That smells good."

"Yes, it does." Eyjan stared at the spit she was handling, where
she squatted. He clasped knees under chin and stared out at the
firth.

"Enjoy this weather while it lasts," he said after silence had
extended itself between them. "It won't for long."

"No, it won't."

"Well, we needn't linger over our repairs."

"No. True."

"After all, we are—what?—two-thirds of the way?"

"Maybe a bit more."

Neither had anything else to say for a span. Eventide waned.

Eyjan poked the fowl with a bone skewer. As she hunched
forward, the unbound hair that she had dropped over her bosom
swung away from white skin and rosy nipples. "This will soon
be done," she said. "You might begin cleaning the fish."

"Yes." Tauno jerked his glance to them and became busy.
Each movement sent a flow of muscles across him.

"We needn't hasten our overhaul unduly," she said, minutes
later. "A breathing spell here will do us good."

"Yes, we've talked about that. Still, we should have ample
time on Bornholm, till Niels hears from us and can come."

"We talked about that too."

"Remember, let me deal with humans. Inuit garb in Europe
is not too outlandish on a man, but a woman——"

"Yes, yes, yes!" she snapped. Redness went over her cheeks,
down her throat, across her breasts.

"I crave pardon," he said in an unclear voice, and raised his
golden eyes to her gray.

"Oh, no matter," she hurried to reply. "I'm on edge. My gut is a-growl."

He made a grin. "Mine likewise. That isn't the sea you hear."

The exchange eased them somewhat. Nonetheless they were nearly dumb while they finished preparing their meat, and held no converse white they ate it except a few words about how savory it was and how pleasant the fire.

When they were through, Tauno fetched more wood and stoked the blaze. Early night was falling, the strip of sky gone dusk-blue, a deeper violet in the niche. Their vision found ample light. They sat down on opposite sides for enjoyment of red, yellow, blue flicker with coal-glow at the core, homely crackle, pungency of smoke.

"We ought to retire, I suppose," Tauno said, "but I'm not sleepy yet. You go if you like."

"I'm not sleepy yet either," Eyjan answered.

Both gazed into the flames.

"I wonder how Yria fares," she said at last, quite low.

"We'll learn."

"Unless Niels and Ingeborg failed."

"In that case, we can hit on something else."

"How I hope they've not suffered evil," Eyjan whispered. "Well-nigh could I wish to believe a god would help them if I prayed."

"Oh, they're tough," said Tauno. "I dare look forward to seeing them again."

"I also. Niels is . . . I like him better than any other human I've known."

"And she—— Whoof!" snorted Tauno, squinching his eyes and fanning his nose. "Suddenly the smoke's become mine alone."

Eyjan lifted her face to him. A half moon made frosty his greenish-fair locks and threw soft highlights on the wide shoulders where firelight did not reach. "Come over here," she invited.

He stiffened, then did. Side by side, flanks touching, they held out palms to the heat and gazed straight before them. Time blew by, over the clifftops.

"What will we do, waiting at Bornholm for news?" Eyjan finally asked.

Tauno shrugged. The movement passed his arm along hers,

and he swallowed hard before he could say, "Take our ease, no doubt, apart from chasing food. We'll have earned that."

Her bronzy tresses brushed him as she nodded. "Yes, we've done much, haven't we? . . . you and I."

"And more is ahead."

"We'll meet it together."

Somehow their heads swung around, somehow they were breathing each other's breath, the clean smells of each other, and her mouth was an inch from his. They never knew which of them reached out first.

"Yes, yes," she half sobbed when the kiss came to a pause. "Oh, yes, now!"

He pulled back. "Our mother——"

She threw herself against him. Behind softness, he felt a heart that slammed even faster than his. Laughter gasped in her throat. "Too long have we fretted about that. We're merfolk, Tauno, darling." In firelit splendor she leaped to her feet, tugged at his hand. "Over there, on the turf, we have a bed . . . only now do I know how I yearned."

"And I." He stumbled up. She nearly dragged him along, and down.

——The moon was sunken behind the cliffs. Stars glistened small.

Eyjan raised herself to an elbow. "It's no use, is it?" she said bitterly. "Nothing is any use."

Tauno threw an arm across his face where he lay. "Do you think I am glad?" he mumbled.

"No, of course not." Eyjan beat fist on thigh. "The Christians can exorcise us," she cried. "Why in the name of justice can we not exorcise the Christians?"

"There is no justice. I'm sorry." Tauno rolled over so his back was to her.

She sat erect, regarded him, ran a hand along his side till it came to rest on his hip. "Scorn yourself not, brother mine," she achieved saying. "There are worse curses. We both have a world for living in."

He did not speak.

"We will remain comrades. Brothers in arms," she said.

The toilsome journey behind him became merciful. He slept.

——He woke and saw different constellations. The fire had died, frost deepened, his body had been burning the food in it for warmth; hunger prodded him anew. He stretched and smiled. Memory washed back like a tide race. He snapped after air.

Shortly he noticed that Eyjan was absent. He frowned, rose, peered. She could not be hidden from him in this narrow space. Where, then? With Faerie perceptions, he cast about. She had not re-entered the water. Hence the footpath . . . aye, her spoor, faint but clarion-clear, thrilling through his blood.

There he paused. He guessed what she had gone for, but he could be mistaken, or she could meet danger in these Christian wilds. Decision hardened. He strapped on knife, took up harpoon, and started off.

The moon was down. Above the steeps, a ling-begrown slope descended toward moorland. Rime and patches of snow whitened its grayness. Tauno padded fast along the trail, which followed the coast until it bent south into a shallow dale. This sheltered a croft grubbed out of the heath: for a meager yield of oats and barley, but chiefly for sheep that ranged afar in summer. He saw their fold, the hayricks, a pair of huddled buildings. Beyond rose a Viking grave-mound and the snags of a Pictish keep.

The trail led thither. Tauno followed. As he approached, a couple of dogs came baying; and as ever, when they had winded him they whimpered and fled.

A softer noise caught his attention. He crouched, ghosted closer, till he could see through the open door of a shed. A woman—aged by toil, for all that she rocked a babe in her arms—stood within, weeping. Two half-grown daughters slumped at her feet. They shuddered with cold; none of the three wore aught but a shift, that must have been hastily thrown on.

Tauno proceded to the cottage. Under the low eaves of a peat roof, light glimmered past cracks in shutters. He laid his ear against a wall, strained his senses.

They told him that four human males were inside, loudly breathing; and Eyjan, who yowled like a cat. While he listened, one fellow shouted. Straightway she called, "You next, Roderick!"

Tauno's knuckles whitened around the harpoon shaft.

——Well, he thought long afterward, he had none but himself to thank, and what import had it anyhow? A chuckle rattled his gullet as he imagined what the crofter and the crofter's sons had felt when she came naked out of night and beat on their door. The amulet would make her able to purr whatever she chose to them: belike that she was indeed of elvenkind but no mortal threat to life or soul; she feared not the Cross, she could name the name of Christ. They had not questioned their luck any further.

Tauno returned to camp. When Eyjan arrived at dawn, he pretended he was asleep.

III

Now that the vodianoi was gone, winter had become for the vilja altogether a time of aloneness. There was nothing else in the water but fish, that never were company and in this time of year grew sluggish, seldom delighting her with their gleaming summer grace. Frogs did not croak in twilight, but slumbered deep in bottom mud. Swans, geese, ducks, pelicans were departed; what fowl stayed at the lake were not swimmers or divers, and their calls sounded thin over snow and leafless boughs.

The vilja floated, dreaming. White and slim she was in the dimness. Her hair made a pale cloud around her. Great eyes, the hue of the sky when it is barely hazed, never moved, never blinked, never took aim at anything that a living creature might have seen. Nor did the slight roundness of her bosom move.

Thus had she drifted for days, weeks, months—she reckoned it not; for her, time had ceased to be—when the water stirred with an advent. As the force of it waxed, she came to awareness. Her limbs reached out, took hold, sent her in an arc and a streak toward shore. Faint though the undulations were that she raised, the new-comer felt them and swam to meet her. At first a wavery shade, he swiftly became solid in the view. Warmth radiated from him, strength, life. His motion made streams, gurgles, caressing swirls; bubbles danced upward.

He and she halted a yard apart and lay free a while, regarding each other.

He was not naked like her; besides headband and knife belt, he had a cloth wrapped about his loins. Huge of stature, fair-skinned, golden-haired, green-eyed, he hardly differed from or-dinary man save in his beardlessness, webbed feet, easy breathing under water. Yes, hardly: to one of the halfworld, the outward

unlikenesses were little, set beside the blazing identity. In him
was a human, Christian soul.

"Oh, welcome, be very welcome," the vilja murmured when
she had gathered courage. Her tones, which reached his merman's
hearing clearly, were tremulous as her smile.

Sternness replied: "Why do you think I am here?"

She retreated. "You . . . are you not he . . . memory is like mist,
but an autumn and an autumn ago—you drove the vodianoi
hence?"

"That which then was me did so," said the deep voice.

"You were frightened of me." The vilja could not but giggle.
"Of me! You!"

Mirth released joy. She cast her arms toward him wide apart
for him. "You've learned I'd not hurt you? How that does gladden
me. Let me gladden you."

"Be still, foul spirit!" he roared.

Bewildered, she shrank back from his wrath. "But, but I
wouldn't hurt you," she stammered. "How could I? Why should
I wish to, I who have no one for friend?"

"Tentacle of darkness——"

"We'd be happy together, in the summer greenwood, in the
winter waters. I'd warm me at your breast, but you'd have me for
your cool cascade, your moonlit leaf-crown——"

"Have done! You'd haul men down to Hell!"

The vilja shuddered and fell mute. If she wept, the lake drank
her tears.

The other calmed. "Oh, you may not know yourself what you
are," he said. "Father Tomislav wonders whether Judas really
knew what it was he did, until too late."

He stopped, watchful. Seeing his fury abated, she eased in her
quicksilver fashion, ventured the tiniest of smiles, and asked,
"Judas? Should I know him? . . . Yes, maybe once I heard—but
it is gone from me."

"Father Tomislav," he said like the stroke of an ax.

She shook her head. "No." Frowning, finger to cheek: "I mean
yes. Somebody dear, is it not? But remembering is hard down
here. Everything is so quiet. Maybe if you told me——" She
tautened. Her eyes grew yet more enormous. "No," she cried,
hands uplifted as if against a blow. "Please don't tell me!"

He sighed, as best he could underwater. "Poor wraith, I do believe you speak truth. I'll ask if I may pray for you."

Resolution came back. "Just the same, today you are a lure unto damnation," he said. "Men fishing the lake for the first time, this past year, would glimpse you flitting through dusk; some heard you call them, and sore it was to deny such sweetness. They will be coming in ever greater numbers. You must not snatch a single soul from among them. I have come to make sure of that."

She quailed, for this was he who had prevailed over the vodianoi.

He drew his knife and held it by the blade before her, to make a cross of sorts. "For the sake of the man who baptized me, I would not willingly destroy you," his words tolled. "It may be that somehow even you can be saved. Yet certain is that none must be damned . . . on your account.

"No more luring of Christians, Nada. No more wanton tricks, either, raising a wind to flap a wife's washing off the grass, or stealing her babe on its cradleboard while she naps at harvest noon——"

"I only cuddle them for a while," she whispered. "Soon I give them back. I've no milk for them."

He did not heed, but went on: "No more singing in human earshot; it rouses dreams best left asleep. Vanish from our ken. Be to the children of Adam—born or adopted—as though you had never been.

"Else I myself will hunt you down. I will carry the wormwood you cannot bear the scent of, and scourge you with it, once and twice. Upon the third time you offend, I will come bearing a priestly blessing on me, and holy water for sending you into Hell.

"In Hell you will burn, you thing of leaves and mists and streams. Fire will consume you without ending, and never a dewdrop, never a snowflake will reach you in your torment.

"Do you understand?"

"Yes," she screamed, and fled.

He hung where he was until he had lost all sight and sound of her, until it was indeed as if she had faded into nothingness.

IV

EARLIER in spring than skippers liked to fare—before the very equinox—a ship left Copenhagen for Bornholm. After a rough crossing through the Baltic Sea, she docked at Sandvig on the north end of the island, where it rises in cliffs to the stronghold called Hammer House. Her crew got shore leave. Those who had engaged her hired horses and rode to a certain unpeopled cove.

Gray whitecaps blew in, beneath a pale, whistling sky. When they withdrew, the rattle of pebbles sounded like a huge quern. Gulls flew about, mewing. On the sands were strewn brown tangles of kelp, that smelt of the deeps and had small bladders which popped when trodden on. Beyond those dunes and harsh grass was a moor, with wide heathery reaches and a bauta stone raised by folk long forgotten.

The merman's children waded ashore to greet their guests. They were unclad save for their weapons, talisman, and what remained of their aureate arm rings. Tauno's wet hair hung greenish-gold, Eyjan's bronze-red with the same faint seaweed under-tint.

Ingeborg and Niels sped into their embrace. "Mercy of God, it's been long," the young man quavered, while the woman could merely cling tight and cry.

When a measure of calm had returned, Tauno stepped off a pace, holding Ingeborg by the upper arms, and looked her over with care. "I see you've done well," he said. "Not just good clothing and the marks of hardship gone. You have a kind of peace within you, am I right?"

"Now that you are here," she answered unevenly.

He shook his head. "No, I mean that hugging you, I feel you

no more being always ready for the world to smite you. Have you prospered, then?"

She nodded. "Thanks to Niels."

"Hm," Tauno said. "I've an idea Niels has much to thank you for."

Ingeborg had been studying him more closely still than he her. "It's been worse for you, hasn't it?" she murmured. "You're haggard . . . and *I* felt you shiver. Have you failed in your quest?"

"We have not finished it. But here is a resting place." Again he gathered her in. "I've missed you, I have."

She gripped him so the blood went out of her nails.

Meanwhile they had not quite ignored what passed between Eyjan and Niels. The merman's daughter had kissed fondly enough, but thereafter asked: "How fares it with Yria?"

"Margrete," Niels replied, wincing. "She is none but Margrete any more." He searched for words. "We got her share safely to her. Not easy; the hangman's shadow lay over us after the Junkers sniffed gold, until we found us a haven. We did, though, and this day she dwells in a house that'll see to her well-being. But—— She is not ungrateful to you . . . but more pious than most. Do you understand? She's happy, but best you not seek her yourselves."

Eyjan sighed. "We expected naught else. That pain is leached out of us. We've done what we can for Yria; henceforward let her in truth be Margrete."

She considered him, where he stood in the bleak air with his locks fluttering, before she inquired further: "What's your place in the world these days? What plans for the morrow do you nourish?"

"I'm doing well," he told her. "If your own search is not ended—if I can help you in that, or aught else—you need but tell me." His voice cracked: "Even if it means bidding you farewell forever."

She smiled and kissed him afresh. "Let's not speak thus as yet," she said. "While we waited for you, with scant else to do——"

Ingeborg saw what happened on Tauno's face. She kissed him in her turn; he seized her to him; her hand wandered, and suddenly he laughed.

"——we built a hut on the far side of yonder headland, for

your coming," Eyjan said. "It can soon be warm and firelit. Wherever we may go afterward, glad memories make light freight."

She and her brother walked behind as the four left the strand, that their bodies might shield the humans from the wind that streaked in off the sea.

V

ALTHOUGH much remained for him to learn, Niels was fast becoming worldly-wise. He was in partnership with an older man who supplied experience to match the money Niels could put into the shipping trade. When that merchant grew sufficiently aged to wish retirement, several years hence, and the younger took over entirely, their company should be as well off as any outside the Hansa, and able to hold its own in rivalry with the League. Meanwhile the business gave them connections to many kinds of people, as did also its curious alliance with the bishop of Roskilde. Moreover, Niels had found positions for his brothers and sisters, places chosen so that each might win contentment, prosperity, and the favor of powerful men. (His mother he simply gave a life of ease, which she was soon devoting to gardening and good works.)

Thus, what Niels did not know, he could find out; what he could not do himself, he could get done for him.

Of course, this was not always possible overnight, especially when the strange reason for an endeavor must be kept secret. His plan was that Tauno and Eyjan take ship for Dalmatia, with letters from Church and Crown to ease their way after they arrived. That required creating identities which would make plausible their hiring of a vessel. He must feel his way forward with utmost care, lest suspicion rouse in someone. This required weeks, and his presence in Copenhagen—theirs too, for consultation at need and for practice at behaving like proper mortals.

Besides, neither he nor Ingeborg could have borne their absence, now when they were again in Denmark.

"Ah, ah, ah," the woman breathed. "That was wonderful. You are always wonderful."

Warm, wet, musky, tousled, she brought herself as tightly as she was able against the merman's son. He embraced her with one arm, laid a thigh across hers, and toyed with what he could reach of her. A taper cast soft glow and monster shadows around the bedchamber.

"Love me more, as soon as you can," she whispered.

"Will you not grow sore?" Tauno replied, for he had the strength of his father in his loins.

Ingeborg's chuckle held more wistfulness than mirth. "That's not the kind of soreness which hurts me." Abruptly she caught her breath and he felt her jerk in his grasp.

"What's the matter?" he exclaimed.

She buried her contenance between his neck and shoulder. Her fingers dug into his flesh. "Your being gone, *that* hurts." The tone shivered. "It's never less than an ache throughout me; often it's like a knife twisting around. Give me everything of you, beloved, while yet you may. Help me forget, this night, that soon you'll leave. Afterward there'll be time for remembering."

Tauno frowned. "I thought you and Niels were happy together."

Ingeborg raised her eyes. Candlelight trembled on the tears in them. "Oh, we're fond of each other. He's kind, mild, generous...and, yes, he has a gift for making love...but nothing like you, nothing! Nor is he you, in your beauty and brilliance. The difference is like—like the difference between lying in a summer meadow watching clouds pass by overhead—and being a-wing in the wind that drives them, the sun that makes them shine. I cannot understand how your mother could forsake your father."

Tauno bit his lip. "Glad she was at first to go undersea with him, but as the years wore on, she came to know in her marrow that she was not of Faerie. Never has such a union failed to wreak harm, on one or on both. I fear I've already done you ill."

"No!" She scrambled back, sat up, and gaped at him, appalled. "Darling, no!" Mastering herself: "Only look about you. See me here in a fine house, well fed, well clad, no longer a piece of sleazy merchandise; and this is your doing at root, yours, Tauno."

"Hardly mine alone." He remained stretched out, his gaze on the ceiling. "Besides, you spoke of hopeless hankering—which may, I suppose, imperil your soul——Aye, best I not linger here, much though I'll miss you in my turn."

"You will?" she cried, and bent over him. Her hair tumbled down to give its own caress. "I've not been bad for you, then?"

"No, Ingeborg," he said most gently, and looked straight at her. "You've bestowed more on me than you will ever know. Therefore I should leave, before I give you a wound that eternity cannot heal."

"But we have tonight!"

"And tomorrow, yes, and morrows beyond." He drew her to him.

Niels came home from church grim of appearance. Eyjan, attired like a lady, met him at the door, saw, and quietly led him to a side room where they could talk unheard. "What's wrong?" she murmured.

"Today Father Ebbe, my priest, asked me why my house guests are never at Mass," he told her.

"Oh, has he heard about us?"

"How could he not? Servants and neighbors do gossip." Niels scowled, hooked thumbs in belt, stared at the floor. "I, I explained . . . you've secret affairs in train which'd suffer were you recognized . . . and accordingly you go to a chapel elsewhere. He said no more, but his mien became graver than is his wont. No doubt he's aware I sleep with you, and Ingeborg with Tauno—and in Lent, in Lent—though we've neither of us confessed it to him. Yet before Easter, we must confess, that we may then take Communion."

"Will that be dangerous? The two of you are openly unwed."

He glanced up, with a crooked smile. "Such is naught uncommon. He sets us a few Aves for it, since he takes into account the good works we do with our money. But if we tell him we're again bedmates of you . . . you halflings . . . and not because it happened thus when we'd small choice about companions, and were in a worthy cause—but of our unforced will—I fear he'd command us to expel you at once. If we refused . . . aside from our souls, even our safety on earth, excommunication would ruin our chance of helping you."

"Why, there's an easy answer," said Eyjan blithely. "Admit the swiving, but not our nature. Also, Tauno said I can come along to his services—I doubt the images would turn from us—if you'll tell us what to do there."

He shrank from her. "No!" he choked in horror. "You know not what you say!"

She shook her red head impatiently. "Belike not. Little about your Christendom makes any sense to me." Plucking at her gown, she muttered a curse. "Could I but shed this stinking thing and bathe me in the waves——"

"My guilt is deep enough already." Niels' voice shuddered. "To take the Sacrament with an unconfessed sin upon oneself— when Satan sees me thus, his fires lick their chops for me."

Trouble came to Eyjan. She stepped forward and captured his hands in hers. "We can't let that happen to you, Tauno and I. We'll make our own way south—start at this very dawn——"

"No." His words stumbled in their haste. "Forsake you two dearest friends that I have? Never. Stay."

As if her presence had inspired him, he went on in sudden half-happiness: "See here. I can arrange that we be shriven just before Easter, and you depart just after. Then I don't think Father Ebbe will make the penance too harsh. He likes to preach about what a man owes his shipmates."

She groped for comprehension. "Suppose you die before you carry out that rite—or suppose he wants you to renounce us forever, and you don't really intend to—are you not damned?"

He took a foursquare stance. "Maybe, maybe not. I'll risk it. And I'll try to repent later, but never will I regret having kissed you." His look went over her tall fullness as an exile returned might walk step by step over his home-acre. "Instead I'll yearn for you, waking and dreaming, in every heartbeat left me; and I; I'll pray for death and burial at sea, Eyjan, your sea."

"You mourn too soon." She laid arms around his neck. "Don't. We've many kisses to give yet, Niels."

Presently she said, laughing, "Well, dinner's not for a while, and here is a couch. Yes, let's grab what comes our way, before the ebb tide bears it out of reach."

"Good news," the young man informed Tauno. "At last we've Christian names for you twain."

"But you've given us those," his comrade responded, surprised.

They had ridden from Copenhagen to be alone and because it was a sweet spring day. The common which they were crossing was vivid with new grass; in the distance, leaves made a green

mist across the top of a woodlot. Against overarching blue, storks
were returning, harbingers of summer, bearers of luck. The breeze
was fresh, loud, full of damp odors. Hoofs thudded on drenched
soil with almost unhearable softness.

Niels ran fingers through his hair. "You'll recall those names
were the best we could think of on short notice," he said. "I've
given out that they're false, used by you because you're on confidential business. Now we're ready to come out into the open"—
he grinned—"for a proper disguise is on hand. Best you and I talk
first, since you must needs play the man's part."

Tauno's mount shied. He brought the beast under control, but
Niels chided him for using the bridle too heavily. "Horsemanship
is another art you'd better learn if you'd pass yourself off," the
human warned.

"Say on," the other grunted.

"Aye. What took this long was, mainly, searching out what'd
be possible for you. We want no hazard of somebody who meets
you protesting that he knows your district well and has never heard
of any such person. Certain documents were advisable too, but
easier to arrange for; my amanuensis is a cunning rascal.

"Well, you shall be Herr Carolus Brede, a squire from a far
corner of Scania—that's the Danish territory across the Sound,
did you know? Some of it's thickly wooded and little traveled.
Though you're not rich, you're well-born. A forefather of yours
was a nobleman attending Queen Dagmar of beloved memory,
when she came from Bohemia to wed Kind Valdemar the Victorious a hundred years ago. You've learned about ties of kinship
reaching still further south, into Croatia, and decided to see if this
is true and if aught can be made of it. You've been secretive lest
agents of the Hansa grow alarmed at the chance of trade agreements
outflanking them, overland through the Empire, and maybe even
try to murder you. Though that chance is not great, as every
sensible man will realize, still, it's enough for my company to
take the gamble of providing you a ship and crew. Besides, I trust
they can dicker for whatever cargo they bring. My plea in turn
ought to get you royal and episcopal letters of recommendation,
if only because the Danish lords will be curious to know more
about the Croatian."

Tauno crowed and shook his head. "Bones of my mother, but
you've changed," he exclaimed. "I can't hear at all, in those
elegant words, the plain crewman of *Herning*. In fact, the torrent
of them carries me off."

Niels frowned. "You'll have to learn how to swim in them, and many more of the same kind. Else you'll betray yourself, likely to your death—yourself and, and, Eyjan."

Skin stood taut on the knuckles above the reins. "Yes, what of her? How'll she fare?"

"She'll be Lady Sigrid, your widowed sister, traveling along with the avowed purpose of making a pilgrimage and the unavowed one of making a better match than she could in Denmark."

Tauno gave him a hard stare. "My sister? Why not my wife?"

Niels gave it back. Invisible sparks flew. "Do you truly want that, you two?"

The Liri prince whipped his horse into a gallop.

Rain sluiced from heaven, brawled across roofs, made rivers of city streets. Lightning flared, thunder went on huge wheels, wind whooped.

A tile stove heated the main room of Niels Jonsen's house; candles threw light on wainscot, hangings, carven furniture. Ingeborg had dismissed servants and had closed doors, that she might continue Eyjan's lessons in womanly deportment.

"I'm no proper dame myself, of course, but I've watched their kind, I've studied how to imitate them, and you walk too proudly."

"Ha' done!" yelled the merman's daughter. "You've gorged me with your nonsense." She paused, quieted, offered a smile. "Forgive me. You're doing what you can for us, I know. But it's so hot and close in here, this wool clings and itches and stifles my skin, I can't endure more."

Ingeborg watched her for a while that was silent except for the storm battering at shutters. "You must endure," she said finally. "It's the lot of women, and you're to be a woman while your journey lasts. Never forget that, or you could betray Tauno to his death."

"Well, but can we stop for today?"

"Aye, perhaps best we do."

"Let me draw a gasp or two ere we meet your world again," said Eyjan. In motions which had become deft, she peeled the raiment off her and cast it violently down. Naked, she went to a sideboard and filled herself a goblet of mead. "Would you like some?"

Ingeborg hesitated before she said, "Yes, thank you. But beware of getting drunk. That's for whores and slatterns—and men."

"Is everything for men in your Christendom?"

"No, not really." Ingeborg took the drink handed her and found a chair. "We learn how to worm a great deal out of them."

"Undersea, nobody had to play worm." Eyjan well-nigh flung a seat into position opposite her hostess, and herself into it.

"But we on land bear the curse of Eve. How often I've heard told me the word of God—'*in sorrow thou shalt bring forth children; and thy desire shall be to thy husband, and he shall rule over thee'*—" Ingeborg clutched her chair arms. She would never bring forth children.

Eyjan saw and tried awkwardly to give comfort. "You've become better off than most, haven't you? Niels is pleasant to live with, and I've seen how he wants your counsel on different things; you're no mere pet of his."

"True. Yet I'm his kept woman, whom no respectable housewife will have to do with if she can help it. Nor, of course, any respectable man. They greet me politely enough, those merchants and nobles and sea captains, but a greeting is where it stops. What they talk to Niels about, I may or may not hear from him afterward. And he's busy, must be much away from home. I can't bring down his standing by growing friendly with any of our servants. Oh, less lonely was that shack on the strand." Ingeborg uttered a laugh. "I don't suppose it's in you to pray thanks for what you have, Eyjan, but be glad of it."

"Have you no better hope, then?" the Liri princess asked low.

The woman shrugged. "Who can tell? I do know full well how lucky I am, and learned years ago how to keep an eye cocked for the next chance that flits by."

"As Niels' wedded wife——"

Ingeborg shook her head, hard. "No. He offered me that, but I could see how relieved he was when I refused. What does he want with a former harlot who has no family connections and can't even give him sons? No, when he weds, out I go...oh, quietly, honorably, his protecting hand over me as long as we both live, and maybe a sleeping together now and then for old times' sake—nevertheless, out."

She struggled with herself before she could say: "If ever he does wed. His passion for you may grow too strong in him. With me he can be frank about it; many's the time I've held him close while he wept for you; but another—Spare him that, Eyjan, if by any means you can."

"How?" asked the other. "Your ways are not mine." After a
moment: "Is that immortal soul of yours truly worth a woman's
having?"

Ingeborg shivered. "God forgive me," she breathed, "I do not
know."

Spring ran wild with blossoms and birdsong, a season of love,
a season of forgetfulness and farewells. The cog *Brynhild* raised
sail, slipped her moorings, and departed on the tide. Until she was
hull down, Ingeborg and Niels stood on the dock, waving.

Then: "Well," she said, "we had them for that span."

His fist was clenched as if to strike, his vision lost along the
horizon. "She promised she'd come back," he mumbled. "At least
once, to tell me how she fares. If she can. If she lives."

"In the meantime," she told him sharply, "*you* have your work.
I . . . should look wider about me than hitherto, I suppose." She
took his arm. "No use dawdling here. Come, let's go home."

On deck, Tauno watched land, water, sails pass by, drank deep
of the air, and said, "Finally we're out of that stinkhole! None
too soon. I felt myself starting to rot."

"Are we better off here?" Eyjan replied. "They cared for us,
yon two."

"Aye, they've been staunch."

"More than that. What they spent of themselves on us—where
else can we find it, ever?"

"Among our own kind."

"If those are as we remember them. And even if they
are———" Eyjan's voice trailed off. After a stillness, during which
the ship bore onward until the last spire in Copenhagen was lost
to sight, she finished: "This will be a long voyage, brother mine."

As the days and weeks of it lengthened, *Brynhild's* men grew
aware of something uncanny about their passengers. Not only
were Herr Carolus and Lady Sigrid curt-spoken, downright
moody, given to hours on end of gazing across the waves or up
at the stars, or to staying latched in their cubicles, with the command that they desired no meat or drink brought them. No, a
couple of mariners thought they had glimpsed one or the other
slipping forth by night and overside. Nobody saw either of them
climb back aboard; however, the owner had issued an odd standing

order, that a rope ladder always be trailed aft for the sake of a
hand who might fall into the sea—as if sailors could swim!
Whether or not there was anything to this (Captain Asbern Ri-
boldsen reminded his crew of what a notoriously superstitious and
gullible lot their sort was), certainly the two never joined in common prayer, but said they would liefer perform their devotions in
private. Devotions to whom? The mutter went that here were a
sorcerer and a witch.

Still, sureness about it was lacking. Carolus and Sigrid gave
no outward offense, nor did any grave trouble arise for the ship.
At the same time, foul winds and dead calms showed that nobody
was hexing the weather. Moreover, Niels Jonsen and his partner
were known as fine fellows who'd surely not beguile poor seamen
into trafficking with evil. He had let the crew be warned that this
was a singular voyage, unlike any that they had heard tell of,
venturesome as a cast of dice in a Visby tavern . . . but with good
pay, good pay.

Thus, however much folk puzzled, things went peacefully on
the whole: down the North Sea, through the English Channel,
around Britanny, down the Bay of Biscay and along the Iberian
shores—with a wary lookout for Moorish cruisers from Africa—
and through the Gates of Hercules. Thereabouts Captain Asbern
engaged a pilot to show the way onward. It helped much that Herr
Carolus knew the language of that Majorcan adventurer (how?).
And so, toward midsummer, the cog reached Dalmatia, and
worked her way up that coast.

VI

WITH horses and servants engaged in Shibenik, Herr Carolus and Lady Sigrid took the road to Skradin. The satnik had sent a message ahead from town to castle, and the zhupan had dispatched a military escort for his distinguished visitors. The party made a brave sight as it wound into the mountains, metal agleam, plumes and cloaks tossing in many colors, hoofs plopping, harness jingling, beneath cloudless heaven. Warmth baked strong, sweet odors out of the beasts, ripening fields of grain and hay on the right, greenwood tall on the left.

Nonetheless Tauno wrinkled his nose. "Faugh, the dust!" he said in Danish, which lent itself better than the Liri tongue to such matters. "My insides are turned to a . . . a brickyard. Can you believe merfolk would freely settle down ashore?"

Her palfrey beside his gelding, Eyjan gave him a stiff look out of the wimple that concealed her mane. "It may not have been freely," she replied. "What *did* you find out?" As the man of them, he had necessarily done the talking, Panigpak's gift hung inside his shirt. Eager to converse with such a stranger, the Croatians had left him no time until now for any real speech with her.

"Little," he admitted. "I dared not press the question hard, you know, when it's not our ostensible business. And I'm not skilled at slyly sucking his knowledge out of anybody. I could but remark in passing that I'd heard rumors and was curious. Folk shied away from the subject. That seemed to be less because they thought it uncanny than because those above them have discouraged mention of it."

"But you did confirm that merfolk are living there where we are bound?"

"Aye, and also that sometimes they come down to the coast by two or threes, and swim about. That would be needful for their health, of course, but it's said they do useful tasks like charting shoals and finding out where fishing is best. Lately, as well, a number of males have departed on ships, in the service of the duke or whatever his title is here. A war is starting up; I'm not clear as to why or who the enemy is." Tauno shrugged. "Our host to be can doubtless tell us more."

Eyjan regarded him closely. "Under that sour mien, brother," she murmured, "you're a-tremble to meet them again."

"Are you not?" he asked, surprised. "It's been a weary search"—voice and eyes dropped—"and this latest voyage the loneliest part of it all."

Her own gaze grew troubled and she averted it. "Yes. On *Herning*, and later in Denmark, we had two who loved us."

"But our own people——"

"Wait and see." She would say no more. Tauno felt downright relieved when the captain of the guards drew close and engaged him in respectfully fascinated colloquy.

Though the birdflight distance between Shibenik and Skradin was not great, the road twisted far to avoid the woods, and departure had been somewhat belated. Thus the sun was low when folk reached the village, its rays golden through cool air, shadows huge before it. Riding along a street toward the castle, the merman's children glanced about with heart-quickened interest. Houses were wooden, roofed with turf or thatch, as in the North; but the style of them, and the gaudy paint on most, was foreign, as was the onion-domed church at one end. Humans who paused to stare at the procession were often tall and blond, but mainly round of skull and high of cheekbones, their garb of a cut and ornamentation never seen at home. They appeared well fed, and they did not cringe from the soldiers but their men offered cheerful hails. As elsewhere in Dalmatia, women kept meek in the background, several of them more heavily burdened than was common in *Brynhild's* country.

Abruptly Tauno stiffened in the saddle. His stare went from a shawl-wrapped face, across whose brow stole a greenish curl, to bare, webbed feet below the skirt. "Raxi!" he bawled, and jerked on the reins.

"Tauno, is it you, Tauno?" the person cried in their olden language. Then she shrank back, crossing herself over and over as the Hrvatskan words poured from her: "No, God have mercy, Jesus have mercy, I mustn't, Mary help me——" She whirled about and ran stumblingly around a corner, out of his view.

Tauno made as if to leap down after her. Eyjan seized him by the wrist. "Hold, you fool," she snapped.

He shook himself, caught his breath, fell still, clucked his horse back into motion. "Aye, they are a startling sight," the guards captain said. "But fear them not, my lord. They're good Christians now, good neighbors, loyal subjects of the King. Why, I'm thinking I might marry a daughter of my own to some young fellow among them."

Beside Ivan Subitj to welcome his guests was a priest, not the zhupan's chaplain but a robust, rough-clad graybeard introduced as Father Tomislav. While a repast was being prepared, and Lady Sigrid resting in the chamber lent her, these two discoursed privately with Herr Carolus.

That was high in the watchtower, where a room commanded a splendid overlook across the countryside. Westward the sun had dropped under the forest which hid the lake. Light still tinged wings of swallows and bats which darted around a violet sky. Thin mists were rising to sheen across the fields. Closer gleamed the conjoining rivers, farther to northward and eastward the Svilaja peaks. It had grown very quiet outside.

Dusk softened Ivan's mutilated face, but there was iron in his voice as he stiffened on his bench and ended a time of amenities: "I sent for Tomislav, Gospodar Carolus, because he of everyone knows most about the merfolk—maybe more than they do themselves—and I understood from reports brought me that you were inquiring about them."

"That was kind of you, sir," Tauno replied uneasily. He wet his lips with a sip of wine. "You needn't have gone to so much trouble or, or keep so close a watch on me; but thank you."

"Naught is too much for a nobleman from abroad who may be establishing connections among us. Maybe, though, you'd like to tell me, Gospodar—since it doesn't seem nigh your purpose— why you are this interested in the merfolk?" Like a whipcrack: "I can't imagine why else you'd have come to this offside place."

Tauno's free hand found comfort in the hilt of his knife. "Well, we do have a race of the same kind in Northern waters."

"Bah!" burst from Tomislav. "Stop that nonsense, both of you. Ivan, your manners are abominable. If you suspect this wight is a Venetian spy, say it forth like an honest man."

"Oh, no, oh, no," protested the zhupan hastily. "However, we do have a new war, and in the past couple of years we've met such weirdness—— My duty is to be careful, Gospodar Carolus. And truth to tell, you haven't sounded as if you knew these Hrvatskan kin of yours as well as you might, considering how perfectly you speak their language."

"Does that make him hostile?" snorted the priest. "Look here, not only have the merfolk worked no evil, they do vital service. And surely the coming of that many pure Christian souls makes God smile on our land." His tone changed, fell to a near whisper beneath which lay a sob. Tauno saw tears start forth. Yet joy welled up from the depths: "If you want a sign on that, Ivan, why, remember the vilja is gone. This spring she came not out of the waters to haunt the woods. Nobody has found one trace of her. If...if she really was the phantom of...a suicide...under judgment...then God must have pardoned her and taken her home to Paradise—and why else but that He was pleased at the salvation of the merfolk?"

His heart a lump within him, Tauno asked slowly, "So it's true what people seem to believe, that they were baptized and lost all memory of what they had been?"

"Not quite," Tomislav answered. "By rare grace, they keep their past lives, their knowledge and skills in aid of our poor countrymen. It's a long story, but marvelous."

"I...would like to hear."

The humans considered Tauno for a silent while, wherein darkness thickened. Ivan's gaze grew less distrustful, Tomislav's ever more kind.

At last the zhupan said, "Well, I suppose there's no reason why you shouldn't. I make a guess you've surmised most of it already. I think, too, that you've your own reasons for being here, which you've not let out; but I dare hope they're innocent."

"Better than innocent," Tomislav added. "Andrei—Vanimen that was—he told me about certain children of his who were left behind.... You needn't say more till you feel safe in doing it, Carolus. Let me help you understand that you're among friends. Listen to the tale, ask whatever questions you will."

• • •

Even ashore, Tauno could move snake-softly when he chose. None saw him glide from his room, down a corridor and a stairway, forth into the shadow and mist of the court, through an open gate where a pair of sentries nodded at their pikes. Once out among the villager homes, he stalked upright, for nobody was awake and no dog would dare bark. The sky was clear, amply starful. Evening chill had quenched the stenches of habitation enough for his nostrils to pick out the odors he sought: a hint of waters more deep and broad than any baptismal font.

Already several merfolk dwelt in human households. He passed them by. Nor did he consider seeking the settlement on the lakeshore which others, who were now fishers, shared with children of Adam. A few small dwellings, fragrant with fresh timber, had arisen on the edge of Skradin for the rest of the newcomers. These were chiefly females . . . no, women, he thought, mortal women who must in propriety no longer go adventuring.

A certain blend of cool fleshly scents brought him to a door whereon he knocked. Ears within had kept their Faerie keeness. A voice called, "Who is it? What will you?"

"It is Tauno, Vanimen's son," he answered. "Let me in, Raxi, lover that was in Liri."

He heard whispers, scuffle of feet, fumblings about. The time seemed endless before the latch clacked free and the barrier swung aside. Two stood beyond. They had thrown on shifts, but he knew them at once: Raxi, the merriest lass in his tribe, and lean blue-tressed Meiiva who had been his father's special friend.

He felt the unsureness of his smile as he spread his arms wide. The girl gasped, sprang back, buried face in hands. Her older companion remained calm, yet it was with an effort that she said, "Welcome, Tauno. How good to know you live, you and Eyjan— and to have you here at last——But you must cover yourself."

Tauno glanced down. When he left his bed, he had not bothered to don clothes anew, save for knife belt; the spirit bone hung always around his neck. "Why, we're alone, Meiiva," he replied in a puzzlement that was half fear, "and you both know this body well."

"I am not Meiiva any more, Tauno, and she, my sister in God, is not Raxi. We are Jelena and Biserka." The woman turned about.

"Wait here. I'll fetch you garb." The door closed.

It reopened shortly, a crack, and she reached out a coat. He belted it around his middle, sniffing with a thrill that it was his father's. When Meiiva—Jelena—let him into the humble building, whose rafters made him bow his head, she had lighted a clay lamp from the fire banked on the hearth. "That's better," she said, and actually touched his elbow. "Be not ashamed. You've everything to learn. Sit down, dear, and let me pour you a stoup."

Dazedly, he settled onto a chest. Biserka crouched in the opposite corner. Her look upon him was—fearful? Wistful? He could not tell, but he heard how quickly she breathed.

"Why are you here too?" he asked her roommate.

"Andrei, your father, my husband, is off to war," Jelena explained. "For seemliness as well as shared help, I invited Biserka to come stay here meanwhile. She's unwedded, and, well——" Aforetime frankness was gone; it was hard to finish: "She had a home with a family, but the eldest son was beginning to show lust for her, and that would not be the best match she could make."

"*You*, Raxi?" Tauno blurted. "Why, I sought you tonight before all others!"

Jelena sighed, though in the dull yellow glow her cheeks smoldered. "I know. May the merciful saints aid me in remembering what you are, and not to blame you but to try to show you the way onward." Having filled three bowls with mead, she brought him one. "Dismiss carnal thoughts, Tauno. This is not Liri, we are not what we were, and God be praised."

"Well, there are some hussies!" flared from Biserka. She huddled back, crossed herself, and added fast, "Ask not their names."

"Surely you'll find one of them among us who were merfolk," Jelena said, where she stood tall above Tauno. "We're too newly born. How I pray we'll never soil the spirits in us, fresh from God's hand!" She paused, stared beyond him, and mused, "Oh, we will, I fear. To feel sure of our own righteousness, that would be a mortal sin in itself, pride. But may we always have grace to repent when we fall, to keep striving." Her glance sharpened and speared him. "If any man would seduce us, let him bear in mind that we can yet wield edged weapons."

"Then you do recall your past lives?" he mumbled.

She nodded. "Aye, though they seem strange, dim, like a dream that was long and vivid but is fading. We've awakened,

you see. There before the altar, we awoke from the half-life of
beasts to life eternal." Suddenly she, who had been strong as
Vanimen, wept. "Oh, that moment, that single first moment with
God! What . . . remains . . . to abide for . . . but the hope of
finding it again, forever, in Heaven?"

A waning moon had cleared eastern heights when Tauno entered the forest. It had not taken him long, for he ran the entire
way across plowlands; stalks and ears of grain left welts in revenge
for his trampling. However, the hour had been late when he could
finally win free of the women, cast off his father's coat at the
door, and bolt.

It was not that they cursed him. They had been affectionate
in their pleading, their wish that he too take the gift of an immortal
soul. It was not even that they were utterly changed, flesh once
delightful now housing an alienness greater than that which sundered him from the tribe of Adam. It was that—he thought, somewhere in his staggering mind—that they were carriers of doom.
In them was the future, which held no room for Faerie. When he
sprinted, he did not only seek to work out some of the despair
wherein his quest had ended. He fled the unseen, while stars
looked down and hissed, "There he is, there he goes, that's his
track to follow."

The breath heaved raw in his throat before he found shelter.
This was below an oak, for it spread darkness and upheld mistletoe.
At last he moved on into the wilderness, toward the lake he could
sense afar. He would bathe in yon waters, fill his lungs with their
cleanliness, maybe catch a fish and devour it raw like a seal or
a killer whale. Thus he would regain strength for returning to the
castle and whatever was going to happen there.

Trees gloomed, underbrush entangled a heavier murk, on either
side of the game trail he took. Moonlight filtered in streaks through
the crowns, to glimmer off vapors which streamed or eddied low
above the earth. It was a touch warmer here than out in the open,
damp, smelling of growth a-drowse. Rustlings went faint, a
breeze, an owl ghosting by, the scutter of tiny feet. Once a wildcat
squalled, remotely, noise blurred into music by all the leaves
around.

A measure of peace lifted within Tauno. Here was a remnant
of his world, the wildworld, which lived wholly within itself,

loved, slew, begot, suffered, died, was born, knew delirious magics but never would probe and tame the mysteries behind them nor peer into a stark eternity. Here were spoor of Faerie . . . the spirit bone brought names into his awareness, as if he had always known them . . . Leshy, Kikimora, also flitting restless, shy of him but——

But what else was it he winded? No, he caught this one sensation otherwise, in his blood, part fear and part unutterable yearning. His pulse thuttered, he quickened his footsteps.

The trail swung around a canebrake, and they met.

For a time outside of time, both halted. In their sight, where a human would have been well-nigh blind, each stood forth white against enclosing many-layered shadows, as if having risen from the fog that smoked about their feet. She was much the paler; it was as though the fugitive moonlight streamed through thinly carved alabaster, save that when she did move it was like a ripple across water. Very fair she was in her nakedness, with the slim, unscarred curves of waist, thighs, breasts which bespoke a maiden, with delicately carven face and enormous, luminous eyes. Her hair made a cloud about her, afloat on the air. She had no color except the faintest flushes of blue and rose, as upon snow beneath a false dawn.

"Oh," she whispered. Terror snatched her. "Oh, but I mustn't!"

And for his part, recalling what he had heard that day, and earlier from his father, he shouted, *"Rousalka!"* and whipped out his knife. He dared not turn his back.

She vanished behind the underbrush. He stood tensed and snarling, until he decided she was gone and sheathed the blade. The intimations of her drifted everywhere around, maddeningly gentle, fresh, girlish, but he knew little of such beings; their traces might well linger. . . .

Would they?

Why, he had the talisman to ask. He need but ease himself, think in Hrvatskan about what he had seen, and let knowledge flow upward. Muscle by muscle, he summoned calm, until he could know and could call: "Vilja. Stay. Please."

She peered around the brake; he barely glimpsed an eye, the gleam of a cheek, the delicacy of an elbow. "Are you Christian?" she fluted timidly. "I'm forbidden to come near Christians."

So she was no menace; she was merely beautiful. "I'm not

even a mortal man," said Tauno against a rattle of laughter.

She crept forth to stand before him at arm's length. "I thought I could feel that," she breathed. "Would you really like to talk with me?" She kindled, she trilled. "Oh, wonderful! Thank you, thank you."

"What is your name?" He must needs gather courage before he could lay down: "I hight Tauno. Half merman, half human, but altogether of Faerie."

"And I——" She hesitated more than he had. "I think I am, I was Nada. I call me Nada."

He reached out to her. She tiptoed close. They linked hands. Hers were night-cool and somehow not quite solid. He thought that if he took a real hold upon them, his fingers would part their frailty and meet each other: wherefore he gripped as tenderly as he was able. The clasp shivered.

"What are you?" he asked, that he might hear it from her own lips.

"A vilja. A thing of mist and wind and half-remembered dreams—and how glad of your kindness, Tauno!"

Desire, long unslaked, was thick within him. He sought to draw her close. She flowed, she blew from his embrace, to poise trembling beyond his reach. Fear and grief worked their ways across her countenance, which was young to behold but inwardly had grown old. "No, Tauno, I beg you. For your own sake. I'm no more of the living world. You'd die, yourself, if you tried."

Recalling how Herr Aage had risen from his grave to comfort Lady Else his beloved—simply to comfort her in her misery—and what came of that, Tauno shuddered backward from Nada.

She saw. Briefly, her aloneness ruled her; then she straightened her shoulders (there was the dearest hollow between them, right below the throat) and said, with a shaken smile, "But you needn't run away, need you, Tauno? Can we not abide a while together?"

They did until morning.

VII

ANDREI Subitj, captain in the Royal Navy of Magyarország and Hrvatska—he who once was Vanimen, king of Liri—turned from the window out which he had been gazing. This was in Shibenik, on an upper floor of the mayoral palace. When such an officer took special leave from the war and came south, in answer to a message from the zhupan, he could have whatever place he asked for. Day had waned while he and Eyjan held converse. Towers stood dark against deep-blue gloaming, above walls and battlements within which links bobbed along streets. Bells pealed a call to vespers. Andrei traced the Cross.

"And thus we know each what has happened to the other," he sighed. "Yet what do we truly know?" Tall in a gold-broidered kaftan, his body moved across the carpet with more firmness than his voice. "*Why* would Tauno not bestir himself to come this short way and greet me?"

Eyjan, who was seated, stared at the hem of her gown. "I can't tell," she replied. "Not really. He said there was no use in it, that you simply are no more the father he sought. But he says little to anyone these days, nothing that might reveal his mind."

"Not even to you?" Andrei asked as he took the chair opposite hers.

"No." Fists clenced in her lap. "I can but guess that he's poisoned with bitterness against Christians."

Andrei sat straight. His tone crackled. "Has anybody done ill by you twain?"

"Never. Far from it." The red head shook, the gray eyes lifted to meet his. "Although we admitted early on we'd been lying to him—for we couldn't well stick to our deception after our kin

230

recognized us—Ivan did not resent it. Rather, he increased his
hospitality, and that in the teeth of his chaplain, who's scandalized
at having two creatures like us beneath yon roof. Ivan's actually
doing his best to keep our secret from leaving the village, that we
may fare back to Denmark without hindrance if we choose."

"Of course, he hopes to convert you."

"Of course. But he doesn't pester us about it, nor let Father
Petar do so." Eyjan smiled a bit. "I see Father Tomislav more
gladly, aye, as often as may be. He's a darling. Tauno himself
can't slight that man." Her thought veered. "Something strange
is there too. I know not what or why . . . but Tauno is very mild
with Tomislav . . . almost the way one might be with somebody
who'll soon die but doesn't know it. . . ."

"How is his daily life? And yours, for that matter?"

Eyjan shrugged. "As an acknowledged sea-wife, I'm not fast-
bound the way a Croatian woman is. I can swim or range the
woods, provided no man sees me. Around mortals, however, I
think it best to act the lady. There I pass most of my time learning
the language, since Tauno keeps the amulet. Often the maidser-
vants and I will sing together; Ivan's wife joins us now and then,
or his son." She grimaced. "I fear young Luka is getting much
too fond of me. Unwillingly would I bring woe on their house."

"Tauno?"

"How can I tell?" Eyjan said roughly. "He goes off into the
wilderness for days and nights on end. When he returns, he grunts
that he's been hunting, and is barely courteous to folk. I bespoke
my idea that he hates the Faith for what it's done to his people.
Though why he shuns me——"

"Hm." Andrei cupped chin in palm and gave her a long regard.
"Might he have found a sweetheart in some distant hut? I'm sure
neither of you can have a lover in Skradin."

"No," she clipped forth. "We cannot."

"And time in a single bed hangs heavy. Ah, I remember. . . . If
he's not beguiled a mortal girl, well, Faerie beings do haunt these
realms——" In shock, Andrei saw whither his thought was leading
him. Again he crossed himself. "Jesus forbid!"

"Why, what harm, if he who is soulless couples with an elf?"
Eyjan gibed.

"I'd not have my son lured beyond halidom. He might die

before he's saved." Andrei's look steadied upon her. "You might, my daughter."

Eyjan was silent.

"What are your plans?" he inquired.

Unhappiness freighted her words: "I know not, the less when Tauno keeps apart from me. We promised our Danish friends we'll rejoin them when we're able. Thereafter—Greenland?"

"No fit place for you, who have seen far better." Andrei hesitated. "Luka Subitj would be a forbearing husband."

Eyjan grew taut. "I'll never wear the bonds they lay on women here!"

"Aye, you'd be freer in Denmark, and I like what you've told me of that Niels Jonsen. Get christened, wed him, be joyous."

"Christened. Become . . . your sort?"

"Yes, age and die in a handful of years, and meanwhile live chaste and pious. But you will live in the blessing of God, and afterward in His very presence. Not until you've taken this bargain Christ offers, can you know how measurelessly generous it is."

With eyes as well as tongue, Andrei pursued: "I understand. You dread the loss of your wild liberty, you think you'd liefer cease to be. I give you my oath—not by the Most High: not yet— by the love I bore for your mother and bear for you, Eyjan Agnetesdatter, I swear that in humanness you will win release. It will be like coming alone out of winter night into a firelit room where those whom you hold dearest are feasting."

"And where I see no more stars, feel no more wind," she protested.

"Faerie has had its splendors," he replied. "But are you not wisest to give them up while they are in some part as you've known them? Oh, Eyjan, child, spare yourself the anguish of seeing the halfworld go down in wreck and feeling that same ruin in your own breast. For it will indeed perish, it will. What happened to Liri was but a foretaste of what must happen to all Faerie. Magic is dying out of Creation. A sage man showed me that, and I'd fain show you it, though each word scourges me too, if you'll stay here till I must return to the fleet.

"Do what is kindest, to those who care for you as well as yourself. Leave Faerie where you can find no happiness, whatever you do, wherever you range. Accept the divine love of Christ, the honest love of Niels and of the children you bear him; and one day we will all meet again in Heaven."

His tone sank, he stared beyond her and every wall. "Agnete also," he ended.

How much like Tauno he is, she thought

In summer, when trees gave shade against the sun, a vilja could move about by day. Nada danced through the forest in a swirl of tossing hair. Among shrubs she dodged, overleaped logs, sprang on high to grab a bough and swing from it for a moment before she sped onward. Her laughter chimed, "Come, come along, sluggard!" Her slenderness vanished into the green. Tauno stopped to pant and squint around after tracks of her. Suddenly her palms clapped over his eyes from behind, she kissed him between the shoulderblades, and was off again. Cool though her touch had been, it burned a long while in his awareness. He blundered on. Unseen, she sent breezes to fan him.

At last he could go no more. At a dark-brown, moss-lined pool he halted. Trees crowded around, huge oak, slim beech, murky juniper. They roofed off the sky, they made a verdant dusk bespeckled with sunflecks. Butterflies winged between them. It was warm here, the air heavy with odors of ripeness. A squirrel chattered and streaked aloft, then he was gone and the mighty silence of summer brooded anew.

"Hallo-o!" Tauno shouted. "You've galloped the breath out of me." Leafy arches swallowed up his cry. He wiped off the sweat that stung his eyes and salted his lips, cast himself belly down, and drank. The pool was cold, iron-tinged.

He heard a giggle. "You have a shapely bottom," Nada called. He rolled over and saw her perched on a limb above him, kicking her legs to and fro. They would catch a beam of light, which made them blaze gold, then return to being white in the shadows.

"Come here if you dare and I'll paddle yours for that," he challenged.

"Nyah." She made a face at him. "You wouldn't. I know you, you big fraud. I know what you'd really do."

"What?"

"Why, cuddle me and pet me and kiss me—which is a better idea anyhow." Nada floated, more nearly than jumped, to earth.

Blackberries grew beneath the tree. She stopped to gather as many as her small hands could hold before she came to kneel by Tauno, who was now sitting.

"Poor love, you *are* tired," she said. "Wet all over, and surely weak in the knees. Here, let me feed some strength back into you."

Herself she was dry-skinned, unwinded, ready to soar off at any instant. She would not sleep when he did, nor did she share the fruits she placed in his mouth. The dead have no such needs.

"Those were delicious, thank you," he said when she was through. "But if I'm to stay out here much longer, I'll require food more stout. Fish from the lake; or, if you'll help me quest, a deer."

She winced. "I hate it when you kill."

"I must."

"Yes." She brightened. "Like the great beautiful lynx you are."

She stroked fingers across him. He touched her in turn, caresses which wandered everywhere. They could never be strong, those gestures. She was too insubstantial. He felt rounded softnesses, which moved in response to him, but they had no heat and always he got a sense of thistledown delicacy.

What had formed her, he knew not, nor she. The bones of Nada, Tomislav's daughter, rested in a Shibenik churchyard. Her soul dwelt in an image of that body, formed out of . . . moonlight and water, maybe. It was a gentle damnation.

Damnation nonetheless, he reflected: for him as well.

"You hurt yourself," she exclaimed. "Oh, don't."

He wrenched his glance from her. "Forgive me," he said in a rusty voice. "I know my bad moods distress you. Maybe you should go for a run till I've eased."

"And leave you alone?" She drew close against him. "No." After a space: "Besides, I'm selfish. You lift *my* aloneness off me."

"The trouble is just that . . . I desire you . . . and found you too late."

"And I desire you, Tauno, beloved."

What did that mean to her? he wondered. She had died a maiden. Of course, she had known, from seeing beasts if naught else, what the way of a man with a woman is; but had she ever truly understood? Afterward she was not one to ponder, she was a spirit of wood and water, her heart gone airy; and what might be the desires which reigned in her? Did any?

Beyond the wish for his company—was that what had captured him, her own swift adoration? She was so utterly unlike Eyjan, perhaps he had unwittingly fled to her. Yet other women lent refuge likewise, and they could quiet his loins and give him comradeship which endured, not this haring about with a ghost. Ingeborg——

Tauno and Nada laid arms around waists. Her head rested on his muscles; he could barely feel the tresses. It restored his calm, the pain-tinctured joy he found with her. Surely this could not go on without end, but let him not fret about the future. Forethought was no part of his Faerie heritage, and he had disowned the human half. In the presence of Nada, beauty, frolic, muteness together in awe below the stars, he lost himself, he almost became at peace with everything that was, this side of Heaven.

"You're wearied," she said at length. "Lie down. Have a nap. I'll sing you a lullabye."

He obeyed. The simple melody, which her mother had belike never sung to her, washed over him like a brooklet and bore away care.

He was content. Let flesh and blood wait until some later time. The vilja would never betray him.

Summer descended toward autumn. At first the fields were crowded with peasants stooped above sickles, or following to rake, bind, shock, cart off, and glean. They labored from before dawn till after sunset, lest a rainstorm rob them, and tumbled into sleep. The work was still less merciful than usual, because all signs portended a winter early and harsh. When at last the garnering was done, everybody celebrated titanically. Meanwhile, each night the stars came forth seeming more remote than ever through air that quickly grew chill.

In one such darkness, Tauno and Eyjan walked along the riverbank. She had insisted that they have a real talk. He yielded, grudgingly, but said he felt too trapped between walls.

A glow above eastern peaks portended moonrise. Erelong it would be the harvest moon that lifted. Carl's Wain loomed immense, as low as it glittered in the Dalmatian sky; higher blinked the Pole Star, to show Northern folk their way home. Frogs and crickets were silenced, only the purling stream had voice. Unseasonable hoarfrost lay upon sere grass. Tauno felt it under his feet, for he had shucked his clothes once out of sight of Skradin. Eyjan had not; hooded cloak and flowing gown did what they were able to hide the fullness of her.

After a mile or two, she took the word: "Captain Asbern sought me out while I was in Shibenik. He warned that if *Brynhild* doesn't start back soon, she'll have to lie over till spring. Already there are few masters who'd embark on so long a voyage."

"Yes, we knew that," he replied.

"But did you, at least, think about it?" Eyjan paused, except for her footfalls, before she continued. "I've learned about human ways of late, maybe more than you've condescended to do. It would be costly for Niels to have ship and crew a year or more agone. And that wretched war—Father back at the siege of Zadar, where he could be killed without ever having seen you. . . . Well, I've been told our documents may not protect us from the Venetians. A commerce raider of theirs may decide the King of Denmark and his bishops are too far off to be a threat. The later we depart, the worse our chances."

"Why, then, we can let the ship sail," he told her. "But what's in Denmark for us?"

Alarm replied: "What's for us here?" She caught his hand. They stopped in midstride. "Tauno, what is it that keeps you in the wildwood?"

He answered the first question. "Well, true, we found our kin and they're merely another lot of mortals. You must indeed be weary of the lady's role. So leave if you wish."

She searched his countenance. It was visor-blank, though hers quivered. "Not you?"

"I think not yet. But go you, and give Ingeborg and Niels my greetings."

"You promised you'd return to her for at least a while."

"I will, I will, when the time is right," he snapped.

"You've changed, Tauno—in a way, more than anyone else from Liri."

"Unless what I am now was ready within me, like a thaw in a frozen pond. Enough. I care not for chatter about myself."

As he watched her, his mood softened. "Aye, do hail Ingeborg from me, if you return," he said. "Tell her I've not forgotten loyalty, wise counsel, patient helpfulness, and, yes, how dear she was when we joined. I could wish it were in me to love a mortal woman as Father did Mother." He sighed. "It isn't."

She looked away, but did not ask whom it was he could love.

"What of yourself, though?" he went on. "After you've spent a few weeks or months with Niels, where will you go?"

She braced herself. "I may go no farther at all," she said.

"Hoy?" he barked, astounded. After a minute: "Well, yes, his leman while he remains young. I can see where that would be pleasant. He'd leave you your freedom; and after he grows old——"

"I would grow old with him."

Stubbornly, against his stupefaction, she urged: "You should listen to Father. He's right, the Faith is *true*, and we're not condemned, it's just a matter of choosing to take what it promises . . . and Faerie is doomed, Tauno. . . . I wanted to be sure we two spoke together this night, because tomorrow I fare to Father Tomislav in his parish and pray him to tell me more. Won't you come along?"

"No!" he roared, yanked loose from her grasp and made a fist against Heaven. "Eyjan, you can't mean that——"

"I'm not quite sure, but——"

"Crawling before a God Who twists and breaks what He made—— At least Odin never claimed to be just."

Her own strength rose to straighten her back and level her gaze. "Be glad that God is not just," she said. "He is merciful."

"Where was the mercy for Nada?" He whirled about and ran. She started to follow, then stood where she was.

Far in the west, the moon still made the lake tremble with radiance; but the east was whitening, stars above yonder treetops were gone, and up there, like a gleam of bronze, an early hawk was at hover. On earth lay a frosty silence.

Tauno and Nada stood side by side on the shore. The vilja's mood was more grave than formerly. "You are always good to me," she murmured, "but oh, at this meeting, somehow, kindness has glowed from you. I felt it, I feel it yet, as once I felt sunshine."

"How could I be other than kind, to you?" His tone was harsh.

In her pensiveness she did not notice, simply squeezed the fingers he had intertwined with hers. "You make me remember things like sunshine," she told him. "With you by me, I'm no longer afraid to remember. I know you'll take away the hurt."

"You, you help me forget."

"What? But you'd not want to forget, would you? Your wonderful sea, that I never weary of hearing about. I, though, I was no more than a silly girl who stumbled into such woe that she drowned herself. Yes, I did; today I dare know it, though I can't understand how I ever got that bewildered." She smiled. "And over a boy, a mere boy. You are a man."

"A merman."

"Well, whatever, Tauno, dearest. Do you know what's become of Mihajlo? I hope he's cheery, wherever he is."

"Yes, I hear he's doing well."

Her look upon him grew disturbed, for he was grimly staring out across the water. "You've been wounded by something new," she said. "Can I help? How I wish I can."

Surprised, for never before had she shown perception so close, he let slip: "I may have to leave soon. My sister, that I've told you about, she thinks we should and I fear she's right." Deep in his gullet: "As far as her reasoning goes; no further."

Then Nada had recoiled from him, one hand across her open mouth to bar a shriek, the other palm thrust outward in denial. "No, no, no! Tauno, why? Please, no!"

She crumpled together and wept. Not until tonight had he seen that.

He knelt to enfold her in his arms. The slim form clung, he stroked the loose hair of a maiden, he vowed he had misspoken himself and not for anything, ever, would he be sundered from her, and all the while he knew he was being as crazy as she had been when she ended her bodily life.

VIII

On the feast of St. Matthew the Apostle, the daughter of Andrei and Agnete was christened by Father Tomislav in his church. The name she had chosen was Dragomir. In Denmark, that had become Dagmar, which means "day maiden."

Tall she stood before the alter, clad in white as though for her bridal, ruddy locks braided and covered as beseems a woman in the house of God. Beside her were her father, back again from the war for this moment; his wife Jelena; Ivan Subitj and his own lady. The dark little building was full of folk from the zadruga and her kindred of Liri, as many as could pack in. At the forefront stood Luka, with a look of hopeless yearning. At the back was Tauno. Some had said it was not right to let him in, but the priest had replied that he was her brother, and in any case there was inevitably much improvisation in this rite, and besides—who knew?—the spectacle might by sudden grace unseal his breast. He kept arms folded and countenance rigid.

Costly was the incense that scented the air, a gift from the zhupan. Fervent was the special prayer which Tomislav spoke, and radiant his face when he bade everybody kneel, took the water, and signed the brow of Eyjan. "I baptize you in the name of the Father, and of the Son, and of the Holy Ghost. Amen."

Dagmar gasped and nearly fell. Andrei laid his arms around to steady her. Himself gazing Heavenward, he whispered, "Agnete, rejoice."

The rest was soon done. Meanwhile she shed tears, but that was because she had no other way to utter forth her bliss. The sobbing ceased when she rose, and after exchanging embraces she walked out upright.

The weather had turned unseasonably cold. Wind drove clouds across a wan sky and soughed in leaves that were fast changing color. Shadows came and went. People who had been waiting at the door crowded around to bless Dagmar and welcome her to Christendom. They had prepared a modest meal of celebration. On the morrow the visitors must leave—she for the harbor, where *Brynhild* lay clear to sail.

Tauno, who had barely greeted his father that was, and had not knelt in church, stood aloof beneath a pine, as if to refuse a share in winter. It was a time before Dagmar could break free of her well-wishers and seek him out. None followed, as ill-omened as he seemed, roughly clad and armed with a spear.

She stopped before him and held out her hands. He made no response. Her veil and gown fluttered wildly, pressing cloth against hip and bosom. Nonetheless she was virginal. Perhaps that was because of an inner solemnity which no Faerie being could ever know.

Since he kept silence, she drew breath and spoke: "Thank you for coming. I wish I knew what else to say."

"I had to bid my sister farewell," he answered. "She was dear to me."

Her lip quivered. "But I *am* your sister!"

He shook his head. "You're a stranger. Aye, we share memories, we who shared a womb. Dagmar, though, is no mermaid; she's a veritable saint."

"No, you mustn't believe that. I'm sanctified this day, like any infant newly received into Christ's flock—yet I too will fall by the wayside over and over—but I dare hope I may repent and win forgiveness."

"That was not Eyjan talking," he said wryly.

Her head drooped. "Then you refuse salvation?" He stood leaned on his spear. "At least you can't stop my prayers for you, Tauno."

At that, he grimaced. "I've no wish to cause you pain."

"You'd gladden me if you'd fare home with me."

"No. I've plighted a certain troth here. But won't you wait until spring? Else it could be a stormy passage."

"We are in God's keeping. I must go to my rightful man, lest he die in his sins."

Tauno nodded. "You are Dagmar in truth. Well, greet them from me, and may luck swim with all of you."

He turned and strode off into the woods. When he was out of sight, he ran as if hounded.

Nada was not in the glen where she and Tauno commonly met, nor anywhere near. He strained his senses and skills that were of Faerie but could find only the dimmest spoor. Often the trail broke and he must cast widely about before he caught further traces. These showed in their far-scattering directions, and their own character, that she had been roving about distraught. The knowledge drove him frantic.

It took him a pair of days and nights to track her down. He did on the evening of the equinox. By then he was beside himself, and lurching with weariness.

Cold had deepened, gnawing inward through windless air. The sky was low and flat gray. She stood on the shore of the lake, which reached steely from a forest gone brown and yellow, a few splashes of blood-colored maple or somber evergreen, many boughs quite bereft. Her figure was tiny, lost, a wisp of pallor.

"Nada, oh, Nada," he called, and stumbled toward her. His voice was hoarse from crying out while he searched.

"Tauno, beloved!" She sped to his arms. He folded them with vast care around her frailty. She felt almost as frozen as the day, and shuddered against him. Their tears mingled when they kissed.

"Where have you been?" he blurted. "What's the matter?"

"I was afraid——" she whispered.

He stiffened. "What of?"

"That you might not come back——"

"Darling, you knew I would——"

"——before I must go under."

"Under?"

"I shouldn't have feared. I'm sorry. I should have trusted you. But I couldn't think very well, it's been so bleak." She huddled still closer. "You're here."

Terrified, he said into the thistledown locks: "What do you mean, what must you do?"

"Go under. In the lake or a stream. Didn't you know?" She pressed outward, slightly but enough for him to mark. He released her and she stepped back a pace to regard him. What blue had been in her great eyes was nearly faded away.

"In winter, the sun is not too bright on the water for me," she told him; "but the bare woods give no shelter from it. In the depths I find shadow. Surely you've heard this."

"Yes——" He glanced earthward. The spear he had dropped lay between them. "Yes, but——"

"Erenow I could stay later awake. This fall, we're bound straight into winter." A dead leaf drifted from its twig to her feet.

"When must you leave?"

She hugged herself against the chill. "Soon. Today. Will you be here in spring, Tauno?"

He undid his belt. "Why, I'll be at your side."

She shook her head. Where he was now trembling and stammering, she had gained an odd clarity (and did she look more than ever translucent, a mist-wraith?). "No, dear love. I will float among dreams. Seldom could you rouse me, never for long. And there's naught of your sea in yonder tomb-quietness. You'd go mad."

He kept at work on his garments. "I can come ashore termly."

"I think that would be worse for you than if you stayed up the whole dark while."

For a span the vilja gazed steadily at the merman's child. She had grown wise, had little Nada, in this twilight of her year.

"No," she said at last. "Abide my return. That is my wish." After another stillness: "Nor wait in the woods. Seek out mankind . . . for we've no elven women in these mountains such as you've told me of . . . and how often I've seen your desire that I cannot ever fulfill. My dreams down below will be happier if I've known you're with someone living."

"I don't want any."

Horror smote her. Crouched back as if beneath a whip, she wailed, "Oh, Tauno, what have I done to you? Go while you can. *Never* come back!"

The last garment dropped from him. His very knife lay fallen across the spearshaft, and he wore nothing but the spirit bone. She shrank further away and covered her eyes. "Go, go," she pleaded. "You are too beautiful."

Like tall waves joining, her despair met his and he was overwhelmed. "By the nets of Ran," he choked, "you're mine. I'll make you mine."

He sprang forward and seized her. She wrenched her mouth from his raking kiss. "It's death for you!" she screamed.

"How better to die . . . and be done——?"

They struggled. Dimly he knew he was being savage to her, but the force of it possessed him. "Nada," he heard himself rave, "yield, be kind to me, this is what I want, and you'll remember——"

She was out of his grasp, she had escaped him as might the wind. He lost footing and tumbled onto the withered turf. When he raised his head, he saw her yards off. She stood white against hueless water and sky, murkful trees, merciless cold wherein no breath showed around her. From her right hand hung the sigil.

He groped erect and staggered her way. She drifted backward. "I can easily leave you behind," she warned. "I'd liefer not have to."

He stopped and stood swaying, "I love you," heaved out of him.

"I know," she said with infinite tenderness. "And I love you."

"I didn't mean harm. I just wanted us to be together, truly together, the one time—if else we must be sundered forever."

"There is a third way." Calm had come upon her; she smiled. "You've told me about this thing. I'll enter it, and you can have me with you always."

"Nada, no!"

"Could I hope for more happiness than to lie on your heart? And maybe someday——" She broke off. "Stand where you are, Tauno," she begged. "Let me see you while I can, and that be the wedding gift you give me."

He could not even weep.

At first she did look at him as much as she did at the piece of a dead man's skull which she held. But slowly the bird of the Otherworld possessed her, until at last she gazed only upon it as it winged across the new moon. Tauno saw how her form of a maiden grew ever more ghostly, until he could spy the wilderness through her, until she was the faintest glimmer in gathering darkness. And then she was gone. The talisman fell to earth.

He stayed in place for the quarter of an hour before he could go pick it up, kiss it, and hang it back where it belonged.

IX

On their homeward voyage, the crew of *Brynhild* marked how changed Lady Sigrid was. Had the decision of her brother Herr Carolus to stay in Croatia brought that about? Two or three sailors still believed that she slipped overboard of nights to disport herself in the waves. There was no eyewitness evidence, however, and most denied it. They bespoke her piety; now she did join the rest in prayer, where she was the most ardent person aboard, and she spent hours on her knees before the image of the Virgin at the aftercastle, often with tears streaming down her cheeks. At the same time, she was no longer curt and aloof, but quickly made herself beloved by her mild ways and her readiness to listen to the humblest among them. She became almost a mother confessor to several.

Captain Asbern had been doubtful about setting sail this late in the year. He went cautiously, as near the coasts as was prudent, running for haven at the first sign of a hard blow. Thus he did not reach Denmark until shortly before Christmas. But the passage was free of peril, with no more hardship than seamen should endure.

About midday on the feast of Adam, *Brynhild* lay alongside a Copenhagen dock. After learning whose she was, the harbormaster dispatched a boy to tell the owner.

Snowflakes drifted thinly out of a sky already dusking. The air was mild and damp. Scant traffic moved between walls and arcades, beneath overhanging galleries; yet light from windows, smoke from roofholes, savory odors, sounds of bustle and laughter and song, told how folk indoors were making ready to honor the birth of Our Lord. Those twelve days would be like a giant candle in the middle of that cavern which was winter.

Slush plopped under the hoofs of the mules which man and woman rode. Ahead of them, high-booted against muck, went a pair of armed linkbearers. The flames flared and sparked, casting short-lived stars out among the snowflakes.

"We've only time for a few more barebones words ere we reach your house," she reminded. "The whole tale will be days in the telling." She thought. "No, years—or a lifespan—for the understanding of it."

"We will have that lifespan, we twain," said Niels happily.

She clenched a hand tighter than needful around the reins. "It will not be easy. First, this same eventide—I dread—— How . . . what . . . shall I tell Ingeborg? Help me think what may wound her the least."

He flinched. "I was forgetting."

"Blame not yourself. Joy can so easily be selfish. Once I would have forgotten."

"Eyjan——"

"I am Dagmar."

He crossed himself. "Could I forget your own miracle? God forgive!"

"It will not be easy for us," she repeated. "You must needs bear with me more than most men with their wives: I who in flesh and mind am half a mermaid."

"And the other half a saint," Niels answered. A bit of his olden grin flashed forth. "*That* will prove hard on me."

"No, never say such things," Dagmar beseeched. "You'll likeliest find me stubborn, quick-tempered, no real womanly meekness in me, strive though I will for it." She reached toward him. "But oh, Niels, never will I fail in my love for you."

He became grave, took her clasp, observed her through snowfall and dim yellow light. Finally he asked low, "Do you indeed love me, Dagmar? You care for me, yes, I know that, and I've no right to crave more. Yet——"

"I give you myself, since you will have me," she told him in utter honesty. "My inmost heart you have still to win, but my prayer is that you may; and in that quest also, I will fare at your side."

X

INGEBORG Hjalmarsdatter was a Jutish woman of about thirty winters. Early one spring she arrived at Hornbaek, a fisher hamlet on the north coast of Zealand, a day's ride by the shore road from Copenhagen. The men who had gone before her, found a cottage for sale, and comfortably furnished it, had explained that she was a widow of means who wanted a place where she could take refuge, when she desired, from city life, among common people such as she herself had been before making a good marriage.

The dwellers gave her an awkward welcome but were soon at ease. She put on no airs; rather, she was soft-spoken in her funny dialect, and ever ready to help when a need was real, whether for a bit of money or for hours of toil. However, nobody came truly to know her, and unwed men presently stopped paying court. She did not seek out her neighbors, nor invite them oftener than behooved her, nor gossip, nor say much of anything about her past. Alone in her home, she did housekeeping, kitchen gardening, and marketgoing for herself. Each day when weather allowed, she would walk miles along the beach or into the woods. That was not as reckless as it would have been formerly; the King's peace prevailed anew, for a while, in these parts. Nevertheless, no other woman would have dared. When the parish priest counseled her against it, she told him with a smile, the sadness of which matched aught he had ever seen, that she had nothing left to fear.

Time passed. Raw winds and lashing rains gave way to blossoms, plowing and seeding of what fields the villagers held, boats bound forth to reap the waters. Blossoms fell, apples budded, furrows wore a tender green, forest filled with birdsong. On the roof of Einar Brandsen had long been fastened an old cartwheel whereon a family of storks nested, summer after summer. They were thought to be lucky for everyone thereabouts, and indeed the months wending past saw births, confirmations, weddings, large catches, merry holidays. But of course they also saw illness, death, burial, a drowned man wash up on this his own strand.

So time went as it ever had, until a new stranger arrived.

He came westward from the Sound, belike from Copenhagen, since his horse was of the best and his clothes, while sturdy for traveling, were too. He was very big and appeared young, beardless, hair yellow with a peculiar underwater tint, though the foreign-looking face was haggard. The lordliness of his bearing scarcely fitted with the absence of servant or bodyguard.

Nearing midsummer, the sun was yet above the Kattegat, over which it threw a bridge of molten gold. Eastward across the channel its low-flying rays glowed on clouds piled like mountains above Scania, which rested blue on the edge of sight. Elsewhere heaven stood clear, crossed and recrossed by wings. Far out, a few vessels lay becalmed, toylike, their sails also catching the light. Lulling of gentle surf and mewing of gulls were almost the only sounds adrift through coolness. Tang of sea and kelp mingled with odors from plowland and common on the rider's left, and the woods which made a darkling wall beyond them.

Youngsters tending geese shrilled their delight when they saw him and sped to the roadside. A bit stiffly, he inquired how to find Fru Ingeborg's house. His Danish resembled hers but was not quite the same. Could he be a different kind of Jute, or an actual outlander? The children buzzed like bees as he rode on.

Turning up Hornbaek street, he was hardly more talkative to the grown persons who hailed him. "I am a friend bringing news solely for her ears. Tomorrow she'll tell you what she sees fit. Meanwhile, please leave us be."

Countryfolk like these were not shocked that he and she would spend a night together. Some snickered, some showed envy, a few who were more thoughtful recognized that here was no romp; the stranger's manner was anything but lecherous.

Ingeborg's cottage stood near the end of its row, an ordinary building of moss-chinked timber gone silvery with age; thatch dropped low, full of lichen and wildflowers, anchored by cables against northerly gales. Dismounting, the newcomer unslung the bundle tied behind his saddle, took it under the same arm that held his spear, and gave a man a coin to stable his horse. The gathering goggled as he rapped on the door.

It opened; they saw Ingeborg wonderstricken, heard her shout; the stranger immediately stepped through and closed it against

them. A minute later, the shutters were latched and nothing could
be heard from within.

A peat fire on the hearth gave scant illumination, but she had
thriftlessly lit several tapers. They picked out newly installed
stove, table, chair, stools, texture of woven hangings, brightness
of kitchen gear, smoke that swirled among food-laden rafters,
amidst flickery shadows. The cat which had hitherto been her
single housemate had given up seeking attention and slept on the
rushes strewn over the clay floor. Warmth and pungency filled
the room, as if to stave off the night that had fallen.

Tauno and Ingeborg sat on a chest whose top, cushioned, was
a bench with a backrest. A goblet of wine rested on a shelf at his
side for them to share, but it had seen no heavy use, and the meal
she set forth remained untasted. For after the storm of kisses,
embraces, caresses, laughter, tears, wild words of joy had laid
itself to rest in her, he had starkly begun relating his story.

"——I came overland, in hopes I might find something that
would give hope. But the journey was merely slow, hard, and
dangerous. Well, here and there were remnants of Faerie, different
from any I'd ever heard of before. Once I'd have spent much time
getting to know them. Now I found I had no stomach to linger
long anywhere. I reached Copenhagen a few days ago. Niels and
Dagmar made me welcome, but still less did I want the lodging
they gave—too thick with sanctity, no place for my Nada. I told
them naught about her. Instead, I got what I needed to be respectable and came straight hither. Aye, they bade me greet you
kindly and urge your return. They'd like to see you mingling,
taking pleasure, making a match with some genial widower who
needs a mother for his children."

Ingeborg leaned against him, his arm around her waist, hers
reaching across his back to comb fingers through his hair. But she
did not look at him, she stared into that hole of darkness which
was the open door to the rear chamber. The second storm he raised
in her, by his tale, had likewise died down. She still trembled
somewhat, hiccoughed, spoke in a voice roughened and unsteady
after much sobbing; her eyes were red, she snuffled, salt lay along
her cheeks and upper lip. Yet she could quietly ask:

"How is it with you and her?"

He too gazed beyond. "Strange," he answered, no louder. "Her
nearness—like a, a sweet drink that burns—or a memory of a

darling lost, before grief has faded, though more than a memory:
a presence—— Is this how you Christians feel about your dead
who are in Heaven?"

"I think not."

"Waking, I have her with me, as I have my own bloodbeat."
Tauno smote his knee. "That's all—that, and remembrance more
sharp than any other ever—it hurts!" He mastered himself. "But
it quenches too. It is her presence, I said; she has not gone away.
And when I sleep, oh, then she comes back in dreams. They're
like life; we're together, just the way we used to be; because it
is Nada in the sigil."

Ingebord summoned her last strength: "Do you, in these
dreams, fully know her?"

He slumped. "No. We roam and gambol through her homeland
or in lands and seas where I've been and call forth for her. She
grows wide-eyed with amazement...until sorrow seizes her that
she must deny me more than a kiss. I tell her these are simply
dreams and she tells me they are not, they're a meeting of shades
outside of space and time; she's a ghost, she tells me, and if I lost
myself in her I would share her death."

"Oh, don't!" Ingeborg's fingers grew white-knuckled upon his
shoulder. Unvoiced was that he would die like a blown-out flame.

Silence.

"Fear not, I shan't," he said.

"Bless Nada for her care——" The woman drew a ragged
breath. "Yet, Tauno, whom I myself love...you'll not go on
thus, will you? Year after year, century after century, living only
what you've lost...no, what you never really had?" She twisted
about to see him. Her mouth stretched out of shape. "God gave
you no soul. How can He leave you trapped in Hell?"

"It isn't——"

She clutched him with both hands. "Throw that thing in the
sea, in the Pit!" she yelled. "This night!"

"Never." Before the sternness in his countenance, she quailed
back.

Abruptly he smiled. His tone gentled, he reached for her,
touched lips to her forehead. "Good friend, be not afraid. Everything shall be made well. I misspoke me. You were suffering, and
that roused my own ache; but it's very near an end. I give you
my word of honor it is."

Numbed, she gaped at him and mumbled, "What will you do?"

"Why, this," he said levelly. "Do you remember what I told you about the sigil after we returned from Greenland, that the angakok had earlier told Eyjan and me? Faerie scryers I met on the way back from Croatia, they agreed he spoke truth, and added more knowledge to mine.

"Nada dwells in the talisman. But she's not locked there for aye. She can come forth, into a living body, if that person invites her.

"I will do that. Nada and I will become one, in a deeper fashion than I sought. I've delayed just so that I might see how you fare in Denmark——"

She screamed, wilder than before, and cowered from him.

He rose to stand above her, take her temples between his palms, speak anxiously: "Be at peace. Nada is. She's ready to dare this venture with me."

Ingeborg shuddered toward a measure of steadiness. She could not meet his gaze. "Find someone else," she moaned. "You can if you search."

He frowned and let go of her. "I thought of that, but Nada refused, and rightly. It's an unhallowed thing to do: for she's damned."

"But a girl in despair... or a pagan, or——She'd gain, wouldn't she? You... for a husband... and what else?"

"The vilja's agelessness, her power over air and water, while keeping the sun-loving flesh. And, aye, Nada's dear flighty spirit. Such a woman would be of the halfworld."

"You'd find many who'd spring at yon bargain."

"And sunder themselves from God, with who knows what fate after the body at last perishes? That was something which no magician could learn for me." Tauno shook his head. "Nada will not. Nor, in my honor, once she'd explained the evil to me, could I allow it."

Ingeborg lifted face and hands in pleading. "But what will you become?"

"That's another thing which is unknown, I being of Faerie," he replied. "Wherefore I'd fain wait several days yet, and nights, with you, old comrade."

"Are, are, aren't you afraid? You'll nevermore be Tauno."

He raised himself to his full height; his shadow fell huge. "I *am* Tauno Kraken's-bane," rang from him. "Should I fear to take unto me my bride?"

She sat mute, until he touched her and murmured:

"The hour is late. Let's to bed, shall we? Though this night, at least—after what's passed between us—I'm weary to the marrow. Let's just sleep. You understand, don't you Ingeborg? You've always understood."

The second room was where she slept.

Having stolen from him after he was evenly breathing, she kindled a splint at the banked fire and used that to relight a taper. This she carried back. It gave her enough ocher dusk to see him by.

He wanted no blankets, but lay on his right side on the pallet, unclad. Over the length of him, the great thews molded darknesses which stirred as his rib cage rose and fell. A lock of hair had tumbled across his brow, another curled beneath the jawline. A blind calm was on his face. In the crook of an arm nestled her cat, purring.

Herself naked—she felt the rushes beneath her feet, heard them rustle, caught in her nostrils a phantom of bruised sweetness—she went carefully to the bedside. She had taken the crucifix off the wall. From that peg hung the talisman.

("Doff it," she had urged. "This once, that you may rest untroubled in your true dreams."

("She would be lonely."

("I see on you the marks of nature's revenge. Would Nada not want you healed of them?")

She had better not look at him for more than a few pulsebeats. He might awaken. She took the sigil by its thong and slipped back out again, closing the door behind her. Thereafter she could stand freely and by the light of the candle in her left hand behold the thing she bore in her right.

All else receded. The weight was small and was as heavy as the world. The dull ivory became a whole sky whose hollowness roofed her in, through which the dark-headed bird winged in eclipse of a moon; she was the earth below, she was the sea. It closed her off from every sound, it made a hush that snowed down through her, drenched her in its coolness until nothing was in Creation but one enormous hearkening, which was herself.

When silence had been completed, she could hear in her spirit, like a dying echo: ——Who are you? What would you?

——I am Ingeborg, your sister, who also loves him.

She put the candle in a holder and brought the thong across her head, brushing her tresses aside, until the piece of bone lay on her bosom. She parted her breasts that it might fall next her heart. Her fingers she clasped above.

Clear within her, a song of longing: ——Ingeborg. Yes. You have had what I never may. I'm glad to know you. He keeps remembering you. (Surprise) What, you weren't aware? Well, he does.

(Later)——He is yours, however, Nada.

——He shouldn't be. If I'd foreseen, I'd have fled him . . . I hope . . . But now I can't.

——Of course you can't.

(Later, timidly)——Ingeborg?

——Yes?

——I'm frightened, Ingeborg. Not for me, really not. For him. You know what he wants to do.

——Aye. Why do you suppose I'm talking with you?

——But—— You? (Aghast) No! I mustn't!

——Why not?

——I'm damned.

——Well?

——Not you too. I couldn't.

——Not even if this is my dearest wish? asked Ingeborg into the weeping.

——It can't be. You've Heaven before you.

——What's that to me without him?

——We know not what'll become of us . . . you-me . . . on the Last Day.

Ingeborg lifted her head. Candle-glow went fiery across her. ——Do you care?

——I should. For you.

——Nada, come to me. (With the strength of aliveness) We will be the bride of Tauno Kraken's-bane.

There was a moment, though, when Ingeborg went on her knees. The rushes had slipped aside and she felt the cold clay underneath. "Mary," she whispered, "I'm sorry if I've made you cry."

She walked from the sleeping hamlet, down to the strand. While the Danish nights had grown short, they were still dark.

Eastward, thunderclouds had gone to loose their anger elsewhere, and a ghost of dawn was paling the stars. Throughout the rest of the sky they gleamed in their thousandfolds around the Milky Way. Beneath that crystal black which held them, the Kattegat glimmered quicksilver.

She waded out. With no wind behind it, the surf had grown slight, and she was soon in water that merely clucked around her. Neither chill nor the numberlessly lumpy shingle hurt. Instead, they were like promises of a salt streaming that waited farther on. When the seatop kissed her nipples, she went below.

She could not breathe the depths as a mermaid did, and that was a loss, but she did not need to, either, She swam, she flowed, she gave back to the water the infinite endearments it sent gliding everywhere across her. She needed no more luminance than was down here to see how long brown vines with fluttering leaves sought upward from rocks whereto they were anchored, how fish darted like argent meteors, how shoals gave way to deeps and endless mystery. She could hear tides as they rolled around the world in the lunar wake, she could hear dolphins pass news onward from a coast of coral, across immensities she could hear the music of great whales. Beyond, she traced gleams, melodies, magics out of the realms that remained Faerie.

She remembered being Ingeborg and she remembered being Nada, but now she was both and she was neither. What swam was a creature of the halfworld, who could love and laugh and strive and sorrow, could do much that is forever denied to the children of Adam, but could no more know God than can an albatross or the wind whereon it soars. Made free, made whole, she felt ever more keenly how joyful she was. Let her doom take her when the Norns chose. This hour was hers.

Soon, ere folk awakened, she would go back and rouse Tauno.

XI

For his guest Herr Carolus Brede, Niels Jonsen bought a yacht, small enough to single-hand but well enough built for the high seas. Her lading became tools, weapons, rope, cloth, and much else in the way of gear and stores. Rumor went that he planned to open clandestine trade with the Wends, under the nose of Hansa. But when he was ready, he simply dispatched three men and an extra pair of horses to Hornbaek. He and Carolus took the boat north, not south, up the Sound and west along the Zealand coast; and Fru Dagmar came too, though she was with child.

They passed the settlement. Off an unpeopled stretch marked by a tall fir, they dropped anchor and waited. Fishing craft were in view, from which night would veil them.

It came late, for this was the Eve of St. Hans, when the sun is not long nor far below Danish horizons. The sky was violet, so bright that few stars glimmered and they small and secret. Water sheened like burnished silver, changeably etched by cool air that carried fragrances of growth from the land. One could count the trees yonder, or read the palm of one's beloved. On distant hilltops, balefires glowed red; youths and maidens were dancing around them.

Clink, clink, said ripples against strakes. Bird calls sounded afar. Surf made a murmur. Little else broke the hush.

Then a swimmer surfaced and hailed softly in a foreign language. Tauno replied likewise. She drew nigh; he leaned over and helped her aboard. Drops gleamed downward off her nakedness.

They say there that the body of Ingeborg had become more fully rounded than erstwhile, for its muscles gave it the motion of a cat. Sunlight had laved it everywhere. Weather had turned brown braids to deep amber. These things hardly mattered beside the strangeness which radiated from her. The very countenance of Ingeborg had subtly changed, become somehow fluid, both shy and bold, heedless and wise, looking forth upon the world as a lioness might, yet with something of otter, seal, and wide-ranging tern in that gaze.

Tauno and she hugged each other for minutes, mouth to mouth. "How have your days gone?" he finally asked.

"Well indeed." She chuckled. "Besides practicing what you taught me before you left, I've invented a trick or two of my own. But I've missed you hard. I hope the cabin holds a stoutly timbered bunk."

"What?" he teased. "You seduced no handsome young men?"

Shadow-swift gravity fell upon her. "I want none but you, Tauno," she said like a virgin in love.

They had been speaking Danish. Their words distressed Fru Dagmar, as their behavior had. She trod forward. "I've laid out clothes for you," she announced. "Let me show you where they are."

Brows lifted above sparkling eyes. "Why, what need? They'd be shucked before daybreak." Mirth departed as fast as it had come. Arms enfolded the woman. "Oh, blood of my dearest, how good to see you." Stepping back: "And you're to be a mother! That's making you glow from within, did you know?"

"Would that I might rejoice for you," Dagmar answered sadly. "I can but pray."

Tauno plucked the sleeve of Niels. "She ought to have stayed behind, your lady," he said for the man alone to hear. "She's too saintly for this."

"But no less brave than aforetime," her husband replied. "She cherishes a tiny hope we can keep you here, and thus maybe at last win your salvation. I'd like that myself." His smile was rueful. "Also for the sake of your company, my shipmates. After you, I'm apt to find my fellows of earth lacking in salt."

His glance fell on his friend's vivid partner, lingered, sought hastily for his wife.

Tauno sighed. "Spare yourselves, and us," he urged. "We'll miss you likewise. But go we must, and unlikely it is you'll ever greet us again."

Their companions heard that. "Yes, quick farewells are best," said she who had risen from the depths. "Go straightway home and be glad in your lives."

"Have you decided whither you're bound?" Niels asked.

"No. How could we, when it's into the unknown?" Tauno responded. "Westward, maybe to Vinland or beyond. Whole vast realms of nature, Faerie, and man must be there, untouched by Christendom, open for our adventuring." He grinned. "Why, we might become gods." Seeing Dagmar wince and sign herself: "Not that we'd seek to, but we might. Anything might happen, which is why we are going."

"To know as much wonder as we can reach in whatever our spans may be," his leman said eagerly.

"But they'll come to a close!" Dagmar cried.

Tauno nodded. "Aye, Faerie is fey, and the work of such as Niels and you is what will bring it to the end." He squeezed the shoulder of the first, kissed the cheek of the second. "Regardless, we love you."

"And we love you," Dagmar said through tears. "Must we mourn you in eternity?"

"No. No more than you'll mourn this whole world"—the female swept a hand around sea, land, sky, all the light night—"fair though you will remember that it was. We would not be other than we are: *our* part of the whole Creation."

"Ingeborg—Nada——" Bewilderment lowered the grief in Dagmar. "Who are you?"

"Both and neither. A child of sorrow whose mother died in the birthing. May yours be the child of abiding joy. . . . I need a name for myself. May I call me Eyjan?"

This time it was the mortal woman that embraced the woman of Faerie.

The yacht had towed a skiff, which brought Niels and his wife ashore. He was rowing when a yardarm rattled aloft. Tauno made sail fast and took the rudder. His mate called up a strong breeze. Their craft surged forward, north-northwest over the Kattegat, to round the Skaw and find the ocean. Above her mast, catching on their wings the light of a sun still hidden, went a flight of wild swans.

Epilogue

In May of the year of Our Lord 1312 died Pavle Subitj the king-maker. His son Mladen followed him as Ban, tried to complete the reconquest of Zadar, but failed and must lift the siege. He likewise failed to curb feuding among the Hrvatskan clans. Again the Kachitji roved as pirates along the Dalmatian seaboard, again the Nelipitji and their allies strove to wrest power from the Subitji and Frankapani. In 1322, civil war broke out. Making league with Nelipitji, Venice took Shibenik and Trogir at once, Split and Nin soon after. Dark were those decades.

Yet Father Tomislav, beard gone white and hands gnarled into uselessness, could stand before a congregation that included widowed, defeated, graying Captain Andrei, and could preach in a sermon:

" '*For God so loved the world, that He gave His only begotten Son, that whosoever believeth in Him should not perish, but have everlasting life.*' The Saviour's words, when Nicodemus the Pharisee questioned him. Would He have troubled to argue if He hadn't cared? Easier just to say, 'You know what miracles I've done already. Stop pestering Me, fall down and worship, before I throw a lightning bolt.' But He did His best to explain the mystery because He wanted folk to come to Him of their free wills, not afraid of Him but seeking home to their Father.

"God loves us. Never forget that. I think He sends us fewer trials than we bring on our own foolish selves. Be that as it may, hang fast to the knowledge of His care for you. No matter what happens, we are not forsaken. Nobody is. Jesus could consort with publicans, sinners, and pagans. These days we have schismatics, heretics, Jews, Turks, heathen, Venetians—and He loves them the same as He loves you. We stumbling mortals often see no way out of having to fight; but must we hate?"

A sunbeam through one of the narrow, unglazed windows made the old priest wipe his eyes as he went on:

"'For God so loved the *world*. . . .' I take that to mean everything He ever made; and there's nothing He did not make. If you need comfort, think of that. Think how the very dust under your feet is loved. We've seen Him give souls to merfolk; He . . . He forgave a poor little shadow and raised her to Heaven; let us take courage from this.

"I've a notion He creates nothing in vain. That Satan himself, after Armageddon and what follows have shown him the error of his ways, may repent and be shriven. That on the Last Day, not only will our dead be resurrected, but all that ever was, ever lived, to the glory of God."

Father Tomislav was quiet for a space before he said, "Now don't you suppose that's necessarily the truth. I'm sure of divine love, but the rest of what I spoke was only my mind rambling. It's not in the canon. It could be heresy."